For Hanne, who was there with me
and
for Ingvar, who is always there

This novel owes its existence to a group of talented, hard-working people who created a world of dark marvels, let someone like me come for a visit, and bashed into shape the stories I told them when I returned. If you like what you read here, it's thanks to them.

THE BURNING LIFE

Hjalti Daníelsson

First published in Great Britain in 2010 by
Gollancz
An imprint of the Orion Publishing Group
Orion House, 5 Upper St Martin's Lane, London WC2H 9EA
An Hachette UK Company

This edition published in Great Britain in 2010 by Gollancz

1 3 5 7 9 10 8 6 4 2

A CIP catalogue record for this book is available
from the British Library

ISBN 978 0 575 09018 7

Typeset by Input Data Services Ltd,
Bridgwater, Somerset

Printed in Great Britain by
CPI Mackays, Chatham, Kent

Prologue

The station lounge was nearly empty, and the only sounds to be heard were the quiet hum of generators somewhere in the distance, along with an intermittent growling vibration as a starship set off from a nearby port. Through the giant viewports there could be seen the occasional caravan slowly drifting into warp position, the sun glinting off its metal carapace.

The only inhabitant in the lounge sat dead still and gazed out at the ships and the stars in the dark space beyond. He was an old man with wispy grey hair, and average build and height, and altogether not someone one would remember encountering. He had a common name, too, and there were very few traces of him in the station logs that could not be eliminated should a situation arise where he needed never to have been on this station at all.

There was a faint, slow tapping sound, of someone arriving on the other side of the lounge and casually walking over to him.

A voice behind him, of a much younger man, said, 'Thanks for seeing me.'

He turned. The visitor was dressed in simple but stylish clothing of an expensive cut, as befitted someone who worked in administration on a massive space station.

The older man nodded to him. 'I was due to pass through this area. If you have any concerns, I'll do what I can. Though I suspect I already know what this is about.'

The young man said, 'It happened again. Thousands this time.'

The older man sighed.

'It has to be stopped,' the young one added.

'We need to be careful. Wait for an opportunity.'

'We can't wait forever.'

'We have feelers out for people,' the old man told him.

'There are plenty of plans ready—'

'Plans are easy and mutable. We need the right people to accomplish anything of consequence.'

The young man took a long, deep breath. Words held too much power not to be carefully chosen. 'We're working for the same cause. You know I would never doubt that. But it's frustrating. It's so frustrating. *Thousands*, just today.'

The old man nodded in sympathy. He looked out the viewport again, at the myriad of stars that shone in the distance. 'Something will turn up. And when it does,' he said, 'everything will change.'

'It has to,' the young man said, and started to walk away. 'Because until we take care of the problem, every one of those lives was lost for nothing.'

PART I

Life

1

'We will eat the body and sanctify its blood, to let it be born again.'

The apartment felt sucked dry of air, replaced with a gaseous formaldehyde that put everything and everyone in stasis. The attendants had formed small clusters, the men standing and facing the floor in grim silence, the women sitting, crying and comforting each other. It was a young man's apartment, little more than a studio with a small bedroom off to the side. The door to that room was ajar.

Drem Valate, so numb of emotion he felt like a sleepwalker, went and hugged his grandmothers. Each of them had a necklace with a tiny golden vial, and each fingered theirs incessantly. 'We will consume him, dear,' they were saying in a shivering stammer. 'We shall take him into our fold and make his blood our own.'

It was an old prayer of the Sani Sabik, spoken in hard times, and they murmured it like an endless litany. 'We will eat the body and sanctify its blood, and we will consume him until he is gone, to let his soul rise again.' They did not cry, for they were too old and weary, but the words fell from their mouths in droplets.

Drem let them go and looked around the room, still avoiding the sight of that half-open door. It was dawn on the colony. People stayed away from the windows, as if the Red God might come and take them away, and through the glass Drem saw the first rays of the nearest sun glide their cold way over the colony dome.

He wondered momentarily if he should walk about and talk to everyone, but he knew it would merely delay the inevitable. He went over to the bedroom door, opened it, took a deep breath and stepped through.

It was dark inside and the air was even heavier. The curtains were closed. There was little decoration: some plants in sealed minidomes, and a couple of holoposters on the walls, cycling through images of space. In the corner stood an inconspicuous machine, dark and quiet, laced with all sorts of wires and tubes that had now been wound up in a loop and left to hang off one side. The sight of that machine felt even more like a death sentence, Drem thought, than the body lying on the bed. You died not when you expired, but when your life was neatly packed away.

His brother had needed that machine. He hadn't been tied to it; he merely plugged in twice a day for a few minutes and otherwise lived a relatively normal life. Drem had been helping him save up for a more mobile unit. It was just the two of them now; their parents had died years ago on a blood-harvesting excursion.

Drem, on reflection, supposed it was only him now.

He sat down on the edge of the bed and remained quite still for a long time, looking intently at the machine. His fingers, meanwhile, blindly found their way to the body of his brother. They held his heavy hands, stroked his cold, inert cheeks, and ran slowly through his lifeless hair.

Drem wanted to cry but couldn't. He wanted to scream but couldn't. He wanted to think of Leip alive, to imagine some course of events by which none of this was even a reality, but those thoughts were opaque and he was too numb to grasp them. Some part of him, he knew, had realized that everything had changed and had put up a rock-solid dam to stem the flood. There would be no proper grief until everything was over, until Leip had been bled and the rituals completed.

Drem sat there until he began to hear whispering at the door. He got up, kissed his brother's forehead and left the room, letting one of his grandmothers take his place. The light outside the windows felt preferable to the bleakness in the house – the presence of a dead body, in and of itself, did not bother Drem, but the immense and silent anguish he saw on everyone's faces, and probably reflected in his own, was becoming unbearable. He headed out into the yard, and took a long, cold breath of morning.

It was early enough that he could still see trails in the sky from the night's shipping traffic. The entire colony was attached to a moon in wide orbit around the sparsely colonized planet below, and functioned both as a delivery port for arriving interstellar shipments and, to a lesser degree, an assembling plant for various pieces of technology sent up from the planet and bound for somewhere else in dark space. Drem had been raised in another section of the colony, one located nearer to the outlying landing base, and had grown used to the silent tremors of starships taking off in the dark. In wintertime, he and Leip had sometimes sat by the window, long after they should've been in bed, watching the bulging columns of smoke as the daily shipments of raw materials were readied to be flown back planetside. Drem and Leip would look at each other, grinning, then in unison place their hands on the windowsill, palms flattened. A few seconds later the soundless vibration from the launch would hit, travelling from the airless landing strip through the metal of the colony and the stone of its mother asteroid, through the atmospheric shield and the ground beyond, up the walls of the nearest houses and into the bones of their hands, the boys giggling like mad.

Drem rubbed his eyes and realized he was crying.

Someone approached him and softly cleared his throat. Drem looked up and saw a middle-aged man, grey of beard and hair, dressed in the familiar red-and-black garb of the Bleeders. They were the combination law-enforcement and religious sectarians of the Sani Sabik. If you ever needed either a priest or a policeman, you'd find a Bleeder. They presided over every religious gathering, acting as everything from midwives to funeral directors, and it was an old joke that you literally had a Bleeder watching over you from the moment you were born until the last breath of your life.

'Hi, Father,' Drem said, not bothering to wipe the tears from his face.

The Bleeder sat beside him on the grass. 'Hello, son. I'm Brother Theus. I understand there's been a loss in this house.' His lips were fixed in a tempered smile held in place by the many wrinkles on his face – a deep concern woven with experience. Drem didn't dare assume how much of it was genuine and not merely the result of years of practice with the grieving, but he found it calming nonetheless and felt thankful towards the man.

'My brother,' Drem said. 'Died in his sleep last night, apparently. He was ... well, I don't know.' He sighed and looked at the sky. 'He'd been having some trouble, what with the sickness and all. But nothing that should've caused something like this.'

'Sickness?' Theus asked.

'Sabik's Sepsis. It wasn't severe, but it caused a whole damn headache of problems. Leip had a haemopurifier that he used twice a day, and it helped, but you can't be sick the way he was and get out of it unscathed.' Drem's ears caught up with his mouth. 'Or get out at all, apparently,' he added with a sigh.

'It is always hard when a child leaves the family,' Theus said.

'Oh no, he was an adult. Not old, but in his twenties,' Drem told him.

'Your brother had *permanent* blood poisoning?' the priest said to him. It was barely a question and verged on judgement. The worry wrinkles on the old man's face increased, but Drem now found them less comforting.

'Is there a problem?' he asked the priest.

'I must go inside, my son, and see the family. Are you the closest living relative to the deceased?'

'Yes, Father. I am.'

'Then we will need to talk.'

The next day Drem, with a head full of thunder, went to his grandmother's house to meet the family for the wake. People would be coming and going all day. They had a young man to bury, and, Drem had discovered, a terrible problem to solve.

The house smelled sweetly of spices, and of flowers left to dry in the air. Derutala, known to the family as Granny Deru, had been baking and cooking all day; mostly, Drem suspected, out of a need for something to do. When he came in she was in the kitchen, busying herself with an oven that only she could use without burning its contents. Everything was made of steel and patience here, including Granny Deru.

Drem made his way into the living room. His cousin Vonus was there, standing by a shelf and inspecting the metal picture frames. Vonus's wife sat in a chair beside him, cradling their infant child. They were only a few years older than Drem and still building a life. At the other end of the room stood another man whom Drem had seldom seen and had not been expecting: Dakren, his father's brother, a much older man with grey hair and grey eyes.

The infant gurgled happily, and Drem smiled at it. Its mother smiled back at him but with deep furrows of worry in her brow.

Vonus said, 'How are you doing, Drem?' in that low voice people reserve for the traumatized, as if sound waves might break them apart.

'I've had better days, thanks,' Drem said. 'How are you?'

Vonus took his time to phrase the reply. 'I'm doing all right, though I have no idea what's been happening over the past few hours.'

'The priest spoke to you, too, did he?' Drem asked.

Vonus hesitated and looked to his wife. She nodded. 'Yes. I think he spoke to most of us there.'

Drem looked at the picture frames Vonus had been inspecting. Theirs was a large family, which was common on a workers' colony. Their little community was sitting on a rock floating in the deeps of outer space. There had been nothing natural here: no atmosphere, no running water, no geothermal heat, and no life. It had taken a long time to give this place anything resembling habitability, and it took no more than a look through its dome to remind the viewer just how tenuous that existence was. In a place like this, people clung to whatever provided the safety and comfort they needed to prove their mastery over their own lives. It made for strong faith, sometimes heavy drinking, and plenty of children.

'I had a talk with him, too,' Drem said. 'Twice, even. First one was yesterday morning, when he came to comfort us on the loss of my brother. Then again early this morning, when he told me what this meant for me and this family.'

He glanced at Dakren, who offered no comment. Drem went on, 'Leip had a special kind of blood disease. It's rare but not unheard of. What *is* rare is for the Sepsis to last into adulthood, because for almost everyone who gets it, it starts to fade rapidly by age four, and by the time puberty starts it is usually gone for good. But not for my brother.'

The little family sat in dead silence as Drem continued, 'As we found out when he was first diagnosed, this condition, among the many other things it made Leip suffer, left him unable to donate blood when required for rescue work or ceremonial purposes. If we were still in the Amarr Empire, this wouldn't matter.'

Vonus and his wife winced. The mention of the old world, which their nation had left a long time before any person in the room had been born, was still not done idly. The exodus had taken place for complicated reasons and left wounds in both factions, which, despite the Blood Raiders' extremism, still shared a substantial amount of core beliefs.

'He'd have been treated like any other person with a permanent illness, no more nor less. But this is the Sani Sabik, where we worship the blood. We have ships out there somewhere, raiding the skies in our name, and in the empires they use us as monsters to frighten their children.'

Drem reached out and plucked from the shelf a small picture frame, set slightly aside from the others. It cycled slowly through pictures of his brother, one smiling face morphing into another. 'Apparently, an adult having poisoned blood, to a member of the Sani Sabik, is a sacrilege. The very idea defies the Red God's laws. I thought I knew a lot about the rules of my faction, but I did not know about this.'

He gently stroked his thumb over the image, then put the frame back on the shelf and turned back to his family. 'Leip cannot be buried. He can be kept in stasis for as long as it takes, because we Sani Sabik are good at keeping people *fresh*.' He spat the word. 'But he can never be buried, not unless by some miracle we convince the clergy to write his name in the Books of the Dead.

'The alternative is that he be stricken from existence, as if he had never lived at all. All records of his life would be expunged, insofar as such a thing is possible. When the priest told me this, I was too numb even to answer, so he added one last streak of piss to this whole disgusting mess.'

Drem looked at Vonus's child. 'Until this matter gets sorted out, no more children in the family can be brought into the fold. Not even this beautiful little thing here.'

He kneeled and stroked the child's head, smiling at it. 'Until my brother's life has been erased from existence,' he said to it, gently, as if he were soothing it to sleep, 'you simply won't exist. You won't go to school, you can't go to the hospital, you'll be banned from our churches. In their eyes, you won't even have a name.'

'Drem . . .' Vonus said.

Drem got up and faced his uncle, 'Adult relatives are safe. Their rights aren't infringed at all, because if they were, the clergy knows that they would revolt. So instead they go after the children, because Blood Raiders understand people's weak points and they know it'll turn you against me.' He smiled faintly. 'Understand, if I could kill this priest, I would. If I could walk up to him, with his understanding smile and his wrinkles of worry, and shove a nail so far into his eye that it would penetrate not only his brain but those of every single clergy member in the Sani Sabik, I would do it without a second thought.'

Behind him, he heard a gasp from Vonus's wife. He turned back to her. 'But I can't, obviously. I can't do much about this at all. There are special dispensations for those with money and connections, but we have neither. My only option is to have Leip stricken off the list. That, or see every new child in this family be turned into an outcast.'

He sat down on the floor. 'Is this what the priest told you?' he asked the couple.

Vonus cleared his throat. 'He said that there would be a problem of a clerical nature, and that we would need to convince you to make the right choice. He also mentioned the striking commission.'

'Which I would be paid as compensation for losing my brother, or whatever half a life's the Sani Sabik think he had. It would even be enough to buy me passage off the colony, away from the memories I'd leave rotting in the ground.'

'Will you consider it?' Vonus's wife said, too loudly. 'Will you please consider it?'

'No,' Drem said. He saw tears form in her eyes, and looked away, shutting his own eyes and rubbing his fingers over them.

'What do you need?' said a dim voice from the other side of the room.

Dakren was a rare presence at family gatherings. He worked closely with the Blood Raiders, the sect of Sani Sabik who spent most of their lives in space, hunting down, attacking and harvesting the blood of non-believers for various purposes, scientific and liturgical. There was money in that life, and honour, and not a little craziness. From what Drem had been told, Dakren had gotten both of Drem's parents involved with these harvest missions. Then on some trip into deep space their victims had fought back, and all Blood Raiders ships on the venture had perished. Dakren had rarely spoken to Drem since.

Drem looked at him now. 'I need my brother to be given a funeral and a line in the Books of the Dead. I need the clergy to approve his ascension. And I need to punch a priest in the face, but that can wait.'

Dakren gave a thin smile. 'I'm familiar with what it takes to finagle one's way into the clergy's good graces. The traditional way is to perform a special service to the Blood Raiders, but it can also be accomplished by donating substantial amounts of money.'

'Seeing as how I can do neither, it's not really an issue,' Drem said. 'I hear the service has to be something that's demonstrably in the favour of the Sani Sabik as a people. It can be a new type of highly valuable technology, or a service in the diplomatic favour of our faction, or just something that saves the lives of a lot of our people. I imagine whoever designed Leip's haemopurifier got an easy pass,' he added in a bitter tone.

Dakren was silent. Drem watched him closely, then said, 'I have tried and tried and tried to figure out a way for this. I have thought harder about this than anything in my life. Do you have any idea,' he asked the old man, 'how it can be done?'

'It's a difficult matter,' Dakren said and looked out the window.

Drem sighed, got up and left the room.

He wanted to leave the house, but he was afraid that it would look as if he had abandoned his family, and he did not want to add even more drama to their worries. Also, if he left now, feeling like he did, he feared he might wander off until he had left the colony and this life altogether, his brother nothing more than a name crossed out on a list. So he went to his grandmother instead.

Granny Deru's kitchen was small but felt big. It was always the brightest place in the house and felt the warmest. Nothing here was pure decoration; this was a place where things were put to use, and it seemed to have taken on the aura of the people who'd been there. The room felt alive and quietly breathing, and was eternally scented from good food and baking.

Granny herself now stood by the kitchen counter, dotting a cake with dark berries. On the wall in front of her hung a varnished wooden plaque with a large gold-and-silver vial affixed – the vial itself golden, and silver drops pouring down its sides. On the wall to the side was a needlepoint embroidery, red on white, with the words 'Babies Need Blood'. Granny Deru was humming to herself – some old song Drem remembered from his childhood. He cleared his throat.

'Oh, hello dear,' she said, as if he'd popped over for a visit rather than just cross rooms. 'How are you holding up?'

'I'm not sure,' Drem said. 'Still on autopilot. Don't really dare stop and think.'

She gave him a sideways glance. 'I've already lost one grandchild, dear, and I'm not going to have another burn himself out. Talk to your gran, now.'

Drem leaned against a wall, hung his head and pinched the bridge of his nose. 'I know, Gran. I know. But everyone is still in shock, and the clergy's made a mess, and if I start trying to unravel this massive knot of feelings that's inside me, I don't think I'll be able to stop.'

Deru placed the last berry, wiped her hands and put the cake into the cooler, then got out a large bowl and several big boxes. She opened each box and began picking out cookies of various sizes and shapes, arranging them in patterns in the bowl. 'It's a nasty business we're in, dear. Did you talk to Dakren about it?' she asked without looking at him.

'I did.'

'And what did he say?'

'When I asked him if he could help, he said he couldn't.'

'Did he now, dear? That's certainly a shame,' she said, quite blithely.

Drem looked sharply at his grandmother as she busied herself in the kitchen. 'Yes, Gran. It is.'

She had put away all but one box of cookies when his resolve broke. 'All right, Gran. Please. Explain it to me.'

Granny Deru looked at him and smiled her old smile. 'I know the men in this family, Drem. Most of them I've known since they were standing in this very room, with scabbed knees and teary eyes, pleading for a cookie. I remember you, even, and look what a determined young man you've become.'

Before Drem could respond, Gran continued, 'Dakren was a boy once, just like you were, but that was a long time ago, and he has seen darkness I hope you never encounter. He has that rarest of talents, which is how to understand a problem and find a solution to it, whatever the cost. If something is broken he will look at it from all angles, until he understands both its original function and the nature of the break, and he will find a way to fix it. If it cannot be fixed at all, he will not even try, but if it can, he will always look at the worst-case scenario and work his way up from there. He's a lot like you, really, except he's had more practice in dealing with evil.'

Drem had a million questions, but anger overrode them. 'And who decides who's evil – the clergy?' he asked.

'There are all sorts of evils,' Gran said, and left it at that.

'So you think he can help me?'

'He has worked with some very powerful people in his time. And he's always looked after you and the rest of this family. I will be very surprised if he cannot find a way to sort all of this out for us. But it will come at a cost.'

Before he even spoke he had halfway decided to seek Dakren's help, whatever it demanded of him. 'Gran, if this can be solved . . . I can't imagine what he would ask that I could refuse.'

'That's good, dear. Because Dakren will want his part acknowledged, likely by asking your forgiveness.'

Drem stared at her, and incomprehension gave way to dread. He said, 'I don't know if I—'

'Here's what you're going to do,' she said, checking briefly on something that was baking in the oven. 'You are going to get your head right. You are going to realize that keeping this family intact – and you with it – matters more than anything. It trumps your anger over Leip's death and your business with the clergy, and whatever feelings you have toward Dakren. You should have settled that long ago instead of letting it poison you. Now's your chance to get it done.'

The silence settled in the warm air.

'How do you feel, dear?' Granny Deru asked him.

Drem inhaled deeply. 'I'm not sure. I'm trying to do what's right. I'm not sure what good it'll accomplish.'

He picked up a cookie, looked at it, and put it back in the bowl. 'But I suppose that's the wrong way of looking at it. Right now I just want to help those I can.'

'Doesn't feel so bad, does it?' Gran said with a smile.

It struck him that he couldn't remember the last time he'd asked her how she felt, about anything. 'Who helps you out, Gran?' he asked. 'Who listens?'

'God listens to me, Drem. Now get to the door, I heard someone come in.'

And he thought it might all work out, right until he went to the door, opened it and found nobody there at all. He walked out in the yard and noticed faces looking out from other windows nearby, then people coming out of their own houses.

A tremor made him look at the ground. The grass was swaying. When he looked back up, to the dome and the space beyond, he saw what he first thought was a new sun, its orbit somehow heading his way.

The missile exploded on the colony's shields, splashing oily fire over its dome. Further in the distance, Drem could see another volley of deathbringers headed his way.

With every hit, the colony trembled. Drem could hear things falling off the shelves in Gran's kitchen. Through the dome he saw a starship approaching the colony, massive even at this great distance. Its missile bays were dark eyes, open and gazing directly at Drem. Another missile launched, starting off as a trail of dust, then picking up speed so rapidly that before Drem could think, it had reached the dome. He dropped instinctively to his knees just as it exploded, setting the entire sky awash with flame.

Several Blood Raider vessels entered the area in defence. The sun glinted off the starship's metal hull as it turned to face them. Its guns swivelled, too, focusing on the leader of the Blood Raider armada, and those guns were so large that Drem actually saw them kick back as they pumped volley after volley of projectiles into the Raiders' craft. Missiles swiftly followed, and the corona of explosion as they tore through shields and armour was agonizingly beautiful. Drem stood there transfixed, knowing that he would likely never see something of this magnificence for the rest of his life, brief as it was going to be. It was like the Red God had come for him at last, and brought Armageddon along for the ride.

One Blood Raider ship exploded in a minor nova. The attacker's guns turned and started firing on the next one. Missiles swept across the sky.

The entire fight was over in minutes, and yet seemed to Drem to take a lifetime. By the time the last Blood Raider vessel fell apart, he briefly had time to wonder how his own death would look to those crewmen who'd made it to their escape pods.

The ship turned back to the colony, its black eyes like those of a god turning its face on a doomed people, and Drem had the crazy thought that somehow he had brought this upon them, all of it – his brother's illness, Vonus's christening troubles, Dakren's need for forgiveness, and now the death of them all. He did not move. There was nowhere for him to run. The Red God was in power now, and nobody else. He felt awash with relief, followed by guilt.

The walls of the dome, transparent until now, went opaque, like the blindfold of the execution victim laid over the eyes of an entire community.

The world tore itself apart around him, and somewhere along the way it took him, too.

2

'It's important that you get this right. No screw-ups this time,' Ralea said. 'That means not leaving him or anyone else on that ship alive. If there are any installations nearby, ignore them unless you've taken out the target vessel. Blowing up that Blood Raider colony wasn't part of the last mission.'

The pilot's image, a halo hovering over the dataprojector on her desk, looked so real that he might genuinely have been sitting in his own quarters, staring impassively at the screen. In fact, Ralea knew she was looking at an artificial projection of him while his real body floated suspended in a vat of viscous goo, strung up with handfuls of thumb-thick cords that served as both communications pathways and security wiring. She, meanwile, was located on a massive Gallentean space station that housed numerous layers of inhabitants, operated a self-contained ecosystem, and orbited a planet in the system.

The pilots she serviced were known as capsuleers, and they were practically the gods of New Eden. When wired into their escape pods, they could be inserted into the hearts of massive starships, interfacing directly with vessel control systems and effectively flying the ships by the power of their minds alone. The ships still had crews, but their duties were relegated to cleanup, maintenance and lower-order operation, and they relied on the capsuleers to keep them safe from harm.

On the screen, the capsuleer's image said, 'The man dies. You get his datasheets. I take the cargo and leave the colonies alone. Done.'

Learning to pilot a ship in this manner was difficult and dangerous, and it had taken the empires of New Eden a long time to establish training programs that would create pilots in sufficient numbers while adhering to acceptable loss limits. The impetus for signing up for such a program – where one might find a profitable and exciting profession, certainly, but one could also be shot out of the burning sky, if not end up a dribbling wreck after a botched neural wiring – had greatly increased when the field of capsuleering started to overlap with cloning technology.

Ralea waved a finger through the confirmation field that floated in the halo beside the man's face. The halo lit up for a moment and then disappeared. She leaned back in her chair and exhaled deeply.

These days, when the sensors that lined a capsuleer's escape pod detected a breach they would immediately deep-scan the occupant's brain – destroying it in the process – and send the contents to a cloning facility, where they would be imprinted on the clean, empty mind of a grown body that had been held in suspended animation for precisely such an occasion. A little later that body would regain consciousness, shaking and trembling and vomiting up ectoplasm on the floor in front of the cloning bay. It was an unpleasant process that did unpleasant things to those who continuously suffered it, but it was better than the alternative. And it had made the capsuleers into an immensely powerful faction.

Ralea was a mission agent, representing the interests of her corporation and responsible for negotiating contracts with capsuleers that would further those interests. Sometimes she asked them to bring something from one place to another. Sometimes she asked them to procure certain necessities, anything from ore to weaponry. And sometimes she asked them to kill.

The four empires – the Gallente Federation, Amarr Empire, Caldari State and Minmatar Republic – were the most powerful and influential entities in the cluster, and at the top of every empire lay the interstellar corporate world: a group of organizations heavily involved with both politics and commerce, whose spectrum of influence ranged from operation of planetside business all the way to interaction with capsuleers, often as proxies acting on behalf of the empires themselves. In theory the capsuleers were tied to factions, but in practice they were a faction of their own, one whose powers held heavy sway over the status of cluster politics. The management of their powers was vital to any corporation, and the mission agents who undertook it on behalf of their corporations were chosen very carefully. Mission agenting was one of the highest-ranking and most stressful jobs in existence. As a result, the agents themselves were nearly untouchable.

Ralea switched off the dataprojector in her desk. She looked around the vast room, taking in the massive screen inset in one wall, which cycled through images of farmlands; the wooden shelves that lined another wall with leather-bound books, which cost a fortune here on space stations; and the wooden desk itself, heavy, varnished oak into which had been carefully planted a few pieces of hi-tech equipment that included the unobtrusive dataprojector. It was a calm office.

She leaned over, grabbed a trash can and puked into it so hard she thought her stomach would tear itself apart.

She caught her breath again, in short wet rasps, then spat out as much as she could, closed her eyes and leaned back in her chair. Without opening her eyes she reached into a desk drawer, picked up a small cleaner bomb and tossed it into the trashcan. There was a muffled thump followed by a hiss of disintegrating matter and a lonely metallic rattle. The sour smell of vomit and bile was replaced by the faint aroma of spring.

Ralea breathed in slowly and let her stomach settle down again. The post-vomit endorphins would carry her through for a while before the next bout of cramps and dry heaving.

She eyed another drawer in the desk. It was a simple pull drawer with no security mechanism and no identity lock. Nothing to indicate it held anything of value.

A tiny cramp roiled in her stomach. She swallowed air with a gulp, and pulled the drawer open. She had put her hand on a rag and a small capsule when a sonorous note rang out and her dataprojector turned itself back on.

It showed a tall man with wispy grey hair and calm eyes. She let go of the drawer contents and touched the vidcast's acknowledgement field.

The man gave a wrinkled smile. 'Hello there, dear. Can we talk?'

She smiled back and keyed him in. Steps sounded across the hall and a few moments later the door opened to let in Alder Gernon, her supervisor. He wore clothing that belonged to yesterday's times, but rather than dragging him back into decrepitude, it heightened his impression of venerability and sound morals.

Ralea rose, walked over to Alder and shook his hand. He had a face that smiled naturally and a personality that lent those smiles great credence, and she adored him for it. He walked on until he got to Ralea's desk, and absent-mindedly stroked his fingers over the worn wood before perching himself lightly on one of its corners. 'Have a seat, Ralea,' he said.

She did, reflexively sitting in one of the client chairs that faced her desk. It had a suede cover, high arms and a soft but thin cushion, and was, of course, made of wood. Meetings with agents were rare but did happen every once in a while. This chair was not meant to make its occupant comfortable, nor encourage him to hang around.

Ralea said, 'If this is about my performance review, last I knew I was rising again. Might even make it to top ten.'

Alder looked over her desk, neat and organized, then back at Ralea. He smiled again. 'How's sleep these days?' he asked.

Her stomach lurched, and she squirmed a little in her seat. 'It's . . . short,' she replied.

'Getting worse?'

'Yes.' She would lie about this to many people, but it never worked with Alder, who had a way of intuiting the truth.

He reached for a pen on her desk and twirled it between his fingers. His twirling felt as if it matched her heartbeat. She hoped she wasn't blushing too hard.

'You know you have the right to take a break,' he said. 'You've earned it. And I don't much like those dark patches under your eyes.'

Ralea hoped he wouldn't catch the whiff of too-fresh air that still lingered near the trashcan. 'Still, sir, I—' she began, but he held up a hand.

'You're still hanging on. Top ten, well, not for a while now. Certainly not after last month.'

Last month had seen Ralea give out missions that led their takers to engage hordes of pirates that turned out to be undercover navy vessels, mine twelve hours' worth of ore that nobody needed, transport combined shipments of livestock and radioactive materials that were of interest only to theoretical biologists by the time they reached their destination, and all in all put people in far too much danger for far too little reward.

When a rep from accounting later asked her about this, she had screamed so loud at him that security had broken down the door to her office.

'You have a good record with us, Ralea,' he said. 'You've done amazing work in the past. But I've sat by too long watching that work take an equally amazing and disconcerting turn.'

'I'm trying, sir. I really am.'

'I know you work yourself hard.' He looked up, into the distance. 'Now, if someone wants to push themselves to accomplish something in this job, I have no problem with that. I'm a hard worker, as my father and his father were, and anyone who makes their way up the ranks by blood and sweat deserves their place. But that work has to be sensible. I don't like seeing good people going down bad roads.'

She looked down. 'Well, I'm trying my best, sir.'

'I know. And I want to make sure you do.' He looked at her for a second, then said, 'You know we're being audited.'

She did. It happened to every company, seemingly for a different reason each time. 'It's the one with the new committee, right? The thing with the DED and the Sisters,' she said. 'I'd heard about it. Less focus on the money, more on infrastructure and the workers. Interviews, things like that.'

'They're focusing those interviews on departments under high stress,' Alder said. 'Command is having a hell of a time with them, but they also want to talk to the enforcers. Security, Internal and the like.'

Ralea's stomach cramped again. She kept her gaze firmly on Alder's face, because she had the oddest premonition that if she didn't, she would see something quite unpleasant. Her heart kept beating fast.

Alder continued, 'Liquidation missions have always bothered the DED, who feel it impinges on their territory, and the Sisters of EVE, who are simply against it. So they want to see some people and have a word with them.'

She felt a tiny trickle of sweat run down her back. Little spots of light were dancing in her vision. 'Sir, please . . . all due respect, but I don't know if I can participate in something like that. I really, honestly have a lot of work and little time to get it done.' She hoped he would take this as a hint that he should leave her to it, but he didn't budge from the desk.

'I know,' Alder said. 'But it has to be done, and it won't be as bad as you think. They just want to talk, Ralea. It might do you good to have a word with them.'

The spots of light were shifting to the edge of her vision, replaced by a blackness that seemed to be taking on solid form even as it grew. 'Sir—'

'It's for the good of the company. And I will make sure it gets noted on your next performance review.'

'But I don't—'

'Ralea,' he said, 'let me . . . let me make this clear to you. You are going to see these people. All right?'

'All right, sir.'

'Good.' He smiled and got up. 'Working late tonight?'

'Always, sir.'

He stood still in brief thought, and in that second his profile skewed. His head elongated, its skin stretching out to show a vast network of blood-red veins that covered his head like rivers of magma on a barren planet. The flesh on his face was drawn taut, exposing the greyness of his eyes as they clung to their sockets, a rictus-like smile baring yellowed teeth, and a nose that now looked like a hardened beak. Behind him, the light spots had turned ashen and caught on the wall of the bookshelves, where they pulsated gently and drifted toward one another like tarry insects creeping their blind way forth. This wasn't some brief start of a migraine or bout of exhaustion, Ralea realized in creeping terror; it was a full-blown hallucination, and she needed to do something damn fast.

'Ralea,' Alder said with that gaping maw, 'where do you see yourself going in life?' His tongue was a lizard's tongue, whipping around in his grimy mouth.

'To the top, sir', she said instinctively but heard the lack of conviction in her own voice. The black mass on the wall was extending its feelers, gripping on to surfaces and slowly making its way towards the floor and the ceiling. It was bulging so profusely that the room itself looked to be breathing, covered in tar like the lungs of a mining colony worker. Ralea could no longer tell if the blackness was one big entity or several small ones, crawling over one another. As it crossed behind Alder his eyes took on its colour, the irises and the whites turning ashen, then black.

From what seemed like a million miles away, her boss did not sound pleased. 'Anything else?'

'Sir?' She blinked and refocused on Alder, who was leaning his head to the side. He was half-smiling and his teeth were too sharp. His eyes were so dark, she didn't know if the black mass was poking out through the inside of his head, or if he merely had empty sockets that she was looking right through. The mass was still pulsating, in tune now with the cacophony of Ralea's beating heart.

'Are you sure you're getting enough sleep?' his voice asked. Behind him, the black mass had spread down to the floor, reaching for the feet of the desk itself. Ralea's sole intent in life at this very moment was to get the man out of her office before she started to scream.

Alder seemed to sense this, for he got up wordlessly and slowly walked over to her. She stifled a whimper as he put a veiny hand on her shoulder.

His maw opened, and she heard the voice say, 'I hope the meeting will be productive for both of you, dear.' There was an undertone of sadness that echoed through Ralea's visions. She wondered how this creature could sound so mournful.

He walked to the door. She watched him leave, then looked back to the wall and found it perfectly blank and normal; the floor and ceiling equally so.

Trembling and cramping started up again. Ralea got up and walked back to the desk, one slow, careful step at a time. She did not want to panic or fall, or think about heartbeats and lizard-like men. She reached into the top drawer and pulled out the cloth and the small vial of Mindflood, sat in her chair, turned all communications firmly off, poured a good dose of liquid from the vial into the cloth, put it over her face, leaned back and inhaled as deeply as she could.

The cramps passed away, as did everything else.

Ralea came out of the fugue a couple hours later – relaxed, serene, all delusions absent from her mind – and turned on communications. It was bad form to be unavailable for too long. She felt fine; the thought rolled through her head like a mantra. *I'm fine and I'm good and I'm fine. No more visions. Moving on.*

The evening pilots rolled in slowly, reporting their conquests. Ralea didn't have the energy to make herself presentable, so in lieu of live comms she had her communicator cast up its own projection of her. Agents weren't always ready to roll on camera – she'd handed out mission assignments while picking her nose, brushing her teeth, and, on a few awkward occasions, sitting on the toilet – and the capsuleers were for the most part more interested in the rewards for their tasks than in making small talk.

One report in particular caught her eye. The capsuleer in question had failed to complete a mission that involved an attack on a pirate outpost. She had to verify and flag all failures for evaluation, so she requested more information from the datastream and was rewarded with some grimly funny notes about how the man had apparently managed to secure the stable of prisoners he'd been sent to rescue, only to end up – accidentally, she hoped – jettisoning them into the sun. The list of damages was no better, either, and she saw with a roiling dread that some of his targets had had nothing to do with the mission. But the day had not left her enough energy for commiseration, so she put it out of her mind and quickly finished the mission datawork; though she couldn't help thinking that if she could, she would let the projection do all the work for her. Capsuleers still managed to touch a dark nerve in her, no matter how long she had worked with them.

She reached again for the Mindflood. The first dose had mostly evaporated from the cloth, but when she put it back over her face she found it had enough left to keep her in a meditative state. She felt as if she could go on like this forever.

A glimpse at the clock that hovered in her vidcast showed that evening had fallen. Lights would have been dimmed outside her office, and the only people still working in this area would be agents like her.

The air rang out with a short note, and her dataprojector blinked into life. Ralea called up the image but kept her own projection rolling while her other hand instinctively reached for an adrenaline shot in her drawer. Alder could not be allowed to see her again in this state.

The face on the vidcast turned out to be of a woman her own age, rolling her eyes and swaying back and forth on her heels. Ralea put away the rag and adrenaline boost, and buzzed her in.

Heci – her best friend and a fellow agent – walked in and immediately loosened the band of her blonde hair, letting it cascade to her shoulders. She leaned over the desk and kissed Ralea on the cheek, and if she noticed a haziness in Ralea's eyes, she didn't say a word about it. She handed over a box of Caldari takeout, complete with silver tongs. Neither woman was Caldari – they were proud citizens of the Gallente Federation, which didn't get along with the Caldari State at the best of times – but good, greasy food was universal.

'Thanks,' Ralea said gratefully. The smell of the food made her realize she had in fact been starving all day.

'You look like shit,' Heci said.

Ralea laughed. 'Thanks. Yeah. Pretty tired, but holding on. You going out tonight?'

'I've been promising Jan a night off for ages. We keep meaning to watch a holovid and eat all kinds of crap, but I always call it off. Figured I'd surprise him this time.' She raised one hand, holding up a large bag of snacks and a disc with the Quafe logo. 'We missed this one when it was on, and I picked it up on a whim. Turns out it's a teen comidrama completely sponsored by Quafe, and I can't wait to watch it. We haven't had a good laugh in ages.'

'Throw some crap at the screen for me, OK?' Ralea said. 'But it's a three-hour flight from our station to his, isn't it? Will you be coming to work tomorrow?'

'I'll try,' Heci said with a sly wink. 'Tired, sore, and with a glowing, sleepy grin, but I'll be here.'

'You're a *slut*,' Ralea said.

'You should just see the things Jan can do with chocolate.'

'Oh, get out.'

'And you know that Quafe soda? It tastes so much better when it's being licked off.'

'Git!' Ralea shouted, laughing, and threw a piece of pasta at her. Heci ducked as she rushed out of the room with her bag, making loud slurping noises before closing the door behind her.

The screen on the wall faded from an afternoon on some planetside grassland to its darkening dusk, with stars starting to glint faintly in the sky. Ralea stared at it while eating, and imagined she was sitting out in those fields with nothing to do but watch the world go by and stuff her mouth with deep-fried food. In theory she could have walked out the door and done exactly that, leasing space on some poor planet in the low-security regions and buying herself a small cabin and an unlimited account at every restaurant on the continent, but she couldn't imagine leaving this place. It was not merely the people she cared about who tied her to it, but the work itself. It was challenging and fascinating, certainly, if one managed to not think too much about its nature.

She hoped Heci's evening would go well. Jan was her latest boyfriend in a long line of men likely too numerous for even Heci herself to keep count of. He sounded like a stable guy from what Ralea had heard of him, which might mean Heci would hold on to him for a little longer; or might not. She loved her friend dearly but doubted that she could change her ways for long, no more than Ralea could, no matter how destructive, dangerous or empty they might be.

There was something that drove them on, a need or a hunger neither woman had ever been able to put into words, though they understood it and recognized it in one another. It had brought them to the top of their profession and kept them there, friendship intact – a rarity in a corporate world rife with burnout, backstabbing and difficult personalities – and it had certainly made them rich enough to afford any life they chose. But they stayed on as agents, stuck fast in the dizzying heights of that apex by the same force that had propelled them there, and they gave to it everything of themselves that they could.

Ralea finished off the rest of the Caldari junk food and threw the box into the empty trashcan, then licked the tips of her fingers, called up the vidcast again and started going through the mission reports.

The bell rang once more. Ralea groaned deeply, taking out the adrenaline syringe again, and called up the visitor's image. It was not Alder, but a beautiful and completely unknown black woman who looked a little younger than Ralea. Her hair was long and braided, her face had only the slightest trace of makeup, and Ralea felt a quick surge of hatred for anyone who could presumably work a full day and still look like that. She put away the syringe – she could fake out a stranger – and with the tips of her other hand stroked the grease off her mouth before hovering them over the entrance field of the cast.

The woman walked in and Ralea saw the Sisters of EVE logo on her dress.

'My name is Shandra Neore,' she said. 'I'm with the Sisters and DED joint effort, the ones auditing your company, and by the look on your face I can see you know why we're here.'

Ralea hadn't realized her disgust showed so clearly. Her stomach lurched, and she tried to pull herself together. 'I'm surprised the Sisters are even operating at this level. I thought all you people did was rescue victims out of burning deepspace colonies.'

'Everyone needs someone to watch over them. Even agents. Some of our work is in direct response to the disasters your own profession has brought about.'

'What can I do for you at this hour, Miss Neore?'

'I have some data for you to review for the meeting. It'll be scheduled in a week's time or so, at your convenience.' She put a small, circular datadisc on Ralea's desk.

'You couldn't send it to me?' Ralea said. Her stomach lurched again. It felt like her fingers were trembling a little, but when she gave them a quick glance, they appeared perfectly still.

'I work with people,' Shandra replied. 'I wanted to meet you beforehand, give you a chance to match a face and a voice to whatever you see in my notes.'

Ralea nodded. 'Miss Neore, I'm sure we'd get along fine if we met socially, but just so you know, once we go into that meeting, we're going to be at opposite ends. I don't know if a late-night visit to my office is going to ameliorate that. But thanks for the effort nonetheless.'

Shandra shrugged. 'Never hurts to talk,' she said.

Ralea knew she should take this chance to end the conversation, she really should, but she'd had a rough day, and the carbs from the Caldari food combined with her increasing physical discomfort were giving her just enough anger for a dumb fight, and she could not stop herself from leaning in and quietly asking with just the slightest tone of irony, 'Why do you do it?'

The Sister regarded her for the longest time. 'What else can we possibly do?' she said at last, in a voice that held echoes of both rancour and amity.

With a half-quelled snort, Ralea leaned back in a chair and looked down her nose at the woman. Audits pitted people against one another, risking jobs and departments, even the entire company. Ralea would have to work overtime to keep even her own job out of the line of fire.

Shandra returned the look and said softly, 'Thirty thousand.'

Ralea closed her eyes. A headache was now poking at the inside of her brain, begging to be let out. 'What?' she said.

'That's the death toll on your watch this week. I know it feels less, but you sign them off by the hundreds in your reports.'

'Get out, please,' Ralea said.

'Best of luck,' Shandra said. 'We are always here.'

Ralea heard her steps recede. The door opened and closed. She kept her eyes closed and her mind as blank as she could. Nausea rolled over her.

When at last she risked a look, she noticed the lights had been completely turned off in the hallway. She sighed and moved back to the reports, then stopped and held her breath. In the frozen, crystallized moment of realization, she remembered that they never turned off the lights in the agents' sector. And she realized the darkness at the door was moving.

Her shaking hands had pulled out the drawer and spilled half the Mindflood all over her hands before the blackness reached her, alive and hissing.

3

Everything was unfocused, fuzzy and bright. Through the haze in his cobwebbed head Drem tried to propel his first conscious thoughts into action.

The world around him was white, which was a good thing. If it had been black he'd still be inside the wreckage. Had he been in any wreckage? He filed the thought away for later evaluation. White was the colour of recovery. He recalled it was also the colour of death, at least in some religions, but it held a lesser significance for the Sani Sabik. Maroon or rusty brown, now, that would have meant trouble.

He suspected he had been doped up, just a little. That was a good thing, too.

Once he could focus his eyes, the first thing he saw was a golden vial on the wall, and relished for a moment the thought that he was back in the familiar kitchen. Except for the smell. There was no smell here.

He turned his head slightly, which brought faint echoes of pain. His left arm was full of tubes. Beyond, in the long eons of distance, he saw a bright window. It was daytime outside, wherever he was.

He closed his eyes but did not sleep. His mind had started moving now. Little memories were trickling in, and he was not at all sure whether he should examine them, or keep them at bay for a while.

A voice to his right said, 'I see you're awake.'

He opened his eyes again and slowly turned his head. The pain was more noticeable now.

To his right side, brought up by a vidcast, was a volumetric head. The head had a face. The face had a gentle smile and a pleasing bedside manner.

'Ah shit,' Drem croaked. His mouth felt dry as sawdust.

AI entities existed in all facets of life in New Eden, usually unseen and out of mind. The one place where common people were regularly exposed to them as humanoid replicants was in hospitals, where they worked in lieu of overworked, fallible human doctors.

Drem regarded the face. It was unmistakably human but had no distinguishing features, and was probably designed to make its patients remember only its vague, benevolent outlines. The face looked back at him, though he got the feeling it was looking through him, or at something he could not see.

He had to ask, if only to keep his mind off other things. 'I've always wondered, how can you analyse me if you're just a hologram? Is there a hidden camera somewhere?' The questions came out in a husky, phlegm-filled tone that alarmed Drem, but the AI didn't raise an eyebrow.

'You are connected to various pieces of machinery that measure all manner of vital functions,' it answered. 'And yes, the room does contain visualization equipment. It is only turned on when you and I are in session, if your vitals spike for an unknown reason, or if you request help.'

The phrasing of 'in session' did not sit well with Drem. The cobwebs in his head were being replaced by the dull cement blocks of pain.

'Right now,' the AI continued, 'it is imperative that you rest and recuperate.'

'Where am I?'

'You're at the Blood Raider military installation in KFIE–Z, constellation XPJ1–6. Delve region.'

The cement block was hacked at, and a piece splintered off. 'That's a whole system away from my colony.'

The AI said, 'Yes. It was.'

He stared at it, not looking at anything.

The AI asked, 'What do you remember?'

He said, 'Not very much.'

'No?'

'Some pain.' He shifted in his bed and winced. 'Well, a lot of pain, actually.'

'Anything else?'

'Nope.'

The AI actually blinked.

Drem stared at it, defiant.

'Your vitals are remarkably stable, but nonetheless you appear to still be in shock,' it said to him.

'What happened to my brother?' Drem asked. 'My brother's body,' he corrected.

'He had already been transported to body storage at another facility. He'll be preserved there unharmed.'

Drem found it very soothing to hear this. It was a little velvet cloth laid over the cement block.

'Do you know what happened?' he asked it.

'I do,' it said.

He lay there in silence.

'Do you want me to tell you?' it asked.

'No,' he said.

Any noises outside were so muffled that he might as well have been imagining them, here in this safe little cloud of white nothingness. But his headache throbbed.

'But I think you better had, nonetheless,' he said.

It told him about the attack during which tens of thousands had been killed, most of them when the colony infrastructure collapsed. The cause was a capsuleer who had turned up in the area and headed straight for a military storage bunker that had recently been erected near the colony. Blood Raider intelligence, or at least what they were willing to declassify for civilians, did not indicate there had been any reason for him to attack the colony itself, only that he had done so after destroying the military bunker along with all other ships in the vicinity. The Raiders had called in backup troops, but those had only served to delay the capsuleer before they, too, were annihilated.

The attacking capsuleer's goals were unconfirmed. He was likely hoping to retrieve salvage, which, the AI reassured Drem for some stupid reason, would have been a futile endeavour. As if reframing the event as even more pointless and random would change its outcome at all.

The pilot had not blown up the colony itself, but taken down its shields and outer armour, and wrecked its infrastructure to the point that it collapsed in on itself. Thousands had expired immediately from the oxygen blowout in the hardest-hit areas, and more had lost their lives in the fiery aftermath. Drem, one of the few survivors, had been saved by rescue forces and brought to this Raider hospital facility on the military base.

Drem thought of himself being transported unconscious between the stars on some makeshift litter, but the image of his brother cropped up unbidden: eyes closed, body in a sealed capsule hauled the other way to some vast storage facility.

He came to a horrible realization.

'My family? My grandmother, my uncles, all the people who were with me in her house?'

The AI hesitated, and Drem realized it was checking its databanks. His family was now a matter of record.

'Only a handful of people survived the attack,' it said. 'There were no other survivors in that particular area of the colony.'

Drem saw the face of Granny Deru saying everything was all right. And he realized that everything had truly and utterly gone to pieces.

'Do you have any questions?' the AI gently asked him.

He squeezed his eyes tightly shut, intent on not crying. 'Why didn't he just kill us all?' he croaked. 'Why'd he even bother to leave me alive? Why not blow up the entire fucking place and end it for good?'

The AI said, 'Our estimates indicate he ran out of missiles.'

Drem laughed and laughed and cried until the tubes in his arms put him back to sleep.

The rehabilitation started not long after. It was agonizing, which helped Drem get through his days. He took all the intangible pain and grief that hid inside him and realized them through physical suffering. When he pushed himself almost beyond his limits, he felt he had achieved something as if in a battle he did not even understand; and he also had to admit that he liked punishing himself simply for being alive enough to feel the pain at all.

He could not move about properly, and the possibility that his condition might relapse was real enough that he had not yet been granted his own quarters. Most evenings he spent in or near his hospital room. Sometimes he'd watch holovids or, when in need of a more immersive distraction, engage in any of the emulation programs the military colony had to offer.

'Most of these programs would normally be classified,' the AI told him one evening, with a barely audible touch of synthetic pride. 'But you're a Sani Sabik, a survivor and an honorary guest, and your well-being trumps bureaucracy.'

'That's good to hear, though I'm not sure how honorary I am,' Drem said. He tried not to think about the lack of faith this implied in his hosts' belief that he could ever put the data to valuable use.

'Oh, you've been noticed. Several high-ranking military operatives even wish to meet with you and give you a tour of their respective stations,' the AI told him. This was not the first time he had heard of this, though the AI usually approached the subject more tangentially. He expected it felt it could be a little more honest with him now.

'I thought under normal circumstances the Blood Raider elite did not mix much with the rest of the Sani Sabik,' he said. It wasn't phrased as a question, but he expected an answer.

'There has been considerable interest in your case, particularly from representatives within our faction,' the AI said. Drem interpreted this as a diplomatic way of saying the brass wanted to patch things over and keep him from asking anything confrontative in public, such as why their forces let the entire colony fall to a capsuleer.

He liked the AI. It was an engaging companion, in the way of those who are courteously knowledgeable and have a genial interest in listening; and its voice, so carefully modulated, felt like the gentle beats of a clock.

'How do you feel about that? About being honoured for your position?' it asked him. He shrugged; the AI regularly tried getting him to open up about how the attack had affected him, but he had deftly avoided all attempts at counselling.

'Tell me about capsuleers,' he said instead. 'I know what they are, but tell me more.'

'What do you want to know?' the AI said. It seemed to hold no rancour at the change of subjects. Drem wasn't sure the emotion was part of its programming.

'I want to know how they live, and behave. How they hunt. They're these mythical beings, angry gods of the skies, but they must have some ties to the rest of the world.'

'Precious few. Outside of secure station environments, where they are effectively isolated, capsuleers' primary interactions with non-capsuleers are conducted through the agent system.'

It explained how agenting worked, meting out kills to the capsuleers in a manner that reminded Drem of a vast cold machine, grinding its gears over the dust of people's lives. It made him think very hard about what had happened and how.

This was how he functioned. He had always been like this. Problems, even the ones that amounted to the worst events of his life, spurred the analytical part of his mind into vicious life, calling forth a cavalcade of thoughts that morphed endlessly into plans. The ability was so deep inside him, he could barely comprehend it on a conscious level. At most he could envision those thoughts through symbols: an idea would start out as a small red molten core, then slowly unravel its lines like an anemone unfurling its arms, each one of them separate but still connected to the core.

Once the AI had finished, it waited in silence for Drem to respond.

'I'd like to know more,' he said at last.

'Excellent. Anything you want to know about the outside world is healthy and will do you good. Fire away.'

He asked more questions. He let the data sink into him. Slowly, the core started to glow.

The AI, believing this to be a sideways entry into proper therapy, gaily obliged him in the conversation, which wore on late into the night. There did come a few moments where its processes registered that something might be wrong beyond its capability to measure. Its every mention of Drem's family was met with no response, as if they were not merely being ignored but completely blocked out; and while Drem would acknowledge comments that related to his brother's life, any attempt to bring up the boy's death would culminate in utter silence.

As soon as he could walk the length of the station without suffering painful muscle cramps, Drem requested an audience with the highest-ranking Blood Raider representative willing to see him. He was eventually given passage to a nearby military colony that operated as part command centre for the local Raider garrison, part carcass drop-off site, and part training grounds for new operatives.

It was located on a massive asteroid whose insides, either naturally empty or hollowed out by construction efforts, had been filled up with colony sections. The whole colony looked like a metal seed ready to flower from the rock that contained it, glittering in the light from the nearest sun. Drem, who had not often seen his own colony from the outside, was amazed that any race of humans could insert themselves so thoroughly into a hostile environment that it looked almost as if it had given rise to them. But then, the Blood Raiders were particularly adept at insinuating their way into other people's lives, and at adapting their surroundings to imply in such a myriad of ways that their presence had been needed all along.

They flew into a tunnel that took them deep inside the station's core, upon which the ship cut its power and was thereafter pulled in by some unseen force. The tunnel was very well-lit, as was the hangar they eventually settled in. Lighting was one of the most important parts of operating any space colony, often considered second only to the planning of spaces and ceilings, and it was an unwise colony overseer with a surfeit of faith in his diplomatic abilities who did not pay heed to a station's light levels. Electricity, even on a deep-space colony, was a low price to pay for crowd control.

Drem had sat apart from the few other passengers on the flight, all of whom were enlisted men who had little to no interest in him, and while he'd been grateful for the opportunity to gather his thoughts, it felt good merely to sense his presence register with someone else. A representative met him as soon as he got off. The rep was nominally a public relations agent but had the unmistakable air of a military man, and his clothing, which was a grey infused with the darkest golden red, looked crisp and pressed.

'My name is Raseren Arkah. Welcome to our barracks,' he said.

'It's my pleasure. Thank you for having me,' Drem told him. He expected to shake the man's hand, but Raseren stood stock still.

'The station overseer awaits, but he asked that you be given a tour of our facilities first, if you're willing and able.'

'That would be fine,' Drem said.

'We'll see the training areas first,' Raseren said and set off.

Their walk brought them to large halls with high ceilings that ended in transparent nanoalloy and black space beyond. There was the stink of sweat in the air, and thuds all around as hundreds of people landed on mattresses or pounded on padded obstacles.

'There's so many of them,' Drem said in amazement.

'The Blood Raiders are a strong faction,' Raseren commented straightforwardly.

'All engaged in combat work, too,' Drem added as he watched the recruits throw each other back and forth.

'We focus on close-quarters work here. Practical activities that work during boarding and invasion.'

'Not necessarily the first thing that comes to mind for use in interstellar warfare,' Drem said.

Raseren seemed amused by this. 'There is an entirely separate school of tactics and starship combat located elsewhere on the colony. Command does not want the recruits to get too comfortable at their desks before they've gotten their hands dirty.'

'I suppose being choked out or punched in the face a few times dials down the arrogance,' Drem said. The throws and takedowns beat dull thuds on the floor, which he felt through the soles of his feet.

Raseren nodded. 'It drives them to constant improvement.

However well they do elsewhere, they will always remember the painful alternatives that await if their interstellar tactics fail them.'

They passed through several rooms, each progressively smaller and barer than the last, until they were walking down empty corridors. The smell turned from sweat to antiseptic, the colours morphed from muted dark to a bright white. It was very quiet.

After passing through a final gateway whose two doors were hermetically sealed, the cloudy air in between them full of micro-disinfectants, they entered the medical section. All around them were small rooms with walls of varyingly tinted glass. Most of them were entirely translucent, if not transparent, and had teams of white-clad students busily working on various things organic.

'The pressure's really on in this place, isn't it? There is no privacy here,' Drem said. Even the rooms with slightly opaque walls were lit so brightly that the students' silhouettes shone through like moving X-ray images.

'Part of the cadets' studies involves the ability to operate under duress and inspection. These are the least of the pressures they'll be working under when they join the Blood Raiders proper.'

Drem glanced into a few rooms as they passed by. Most people were engaged in some manner of medical activities, he surmised, based on the amount of sharp, small metal equipment they appeared to be using.

'Those are some of the strangest body dummies I've ever seen,' Drem remarked. He peered and said, 'Some have their flesh completely missing.'

There was no response. The thought occurred to him that some of those might not be dummies, and he returned his gaze firmly to the back of the representative's head.

They kept moving, Raseren keeping up a quiet dialogue on the great medical advances achieved by the Blood Raiders in recent years and the renewed scientific interest in the properties of human blood. From the corner of his eye Drem saw the inhabitants of one room go into panic. Their agitation was followed by a silent splattering of maroon all over the walls of their chamber, blotting their fate from sight.

'People need to stay focused,' Raseren said expressionlessly.

They passed a sign that said DROP-OFF HANGAR & OFFAL STORAGE. Drem was not offered the chance to see this section, nor did he ask.

At the end of the medical section they were disinfected again and passed through another set of sealed doors, as if shifting from one organ to another. This section looked much richer than the rest, and while the direct light levels dropped slightly, the ambient lighting increased, as did all the decorative objects hung on walls or standing on wooden bookshelves. They walked over hand-woven carpets that had been specially fitted to the shape of the area and the furniture it contained. Even the metal in the walls was clean and polished, unlike the cement-and-dirty-iron constructions Drem had grown up with on his own colony. Tall banners with various Blood Raider sigils were hung at regular intervals.

The representative slowed his gait to give Drem a chance to inspect the contents of the shelves. Most of the books were leather-bound religious tomes of one sort or another, and the unlabelled artefacts that dotted the shelves had a holy theme to them: plasti-sealed bones; air-sealed canisters of a handmade nature; even small fragments of calciferous rocks, many covered in faded brown spatters, which Drem presumed had come from someone very holy and quite dead.

'This is the combination theology and command section,' Raseren said. 'It is not possible to rise high in the ranks of the Blood Raiders without being intimately familiar with our faith.'

Drem nodded. He knew his theology as well as anyone else who'd been raised in a religious household – albeit with a few notable gaps in that knowledge, he bitterly thought – but most of these texts and items he'd barely heard of.

The representative continued, with a slightly more passionate timbre, 'A person cannot do what we do unless they understand, as fully as is humanly possible, why we do it. Not the science or the power, nor the fear it engenders in others – and we should never deny that we reap those benefits – but the closeness to the Red God it entails. Discussions on this topic have gone on for decades.'

Drem nodded again. He got the feeling the rep was using the exact same speech on him as he did on new recruits, but there was no doubting the man's strength of feeling on the subject, nor the singular focus he likely possessed. At no point had he asked Drem about his family and his loss, and while Drem supposed he should take it as an insult, he merely felt relieved.

They came to a handleless door of old, darkened wood, which looked entirely out of place in the metal wall surrounding it. The rep held up a hand near a biometrics scanner in the wall, waited until it was greenlit, then pushed at the door, which swung silently open.

The circular room on the other side was large but not high, and while the organic theme of wood, leather and dead earth continued alongside the curving walls, the furniture looked modern and very functional. It included a vast round table with a black, matte glass plate that Drem didn't doubt had excellent vidcasting abilities. He suspected this room was as much a tactical bunker as a haven of worship.

At the other side of the table sat a man whose skin was nearly white. The veiny streaks in his head, on his throat and the back of his hands lay spread out like a torn net. His dark hair was cut short and his clothing tightly covered a body that appeared shorn of excesses. His face had no beard, a share of scars, only a few wrinkles, and eyes of a colour that Drem couldn't possibly determine from a distance. It was impossible to tell his age; he might be thirty or two hundred.

The representative reverently whispered, 'This is Carlen Jore, the man you requested to meet,' then backed out and closed the door.

When the ghost of a man opened his mouth to speak, Drem expected the throaty croak of an octogenarian. What he heard instead was a dulcet and powerful voice, the kind that felt like it could both shout down walls and talk someone off a ledge.

'Be assured,' the voice said, 'that I speak for the Great Master when I say how very sorry I am for your loss.'

Drem nodded. The master in question was Omir Sarakusa, the infamous head of the Blood Raiders and altogether not a man Drem expected much sympathy from.

'I understand you have a request,' the voice continued. It was much too strong to come from such a trimmed, marked, frail body, and Drem wondered whether he was seeing an old man with great reserves of vitality or a young man taken seriously ill.

'I do,' he replied. 'I want revenge for my family.'

'Who is it you want harvested?' Carlen seemed unmoved, but Drem thought he could detect a heartbeat, or merely the quickening of one, through those blackened veins. He swiftly walked over to where the man was sitting, took a seat beside him and persisted, 'The capsuleer who murdered my family and everyone else on my colony. Track him down, find his ship and his pod, trap them, board them and take him into our custody. Bleed him, but not to death. You must keep him alive for a long time. I want to see him. I want to use him as an example, to everyone who's been asking about my case, of what we do to those who defy us. And eventually . . . I want him to die a painful death.'

Drem caught his breath. Carlen said nothing in reply. The room smelled of silence and age, of dead things long gone to dust.

'This is not possible,' the man's ageless voice said at last.

Drem moved to speak but Carlen raised his hand. The veins in his palm were throbbing. 'I am not heartless, but as a representative of the Great Master, I will not coddle you with lies. Listen.' He stood up, slowly, and drifted past Drem, talking into the air. 'If we were to do this at all, and pool into it resources that are currently being spent on protecting the interests of our people, we would have to either find this capsuleer or entice him to return. Even if he came alone and unguarded, we would lose ships and people in the ensuing battle. Were we to emerge successful, at whatever price, we would have to capture the man's escape pod and disable it in some manner, lest he simply self-destruct and awaken safe in a cloning facility far beyond our reach. I am not informed of the latest science to do with capsule technology, but I believe it is entirely possible that the mere attempt to extract the human from his pod might kill him, or at the very least trigger some defence mechanism to that effect.'

Drem was breathing too fast. His head swam. The lights in the room felt too bright, even as Carlen walked away from him and receded out of focus.

'And that is assuming,' Carlen's voice continued through the encroaching haze, 'that we would even be allowed to attempt this. Believe me that I am sorry for your loss, as I would be for anyone who had suffered at the hands of a capsuleer, but there is a political cost to this that simply cannot be ignored, distasteful as it may seem. We have a . . . relationship with the capsuleers.'

Drem flew to his feet. The room swayed a little. In his hyperventilated stupidity of the moment, he thought how strange it was to hear a Blood Raider, the vampire of the skies, speak of someone else as distasteful.

'Yes, they cost us dearly,' Carlen said, his back turned to Drem. 'It's a terrible price to pay, but we often take our lives from them in return, harvesting the crews of their ships.'

'You're trading our people for theirs,' Drem said with more rancour than he knew he had.

Carlen said, 'What other faction would dare to constantly bring us ships crewed with thousands of humans from all over the world, lose it all in battle, have us scoop up the refuse of escape pods, and yet not start waging total war on us? The capsuleer crews account for a substantial part of our pickings.'

Drem could not keep his voice level any longer. 'What kind of beast are you?'

Carlen finally turned, and the look he gave Drem was as dark as the veins on his throat. 'A wise one,' he said. 'Would you bring down upon our heads a plague of capsuleers? Do we not have enough trouble dealing with them already? Do you even know how much it would cost in money and raw intel merely to go after a single one of those animals?'

'He destroyed our people! He destroyed my family!' Drem shouted at him, beating so hard on the glass of the table that it rang with his blows.

'And we shall prevail,' the man said in a tone now sanctimonious and infuriatingly calm.

Drem tightened his grip on the chair, with the budding idea to rush the man and break it over his poisonous head. Carlen seemed to notice this, for he lowered his head a fraction and in an even quieter tone said, 'If you do anything other than walk out that door, it will be the last action you ever take.'

Drem considered it – but Carlen added, 'And your family will have lost their lives for nothing. Their memory will be disgraced by a coward who lashed out at one of his own.'

This brought a hesitation, and when the Blood Raider added with undisguised disgust, 'Do something with your life, such as there is left of it,' Drem's fighting spirit left him completely. Through some unseen signal the door opened, and it was now flanked with guards.

The man pointed his black-veined hand outside, into the unknown.

'How did it go?' the AI asked him.

Drem kept silent and calm.

The AI added, 'Your vitals are more stable than ever before. I think the trip was therapeutic for you.'

Quietly, hiding his disgust, Drem said, 'It was. Now I just need to get back on track with my rehabilitation.'

The AI looked at him with its unseeing eyes. 'You're still grieving,' it said.

Drem ignored the subtle warning. He opened up the selection screen for the station's emulation programs, and was grimly pleased to see that his access had not been restricted. He browsed through the selection.

'I'm fine,' he lied. 'I have some more questions.'

'Yes?'

'About the region. And the Blood Raiders. And our military.' He found the program he was looking for and started it up. It was more extensive than the ones he'd engaged in so far, much more extensive, but that was all right. He had time, and purpose.

'Oh good,' the AI said. 'You're showing a bit of local interest.'

'And the vessels stationed here,' Drem said. Before his eyes, the piloting program ran through its opening cycles.

4

The two women sat firmly at their tables in the outdoor café. It jutted out of the side of the building, high over the surface below, built over with a transparent shield that occasionally let through little gusts of air. Plants grew out of every wall, carefully placed in between metal and marble plates, and much of the architecture was gently amorphous in the manner of a wind-worn article. The place felt naturally raw, like a rocky cliffside opening in a mountain; and was yet another odd reminder of how the most expensive thing on a space station was the convincing illusion that one wasn't in space at all.

In tandem with the outdoor theme it was a naturalist café, attended by people who were either completely into that lifestyle – the ones who would order drinks the same colour as the plants and imbibe them with every sign of enjoyment – or the ones on the other side of that lifestyle; the ones with red eyes and unkempt hair who stared at their drinks the colour of plants with every sign of utter dread and disgust.

'Talk to me,' Heci said.

'I'm not doing too good.' Ralea's hair was matted and shiny with filth. Behind it, her face was covered in red blotches from overstrain and exertion; as were her eyes, with large red veins snaking through their whites. She had never thought it would turn out like this.

'I can tell,' Heci told her. 'You look like you're going to puke in that drink.'

'Don't tempt me.' Ralea's voice was raspy. She'd been found lying on the floor of her office, hissing and gasping, by the night guards on their rounds. They had escorted her to her personal quarters, fearful of their own jobs lest they bring her to the infirmary and later find they'd ruined her career and their own with it.

She'd lain on the floor of her own home for the remainder of the night and most of the next day, alternately frozen with fear and screaming at nothing, clutching the cloth of her increasingly filthy clothing and watching the blackness seep out of every crack in the wall. She hadn't dared use her secret stash, lest it push her completely over the brink. At last she'd heard from Heci, who had dragged her out of there.

Ralea leaned back in her chair, rubbed her eyes and breathed deeply. Living did not come easy right at this moment.

The breeze was refreshing in the café, high over the ground. The brief gusts of wind kept nudging her hair in front of her face. There was no view straight down – the last thing you needed on an unsettled stomach was to see how dizzyingly far it was to the ground – but the view in the distance was magnificent: massive sharp towers jutting out of the ground like shards, and vistas of grassland dotted around like little wounds in the metal skin of the station. Ralea registered none of it.

'It's the drugs,' Heci said.

Ralea nodded.

'Talk to me,' Heci pleaded again.

Ralea kept looking out at the vistas. She imagined that if she took a running jump off of the restaurant, and crossed the multiple layers of suicide security installations put in place for this exact kind of mindset, she might feel like she was flying for a few precious seconds.

'I can't,' she said. Her skin itched, and her clothing felt as if made of raw crystals, stinging cold and simultaneously biting hot.

'Talk to me,' Heci repeated.

'I don't know what to say,' Ralea told her in a whisper.

'Maybe I can help,' Heci said.

The light wasn't bright but it made Ralea's head throb. She tried to compose her thoughts. 'I don't even know what "this" all is. Or who I am any longer, except some freaked out, druggie, broken-down weakling.'

'Fucked if I'm going to let you play the pity-me martyr card, either,' Heci said. When Ralea looked at her, she took a grinning sip of her drink. 'You're in deep water, hon, and I'm not going to push you under. But you still need to talk. Tell me about something, anything, even if it has nothing to do with this.'

'Like what?' Ralea said. The nausea came and went like waves on the ocean.

'Tell me about your first day at the corp,' Heci said.

'Can't.'

Heci leaned over and took her hand. 'Then go further back. Start at the beginning.'

'Of yesterday?'

'Of your life, sweetie.'

Ralea gave her a puzzled look.

'I need the diversion, believe me,' Heci said. 'And you need to start talking.'

Ralea noticed that her friend's eyes were also red. She took a deep breath, filling her lungs with the fresh air that stroked her face.

'I was born rich.'

Heci watched her; then, when nothing else was forthcoming, asked, 'What was your home like?'

Through the fugue of pain and dehydration, Ralea cast her mind back to old times. 'Not unlike this, actually. Planetside, but inside a dome. It was a wonderful life, very safe.'

'Sounds secluded?'

'Oh yeah. I was a protected princess.' The memory of her youth warmed her mind like soothing currents. Ralea continued, 'For a long time it was all I wanted. I loved to study, so that's what I did. But there's no consequence to that kind of life. You never move yourself. You're driven, hovered, shuttled or flown everywhere.' She thought this over, slowly breathing in the fresh high air. 'There was no connection between anything at all. I lived in a bubble, perfectly safe, and I guess I was happy there for a while. Which was wrong, because we both know nothing good ever comes to stay without hard work behind it.'

'Absolutely,' Heci said, but Ralea noticed she was looking away, idly stirring her straw in her drink.

'Anyway, despite the isolation, I loved it. Living with my parents at their huge mansion planetside, learning about the world and the way it works, and always imagining that I'd have a wonderful career in some profession I just couldn't quite nail down yet. Eventually, as you probably figured out a long time ago, that became a bit of a problem.'

Heci gave a grimacing little smile. ' It must've been hard to break away.'

'Well, it wasn't so much breaking away as ...' Ralea sighed, and brushed the hair from her face. 'I don't know. I hit that point in my early teens when I realized, simultaneously, that I was a really bright girl with enough financial backing to find major success in anything I wanted to do, and that I had no goddamn clue what to do with my life. The only valid measure of accomplishment was the approval of those closest to me, so eventually I developed this crazy need to validate myself in their eyes.'

She paused, took a sip of her drink. 'They didn't neglect me, you understand. They weren't the kind of parents who throw money at their kid from a distance.'

'I'm sure they didn't,' Heci said kindly. 'It sounds like they were very loving.'

Ralea nodded. Her body felt more at ease than it had for a while, not just during the last night of craziness but the weeks and months of what she was now seeing as a slow-motion collapse. This storytelling, the treatment of her own life as a distant thing, gave her a bit of needed distance.

She said, 'They were simply the only reliable indicator of accomplishment in this world of plenty I inhabited. What happened then, as it had to, was I became driven to work harder and harder, eventually reaching the point where the drive was all I had to prove I was really a person. Some things went pretty badly wrong along the way—' this brought Heci's gaze back to her like a whip, but her friend didn't ask, '—but it only . . . I don't know.' She thought it over. 'Strengthened my resolve, I guess.'

'That's a beautiful way of saying that work is all you had.'

Ralea nodded again. 'When I was chosen to work here, so far from where I grew up, it was a great honour and I took it as confirmation that I'd been on the right path all along. I was the only one from my family ever to move to a station, and even if I was just a mid-level datagirl and wouldn't do anything important for years, I could see myself rising eventually. Commander, maybe, or CEO. Or an agent.'

'And work just as hard to get there,' Heci said, 'no matter how much it wore you out.'

'Precisely.'

Heci took a sip of her drink, grimaced and stirred it with her straw. 'You have to be incredibly clever, resourceful and tenacious to rise this high.'

'Yeah.'

'So when did we start being so fucked up?'

Ralea, whose red-blotched paleness had gradually been assuming a more human colour, couldn't help but laugh at that. 'I don't think we did,' she said. 'I think we've just kept going the same way we always have.'

'Unstoppably.'

'Yeah.'

'And we never think the road is going to run out,' Heci said sadly.

'It doesn't. We do,' Ralea said. She thought for a moment, then plunged in. 'I started doing drugs.'

A quick glance at Heci's face revealed that this was no big news. Ralea continued, 'At first it was no different from all the caffeine and sugar I'd ingested as a student. When I needed better performance I found the tools to do it, and if that was a cup of coffee or some sugary crap, then damn it, I was going to use it, and to hell with the consequences.'

Heci gave her health drink a look, sighed, and looked back at her friend.

Ralea continued, 'I drank my first cup of coffee in the kitchen at home when I was fifteen and trying to stay up to study. It didn't make me feel grown up. I ate my first strip of Red Exile when I was twenty-one, living on a space station with half a year's work experience and a huge project on my back. It didn't make me feel more mature, or sexy, or deviant. It just kept me awake and functioning. And all the while, I had that goal in mind. Mission agent. Top of the corporate ladder. People say it's management and command, but that's wrong; those are all politics and happenstance. Agents are the important ones. Agents make it on their own worth and nobody dares touch us.'

'Come on, let's grab a little air,' Heci said. They got up and walked over to the edge of the veranda. Ralea's body still hurt from the recent wringing, but she enjoyed the motion, and the zephyr was becoming more soothing. It was good to be going somewhere, even if only for a little while.

'When did you lose control?' Heci asked after they'd rested their drinks on the parapet.

Ralea thought this over. 'When I made agent. When I saw the paperwork on my first kill mission.' She looked at Heci. 'I know it's not something we talk about. Nobody talks about it. But those people were dead. I killed them.'

'You haven't killed anyone. We go over this in training and then again in the realignments,' Heci said in a soothing tone. 'Everyone loses a bit of sleep now and then. But we're not bad people.'

'First time it truly hit me was a week into the job, when the obsessive-research part of my personality took over and made me look over the full list of deceased. Not the shorthand they send us, which you can sign off in a blink along with the cargo, livestock and scrap metals they report in the salvage datastreams, but the actual, detailed lists of names. It took some digging, because they don't want you to do this, but once I unlocked the names I also discovered how to look those people up in our databases.'

'That,' Heci said, 'was a bad idea.'

'It was a rotten goddamn idea, done by a rotten goddamn know-it-all who thought she'd be better off if she faced the facts.'

'How long could you stand it?'

Ralea took some time to answer. Eventually she said, in a chastened voice, 'I broke down crying after the fifth or sixth face, staring at me from the dead screen.'

Heci nodded. 'Same here.'

'And you know what made it worse? There was so little information on them! We've got one of the most extensive databases in the world – we have to – and for many of these people there was barely a picture and a next of kin.'

'So what'd you do?'

'Drugs.'

Heci looked askance at her.

Ralea said, 'I was adapting, I thought. I'd been using them for a while to keep me focused, and then I used them to numb myself up a little. It was about staying productive, and being happy with it. Making myself happy.'

She sighed. 'Aside from that, I did basically the same as you and anyone else. I kept on going. Dropped the pictures, never looked at them again, never thought of – well, that's a lie. Thought of it a lot, always have, but never acknowledged it.'

She brushed back her hair again, and gently rubbed the skin of her hands. 'The job was there and I worked hard, but eventually I had to admit that I had changed. I was no longer an outsider from the world, looking to make a place in it. I had very much become a part of the world, and I'd become something very specific, if only I dared put a name to it. But if I did that, if I gave it that acknowledgement, it'd all be over. So I kept working, and I never again looked at the names, and in every goddamn moment of weakness since, the drugs have been there to catch me.'

Heci looked over the view. Hovercars were passing each other in the distance, en route to somewhere. 'We've been working for years. How long has this been a problem?'

'Since the hallucinations. And the vomiting.'

Heci raised an eyebrow.

'I'm not sure how long,' Ralea admitted. 'Weeks, months. Years. I'm doing a far higher dose now than when I started, but shit, it's not like there's any kind of scale on these things.' She pointed her finger at some unseen marker in the sky. 'This is the level you can stay at without having a breakdown.' She raised her hand a bit. 'And this is the level where you go batshit ... It's not like they go over that stuff in training.'

'So what's happening now?'

Ralea took a deep breath. She put her drink down on the floor and clasped her hands together behind her neck, like a prisoner contemplating her execution. 'I'm losing it, Heci. That's the long and the short of it. I finally reached the top and every day, even as I'm sliding back down, I try not to think that it made me into a monster. The drugs made me perform and they've made me forget. And now they don't even work.'

'What is it you see?' Heci asked her.

'Monsters and blackness.'

'And you can't stop it?'

Ralea shook her head. She picked up the glass again, took a sip. 'Withdrawal isn't a problem. At least, I don't think it is. It might be. I've got savings, I can pay for whatever they have to do. The problem is, I don't know what I'm doing myself, anymore. I've spent the last thirty-six hours variously screaming obscenities at my walls, shivering in cramped fear, or trying to drink some water and hold it down for more than five minutes. The thought of going back to work ...' She trailed off.

'How long has it been since you last used drugs?'

'About two hours. Took some before I crawled out to meet you this morning. Before that ... I don't know. I used a bunch of my hidden stash at the apartment, trying to claw my way out of the tremors, but I don't know when or how much, or even if it helped.' She looked pleadingly at her friend.

Heci took her head in her hands, leaned in and kissed her on the forehead, then leaned back and looked directly into her eyes. 'You get a grip on things. And you leave your job.' Ralea tried to shake her head but Heci held it tight and said, 'No. You don't get to run away from this. You look like you crawled out of a grave, and I've seen you heading that way for a long time now.'

'I . . . can't . . . quit,' Ralea whispered. She was trying not to cry, and failing.

Heci let go of her head and grasped her in a tight hug. Ralea trembled with quelled emotion that she didn't dare let out.

Stroking her hair, Heci said, 'Jan cheated on me.'

Ralea whimpered and held Heci tighter.

'Found him in bed with someone else. He said something that I didn't hear. I put down the snacks and holovid, and left his quarters. He didn't run after me, which hurt, but I'm glad for it.'

'I'm so sorry,' Ralea said, her voice muffled through the fabric of Heci's shirt.

'So am I. I'm sorry I let you fall this far. I'm sorry I've let myself do the same. This place is poison and this job is poison and this world does nothing but break us down until we're dust under somebody else's feet.'

'You haven't made my mistakes,' Ralea said. 'You don't do drugs. You don't have freakouts or hallucinations.'

Heci shook her head. 'You know what that scene with Jan made me want to do? Fuck. Anyone. Just find someone out there, without a name or a face, and let him use me all up. Same as it did when I had my turn at looking up the names, way back when. I'm no holier than you are. I just find a different kind of release.'

The two women stood there, holding each other. The breeze stroked their hair.

'I'm leaving,' Heci said.

'What?'

'And you're coming with me.'

Ralea broke the hold and stared dazedly at Heci. 'What do you mean? You can't go. We can't go! Go where?'

'Anywhere but here, hon. We need to get you cleaned up and give my stupid heart some time to stitch itself together.'

Horrified, Ralea said, 'I can't leave!'

Heci stroked her cheek. 'You can't stay, dearest. Or you are simply going to die.'

'I'm not a quitter. Where would we go? I'll just drag myself with me, wherever I end up! What would I say to people? Hey, I'm a worn-out druggie good at hard work and mass murder?'

'The people can go jump through a wormhole,' Heci told her.

Ralea was starting to tremble uncontrollably.

'Withdrawals?' Heci asked.

She shook her head. 'Panic. Attack.'

Heci held on tighter, but Ralea pushed herself out of her friend's grip. 'I gotta go.'

'We do, yes.'

'No!' she said, walking fast away from Heci. 'Not with you. Not away. Not now.'

'Ralea—'

'No! Fuck! Fuck! Fuck you! *Fuck you!*'

She broke into a run and fled the woodland haven in the sky, alone, descending to the metal and concrete below.

The promenade had turned cold with the onset of evening. Ralea's teeth chattered as she walked about. She had no destination in mind, nor much else beside the need to keep moving.

This was one of the highest and most restricted parts of the space station. The more important you were, the closer you could situate yourself to the sun and the skies. Capsuleers could even be glimpsed from here, walking along their special section of the station just a few storeys up. She tried not to look at them. If she had a weapon she might will herself to do something stupid, but the tracking and scanning equipment at this level eliminated those kinds of risks.

She felt detached from herself, not as if she were watching her body from the outside, but as if she were someone else entirely, seeing herself the way a normal, well-adjusted, drug-free person would.

She felt numb; not hungry nor tired, and neither nauseous nor anxious. She was merely there, a biological machine set in constant motion, and now completely unanchored.

She walked past a few bars and went into one, not wanting a drink, but merely to feel a part of something. She did not even sit down before turning on her heel and walking out again; the looks she'd received were of various kinds, none inviting.

Her walk took her past chapels, restaurants, stores and more bars, eventually leaving the higher section and went down to the lesser promenade, where the upper class of 'normal' people resided and did things like buy food or embark on interstellar travel. Down there she dared look up again and saw only the skies, turning darker. Hovercars flew by, looking like ants on the ceiling, and dirigibles skinned with video ads ambled through the air. The tops of the skyscrapers seemed to reach for them, so high and pointed it felt as if the floating vehicles might actually be caught on their tips. The sun's receding rays were reflected in thousands of windows all the way down to the street, with camera drones hovering through the light like gnats over a lake at sundown.

There were trees here, too, and they blocked out the sun from the stores Ralea passed. Everything was here: Amarrian temples and other religious services, Minmatar recruitment centres for anything from ambitious arts and engineering projects to badly masqueraded gunrunning, Gallente hedonism cruises to serve all possible whims and curiosities, and even Caldari offers for anything from proxied investment in new businesses to attendance at major upcoming sports events. She looked ahead and saw the streets of metal and concrete waiting for her, while the flora dotted the landscape at positions just strategic enough to remind everyone they were still in space.

And below her feet, taking care of the refuse, were the little cleaner bugs, skittering around on silent legs.

She wished she were a cleaner bug.

Her stomach lurched.

The view Ralea had of herself from the outside was snapped back in. She felt alone and utterly helpless. Her body ached and trembled.

She stumbled to a tree and held on to its trunk while she vomited. A young couple walked past her, their conversation falling to a whisper. She saw them shake their heads. The skin on their faces was stretched, and their teeth were sharp, and the hands they had around each other's waists were mottled with blackened veins.

Her nails dug into the bark of the wood. She dry heaved a couple of times, spat, forced herself to rise.

The sun was setting and she could not go back.

She marched off, to somewhere, anywhere and nowhere at all.

5

Ships hover in stillness. A series of the smaller ones, the frigate classes, are hooked in with massive electromagnetic anchors the sizes of boulders, and are kept constantly hovering. They are the first guard, ready to fly out at a moment's notice, and there must be no delay on them when they leave.

Farther in the distance can be glimpsed the cruisers, larger than the frigates by an order of magnitude, held in place by massive clamps on strategic support sections of the ships' bulks. The cruisers are kept in their own separate area with plenty of space around them. When the clamps are disengaged, they are not merely moved aside but thrown off by an explosion of incendiary agents so that the cruisers can take off without delay.

Yet farther are the battleships, so large that the naked eye simply cannot take them in all at once. Battleships don't usually stay long on the outer colonies; they require too much space and unless they're coming in with spoils from a successful mission they tend to drain the colony of resources.

There were many exit areas in this hangar, though most of them eventually led to the same central hub. A few side exits led directly to other sections and were meant primarily for various types of emergencies. There was a wide corridor for fragile offal transport, crossed swiftly by quiet people with downcast eyes; and a series of fork-like corridors used mainly for serious injury cases that led directly to the living quarters.

In one of the forked corridors, a door slid open.

Nothing should have passed through that door at this time of day. No one was disembarking or leaving. Alarms should have activated, sirens, drones and electric shielding, but none did.

Drem moved through the door. He did not run, but walked at a pace that implied a definite and time-sensitive purpose.

He passed beyond the shadows of the corridor's overhang and into the hangar proper, and the lights that glinted off the distant starship hulls shone down on his face.

Every faction has its own fleet of ships, the smaller crewable by only a few men, the larger inhabited by thousands. Those ships are designed and indelibly marked as creations of their factions. It is impossible to see a golden vessel belonging to the holy Amarr Empire and confuse it with the hard, angular lines of a ship created by the corporate Caldari State.

Likewise, the hangars in each station have their own visual themes – the Blood Raiders have a vermilion sheen, the colour of a dying sun setting for the last time on an old empire – but if one looks closely enough, hangars and ships are all the same underneath. They simply take different paths to the same destination. A hangar must keep its contents in full working order, ready to bring them into action under great duress; it must retain the right people in the proper places; and it must be accessible and navigable at any point in time. Likewise, a ship must fly through space in whatever direction is required and at whatever speed it can muster; it must keep its crew alive and all its major processes functioning; it must fulfil whatever mission its pilot reasonably requires, whether it be to transport goods, to operate on celestial asteroids and ice crystals, or to attack and destroy.

Drem walked over the metal floor, the sound of his steps washing away into the distance. There was no echo here. The hangar was so vast that he could not see its far side; the distance merely held shadowy silhouettes of ship parts, like tattered monsters crouching in the mist. He wasn't too worried about being caught, but nonetheless stepped lightly. He'd had enough time to learn to walk again, though he still stumbled a bit if he got overzealous. He hoped he wouldn't have to run.

He came to the light pits, deep gaps in the ground that were used to hold ships in place. They were wide – Drem just barely might throw a rock over one – and perfectly circular, their sides lit with a dim blue light when not in use. This section, closest to the exits, had no ships or ship parts in storage, so the unblocked lights from the pits reflected a pale blue off every surface.

Each light pit was stuffed full of complex electronic material that would hold a starship in place like a suction cup. They had no safety boundaries, partly because anything outside the pits might interfere with the ship containment fields, and partly because anyone passing through the hangar on a Blood Raider military complex was expected not to be an idiot. A cadet who fell in would find their pride and colony reputation even more damaged than their limbs.

Drem swiftly made his way past the pits, walking as fast as he could, remaining nonchalant. In the distance he could see the repair sector scaffolding that held spare parts, engine sections and modules that had been split off the main units and were being put through automated testing.

As he got closer, he heard the subdued roar of the automated testing: a hum that thrummed so deep it felt like it echoed in his body. He passed the area as quickly as he could; the broken, dismantled pieces lying around like debris were an unpleasant sight.

Colony hangars contain security systems that cannot by nature be as comprehensive as those of space stations. A colony is often defenceless, far away from any backup forces, not even left with sentry guns for protection, and so must be ready to defend itself with whatever forces it can muster. As a result, its security must not be based on time-locking, full of delays and checks that might impede fighters scrambling to defend against pirates or, even worse, capsuleers.

The worst sources of failure of any kind are human, and thus the security system has inbuilt mechanisms that will tolerate a certain degree of error before it sounds the alarm or locks off any part of the system. A panicking supervisor cannot be allowed to hold back a vital undocking when the colony is under attack, no matter how many buttons he mistakenly pushes.

*

In the lights of the metal floor he saw reflections of engines held in stasis. As he stepped from one section to another, the multifaceted images looked like a myriad eyes, staring down at him in judgement. He stared back, willing himself to remain unseen. The engines were attached to ships, which meant he was getting close. All he needed was to find the right one.

He started breaking up his route, veering from the straight path and walking instead among the frigates. There were no guards in this section of the hangar, but he was not too far from the cruisers and the battleships now, which might have people onboard.

Drem had planned this as carefully as he could. The only place impossible to pass through undetected was the guard section stationed between the personal quarters and the hangar entry area. Drem had gone to considerable effort ingratiating himself with the guards who worked there, playing the weakling civilian who was always up for a talk during the late evenings, and who, thanks to insurance payments for his accident, had no qualms about bringing a little something to help the shifts pass faster. The guards, in turn, had seen no reason tonight why Drem couldn't pass through the guard section and into the hangar entry area; it was locked from the hanger proper and used mostly as an outlook point. Shortly after letting him through, they had seen no reason in anything at all, no sense or conscious thought, thanks to the concoction Drem had tricked them into drinking. They were the only ones who might have been quick enough to catch him after he set off the alarm.

Goodwill and knowledge were essential, Drem knew, but not enough for his plan. Thus, earlier in the day a particular datakey had vanished from a particular pocket, and had proven very useful in passing from the entry area to the hangar proper. The key could be used by anyone as it was absent of bio-heuristics, those kinds of safety measures having been deemed an unnecessary extravagance in a closed colony where most people knew one another and departures were strictly controlled. For these very reasons its owner would not yet have reported it missing, for there was nowhere for it to go, and little but embarrassment to be had from making a fuss.

*

In the olden days of the holy Amarr Empire there arose a blood-worshipping cult called the Sani Sabik. They were powerful and cabalistic, and soon found themselves at odds with the pious ruling body.

The Sani Sabik were hunted down on their native planets, but some managed to escape, settling on different planets to forge a new life of black science and worship. Eventually, a particularly vicious sect of this cult took to the skies again, this time as the hunters. Led by the brilliant madman Omir Sarakusa, they called themselves the Blood Raiders.

It is a constant affront to the Amarr Empire that the Blood Raiders' fleet is based on Amarrian design, modified for the Raiders' needs of tactics and propaganda. Raider ships have the same golden liquid sheen as the Amarr vessels, but are mottled in rust-like vermilion, giving the hideous impression they tore their way out of the Amarrian womb.

The access doors of the frigate soothed open. Drem walked in, silhouetted by the glare that bloomed from inside. The doors closed. A few moments later, various other lights lit up from the frigate: some of them on the outside hull, others shining out through the transparent nanoalloy of its viewports. In this vast field of ships and stars, no one would notice the activation unless they were looking out for it. The ship, a unique Blood Raider creation called the Cruor, powered up its engines.

Had someone been watching, it is unlikely they would have immediately raised the alarm. The ship went through its pre-flight cycles with perfect ease, and the light pits holding it in its hovering place started to disengage. The smooth launch procedure was a clear indicator that the ship's internal security systems had been disengaged with a sanctioned datakey. Notifications would still be making their way to various service boards and guard stations, but the closest line of alert currently lay unconscious on the floor. Undoubtedly someone would eventually request information on the Cruor's mission, but they wouldn't dare lock down the hangar, lest they ruin the colony's response against an impending attack.

The ship was slowly shunted out, its trajectory set. By the time it exited the hangar and was out in space proper, the station crew had realized the error and started hailing it. Nobody knew who was onboard and what their intention was, and before a decision on a chase could be arrived at, the ship had flown away unharmed.

Frigates have small crews and little firepower. They are rarely used in direct conflict but can be made to work exceptionally well as support vessels, stopping enemy ships short and holding them in place for higher-class ships to aim their guns. Depending on the mission, they can be flown by any number of people. Complex endeavours that involve group combat and mass tactics require a man at every station, but simpler, more direct assignments can be handled even by a single, very determined person and a dedicated AI. Nothing much can go wrong, but then, nothing much usually goes wrong with a Blood Raider ship snaking its way through space. Caravans and civilians, even empire navy ships, will give them a wide berth, fearful of the consequences if they engage. Other pirate factions won't enter Blood Raider space. Capsuleers will – they are safe in their clone pods, and their ship crews do not have a voice in the matter – but many of them come simply in search of valuable ore or ice crystals and aren't the least threatened by a single pirate ship heading their way. A brave frigate pilot who has studied the region and found out where the mineable asteroids are located could, with careful planning and fore-knowledge, program the ship's AI to lead him there, without support or sanction.

After a dozen uneventful system jumps the Cruor drew close to yet another stargate. Drem, who had managed the vessel with the dutiful aid of its autopilot, was drenched in sweat from the effort of concentration. The simulation programs had served him well – he knew every facet of them by heart – but the reality of single-handedly piloting a starship was intense beyond anything he could have imagined.

He was so busy handling command that his mind was entirely, blessedly, uncrowded of doubts and other extraneous thoughts. He knew he needed to do this.

In the distance, hovering near the gate, was a group of capsuleers.

Drem kept on his approach. They had no interest in him. The system on the other side of that gate had a Concord security classification of 0.5, which meant that any unwarranted skirmishes between capsuleers would be met with the full force of Concord's security forces. The system that Drem and these waiting capsuleers were in, however, had a security rating of 0.4, which was the statistical equivalent of every man for himself. Concord still monitored fights and assigned penalties to capsuleers' security statuses, but otherwise did not get involved.

Which meant that any unwary capsuleer coming through the gate from the other side would be pounded into dust, while non-capsuleer pirate ships, whose pickings were minute by comparison, could pass by without worry.

Drem liked to imagine these killers of capsuleers felt a fellowship with him.

He could, at any moment, target one of them and change everything. They were primed for battle and would not tolerate any interference. But Drem, who chose not to think that he was a weakling for cherrypicking his targets, avoided all aggression and merely aimed for the gate. He passed through the gate unscathed, into safe space, where the roaming capsuleers would not be on their guard.

Capsuleer attacks are like a typhoon hitting calm waters. There is a complex interplay between the pirate factions, and most of their military actions are part of extended campaigns whereby attacks and counterattacks are carefully modulated and weighed in a long-standing war that both sides know exactly how to fight. But capsuleers are a different breed. They are fearless and mercurial, often caring more about their ships than their crews; they care nothing for their own lives.

By the time he saw a lone capsuleer battleship his heart felt like it would beat its way out of his chest.

The battleship dwarfed his frigate like a planet would a moon. One of its thousands of crewmembers was bound to have noticed him, but that was immaterial. Faint beams crisscrossed the distance between the ship's bulk and a nearby cluster of asteroid fragments. The capsuleer was mining ore. Thin drifts of dusty detritus would be continually sucked into the ship's cargo hold and, until that hold was filled, the ship would go nowhere. Capsuleers had no concerns for anything but their own gain.

Drem set the Cruor on a course toward the battleship. His mind was racing through images: of breaking down the ship's shields, of boarding it near the capsuleer's chamber, overpowering whatever crew he encountered, breaking into the pilot's capsule and slitting his throat. Dreams, all of them, carrying him further down the river.

He activated the ship's targeting equipment and fixed its aim squarely on the battleship. As the large vessel was completely stationary, it was the work of a moment for Drem's frigate to lock on. There was no reaction; he had likely graduated to curiosity but not yet a threat.

He had chosen this frigate carefully. The Cruor was meant for support work as part of a larger strike team. This unit was equipped with lasers, which could be fired almost indefinitely so long as the ship's recharging capacitor could keep up; a stasis webifier that would keep it locked in place; and a warp scrambler, which would block the target from creating a subspace escape route if it had been unwise enough not to equip the proper protection equipment. A lone, random capsuleer, focused on mining in an empty belt, would not likely be ready for battle.

After the first shot, Drem would never be able to retreat. The theft of the ship alone would get him thrown into military prison for a long time. The targeting of another vessel was not, in and of itself, any kind of punishable action. But the attack would register with Concord, holding out sensors in this system, and would eventually reach the Blood Raiders themselves, who would pencil Drem in for a very brief meeting with a very angry harvesting team.

His heart beat fast with the excitement of battle, but his mind felt incredibly clear. This was the difference he would make. His family would thank him when he met them again.

He ordered the ship's AI to start orbiting the battleship at a close range, no more than five clicks. It would be impossible for the battleship's guns, slow and thunderous, to track him so long as he kept up this speed.

Drem checked the status on the Cruor's modules. His weapons were ready to fire, and his lockdown modules were powered up.

He took a deep breath and gave the order.

A wave of purple light emanated from the Cruor, blending in with the dark blue nebula whose clouds surrounded the system. Drem looked over the readings on his holoboard. Success. The battleship wasn't equipped with warp core stabilizers. With any luck it wouldn't have any electronic countermeasure modules to block the Cruor's targeting. It would be unable to move so long as Drem could keep his equipment running at full power.

His weapons kicked into action. The battleship started to target him back, a slow process that Drem tried not to worry about. He focused his attention on the battleship's shield levels instead. The readouts he was getting indicated that he wasn't making much of a dent in them, but he didn't worry. They might have shields, but he had inexhaustible lasers, and he could do this for days, locking a crew of thousands and one angry capsuleer into an endless dance.

Then a chute on the battleship opened, sliding aside with the incredible quiet of a simple and final movement. And out came the drones.

Given the right equipment, along with ideal circumstances and not a little luck, smaller ships can hold larger vessels in their thrall. Battleship capsuleers, whatever may be said for their average levels of foresight and general levels of sanity, are aware of this and tend to prepare accordingly. It is a foolhardy capsuleer who ventures into space completely without protection, whether it be backup from other capsuleers, ship modules that will enable him to take flight if needed, or an army of deadly machines with perfect aim and unquestioning loyalty to their masters. To the frigate captain, drones are not a welcome sight.

Drem's face twisted into an evil grin. The drones, five of them, targeted the frigate. His screen projected warning after warning: shields had dropped, shields were depleted; armour had dropped, armour was depleted; hull integrity was compromised . . .

Drem, feeling like a mad fool, laughed to himself and waited. In the event of hull disintegration the frigate's command section was designed to be sheared off and function as an escape capsule, but a few stray shots from the drones could tear it to pieces, and in the absence of a rescue fleet it wouldn't survive for long either way.

There was a single silent burst of light, bright as the sun, and the Cruor exploded.

6

As Ralea wandered through the station's business and residential sector, she didn't know whether she was looking for remnants of her rapidly disintegrating life, or saying goodbye to a fixed and dangerous shore before sailing blindly for some unknown destination. Her peace of mind wasn't much helped by her intermittent retching, which tended to make for limited conversation with the people she met. The hallucinations had receded for the time being, for which she was thankful. She had screamed at a few people, thinking they were going to attack her, before she managed to get a grip on herself.

There were many residential areas on the station. This was a high-class one. Although Ralea had been here before, she had rarely visited anything beyond these topmost levels – not out of guilt at what she might find, but from a real lack of interest in the sightseeing. She knew from news and hearsay that the deeper one got inside the station the worse things looked and that had been enough to dissolve any curiosity. During her tenure as a datagirl she'd had precious little time for exploring the station's poorer parts, and after she made agent she simply hadn't bothered.

It was late in the evening. The station lights had turned from their usual bright yellow to a dimmed orange reminiscent of planetside streetlights. Ralea had always liked this time of day, and in the interim between missions had often gone down to the entrance of her office building merely to take in the yellowing air.

The lights were high up in the ceiling, like proper planetside lightposts. Most of the central areas in the station's outer sections were directly connected to numerous ship hangars, and since the latter required high roofs to room their vessels, that same height was retained for all other areas in the vicinity. Besides, the station builders had long since discovered the beneficial effects extra space had on the resident population. High and wide areas relaxed people, even cowed them a little, giving them plenty of personal space and reminding them gently of their own insignificance. Low ceilings and narrow corridors, meanwhile, made the crowds nervous, claustrophobic and prone to outbursts. Most of the central corridors were wide enough to let two lanes of hovercraft pass through on either side, with plenty of space left over for pedestrians. Here, as in much darker places, station design and maintenance was an exercise half in economics and half in crowd control.

Ralea spat. It felt like an act of defiance, and gave her a little shock. She realized her calm mindset was unnatural and possibly leading her somewhere dangerous, like a drowning victim that finally gives up on the struggle. The thought frightened her beyond measure, and she spat again, ridding herself of the vestiges of the last retching bout.

She looked at the buildings around her. On both sides were townhouses and spacious rows of apartments fixed together in a resemblance of planetside dwellings. Down on the planet where airspace was cheaper than land, they'd be cheap; here, up in the cosmos, they were incredibly expensive.

One door in particular caught her attention. It was made of wood and had a carved flower motif, thorny tendrils twisting and weaving in an ever-narrowing spiral, ending in a single blooming rose right in the door's middle. The effect was simultaneously tacky and a tad unnerving.

She knew that door. She had stood in front of it before, a different person with different values and, she thought with a shudder, a terrible lack of foresight at what that visit would eventually cost her.

She had not consciously realized that she had been heading for this place, but there was no question that some part of her mind had led her directly here.

Before she could think about it, she walked up and knocked on the door.

It was opened by a middle-aged man of medium build. He was balding, grey, wearing horn-rimmed glasses, rather old-fashioned clothing. He looked like an accountant yet did not seem surprised to see a stranger at his door.

Ralea opened her mouth to speak but could think of nothing to say. After a few endless seconds she garbled, 'Nice door.'

The man looked at his door, regarded it as if it were an object of some interest, then looked back to her. 'It is,' he said.

When Ralea did not respond, he casually added, 'It's heavy oak. I have some wooden furniture as well. It's terribly hard to get up here. You have to have it assembled and built planetside, and pay an arm and a leg to have it transported to station.'

He stood aside and beckoned her into his apartment, a gentle smile on his face. 'Would you like to see it?'

The casualness and normality of the whole conversation made Ralea feel like she'd already lost her mind. She walked in, hearing the door close behind her.

She walked directly into a living room, not waiting for the man to follow. The lights were turned down, casting a sunset hue over everything inside. The walls were decorated in a creamy yellow pattern interlaced with faint orange stripes. Several pictures hung from the walls, cycling slowly through images of landscapes and flowers. One part of the living room was dominated by a sideboard, which had a dark varnish and small golden handles on its drawers and doors. On top of it were a couple of pots overflowing with flora and, lodged in between, a small and quite unobtrusive credit scanner.

The rest of the space was taken up by the dinner table, another massive wooden creation in dark varnish. It was covered with a glass plate on which lay a small lace cloth, and it stood on a thick rug woven in Caldari patterns. The room brought to mind a kind of old-fashioned, upper-class gentility of the sort that had probably never existed outside fiction and certainly never on space stations.

Her host, whose name was Kobol, said, 'It's nice to see you again,' but otherwise stood in silence while she regarded the room. The flowers smelled wonderful, and Ralea leaned over to get a better whiff.

'Have the visions started?' he asked her.

She did not look at him. Instead she looked down at the table, where the credit scanner, that little item of destruction, rested, waiting. In her tired, sluggish mind, she knew what she had to do, but she couldn't bring herself to say it.

From the corner of her eye she saw the monster take off his glasses. 'It's a fairly specialized business, I'll admit, but I do rather well at it,' he said, cleaning the glasses with a small cloth. 'I would say that a good portion of this house and everything in it comes from the trade. Including the drugs my people have been selling to you.'

'I want you to . . .', she started, but her voice faded to nothing. She knew what she wanted to say. She also knew what she needed to say. It terrified her that the two might not be the same.

Feeling increasingly desperate to pick some other subject, any subject, while she got to grips with her own mind, Ralea made mention of Kobol's glasses, and how rare it was to see those.

Kobol smiled and handed them to her. 'Try them on,' he said.

'No, I can't—'

'Go on. What've you got to lose?'

Ralea took the glasses from his hands and put them on, then looked around. 'But . . . there's no difference. I see everything perfectly.' She took them off again, still frightened but astonished too, and handed them back to Kobol.

'I built myself up from scratch. Came from a poor background—' Kobol said.

'Being poor means you wear glasses?' Ralea asked.

'Being poor means you can't afford corrective surgery,' Kobol said. 'It's long since fixed, so these days I wear glasses as an affectation, and a reminder. It's one of the few genuine links I have to my old planetside life.'

'So you didn't start your . . .' She flailed around for a word, found the only one that fitted, sighed and said, 'You didn't start your business here?'

'Nope, started it down on the planet. But I moved up to this station as soon as I could. There's better work here.'

'More contacts?'

'Fewer, actually. But they pay better and the extended business network is much more potent. On the planet, you're only working within the boundaries of the planet's economy and whatever can be manufactured there. Once you get powerful enough you have to start taking an interest in politics, and eventually you become a target for everyone else. On a station you can work in relative obscurity and still make masses of wealth.'

'So you don't want to be tied up?' Ralea said.

'I prefer to stay distant, let's keep it at that,' Kobol replied. 'I'd rather be backstage. Let other people wilt in the spotlight.'

The overlay of normalcy that blanketed this entire situation, conversation and all, pushed Ralea in disgust to say, 'So that's why you deal drugs, is it? You like the control. You don't want to get your hands dirty, so you sit in the shadows and let other people ruin their own lives with your help.'

He looked at her askance. 'You wouldn't have knocked on my door unless you wanted something from me, dear.'

She took a deep breath. 'I want to end our arrangement. I want you to stop dealing drugs to me.'

He didn't appear to have heard her, and nonchalantly asked, 'What do you do for a living?'

'I . . . am an agent.'

The man smiled. 'Then we are in the same line of work. More or less.' He walked over to the wall and turned the lights down slightly, then reached out and reset the picture frames. They blinked, and presented a mosaic of all the available images. Waving a finger through the air like a magic wand, Kobol had the frames scroll through images.

'Addiction has four stages,' he said, not taking his eyes off the frame. It was displaying an abstract piece – bright with clashes full of colours – that was impossible to resolve into shapes. Some of the milder colours might have been people; or not. 'The first is called initiation, where you're experimenting, getting to know the drug, and still feel good about it. It's a source of limitless potential, and the expectations – even the ones that turn out to be completely wrongheaded and naive – are easily the best part.'

He flicked to another image, this one a still life of old farming tools lying on a small table inside a barn. The colours were soft and gentle, though the tools themselves looked terribly sharp. 'The second stage is continuation. That's when you begin to misuse the drug. You have doubts about it, small ones, but hey, you're a grown woman. You can make your own choices. And you're being filled with feelings that you had long since forgotten.'

Again, he changed the image. It was now an austere landscape, clouds over hills, but drawn only in straight lines that intersected at angles; like boxes, each representing a portion of the whole and themselves at the same time. 'The third stage is dependency. You can't break away. You start making excuses and ordering your life around the addiction. It still makes you feel good, but now it's started to let you down, and quite seriously, too. The moments of pleasure feel less habitual, less frequent, and more like respite. You're racing up the river, not sailing down it, and in your lucid moments you may allow yourself to wonder why you started doing this in the first place.'

He chose another image. It was an optical illusion, its subject constantly shifting from strange people working in the fields to stormclouds letting out a torrent of lightning.

'The last stage is withdrawal. You barely survive the attempts to break away and you eventually realize that you cannot stop at all. So you start swinging between extremes. On one hand, you try to accept the life that you've made, to immerse yourself so in its patterns you stop noticing how you're being torn apart, and on the other hand, you start devising increasingly desperate measures to break the habit. But you can't cast off the drug, and so instead of giving it up completely, you try to make it so that it won't poison you any longer; that you'll get its benefits without having it destroy you.'

Kobol switched over to a final image and set it to full display. It was a sunset, over a clear and empty desert.

Ralea, who understood that he had not merely been talking about her addiction to a drug, said, 'You knew I would end up this way.'

He nodded. 'I thought you might.'

'How do you do it?' she asked. 'How do you go on?'

He looked at her, wordlessly. She looked back and felt a tiny flicker alight in the vast darkness. 'The glasses,' she said. She had nothing like that, no broken past of deprivation on which to build her adulthood. All she had was a life that had been far too perfect, now fading away in memory like everything that had come after.

Kobol smiled at her.

'How did you know I wasn't dangerous?' she asked him, half wishing that she had been. She was too tired to think, let alone be a threat to anyone.

'Dangerous people aren't allowed into this level of the station. And besides, the moment you entered my house you were scanned for wiretaps and weapons. I'm quite happy with the monitoring systems I've got set up. I could even tell you what's in your pockets.'

'I could expose you,' she said, weakly.

'You could, yes,' he said. 'You'd take a fall, too, though given where you appear to be right now, I suppose it'd be a shorter one than mine. But I don't think you even want to do that. In fact, I believe I know exactly what it is you want.'

Ralea nodded despite herself. She wanted to cry. Her stomach was churning again, and little spots were creeping into her vision. She blinked hard.

Kobol regarded her. 'Hallucinations?'

She nodded.

He appeared to consider something, then went past her to the sideboard. He pulled on one drawer, whose silver contents glinted in the light, reached deep into it and pulled out a tiny transparent bag. The bag held pills. He held it out to Ralea. 'Here. This'll keep you going for a little while longer.'

She didn't reach for it. He added, in the sweetest dulcet voice, 'I am not letting you go. You owe me, darling. There are debts to be paid that go back years, just like there always are when people with too much money don't think of using it to pay when they're supposed to. I will send my people to you, just like I always have, and I will keep on going with you until you stop.' He took a deep breath.

'And in the meantime, you will take these pills from me. That is not an order. Nor is it a threat. It is a simple matter of fact.'

It was at that moment that it truly hit Ralea: what she was doing here, and what she wanted even as she hated herself for it; and the simple matter of fact indeed that she was headed for the same, same old habit. 'Please, don't,' she said.

Kobol walked up to her, took her hand and pressed the pills into her palm. He then took hold of her head and held it tight to his shoulder. She was too tired to resist.

'There will come a time not long from now when you will need these pills,' he said in a frighteningly emotionless tone. 'Whether it's to prolong your life or end it. They are the best thing available to you right now and, believe me, you will eventually debase yourself for far lesser reward if you live long enough to reach that stage. Take them.'

Her palm slowly closed on the pills. The world swayed, and she leaned against the sideboard, resting her hands on its cool surface. 'Why are you doing this?' she whispered.

'I could say that losing potential clients is bad for business,' she heard him say. 'But that's too simple. In truth, I suppose the answer is . . . because I can.'

It wasn't what he said, though the words would haunt Ralea for a long time. It was his voice: confident, self-assured. Smug in its powers of destruction.

She heard him walk away from her, towards the door. She looked up and saw the credit scanner there, waiting patiently to be fed its blood money.

She picked up the scanner and rushed after Kobol. The blow rang with a sickening crunch, and the drug dealer collapsed on the ground.

Ralea stood over him, breathing quick and sharp. A raw whimper escaped from her throat. She held up the scanner as if to take another swing, then closed her eyes and beat it against the wall instead, two times, three times. Then she dropped it, ran down the corridor, and stumbled out of his door and out of his house and out of his life.

*

The orange lights shone against the encroaching darkness.

Beyond and below had been the mechanical quarter, where no humans could be seen anywhere at all. Ralea was glad. She'd taken one pill already and had been sitting there for what felt like hours with her back against a railing, enjoying the time alone, not thinking very much about anything at all. If she were to encounter any people, she knew that mindset would change.

The Mechanical Quarter, like the Business Quarter above it, was a residential area. It housed the workforce responsible for the capsuleers' hardware. The inhabitants repaired engines, hulls and modules, and every once in a blue moon were responsible for some breakthrough in starship technology that changed everything except, Ralea suspected, the lives of those who'd invented it.

Not that they were powerless. Any engineer proficient enough in their trade to be given a place in the Mechanical Quarter was damn nigh untouchable. But they didn't want much. Profits didn't matter, not like they did in the Business Quarter. From what Ralea knew of these people, their lives revolved around the workings of machines, to the point where the two were hardly distinguishable.

She looked around. It was the cleanest part of the station by far. Businessmen could afford to buy hordes of cleaner bugs, which would leave the streets spotless, but the mechanics simply designed *better* cleaner bugs to eat up the dirt, or miniature sound-wave drones to break it off, or bacterial agents to dissolve it. It wasn't one-upmanship, but a constant search for automated perfection.

The houses could barely be considered that. They were great constructions, low in height but quite voluminous, and the irregular count of windows on various walls indicated that the labs and garages present in every abode did not welcome prying eyes.

There was no wood in sight, no concession to planetside life. Everything here was plastic and polished chrome. Even the gardens, small and flowery, were so perfect as to be practically lifeless. There was plenty of strange machinery in sight, for cleaning and gardening and more cryptic tasks, but not a great deal of security mechanisms. The mechanics, who would know precisely what these systems were capable of, also knew that everything eventually breaks or falls prey to human error, and leaned towards simplicity rather than over-compensation.

Ralea, in the peaceful place somewhere on the other side of desperation and sanity, looked at the doors on the houses and imagined she could see into them, where even more machinery existed and nothing much else at all. At most there would be a drive in humanized form, constructing mechanical devices in a tactile assembly line, until such point as the drive itself gave way at last, broke down, and died.

It was a gorgeous and ordered place, not evil as the business district had been, but only because evil required humanity as a breeding ground. This place was empty of life and soul.

A buzzing noise attracted her attention. On the other side of the street, a monitor drone had collapsed to the ground and seemed to be having trouble rising again. It would lift up for an instant, then crash down, each time buzzing a little louder. It wouldn't be long before the thing expired and got swept away.

She got up, brushed off her clothes and walked over to the drone. It lay still on the ground now, making grinding noises, perhaps trying to cut out its own processes before someone else could.

She had destroyed someone. She had ended him. She had broken away.

She had killed a man.

She had been responsible for the deaths of untold thousands, every single one of which lay on her conscience like a tiny drop of poison, but that had been the extent of her actions.

Not any longer. She was a killer now. One life extinguished, with the consequences that would surely follow.

She bent down to the drone – it was too heavy to lift – and she kissed it.

It wasn't dying, not in any proper sense of the word. It would be repaired or, at most, taken apart and rebuilt in some new fashion.

Ralea, calm and quite completely mad, placed another pill in her mouth and began to walk again.

*

The Artists' Quarter lay on the very edge of the line, the last bastion of spirited life before a descent into much darker places. It couldn't be anywhere else, really, with its anarchic, carefree attitude. Here, on these few corridors, were the people who chose to live in the slipstream, who cared little about days past and nothing about tomorrow. They were kept alive mostly by occasional infusions of money from higher above, where people had their own ideas about amusement.

There was constant music in the air, which entranced Ralea. She passed by drunken revellers, clad in the odd fashions of those who replaced money with inventiveness, and by quiet, sombre-looking types who sat on the ground and exhaled smoke in strange shapes. A handful of people had gotten their hands on customized miniature volumetric projectors and were playing around like children, morphing colourful geometric shapes in mid-air and making them course back and forth like kites in a storm. The flickering lights made Ralea's head hurt. She stopped and closed her eyes to better hear the music.

It was coming from a corner in one of the side corridors. The player, a man Ralea's age, sat cross-legged on a small rug frayed at the ends. His clothing was loose-fitting and mostly in shades of brown and grey, effectively camouflaging his build, though Ralea noticed he had thin wrists and fingers. His hair, a dark brown, went just slightly past his shoulders, and had a faintly oily sheen. Strands hung in front of his face, obscuring it from view, but Ralea still saw the dark curve of his eyebrows, the half-closed eyes, perfectly formed nose, high but thin cheekbones, and the mouth that was arched in the semblance of a faint smile.

He was engrossed in the playing, his eyes closed. In front of him, on the rug, lay a theremax – a thin, black piece of rubbery material, square when rolled out, about the length and width of a forearm. It was entirely unmarked apart from two parallel lines that ran over its surface and segmented the instrument into three parts of equal size. Ralea had only ever heard of these before; they were exceedingly hard to play and required a near-perfect ear for pitch, not to mention musical talent.

To play a theremax you would touch your fingers gently to its black surface, hold them there for a moment, then slowly lift them up. The instrument would begin to hum with a faint but resonating bass note. This was your starting point, your launching pad. From here on, anywhere you moved your hands the sound would follow. Wave them gently back and forth like a fish swimming unhurriedly, and you would amplify the deeper notes, make them envelop you. Lift and drop them gently as if imitating a bird's wings, and the notes would hover hesitantly, then begin to rise with you. Fingers moving individually would multiply notes, meld them, make them twirl like dancers on a stage. If you curled your fingers you would strain the note, as if tying it around them, and if your hand made a fist the sound would choke, desperate to breathe. At last, let go, wave your hands away, and the theremax would fall silent, as if it had never been alive at all.

In front of the instrument was a small felt hat, and in the hat was a credit scanner and a small piece of paper on which was written 'Give'. On the scanner was a tiny digital screen flashing the amount it carried thus far. The amount was quite high, given that the man was effectively a street entertainer, but Ralea thought he was worth it all.

She took out her own card and keyed in a number, then leaned down and touched it to the scanner, which flashed for a moment. The player looked up at her and smiled sweetly. The music changed, taking on a deeper tone, and Ralea could feel it pulling at her. She leaned down and touched the scanner again. The music changed in accordance, seeping all the way into her bones.

From the corner of her eye she saw some of the projector people approach. Neon birds flitted through the air, announcing their passage. The birds flew through one another, insubstantial, their forms constantly changing as new polygons were added on the fly and old ones disappeared. Several birds now surrounded her, flying around her like a little bright typhoon, and the theremax's music switched to a higher-pitched piping that made them whistle to her. Ralea instinctively reached out her hand and tried to grab them.

The smoke exhalers came up from her other side and added their hue to the mix, using their throat implants to let out increasingly complex shapes of all colours. Ralea was surrounded by tendrils of a fog that momentarily held the shape of a leafy green tree before dispersing; and the birds alighted on its branches before flittering into the air again. All the while, the music played on.

One of the faces around her said, 'We can make this go on forever.' She smiled and nodded. A hand was held out, open and beckoning, and she put her card into it. She had nothing now, empty at last, waiting to be filled with happiness.

A voice cut through the haze.

Ralea drifted up into the light, then back out of it.

Someone kicked her. It hurt.

She started to drift up again.

Something was being held under her nose. She *woke* up, flashing into action and jerking upright, eyes wide, gasping for air. She gulped and let out a little scream, but the sound was muffled by whoever was hugging her tight. She couldn't see who but she could smell them, and she trusted that smell. A voice said, 'It's OK. You're OK now. It's fine.'

Her lips were too cracked and numb to form proper words, but she managed to articulate a guttural, 'Heci.'

'You idiot,' her friend said, stroking her hair and still hugging her tight.

She tried to say something more, but it was unintelligible. Heci loosened the hold and held a bottle of water to her lips. 'Drink slowly,' she said as she poured a little into Ralea's mouth. 'I don't know how long it's been since you had any water.'

The drink let Ralea speak a little. 'Neither do I,' she said in a whisper. She looked around. They were in an empty street somewhere on the station, with nothing but vacant, dilapidated huts all around them. She couldn't remember how she'd gotten there, nor much of anything at all.

She looked down at herself. She wasn't wearing her own clothing. Some of it was filth-covered rags she'd never seen; some was cloth that looked like it had been laid over her. 'Is that puke on me?' she asked Heci.

Her friend looked at her shirt. 'Yeah, it probably is.'

Ralea pointed to something on the cloth over her legs. 'And what're those spots?'

Heci screwed up her face. 'Don't ask.'

Ralea grimaced miserably, and Heci gave a deep, trembling sigh. 'Hon, I've taken a leave of absence for both of us. We are leaving now.' She grinned and added, not unkindly, 'You self-destructive nitwit.'

Ralea nodded. With a shaky hand she fished around in a pocket, but the pills were long gone.

'I . . .' she started, but she couldn't say it, and merely shook her head.

'Whatever it is, you're fine now, hon. We're going to sort this out and get you back on track,' Heci said with mock cheer.

Slowly, Ralea turned her head and looked straight at her friend; into her eyes, through her eyes and into some kind of darkness beyond. She said, 'I killed a man. I *killed* a man. Someone is *dead* because of *me*.'

Heci didn't move. Nor did her expression change. It *solidified*: the look of compassion remained what it was, but at the same time turned to utter granite.

'We are going to fix this,' she said quietly. 'We are going to get you out of here and we are going to fix this fucking thing before it destroys both of us, because I am your friend. I am your friend and I am here for you and I will *not* let this thing catch up with us. You're coming with me now, hon.'

Ralea looked at her friend. 'OK,' she croaked.

Heci pulled her up and put an arm around her back for support. 'Can you walk?'

'I think so,' Ralea said. She tried a step. 'Yeah. But keep hold, just in case.'

They walked off slowly, towards the hangars. Ralea didn't know where they were going, but at least she understood what she was leaving behind.

7

'You're one lucky sonofabitch, you know that?'

What came into focus this time was a bearded face, scraggy and pocked like a half-mined asteroid. It was hovering over Drem. He tried to sit up, felt an explosion of pain, and fell back on his pillow with a grunt.

'You'll want to take your time an' that,' the bearded man said. 'Some of those scars you've got are old ones, I'm told, and some of the breaks are ones you've had before.'

Taking great care not to move the rest of his body, Drem gently turned his head and inspected his surroundings. It was another hospital room, though much more homey than the one he'd occupied at the Blood Raider military barracks. The bearded man, whom Drem guessed to be about twice his own age, was sitting in a chair beside the bed, a datapad on his lap.

'Are you a doctor?' Drem asked.

'I'm the one who saved your hide, if that's what you mean. But no, I'm not the doc. They told me you'd be waking up soon and I figured I'd check in.' He waved the datapad at Drem, who saw it was filled with lines. 'Besides, the way work's been here lately, I don't get much of a chance to read.'

'What's your work?' Drem said.

'Saving people,' the man said in a straightforward manner, and went back to reading his book.

Drem thought this over. The last he remembered, the Cruor's

bridge capsule had been ejected out of the ship's crumbling remnants. He hadn't been strapped down, so the shock had flung him against the wall and knocked him out. He should have died. He still wasn't entirely sure that he hadn't; but this did not look like the Blood Raider afterlife.

A thought bubbled up to his consciousness, but he couldn't believe it. It'd be stupid damn luck and stupid damn misfortune all in one.

'I'm with the . . . Sisters?' he asked the bearded man.

'You're alive, is what you are,' the man replied. 'But yeah, you're with the Sisters of EVE. My name is Ortag.' He put the datapad aside and extended a hand, which Drem shook gingerly. The Sisters faction was divided into three corporations, one of which did interstellar rescue work, monitoring the dark space for dangerous situations with the sole purpose of saving lives.

'I'm curious, though,' Ortag said. 'What happened? Some of our contacts sent out a call. Said they'd seen something that, quite frankly, amazed them. Asked us to check up on the action in a particular asteroid belt. You know anything about that?'

In an instant Drem thought of a myriad lies and discounted them all. Anything that made his suicidal trip sound better would be checked with Raider HQ and found out to be a pile of ashes before he could even be back on his feet. He'd be sent back, likely to a court martial and an ignoble death.

There was something he had to know before he talked, though.

'How did I survive?' he asked.

The old man's beard moved to reveal looked like a wry smile. 'The crew on that battleship you attacked could not believe what they were seeing. You impressed them, which is not easy to do when someone's done tours of duty for a capsuleer. So they rigged the drones, had them pull back before you got totally shot. Called us, and we scooped you up.'

For a moment he couldn't even breathe. 'They saved me.'

'You're one of many to them. Your life means nothing, one way or another. And really . . . you were never a threat to them anyway, son.'

Another hand of fate, holding back on the trigger that should've shot Drem into the afterlife.

'I . . . don't know what to say,' Drem said, stunned.

Ortag leaned a little closer. 'I think, my boy,' he said in a low, raspy tone, 'you had better start with the truth.'

After Drem was on his feet Ortag gave him a tour of the facilities. The Sisters had a proper hospital wing in lieu of an offal drop-off station, and the medical rooms were used for healing rather than gruesome examinations, but otherwise it was much the same as the Raider military barracks.

Drem expected that an extradition request was in operation, though he refrained from asking Ortag any direct questions. The old man seemed comfortable with his being on the colony for the time being.

When Drem saw some of the training facilities they had, he experienced enough of a déjà vu that he had to stop for a moment and reorient himself. 'I feel like I've been here before,' he said as Ortag patiently listened. 'Except then it was a Raider military barracks. Which, I suppose, I might be seeing again soon anyway.'

'Oh, the paperwork'll keep you with the Sisters for a good while yet,' Ortag assured him. Drem accepted the comment for what it was: a stay of execution.

He had told Ortag everything about his failed plans, including his motivation for the attack, and while he hadn't expected any measure of approval from the old man he got the sense that his story of the whole debacle wasn't going to cause him to be pushed off the colony any faster. The Sisters were apparently OK with their guest's checkered past.

He was eventually brought to a small meeting room in the colony living quarters. Three walls held laser-etched plaques showing connecting routes between various systems in the current and surrounding regions, while a fourth was taken over by a viewport looking out on to space. There was a black holotable in the middle, at which sat two people: a man and a woman, both around Drem's age.

'These two helped pull you out of the fire,' Ortag said. 'Yaman and Verena, meet Drem.'

Yaman's open face was complemented by his blond, short-cropped hair. He immediately stood up and extended a hand. 'You're on your feet already? Goddamn.' Drem took an instant liking to him.

'Our boy has some experience with calamity,' Ortag added, and to Drem's relief kept it at that. He was sure the two would eventually hear all about him, but he liked that the first impressions were done with a blank slate.

Verena gave a little smile and extended her hand as well. She was just under Drem's height, and had the wiry build of someone whom nature wanted to be thinner but whose choice of profession demanded a great deal of strength. 'Pleased,' she said.

'I guess I should thank you guys,' Drem said, shaking her hand. She had a firm grip, and eyes that were remarkably bright and intense in colour. He suddenly found himself at a loss for what to say.

'You can thank us by keeping out of trouble while you're here,' Ortag said.

'And telling me about the Blood Raiders,' Yaman said, adding in an excited tone, 'I hear they're fucking *insane*.'

Ortag gave the man a look that went completely ignored. Drem just laughed.

'Yeah, I suppose. We do some strange things. It looks pretty normal from the inside, especially if you're a true believer.'

'Are you?' Verena asked.

Drem thought it over. 'I suppose. But mostly because I can't imagine how not to be. It's a way of life, so everything we do, whether it's moving into a new house or dealing with a funeral, it all gets funnelled through civil channels operated by religious authorities. It doesn't matter so much whether you believe in it, because the system does, and the message is always there at some constant, subtle level that you learn to accept and ignore.' Under her unwavering stare, he found himself adding excuses. 'But the strength of my belief isn't the same as, say, Omir Sarakusa's. I've never done a Bleeding, nor really gotten involved in the whole scientific part of it.'

'You must've had some military experience, though,' Yaman said. 'We found you floating in a Cruor capsule!'

'Yeah, about that,' Drem said, embarrassingly stroking the back of his head. 'I stole it.'

Yaman's eyes went wide.

'Yeah. Probably not the most popular man with the Raiders right now, I fear,' Drem said.

'You stole a frigate and flew it into combat against a goddamn capsuleer, all by yourself?' Yaman asked. It was hard to tell if he was more shocked or awed.

'That's about the truth of it.'

'So what happens to you now?'

'That's up to the papermen,' Ortag interjected, keeping his gaze on Drem. 'In the meantime, our boy is our guest, and so long as he keeps his hands where we can see them there shouldn't be any trouble. He'll be joining our training program pretty soon.'

Drem did a doubletake. 'What?'

Ortag said, 'Extradition takes time, and Sisters' protocol is to evaluate your physical and mental condition. You're in OK shape for someone in your shoes but we're not going to send you off unless we're sure you won't keel over on the way. Phys/Men tests are woven into our training routine, so it's the natural place to put you while you're waiting. If you're going to set off red flags I'd rather you do it in public, monitored by plenty of our people, than have you sitting alone in your room thinking up ways to kick God in the nuts. When we finally do hear from the Raiders, I'll make sure you get enough time to get your affairs in order.'

Drem, unsure what to say, thanked him. As an afterthought, he asked, 'Does everyone you pull in and rescue get this kind of offer?'

Ortag shrugged, though he seemed amused by the question. 'No, just people with . . . potential. Understand that this has no effect on your chances among your own people, once they arrive,' he added darkly, 'but until that happens, you're going to be taken care of.'

The next few weeks passed in a blur of pain, sweat, and enlightenment.

The Sisters' training centre was just as vast as that of the Raiders, but their entire training philosophy was the complete opposite of what Drem had known before. Everything was based on fight avoidance, disengagement tactics and a minimization of damage done. Drem, who already knew how to choke a man half to death, now learned to bring people back to life even as they fought tooth and nail against his assistance. Disasters, too – man-made and natural – were a whole world unto themselves. Many scenarios dealt with natural calamities and the resulting structural collapse and fires, while courses in environmental analysis were primarily for tactical safety against human attackers.

He passed the psych tests with ease. He wasn't crazy, they told him, merely grieving, and with a tendency to obsess. This did not come as news to him. He doubted it would make much difference to the Blood Raiders, who had an entirely different view of what madness and culpability were than most other factions in New Eden.

Despite the joy he felt in devoting himself to a new, nondestructive goal, he knew he was living on borrowed time, and would need to escape before the Raiders came for him. Perversely, as this realization dawned in his tired mind, it finally allowed him to properly think about his family's death. Before, he had been so consumed with hurt and blind rage that he had believed he was merely one fatal step away from joining them. Now he saw them at a distance, as one would see some expected event in one's future. Eventually he too would die, and eventually he would meet them all again, his brother included. Until then, they were truly gone. The feeling was equally like having a weight lifted off his soul and having something torn out of his body. It hurt, but he could live with it.

Drem was surprised one day, during a live casualty engagement exercise, when Yaman stepped on to the mat and partnered with him.

'Are you sure it's OK for you to work with me?' Drem said as they got into position. Yaman was playing the role of a victim hit by a multispectral grenade, thrashing about blindly as he tested Drem's ability to keep him under control and undamaged.

'No worries, buddy. I've worked with far crazier people,' Yaman told him. 'Used to be a pirate myself.'

'You serious?' Drem said, then spent the next two minutes in intense silence trying to wrestle Yaman to the floor without getting hit in the groin. Multispectral grenades were nasty things.

'Yeah,' Yaman said at last, after having tapped on the mat in surrender. 'Guristas, born and raised. Didn't get into the shit-heap of trouble you did, but can't say I wanted to spend my life among them.'

Drem, who had in fact started to suspect he would have to make his home among one of the pirate factions, was surprised at this. 'The Guristas have a pretty good reputation, though,' he said. 'Rich faction, lots of money – *lots* of money – and they're willing to do far crazier stuff than I tried.'

'That's about it,' Yaman said, getting into position for their next exercise. 'They're a little too fuckin' crazy for my liking. I like life; man, I *love* life, but I want to have fun while I'm young and have the sense to slow down when I get older. Guristas, they never slow down.' He let Drem get a half-hold on his neck, as a drowning victim might a rescuer, before swiftly turning and maniacally trying to break it off. Drem, hanging on for dear life, wondered briefly what kind of people could be too mad for this guy.

After the match was up, the teams were given a short water break before switching sides. Drem and Yaman took a breather off the side of the mats.

Yaman said, 'Guristas are easy-going as a group, forceful and hard-working, but not always what you'd call reliable and don't always finish what they start. If you've got their favour, mind, they'll break themselves in half helping you out. Nice job on the lockdowns, by the way. You're stronger than you look.'

'Amazing that an organization like that can even function,' Drem said, nodding to acknowledge the compliment. He suspected that part of his strength came from all the pent-up aggression and that another part came from the simple fact that like the Guristas, he was not afraid of injury, which he had certainly suffered, nor of death.

Yaman said, 'Well, they're sensible people, in their way. They just don't mind the risk, neither military nor financial. They achieved total dominance in their sector by being suicidal enough to take on practically anyone or anything they felt like, but also by having keen enough insight into military tactics that they could subtly pick their battles. They were founded by good people.'

'That'd be Fatal and the Rabbit.'

Yaman nodded. 'Yeah.'

'Didn't they steal ships?' Drem ventured.

To his relief, Yaman grinned. 'Yeah, like you. Two Caldari Navy guys, sick of a nation that ground its people to dust and expected everyone to fall into step. They grabbed a couple of Condor frigates, took to the skies, and started their own goddamn faction.'

'And survived to tell the tale.'

'I suppose.' Yaman sighed. 'Those guys lived like madmen for a while, made unbelievable amounts of money and power, until Fatal finally went down for good. Nothing that good can last, man,' he said, in a tone of sadness that told Drem a lot about why an active, energetic man like Yaman would leave the pirate world for rescue work.

'What happened to Fatal?' Drem asked.

'Killed by capsuleers. Happened not that long ago, in the scheme of things. Rabbit's hated them ever since. His people work with them, agent missions and all the rest, same as any other empire, but I'm told he holds a vicious grudge.'

Drem nodded darkly. 'I know how he feels.'

'I dunno if he thinks it's worth it,' Yaman said. 'Supposedly he's gotten . . . calmer, but the kind of calm that worries you. You know? Organization still makes money, though. Even more than before, I heard. They're running out of things to spend it on.'

'I have a few choice ideas for them,' Drem said, trying not to think of his brother or the Sani Sabik decree about his death.

'Don't we all,' Yaman said.

Only a few days later, a simulation rescue found him side by side with Verena.

'Wanted to make sure everything runs tight,' she said to him while they geared up. The colony operated several full-size simulation chambers – great halls filled with both debris and complicated machinery – through which teams of recruits were made to run rescue gauntlets. Each person wore a full-body protective suit and a fully sealed helmet with an overhead display integrated into its faceplate. The suits were the same as the ones used in active field duty, with the addition of biomonitoring equipment used to evaluate the trainees' stress responses. The helmet displays had been specially modified for training duty and would cast their own overlay on the objects in the simulation chambers: metal scaffolding became crumbling towers, stacks of bricks turned into flaming hills of debris, and small transmitters located at strategic locations contained either the potential for wounded victims or surprises of acidic, volatile or electric natures. Electrodes and other transmitters laced through the insides of the trainee suits would provide the appropriate feedback, and serve as ungentle reminders to those who exhibited a lack of foresight.

'You've been with the Sisters for long?' Drem asked, a little nervous. Although he'd done well in these sessions and not caused any trouble, they tested his composure. He didn't like the idea that he might embarrass himself in front of her, or found to be wanting in some manner.

'Ever since I left the Angels,' she said, checking the display pane on her helmet and frowning. The mission would not start for another few minutes; trainees were still arriving and gearing up.

'Wait, hold on. What?' Drem said in astonishment. 'You were a pirate?'

'I was a member of the Angel Cartel,' she said.

'So you were a pirate.'

She said, 'The Angel Cartel is a complicated and extensive organization—'

'Of pirates.'

'—of connected corporate networks overseen by a command group called the Dominations—'

'Pirates.'

'—and have long since grown to a stature that requires them to participate in world politics, though their main agenda is primarily the acquisition of power.'

'Pirates and politicians. The same, really.'

She looked at him askew, with a stern expression that could not quite disguise her amusement. 'Someone from a faction notorious for its brutal and murderous rituals is lecturing me on my background?'

Drem shrugged. 'Most of the Sani Sabik are perfectly normal people who just want to get through the day. The Blood Raiders are crazy, I'll grant you, but they're a minority.'

'So are active Angels,' Verena said, polishing the inside of her helmet's faceplate. 'I think someone threw up on this,' she muttered. 'I can still smell the bacterial cleaners. Anyway, the Cartel is precisely the same. A few people take to the skies, but most of us live on stations, colonies or planets, doing whatever we're good at. They welcome everyone. Which is why they have the most extensive information network and classified data repositories in the cluster, while *you*, sweetheart, have spooky people running human cattle-farms.'

'You say that with such pride,' Drem said, checking his own helmet. It didn't seem to smell of much, except a faint whiff of sweat and spent adrenaline. 'Everyone knows you stole half your tech from the Jovians.'

She rolled her eyes. 'Just because we took one of their abandoned stations, everyone thinks they can give us endless grief over it.'

'Well, yeah.' Drem grinned at her. 'You're the squatters of New Eden.'

'We're the *safe haven* of New Eden, thank you very much. Look,' she said, taking a seat beside him, 'the Cartel's excellent internal organization, its extensive reach, and this prevailing myth that we've got the upper hand because we scrounged our guns from the secret empire, it all makes us a prime destination for anyone looking for safe, lucrative work. Everyone's accepted, regardless of past crimes or origins. If you become an Angel, that's what you are; nothing more and nothing less.'

It sounded like a haven to Drem.

'So what do you think of that, little Raider?' she said with sly amusement.

Drem thought she definitely smelled better than his helmet, but said nothing and nodded.

As they went through the last round of preparations before the simulation, Drem thought of the obvious question. 'Why did you leave?'

'Some things happened,' she simply said, putting on her helmet and locking it into place. 'But I'm planning to go back soon enough, as a Sisters agent. And just so you know, if we pass an electrical fire, I'm totally pushing you in.'

Drem sat down, called up the vidscreen and started reading. The station library lights were yellow and gentle on his eyes, and the soft quietness was a nice break from the noise and hubbub of the training centre.

He had needed something to do – to stay in motion at all times – and even if the results of his research with the Blood Raiders had eventually gotten him into trouble, he recognized that the inquisitive nature which had driven him in those dark times had, in itself, been positive in nature.

The Sisters of EVE, naturally, had databases on all the factions. These were full of information gleaned from rescue missions and were kept under strict confidence. The Sisters were trusted with access to various locations – pirate military colonies, empire outposts, and all manner of war-torn areas – that often held sights not meant to be seen by outsiders.

The Sisters had set up this database not merely to better strategize their rescue missions, but to protect their clients' secrets through basic human psychology. When someone came back from a mission, they would need to talk about what they saw. Specific agents within the Sisters, sworn to secrecy, were in charge of listening to the rescue workers and registering what they said into the database. It pacified the workers, who felt that their voices – and complaints – about the terrors they encountered had been heard; and it accentuated the feeling that these were secrets, meant to be told to the right people and not spread around like gossip.

The information in these databases was stored in layers and made available according to security clearances. The level of security for the real secret stuff was kept tight, but lower levels were safe for most to access. Initially Drem's status as an outsider didn't permit him much access at all, but a few barters with some friends in training eventually had him back in the library with keycodes in hand and curiosity in mind.

He soon found himself spending most of his free hours at the library, retiring to his quarters only when sleep threatened to claim his waking mind. It was not possible to transfer data out of the library's purvey, but Drem had a good memory. He sat there for hours, every night for weeks on end, reading through hundreds of reports of every degree: technological, social, political, taken from both the high diplomats who engaged with these pirate factions and from the low workers who dealt with them in the real danger of the field.

He should have been planning his escape before the Blood Raiders came for him. But in his efforts, night after night, he found himself consistently looking for some hint, some tiny morsel of data, that might lead him to the one thing he knew he still craved: the name of the man who had brought death to his door.

It was late in the evening after a hard day of training and most of the trainees had retired to their quarters, but Drem was too wired to rest. He and a friend called Terden were sitting at a metal table in an otherwise empty cafeteria. When they spoke to one another their voices echoed faintly off the walls.

He had been on the colony for months. He knew he needed to get to Angel Cartel space, or Gurista, but his options for escape were extremely limited. Training season, though soon to conclude, was still in effect and no ships would be leaving the station just yet.

A message had been waiting in his quarters. It said Ortag wanted to see him in the morning. The message did not specify why, but Drem didn't need to be told. His time was up. The Blood Raiders had come for him.

'I don't . . . sleep much, to be honest,' Terden said. 'Every now and then some memory will pop up, of something my people did, and then there's nothing to it but stay awake, not thinking.'

Drem nodded. He knew that one.

Terden was one of the trainees at the camp, a lapsed recruitment agent from a pirate faction called Sansha's Nation. He was a shifty man with deep-set eyes, a head buried inside a mass of unruly hair. His voice seemed to have been born a whisper. It was full of odd hesitations when he started in on a subject, as if his thoughts needed to steel themselves before he could express them, but when he got properly going he rarely paused, letting the words stream out at speed.

His manner was quiet when in mixed company but he greatly liked talking to Drem, whose faction was the only one with a history and culture terrifying enough to match the Nation. Over the course of their training the two men had built a solid friendship.

Drem had approached him for a late-night talk, and Terden, who understood why a man would want to stave off the morning, gladly obliged.

Sansha's Nation was a silent and terrifying kingdom. It was the scorched, broken result of one man's attempt to create a caste-levelled utopia, populated with intellectuals unshackled from the world's corporeal demands and free to tackle the larger issues of life. It had devolved, as they always do, into a tyranny. Sansha Kuvakei was revealed to have created brain implants that allowed mind control, turning his experimental subjects into human puppets whose cognitive faculties were rewired for optimum performance in whatever tasks they were assigned for perpetuity. His secret aim had been to create a subclass of humans who, he was convinced, would happily spend the remainder of their lives in blissful servitude, leaving everyone else free to pursue the sciences and arts. In the aftermath of revelations about these secrets Sansha lost most of his followers – at least the ones who could willingly leave – and was eventually defeated by the four empires, many of whom wanted to close the door on their embarrassing relationships with the madman. The rising empire of Sansha Kuvakei had crumbled to dust, but life crawled about in the ruins. The human zombies he'd created – called True Slaves – had remained true to their implanted drive of servitude and expansion, and still roamed space looking for victims to recruit. It was a toss-up who were more feared, the Blood Raiders or Sansha's Nation. *Drain your blood or lose your mind*; not the best choice a starship trooper could think of.

'I always thought recruitment agents were True Slaves that couldn't even summon the will to leave,' Drem said.

'True Slaves, they . . . they come in many types,' Terden told him. 'They range from barely coherent biological machines to undercover agents, like me, that can function among normal people, when most of those agents are either spies or recruiters, looking for little chinks in the armour of deep-space communities and planning Nation's assaults on them. We're given much more leeway than regular recruits and we're rarely implanted with much more than basic tracking devices, if that; in fact, we're *encouraged* to desert the faction if our conscience demands it. Nation would much rather have their agents committed to the cause than risk having them turn coat and ruin a Nation invasion.'

Terden had deserted, but he kept his conscience to himself. 'Agents leave Nation all the time,' he added.

'Isn't it hard for them to attract new ones?' Drem asked.

'No, it's . . . it's not even hard to get the *old* ones back. I don't know if it's proof of humanity's darker nature or what, but we agents always come back to Nation eventually.'

'I find that hard to believe.'

Terden grimaced. 'When I joined the Sisters, I'd already undertaken a number of Nation incursions into empire space, and been responsible for hundreds of thousands of new True Slaves. You do something like that, Drem, and the darkness waits inside you until you're ready to greet it again.'

'So why did you leave?' Drem asked, not knowing if he wanted the answer.

Terden merely said, 'Saw . . . someone I knew. Anyway, the idea of a True Slave is completely wrong,' he added, running his fingers through his hair and idly scratching his head. 'There's no such thing.'

Drem accepted the change of topic. 'Really? Because there's barren colonies in lowsec space that would probably disagree. If they had any people *left*.'

Terden laughed loudly.

'It's a spectrum, is what I mean,' he said. 'There are so many different types, with the military one being the last and only thing you outsiders ever see, but it's just one of many.'

'Sounds a bit like the Sani Sabik,' Drem admitted. 'Most people think we're all Blood Raiders, as if a nation of millions could even function like that.'

'Precisely.'

'Among the Sani Sabik and all its factions there are people who're up to their knees in blood and screams all day long, and others who spend their entire lives in quiet rooms doing research on theology and science, and then there's just a whole lot of people who merely live in that world and eke out their existence like ants among the demons.'

'Nation is . . . really, Nation is the same,' Terden said. 'The True Slaves stalk the world like giants, but there are those who are only half-slaves, with a much greater degree of autonomy, or who've only had a particular section of their minds taken over.'

'Is that possible?' Drem said.

'It's not the most common setup, but sure, some of them can explore their creative talents as much as they like while their analytical mind belongs to Nation, so they can paint and draw but they can't solve even the simplest maths problem unless their implants allow it. Others have had certain emotions suppressed.'

'Why, because they have freak-outs?'

Terden inspected the table. 'Mmm . . . some of them, yeah. Occasionally there's someone who needs an extra failsafe, but the ones I'm talking about, they come to us asking for that suppression before we even implant it.'

It took Drem's mind a moment to catch up with what he was hearing. He asked in horrified fascination, 'Wait, they seek you out?'

'As treatment, yeah.' Terden kept his gaze on the table, almost as if in acknowledgement of the darkness in their conversation. 'People who've had crippling depressions or any number of other mental illnesses, people who want to end whatever pain they're enduring in their old lives, or to end the lives themselves without an actual death. Nation,' Terden said, 'is the last stop for those whose enemy is the most dangerous one of all. Themselves.'

Drem leaned back and looked at the ceiling. If there had been holes in it, he would have counted them, merely to push out the thoughts that were in his head.

A fleeting thought struck him. 'Your old faction must have access to immensely complex technology. Do all True Slaves look the part?'

'Robots and monsters?' Terden said. 'Depends. You can spot the implants in most of them, and there's a bunch of ongoing projects that I don't want to get into where there's almost more machine than man.'

'More machine?'

'You miss the part about not getting into that?'

'I just didn't think that was possible. The more you shove metal into someone, and take away the body they've grown used to, the less they can usefully operate.'

'There is that . . . There is that, yeah,' Terden said, inspecting the table again. His hair cast jagged shadows on its surface. 'So what you do is either you use as little metal as best you can, or you use as little human as best you can.'

The two men sat there in silence.

'Little human,' Drem said.

'Yeah,' Terden said.

'As in a little ch—'

'Yes.'

Drem looked at the ceiling again and thought of all those stars out there, all those stars and the darkness that held them.

'They have done some research into the opposite end, non-detectable mods,' Terden said. 'But it's not that common.'

'Really? I'm surprised.'

'It's just not that useful. If you've been taken in by Nation, you're already in our space, surrounded by thousands of agents on all sides, so there's no point in making you any prettier if you're not going anywhere, anyway.'

'But what about implanting, I don't know, heads of state or something.'

Terden gave him a look that he would not soon forget. 'If it were that easy, my friend, Nation would already rule the world.'

The ex-agent thought it over, then added, 'There do exist some experimental projects, and I know of at least one procedure where they barely even leave a scar on your head. It's a mix of behavioural theory and brain alteration that involves repeated rewiring of the brain's pathways on a cellular level and basically alters behavioural patterns over time; so really, you'd be hard pressed to notice it if it was done to you. Apart from the occasional drilling into your skull, I mean.'

'And digging into someone's head won't just destroy them?'

Terden gave him a look that indicated his faction had enough experience in the field not to worry about that particular issue. 'In those cases where that's a concern – say that the cranium isn't conducive to direct invasion – the procedure can be accomplished by administering nanoagents.'

'Nanoagents,' Drem said, trying not to think of his friend's offhand comment about direct invasion.

'Yeah. Administered through . . . select points in the body. They'll remain nearly undetectable once they've gone to work and any excess agents will be flushed out of the system, so while the process is even more time-consuming than the direct approach, both in application and the patient's adjustment period, it's far less intrusive. I mean, the subject won't be in any doubt that he's been injected—'

'Good,' Drem butted in, to Terden's clear amusement. He thought to himself that if the Sansha ever developed a method to secretly inoculate people with concoctions like this, there really would be red flags waved in every faction throughout the cluster.

Terden continued, 'But aside from the injection process itself, which is fairly involved, the subject would remain entirely unharmed, and with successive treatments, he could be induced to do almost anything at all, regardless of the risk to his own health.'

'A True Slave,' Drem said.

'A True Slave.'

'How do you know about something like this? Sounds like it should've been kept top secret.'

'Well, it really isn't much use to Nation so I doubt they went to much effort keeping it under wraps. It's an obscure minor project of limited use, and if anyone's heard of it outside Nation, and maybe the Sisters, I'd be surprised.'

'But it's brainwashing. Isn't that something people would be worried about?'

'It is brainwashing, but it requires frequent access to the subject, extensive injections, and a great deal of time to alter their behaviour. What you'd end up with is an implant-free recruit, certainly, one subject to specific triggers and influences, but the effort required is completely out of proportion to the outcome. If we have that kind of access to someone we might as well put in an implant and achieve the same effect, something Nation's enemies know full well.'

'Nation's enemies,' Drem said.

'Well, you know . . .'

'The rest of the world, you mean.'

Terden grinned. 'Yes.'

Early next morning when he entered the meeting room, Ortag was already there, alone. That surprised him. He had been expecting at least a token presence of security personnel.

He hoped the extradition announcement wouldn't immediately be followed by actual deportation. He needed more time. He always needed more time.

'How're you doing?' Ortag asked him.

'I'm all right. Nervous,' Drem admitted. 'I assume you have news for me.'

'That I do,' Ortag said.

'Am I going to like it?' he joked awkwardly.

Ortag shrugged. 'That depends. Probably not. I can imagine a better fate for a person.'

Drem sighed.

'Walk with me,' Ortag said.

They exited the meeting room, walking down long corridors towards the training areas. 'Your time on the colony,' Ortag said. He appeared to think it over. 'I hope it's been good. Short, I know, but there's worse places to be.'

'Yes,' Drem said. Worse places indeed.

'You've done well here. Very well. You impressed us.'

'Thank you.' Drem was surprised at how much that small compliment meant to him.

'Tell me,' Ortag said, taking a turn and heading toward a single room to the side of the training grounds, 'if you were free to go wherever you wished, where would it be?'

'The Angel Cartel,' Drem said without thinking, then cursed himself silently to all hells and back. He hoped and prayed he hadn't just ruined his chances at escaping from the station, or given these people a solid lead on where to find him.

'Really? That's interesting. Almost prescient, in fact.'

'How so?'

'You really have done well here, young man,' Ortag said, walking up to a door. 'In fact, in the history of this colony there's only one person who has outdone you in most of the training routines. Though former pirates are commonplace among the Sisters, the Blood Raiders can still be unpopular among our ranks. We need to take care in accepting them, and in deciding who they will work with.'

Drem's mind was reeling. 'You ... wait, look – what are you saying?'

'I'm saying we have a team that, as a matter of fact, has been looking for a new recruit. Since teams get rotated out on a regular basis, we have also been trying to decide where it is we want to be stationed next, and with your vote it's now two in favour of the Angels.'

'And my extradition?'

Ortag grinned and said, 'It is, in fact, entirely possible that I forgot to file the paperwork on that one. No sense in letting a good man go to waste.'

And as he walked through the door, where he found Yaman and Verena waiting for him, all Drem could think to say was, 'I'm really not being sent back to the Raiders?'

'Not unless you want to, my boy,' Ortag said.

Drem stood there, staring at his new teammates, and marvelled at the stay of execution. Some day the Blood Raiders would come for him. But not today.

Ortag clapped him on the shoulder and said, 'Welcome to the Sisters of EVE, son.'

PART II

Death

8

It was the middle of the night, and the alarm roused Drem from unsettling dreams. He was up and running in a matter of seconds and arrived at the ship in three minutes flat. There was no conversation; everyone was still effectively asleep, dressed in little but underwear, running on ingrained autopilot.

The team had been stationed in Angel space for a few months. They had done remarkably well. Even by Sisters standards, which were high, they were a success.

As the ship arose from the hangar floor and started on the runway course to space, the team took care of whatever ablutions were pressing on their sluggish consciousnesses, then went to their respective safety pods and sealed themselves in. No one ate or drank a thing.

At first, the daily carnage had overwhelmed Drem. He had lived on a pirate colony for all his life, but now for the first time he truly understood the extent of the bloodshed that was an inseparable part of his culture. The factions warred continuously with their regional neighbours, though thankfully both the pirates and the four major empires tried their best to minimize harm to innocents – Drem loathed the term 'collateral damage' – and focused instead on purely military targets. The Angels had their own rescue services, which took care of their active troops, scooping up their escape pods after a flight encounter or an assault on a military colony. The Sisters remained apolitical and did not come in unless non-combatants had been harmed, or the loss was so cataclysmic that the Angel services needed the assistance.

'Everyone hot?' Ortag's voice asked from the speakers.

'One tick,' Yaman's voice replied.

Inside his pod Drem got ready for warp, fitting his head in the cranial socket and adjusting the sticky neck strap so that it adhered perfectly to the sides of his throat. He closed his eyes and tried not to think about what would happen next.

Every time he resolved a situation in which someone's life had hung in the balance, he counted his lucky stars for the people on his team. They matched as perfectly as he could have hoped. Drem was always at the forefront, serving as a tracker and first rescue point. Verena provided immediate backup, Yaman took care of secondary emergency services. Drem had expected those two to work the other way around, but Verena's wiry strength proved invaluable whenever a victim needed to be painfully extracted from a break point, and he'd be hard pressed to imagine a better sight for a frightened and injured colonialist than Yaman's big, blond, happy face grinning through the security helmet as he slyly administered the anaesthesia and mood settlers. Ortag, meanwhile, was happy to hang back and direct the other three, using his extensive experience of rescue operations to ensure they didn't make costly mistakes; Drem quickly started to add his own tactical suggestions during missions, and found them welcomed by the team.

It was a new life, with a new purpose.

'Hot,' Yaman's voice said.

'Hot,' Verena confirmed.

'Hot,' Drem said and exhaled slowly.

In each pod, the neck straps simultaneously extruded the tiniest of needles, which swiftly pumped tranquillizing nanoagents into the receptors' bloodstreams. The team was fast asleep before they left the colony's outer hangar gates. The ship's warp engines kicked in, and it blinked out of existence.

Adrenaline shots awoke them, administered through the same patchwork of needles. Drem's eyes popped open and he took a few gasping breaths before detaching the neck strap and leaning forward in his pod, his head between his knees. No matter how often he went through warp, it always shook him up.

Warp technology was a wonderful tool for transporting large vessels at high speeds across great swathes of space, but the little that Drem knew of it was restricted to a layman's understanding of depleted vacuums, laser-locked fields, tunnel-shaped warp cores, and the fact that all of this agreed perfectly with any machine not saddled with a carbon-based structure, greyish clusters of pyramidal cells, and a functioning digestive system.

After the world had settled a little, Drem unsealed the pod and stepped out. The others were already awake, rubbing their faces and walking about.

Ortag raised his voice. 'Hi-tech factory, guys. Not dissimilar to the one last week at that ugly-ass moon two jumps over, except this one's got higher stores of miniature electronics and other bits that burn in nasty ways. They say the colony was making ship subparts, but nobody's going to tell me it couldn't also be missiles, so watch out for electricity, radioactive seals, and things that look like they're gonna go boom. Rest is in the overheads. Let's gear up.' He shot Drem a strange look that went on for a second too long, then looked away and got busy suiting up.

Drem took a few steps about the cabin, reorienting his post-warp organs to air, gravity and not puking, then went back to his pod and opened the cabinet beside it. His hazard gear hung inside, ready for use. The shimmering black would act like an active reflector when put under light, marking Drem out colourfully to anyone within visual and shouting range, and would be auto-luminescent in pure darkness. Its insides consisted of several layers of protective material that sealed its wearer against toxic materials and a wide range of other dangers ranging from the scorching heat of explosions to the sudden frost of space itself. Drem hadn't yet experienced a blowout bad enough to hurl him outside a colony's shields, and he hoped never to test that aspect of his hazard suit.

'How's yer guts?' Yaman asked.

Drem, hearing the tension in his teammate's voice, grinned and said, 'They're all right. Probably shouldn't have had those eggs for breakfast, though. Fried, on bread toasted in fat, greasy oil—'

'All right, OK,' Yaman said.

'And a heap of butter on the side, smeared all over—'

'Fucking hell, man—'

'Leave the poor boy alone, dear,' Verena said to Drem. 'You both haven't even put on your pants yet.'

This was not entirely true. The team wore clothing of a regular cut, if fairly thin, made from lightweight synthetics that kept the skin temperate and let it breathe. The hazard suit, which Verena was already half into, would go over this, completely encapsulating its wearer.

'How are we for time, Ortag?' Drem asked.

'No reason for you to piss in your suit, if that's what you're wondering,' the man said. 'Take your time.'

Something about the way he'd spoken – the usual dark humour was laced with an unusual tinge of concern – kept bothering Drem, but he put it out of his mind and started to get into the suit.

Putting it on – core frame, limbs, helmet – was a small ceremony. Systems needed to be checked, material integrity tested, and full comfort to be found in this new, pliable cocoon. There would be no option for adjustment in the field.

Once Drem was fully sheathed and looking through his face shield, he was no longer a normal man, nor did he possess the thoughts, anxieties or feelings of normal men. He was an agent of life, dedicated to the purpose of salvation. It was a high-minded and stupidly dramatic attitude, but it helped psych him up for the job at hand while also giving him the emotional distance necessary for any number of agonizing snap judgements.

The first few times he'd been plunged into the fray he had forgotten all about the past. The death of his brother, the loss of his family, the travails he'd suffered since that terrible day, all were pushed far to the back of his mind. The only world that existed was the one filled with smoke, screams of pain, and bodies trapped under fallen support structures or buried in mounds of asteroid ore. The faces of the people he saved or lost were now etched on his mind, staring back at him in agony during every quiet moment.

He blinked and refocused. Reports flashed across his helmet's screen.

'Colony is midsize, so there'll only be a handful of Sisters teams working there,' Ortag's voice said. 'We'll have one in each inhabited section. Angel agents will be shadowing every team.'

That was an unusual proliferation, which indicated Ortag was probably right about the valuable weapons production on the colony.

'They'll also provide advance reports if there's a renewal of hostilities.'

'If?' Yaman's voice said. 'You mean they don't *know*?'

'When they hear, they'll tell us. Finish suiting up,' Ortag said, cutting off that line of inquiry.

This lack of information surprised Drem, who was used to the pirates knowing almost too much about the attacks they suffered. He shifted sections on his screen and looked for data on the assailants. When he saw it, his stomach knotted up again.

It was a capsuleer. Probably on a mission, though Drem would never know.

He took a very deep breath, then checked the security fastenings on his gear and ran final tests on the oxygen and audio filters. A series of soft beeps confirmed audio communications.

'Drop in two,' Ortag's voice said. There was no ceremony, no questioning of whether Drem could handle this. He understood what it was: a test, of his ability to think clearly, stay sane, and save the lives waiting for them in that hellhole of familiar memory.

He sat in his pod again. The inner sections of the cranial socket retracted to make space for his helmet.

Another voice spoke up in his helmet, this one on a private channel. 'Hey.'

It was Verena. 'Hey,' he replied.

'I saw the attacker info. You going to be OK?'

He thought about it. 'So long as I can pull at least one person alive out of that place, yeah, I think so.'

'All right,' she said, kindly. 'I'll be here.'

Their ship dropped into orbit.

They were on an exterior asteroid colony that was unified and ellipsoidal in design, all bad for stability. Had it been embedded inside the asteroid, its shell of solid rock might have absorbed the brunt of the damage and propped up whatever remained, while a more modular structure could have been left with some parts undamaged. As it stood, with this kind of design, if the core gave out, everything would be destroyed.

'He tore the damn place to pieces,' Yaman said in awed horror when they stepped out of the hangar and into the station proper. 'Shit. Remember the blowout at that chem research hub? The one that looked like someone fucked a hole in its side? That's nothing to this.'

Drem looked around and nodded quietly. The colony was barely hanging together. Whatever the capsuleer had fired at it had certainly done its work. Plumes of smoke rose in the distance over countless ruined buildings, and the air smelled bitterly of ashes, machine oils and electrical fires. There was none of the intentional, well-ordered destruction common with pirate faction skirmishes; this place looked like it had simply been shaken to pieces and set on fire. Apart from the occasional cavalcade of noise when another structure gave way to the local gravity, there was utter silence.

'I wish I'd known about the setup,' Verena said to Drem, still on a private channel. 'If you have any problems with this, tell me. Please. I don't like you being put through this.'

'No, it was better this way,' Drem replied. 'If I'd had time to prepare, I would've wasted it seething with anger. This is no different than any of the hundreds of missions we've done so far. Keep my mind empty, do the job, and get out.'

Thinking, in fact, was remarkably superfluous to being a base-level Sisters operative, inasmuch as conscious, over-analytical cogitation was concerned. Instinct and snap decisions were the order of the day. Drem had discovered this the first time he held someone's guts in his hands.

Verena nodded in acknowledgement, and they moved on, splitting up in search of survivors.

One emergency hangar had survived the onslaught, so all survivors still conscious and moving had managed to evacuate. Inhabitation numbers, however, indicated scores of people unaccounted for, most of them assembly line workers. There hadn't been any oxygen blowouts yet, and the ongoing fires were mostly confined to localized factories, so the team still had hope there would be some people alive.

'No Cartel yet,' Drem said.

'Thankfully,' Verena replied.

Most times the team didn't mind the Cartel's presence – its people pulled their own weight and usually showed great care for their own kind – but on too many occasions they put the rescue of resources over people, and Drem felt they sometimes got a little too close for comfort when he and Verena were delicately trying to pry someone out of an unstable structure. Drem didn't mind it as far as his own safety was concerned, but he didn't like outsiders being a threat to anyone else on his team.

'Deploying scouters now,' Yaman said over comms.

'Same here,' Drem said. He laid down a small bag with contents that clinked quietly in the fiery gloom. After sending out a quick command through his overhead, the bag began to buzz. When Drem pulled it open, several small orbs rose out, hovering unsteadily at face height as they oriented themselves. They were mobile sensor clusters grouped around a central AI and encased in lightweight but immensely durable armour. Once they'd compared the archived station data to the tattered remains of reality, they hovered off, flying in fixed search patterns, scanning for any signs of life and reporting their findings directly to the Sisters' scanning gear. No positives came, but Drem still held out hope.

The peace didn't last long. The vibrations in Drem's audio receptors soon picked up a patter that resolved into the thump of running boots. Yaman's voice came in on overlay, saying, 'Here come the fucking troops. I'm hooking them into our talk net before they can start bitching about it.'

The team of Angel Cartel forces wore dark outfits, but unlike the Sisters' gear that reflected available light to shine as brightly as possible, these were merely black as tar. Their one concession to colour was the small silvery patches on their shoulders, bearing the faction logo that always reminded Drem of a one-eyed pirate with a helmet malfunction. He pushed the drones' search to background levels and stepped out in the open to acknowledge the troops.

One of them walked up to him and said, 'Captain Kiel Rhan. I'm in charge of this operation.'

Drem acknowledged the man with a nod and a 'Captain,' before returning to his environmental scanning. His mind was cold with reason.

'Agent, my team will proceed to the repair facilities a click north of here,' Rhan said.

'How many people do you expect to find there?' Drem said.

The Captain ignored the question. 'Meanwhile, Base strongly suggests you Sisters investigate the living quarters to the east.'

Drem called up a map of the colony. 'Living quarters, you say,' he said.

'That's right,' the Captain said.

'That would be the ones right next to what looks like storehouses. Contents unregistered, I'm seeing. I've moved a flight of drones to check it out.'

'Agent, I suggest you follow instructions and report back what you see.'

Ortag came in and said, 'We're all doing our jobs here.' On a private channel to Drem, he added, 'Be careful, son. Time over temper. I know of this guy, and he doesn't like capsuleers any more than you do.'

Drem ignored the warning. 'Captain, my instructions are to save lives, which I won't accomplish by running around and checking every building in this place. There are over a hundred people missing. If the drones find a hotspot I'll be rushing over with the rest of my team, but until that happens we're going to scout out everything. And I'll add,' he said, trying to keep a lid on his anger, 'that those warehouses look an awful lot like ammunition and military hardware stockpiles. Which most of the pirate factions, including my own, tend to stack right next to people's beds, the better to dissuade your enemies from firing on them. My guess is you wouldn't mind us reporting back from that location, verifying the integrity of those living quarters and maybe those warehouses while we're at it. That about right?'

The captain was silent.

'In fact, that's the only reason I can think why we'd go there. Most of the people . . .' Drem paused and thought it over. 'Hang on. Most of the missing are assembly guys.'

'Agent—'

'Shut up for a sec.'

The team heard the Captain's sharp inhalation, but before he could start shouting, Yaman chimed in, 'It's worth hearing our man out, sir. He's pulled people out of the fire.'

The dead calm in Yaman's voice, a far cry from his usual mad cheer, stopped Rhan short. Verena quietly added, 'He's right. There'd be fewer men among your troops if it wasn't for him.'

Meanwhile, Drem had called up schematics of the station and was giving them a long hard look. A specific detail caught his attention. 'Ortag, I need a high-importance relay.'

'Go.'

'Summaries of station work contracts,' Drem said. There was a short delay, then his overhead started scrolling through lines of data. He glanced over it as quickly as he could, grunted in acknowledgement, and said. 'OK, we're heading out. You want to see your people alive, come with me.'

The Captain's patience broke. 'Agent, what the *hell* are you up to? Where are you going?'

Drem had started running due west. 'Ortag, send the bots and the drop drones all to the second sector due west from our arrival point. Yaman and Verena, start running and meet me there. Coordinates are on the way. All Angels in the area, same charge.' He highlighted a location on his overhead and broadcast it. His team acknowledged the messages without question.

Behind him, he heard the thump of feet. Angels might be

insufferably bureaucratic, but if you spoke with authority, they listened.

As he ran, he heard the Angel captain yell at him over the open comms channel, 'You're going to the bars and recreation areas? Agent, timestamp says the attack was at three in the morning!'

Drem, conserving his breath, barked back, 'Timestamp means half hour before bars close. These people work swing shifts, assembly, shit jobs! They weren't sleeping in their quarters at three in the morning, they were awake and drinking!'

'I am not going to let my guys—'

Yaman's voice came over the comms again. 'Hey guys, guess what I found? There's a standalone dataport here, unplugged and all. It probably holds a lot of research data that hadn't yet been shipped.'

'Is it undamaged?' the captain asked, far too swiftly.

'Hang on,' Yaman replied. There was a *BAM* over the channel. 'No,' he said.

The captain inhaled and was about to say something very loud when Drem, who'd momentarily slowed to catch his breath, cut in with deathly quiet, 'Maybe you'd better let us run this one, sir, and let everyone do their jobs. Otherwise, accidents are going to happen.'

There was a silence on comms. Drem started running again, and shortly after heard the tremor of feet trampling their support right behind him.

They arrived at the recreation areas and found them in blasted ruins. Sublevel supports had given way, plunging most of the buildings into a steep fall that was only stopped by the very rock of the asteroid sitting below. Drem sent out scouter drones that wormed their way into various cracks and crevices and immediately reported several signs of life. They were wavering, but Drem didn't yet know whether that implied impending expiration or if the thick rubble was merely distorting their signals.

The drop drones arrived, bulky creations that landed on the ground beside him and disassembled themselves into rescue kits. Drem had his overhead project the route through the debris that would bring him closest to the victims without risking total collapse, then grabbed a handful of spoke bombs from the rescue kit and set to making a tunnel.

Spoke bombs contained pressured meshes of tritanium pins. When set off, the tritanium's contact with air would cause a violent expansion that broke through the bomb's shell along with anything else in the near vicinity. The tritanium would instantly harden, its mesh clicking into place and creating a complex prismic polyhedron large enough for a human to pass through with ease. A series of spoke bombs set off in tactical locations would create a propped-up tunnel through all but the densest of materials. It was a dangerous tool, one that could save lives and obliterate them with equal ease.

Drem cut off his overhead projections, keeping only the heat signatures, and had his display heighten the photosensitivity of his surroundings. This was when the greatest attention was needed; a sign missed could mean a life lost. He readied more spoke bombs and passed into the dark tunnel, quelling any feelings of panic that threatened to cloud his judgement. He couldn't deny the constant, stifling sense of déjà vu he experienced when passing into station wreckage that he knew had been caused by a capsuleer – it truly was unlike anything else the pirate ships ever inflicted – but he refused to let it be a problem, channelling the anger to fuel his purpose. He would not let these people die.

Behind him, he heard the Angel troops follow. He signalled the captain, hooking the man's team into the time signatures of the spoke bombs and into Drem's own tagging capabilities. The captain silently accepted both hooks. His men wouldn't get blown up, and would immediately be notified of any life Drem encountered.

Yaman and Verena both sent signals to Drem, letting him know they'd arrived at the mouth of the tunnel.

He activated spoke bombs as he went along, making his way deeper in. It took him several minutes before he found his first victim, trapped in a tiny alcove under a mass of metal girders and electrical wiring. It was a man about Ortag's age, conscious but clearly in pain, clutching a shattered leg. Drem tagged the man on his overhead, got acknowledgement from the Angel agents, and spoke a few soothing words to him before moving on.

The minutes passed like hours as he made his way through the rubble, tagging victims and occasionally sedating the ones who refused to let him go again. The destruction had been quite incredible, and it was a testament to Cartel workmanship and engineering that the whole colony hadn't collapsed already.

Drem, who needed to say something if only to throw off the silence of the tunnel, remarked on this lucky fact to the Angel agents. One of them – not the captain – said, 'Well, the egger was allowed to attack without response. By the time our guys flew in, he'd gotten what he wanted and gone already.'

The immediate silence that followed gave Drem the impression that something had been said on an Angel-only comms, and he couldn't resist jabbing, 'The Blood Raiders don't wait before scrambling forces for their guys.'

'Rules of the game change when the capsuleers come in,' Rhan said, and Drem heard the quiet anger in his voice.

He decided to risk a little white flag. 'No friends of yours either, are they?'

'If every one of them was gone for good, you wouldn't find me mourning,' Rhan replied, an amazing admission over open comms. 'And if any of you report this to my superiors, you'll soon be involved in a brief and spectacularly unsuccessful rescue mission, I promise you.'

Drem grinned darkly and turned back to the scouting.

It went well, as such things go. When they'd picked out the last man the drones had detected, Drem called for reports from the other Sisters teams and found that virtually everyone was now accounted for. More than a hundred people assumed lost to the world, only to be found again. If this wasn't a reason to keep on going, he didn't know what was.

Those same reports, however, indicated increased instability in the station's core, which wouldn't have been a problem except for the intense damage its outer hull had taken. When the core gave and the hull was unstable, blowouts would inevitably happen.

'All right, let's wrap up,' one of the Angels said. Most of them had retreated out of the tunnels, leaving Drem and his team in there to do any final scouting.

‘What’s up?’ Verena said to him.

Drem was impressed with her. Even through the suit and the silence, she could tell he wasn’t at ease with the situation.

‘There’s too few people here,’ he said on the team channel.

‘That’s . . . pretty much the point, isn’t it?’ Yaman said.

‘No, there’s way too few people,’ Drem insisted. ‘I remember places like this, back on the Raider colonies. There were always illegals, transients who’d come in for a hard seasonal term, get two-thirds their payout in transportables they’d sell elsewhere and one-third in a bar tab. This kind of place, the bars should’ve been full, but I swear to the Red God it’s like some people are missing.’

He hefted a spoke bomb. ‘I want to go deeper. There’s got to be more people down there. They would’ve been in groups and we haven’t found any. Everyone was on file. It’s not right.’

‘You’re sure about this?’ Verena said.

‘No. But I really feel like I need to give it a go.’

‘People, blowouts are starting to look quite likely,’ the Angel captain broadcast to them. ‘Whatever you’re doing down there, you’ll want to finish up quick.’

Drem looked at the other two, who silently looked back at him.

‘We go where you take us,’ Yaman finally said. ‘Make the call, bro.’

Drem looked at the spoke bomb in his hand, then at the ruined colony around him. He was asking them to join him on a deadly, hunch-driven ghost hunt. But it was thanks to the Sisters that he’d been pulled out of wreckage that probably looked a lot like this.

‘Ah, fuck it,’ he said and called up a stability projection on the overhead, then set the bomb and tossed it.

It took them twenty precious minutes, with worried haranguing from the Angel captain, but they found what they were looking for: in the buried mess of what used to be a bar, a buried mess of what used to be human beings. Several dozen pairs of eyes stared out in dead accusation.

Even through the masks, Verena’s face was white with shock. Yaman doubled over and managed to cut off comms just before puking, the spatters covering the inside of his helmet.

Drem let a red river of anger carry him away from what he saw. His mind grasped for something else to focus on, but found only people living their peaceful lives on a colony, and a capsuleer coming along to break it all apart.

The captain's voice cut through the haze. It was very calm. 'Guys, I patched through visual and just saw what you're seeing. I know you're torn up, but we have to get out *now.* Total collapse is imminent. We will take care of this, I promise. We will find their names. But you have to go. Now. Go.'

In Drem's distant stupor as he started making his way back above-ground, it occurred to him that Angels were very efficient, in their own way, and that if he could find one with enough of a conscience to place people over hardware, he'd recruit the man on the spot. Yaman, whose disgusted expression was only hazily visible behind the layer of bacteria currently cleaning his viewscreen and his face, briefly put a hand on Drem's back before passing him by. Verena took his hand and held it so tight he could feel it through the fabric.

It took him a whole five hours, through return, warp, debriefing and retreat to quarters, but he finally reached for a towel that he wrapped around his face, knelt down on the floor of his living room, and screamed until he was hoarse.

Perversely, it was the success on this very mission – of saving the living, but also of finding the dead – that finally got Drem a meeting with the underground.

Ever since he got to Angel space he had been trying to make contacts in the criminal world, feeling his way along its gloomy corridors in the hope that someone would possess the one piece of data he craved. Security codes, staff records, places, schematics, *names*; Drem knew it was all stored somewhere in the Cartel. Someone out there held the key that would – he hoped – help lock for good a dark door in his mind.

But he was an outsider without reputation or credit, a potential spy for any number of organizations. He could not reveal his true identity, and he had neither the money nor the leverage to pry what he wanted from the mouths of the silent. Some of the people he talked to told him openly that he looked too hungry to trust, and a few, to his surprise and discomfort, had now begun to recognize him as a Sisters agent. It ingratiated him with them, apparently, but not enough.

Once he returned from that bloodied mission, an anonymous message awaited him in his quarters. It thanked him for his efforts – which alone was amazing, as not even the Angel top command would yet have received the mission debriefing – and asked him to visit a particular address. It pointedly gave him two full days before the meeting. He appreciated that. He needed more time to unwind.

Drem set off from his quarters, passing through the borders of the Angel station proper and up into the more elite residential areas. He passed through several layers of security along the way, each more intense than the last. At one point Drem was even checked for viral agents by an intent-looking man whose weaponry was not quite concealed about his person. The checkpoint guards did not speak much during the procession, but Drem got the strange feeling that they'd known who he was even before he arrived at their gates.

To his surprise he was not brought to a windowless room, but escorted instead through the guard's cell, down a series of corridors, and finally through an opening into a large, sunny park where small clusters of people slowly walked over the grass. There were trees in the distance, and at least three large ponds that he could see.

The guard pointed him towards a far table, where a grey-haired man dressed in white sat patiently, looking out at the trees. Drem walked on expecting the guard to follow him, but he returned to his post.

As he got closer to the man in white he looked around again. He still did not recognize anyone else in the area. One person in the far distance looked oddly reminiscent of Captain Kiel Rhan, with that same stiff bearing and trim build, but that was as far as recognition went.

The man in white smiled at him, and rose when he approached. 'A pleasure to meet our newest hero,' he said to Drem's embarrassment, and offered a hand. Drem shook it and took a proffered seat at the table.

The air in this place seemed wonderfully fresh to Drem, who spent half his time in crowded Angel commons and the other half in the filtered space of his hazard suit. He inhaled deeply and imagined he was breathing in the air from a forested planet. The sun was setting, and its rays reflected off distant hovercars like raindrops in red summer.

'It's men like you that make me proud to have our organization associated with the Sisters. Your efforts have certainly not gone unnoticed.'

'It's my duty and honour, sir.' Drem wondered just how deeply the Angel criminal element was interwoven with its administration. He suspected that few people knew, or were allowed to live once they'd found out.

'That said, it's rather uncommon to have a Sisters agent look to make connections among our cadre,' the man said. 'Even if he's trying to do it anonymously.'

'I take it I'm not very good at subterfuge,' Drem said a little dejectedly.

'Oh, I don't know. You're still alive,' the man told him with a wry grin that did not quite hide the seriousness of the situation. 'Usually someone in your position would at best end up getting nothing, and at worst end up getting whatever the lower orders think they deserve.'

The man had not yet said Drem's name, nor given his own. Drem found this curious.

Thankfully, the man in white seemed to find his concern amusing. 'Not to worry. This place was designed for trust. Even the table we're sitting at has embedded equipment that encapsulates us in a cone of silence. You can talk freely here.'

'That's certainly appreciated, sir. In fact, I was hoping you'd be the one doing the talking.'

The man's smile did not move. His greying hair, silhouetted against the fading background sunlight, looked like errant wheat stalks in a field. 'How so?' he asked.

Drem leaned in. 'I need the name of a specific individual. Someone whom I know was in a certain place at a certain time, not too long ago, and let his presence be known with a bang. A capsuleer.'

'We cannot provide that information, I'm afraid,' the man said without hesitation.

'But I—'

'My boy, no matter how much good you've done for us, and I'm perfectly aware that you've done a lot, the capsuleers represent a whole different world.'

Drem fought back the agitation in his voice. 'I am not asking you to *do* anything—'

'I know. But whatever reason you have for wanting this man's name, and I don't want to know about it, it'll eventually be traced back to us. We cannot afford that, I'm afraid. Not even if you believe, in this moment of desperation, that you merely want to hear it.'

It was like a retread of his meeting with the Blood Raider. Drem could have stood and throttled this old man, for all of the two seconds it would have taken him until the snipers drew a bead, but he did not. He had another life now. New values, of life over blood. He would not go down the road of self-destruction yet again.

Through the red mist of his vision he saw the man in white say, quite simply, 'I'm sorry.'

Drem sat there and said nothing.

'Was there anything else?' the man said.

Drem shook his head.

The man stood up. 'Then I wish you the best of luck in your continued work, whether it be for us or anyone else who needs your help.'

Drem stood up as well. He nodded at the man and slowly walked toward the exit, making no sudden moves.

He did not lose his grip. He would find a way. He would make this happen, and then he would move on with his life.

The guard led him out of the area by a different route, down grey corridors, and out into the crowds beyond. Drem barely noticed them.

A voice he recognized said, 'That was a stupid thing to ask for,' but as soon as he looked up, whoever had spoken had gone.

He smiled faintly, turned back to the last door he had walked through, and with all the force he could muster he hit it so hard that it visibly dented under his blow.

Before the guards could rush out, he made a swift exit, walking away from the area and toward his own sector of the station, turning off his communicators and disappearing into the gathering dust.

When he finally came home, there was an e-tag on his quarters' access log. It was from Verena, asking him to come to her quarters immediately.

There was nothing in his own home he particularly wanted right now. The anger had subsided, replaced by a dull throb of anxiety and frustration.

Verena's place was in the same sector as his, but far enough that the walk gave him time to wonder what she wanted. He doubted that word of his meeting with the man in white had reached anyone outside that protected circle: his request had been polite, if apparently delusional, and didn't seem to have ruffled any feathers. Besides, if there were any trouble, he'd more likely be hearing from Ortag.

It was very late when he reached her place, but she'd left the halogen on, so he assumed she must be awake. He rang and waited. When she opened the door, he saw that she was dressed in night clothes; spacious, comfortable and thin.

She smiled at him. 'Good to see you. Come on in,' she said and walked away into the apartment. He followed.

They went into the living room. He took a seat on a chair. 'You know,' he said, 'we've been working together for I don't know how long now, and I've never been to your quarters.'

She handed him a drink and sat on the sofa across from him. 'I don't stay here much,' she said. 'I try to stay outside most of the time, be among people. Not much use in being home alone, thinking.'

He nodded in agreement. 'How is it, being back in the Cartel?'

She put down her own drink and leaned back in the sofa, her night gown outlining her body. 'It's . . . not what I thought it would be, to be honest,' she said. 'I wasn't planning to leave the Sisters, but

I did hope I would find something here that I'd forgotten.'

'What did you find?'

'It's the same, in ways that I'd forgotten about. You know how it is when you leave a place you know too well. What you remember are the highlights, which you miss, or the lowest points, which you eventually convince yourself that you can ignore. But there's all this stuff in between, the little annoyances and this . . . this . . .'

'Unnerving familiarity?' Drem hazarded.

'Yes! The faces are different and so is some of the architecture and what have you, but this very place is so much an Angel Cartel station. It couldn't possibly be anything else. Stiffs acting like they're a proper nation with an army, instead of this ragtag bunch of criminals with a hierarchy.'

'At least you guys don't creep out half the cluster,' Drem said, slowly sipping his drink.

She looked at him, then said, 'Shit. I'm sorry, Drem. I'm bitching about my past to someone who can't even go home.'

'It's OK,' he said and shrugged.

She got up, picked up a datapad off a table, and handed it to him. 'Anyway, I asked you over so I could give you this.' She stood by him for a second, then put a hand on his shoulder and sighed. 'I really am sorry. You've just been through hell. How are you holding up?'

'I'm all right,' said Drem, and he meant it. Events of the last few days all faded, overshadowed by the nice calm he felt right at this moment, in this comfortable chair. Close to her.

'I was impressed by how you handled it. Really impressed,' she said in a quieter tone. 'I always am. All those times we've been out in the field, in the smoke and the fire, and I've never seen anyone like you.'

'Thank you,' he said, and before he knew what he was doing he'd taken hold of her hand, stroking it gently with his thumb.

They remained like that for a while, in the potent silence of the room.

'Aren't . . . are you going to read the message?' she asked, nodding towards the datapad in his hand.

He tried to shrug nonchalantly. 'The message doesn't interest me so much, right this minute.'

'I think you should,' she said. 'The guy who had it sent to me was worried that he couldn't contact you. Said he wanted to make sure you got it before you did anything else stupid.'

Drem's thoughts veered momentarily off their libidinous course. 'Anything *else* stupid?'

'That's what he said.' She seemed amused by this, too. The way she looked at him, a little distant but entirely close at the same time, made him feel quite pleasantly unreal, as if he were a toy in some strange game.

He forced himself to look down at the datapad. The message was from Captain Kiel Rhan.

Drem read it in silence, eyes widening with amazement.

'Anything interesting?' he heard Verena say.

'That sly fox,' he murmured, half to himself.

'Did he give you something you wanted?' she said, with an emphasis on 'wanted' that brought his gaze back to her. Now she smiled even wider, and narrowed her eyes slightly. Drem felt his pulse quicken.

From afar, he heard his own voice say, 'No, but he gave me a lead to someone else who might.'

She nodded, as if this were all part of the game. Then she leaned over, taking the datapad from his hands, and straddled his lap.

She was trembling a little from nerves, but that was all right with Drem, because so was he.

She said, 'But first . . .'

9

The starship came out of warp in Luminaire and set its course for the planet of Gallente Prime. By design the journey gave the ship's civilian occupants enough time to shake off the post-warp effects.

'How's the warp on you, hon?' Heci asked Ralea.

'Fine.'

Ralea had been morose and weak for most of the trip, with short, curt phrases constituting all the communication she could offer. Now she sat inertly by the viewports, alone with her friend, and watched the cosmos pass her by.

Heci didn't mind. A loyal friend and a more insightful woman than many might have thought, she didn't get upset by whatever idiosyncrasies other people exhibited, even if she did not comprehend them. She merely believed that these problems were real, and accepted them. She did not extend this courtesy to everyone, but to those who had earned it she gave it unreservedly. In return, Ralea trusted her to choose the right path for them both.

To Heci's surprise, Ralea looked at her and said, 'After years ... I thought it was months but I guess it's been years of being hooked ... what happened in the last few days, I can handle a little warping.'

'We really, really had to go,' Heci said. 'I've been watching the news. A man was found murdered up in the residential areas. They didn't say who he was or what he did, but I know people and I found out.'

Ralea nodded silently. She looked out the port again.

Feeling thankful that they were alone in the viewing area, Heci said, 'He wasn't a nice man, hon. I won't say what you did was right, but I can't say the world will mourn him in any great measure, either.'

'What's going to happen to me?' Ralea asked her. Not tearfully, and not in desperation; but in that quiet limbo of pain and exhaustion that existed somewhere beyond them.

'Oh, sweetie,' Heci said in a tremulous voice and sat down beside her, putting an arm on her shoulder. 'We're agents. That buys us a little time, if they even have a clue it was you. The guy was high-tier on the station and I'm sure he had underground contacts that want to know what happened, but these things take time.' She tightened her grip on Ralea's shoulders. 'The place we're going caters to people like us. They'll let us breathe a little, help you get better, and they won't say a goddamn word to anyone about it. Nobody will find us there. What's important now is that we take care of ourselves, lay low and stay clever.'

'We can't stay there forever,' Ralea said.

Heci sighed. 'No. Other agents and semiautonomous AIs will pick up our slack, and we've got enough money saved up for a very, very long time on our own. But after whatever happened with you and that shitheel, we are now on the run, probably both from the law and from other people like the one you . . .' She faltered. 'Anyway, we'll figure that one out later.'

They fell silent for a while. As she watched Ralea stare out the viewports, Heci noticed that her friend was rocking gently in time to silent music, as if they were sailing on unseen waves. It wasn't an uneasy motion, nor jittery; it was smooth and meditative, the subtle hints of a mind's silent contentment. They were *going* somewhere, which felt enough like a solution that it gave the two of them a little hope.

The ship's viewpoint lounge was dark and quiet, offering an uninterrupted view of the stars. Some viewports allowed hyper-focusing, so that onlookers could curve their view, even rotate it, for a greater visual experience.

In a more normal voice, not the cowed, wispy thing she had been using all flight, Ralea said, 'How strange this place looks.'

Heci looked at her, then shifted and glanced over her shoulder to see what she was looking at. It wasn't their destination, Gallente Prime – the seat of democracy and free living – but its terrible cousin Caldari Prime, war-torn and shredded from a recent invasion by the Caldari State.

She put her hand on Ralea's shoulder and kept it there, squeezing very gently.

Some of the unoccupied monitors started scrolling through ads on Gallente Prime's recreational options, a subtle acknowledgement that they were nearing the link to the dropships waiting for them in orbit. Heci left her friend and headed over to one of those screens, idly browsing through its polychrome offers. There were a million things to entertain visitors, though for Heci the planet held another, more subtle attraction: its open, profligate atmosphere would allow them to maintain their old vices for as long as needed, without fear of reprisal or discovery. She knew, from dealing with demons just as destructive as Ralea's, that one did not simply drop every last vestige and turn into a new person. There needed to be a period of reduction, of weaning and moderation.

Whatever else the planet held, she hoped it would be external rejuvenation and internal rest, in equal measure.

The refuge was a wonderful city, not the largest on Gallente Prime but sizeable enough that it could house several spacious layers, complete with full infrastructure on each: housing, transportation, even woodland carefully grown to match the architecture and the pathways of the streets. A latticework of life and activity.

It was an expensive place, particularly for those who chose to reside in its uppermost layers. The population was a pyramid, with tens of millions making a living further down, whittled down to only a few million in the median layers, and a single million or so at the top. There was no social segregation: if you could afford to move up, you did, and you brought with you whatever lifestyle you chose.

The largest buildings pierced the skies, their spires glinting like rainbows. Architecture here followed the crystal style so favoured in the richer parts of the Federation. Below them, near the ground of each level, the local planet's flora took over, covering not merely the safety gaps between the buildings and nearby roads, but every other hole that could be seen. It was not possible to see down with the entangled branches, the creeping vines, the great bushels of flowers sprouting from all manner of surfaces. A careful eye could spot that some of these plants were not natural neighbours, and that, in fact, they had been genetically modified to form symbiotic relationships, resulting in a natural, sweetly scented web of illusion that gave the constant appearance that the only thing beneath the pedestrians' feet was the soft moss of nature.

The streets themselves, spacious and clean, were pristine in design and appearance. They doubled as scaffolding for the skyscrapers and were thus connected to each side of every building. The general attitude among the denizens of this city was that personal freedom, in whatever interpretation one lent it, trumped all reason. It was considered normal to have people wandering in on the ground floor of every building even if they had no business there, for no other reason than curiosity and, possibly, some need to have a definitive solid structure holding them up for a while. The streets were translucent synthetics with an unscratchable varnish, but the buildings, for all their crystalline exterior, were very much solid brickwork and metal.

The culture was another thing entirely.

As Heci and Ralea passed through the streets, they saw everything one could think of seeing in a world that had all it wanted. Nowhere else were there greater human modifications on display; nowhere was there a higher density of information effulgently broadcast from countless sources. Other senses were assaulted, too: in the grand flora that surrounded every street, embedded launchers would send out wafting puffs of spores that, when inhaled, would carefully enhance longings and emotions subject to the inhaler's location. A journey past a travel agency would find the traveller suddenly excited for adventure; a walk near the matchmaking agency and adult toy boutique would set off several glands that had not entirely expected to go into full operation; and the gods of New Eden help anyone walking past a chocolatier.

Safety limits were, of course, strictly enforced – the keyword was 'enhance', not 'induce' – and any corporation whose advertisement assaults became too intense for the population to handle would find themselves booted down a level, where the natural light was a little murkier, standards a little lower, and competition all the more cutthroat.

Heci allowed their journey to veer toward the level's mildly seedier areas. There was nothing dilapidated or all that dangerous this high up, but the sleaziness was nonetheless quite detectable, overlaid on certain buildings and structures like an oily patina. Lights took on a redder quality, and the emotion spores became all the more singularly focused.

They stopped near a store whose volumetric ads, slowly revolving like glittering ice circles around its building, promised entertainment quite unlike anything else the viewer had seen. Heci read from a distance. 'Alien . . . cheerleaders . . . shooting lasers through their . . . hey, how about that?' she said, turning to Ralea.

Her friend lay half over the controls of her hovercraft, her face white.

'All right, OK, we're going straight to the resort now,' Heci said swiftly. 'Are you strapped in, sweetie?'

Ralea nodded, then let her head slump on to the control board again.

Heci keyed in a towing control. Ralea's hovercraft silently aligned itself behind hers, ready to follow. She set off, slowly at first, with an eye on her friend. As they started moving again, Ralea looked up with bleary eyes and blinked in the sunlight. She seemed to like looking at the trees, but otherwise exhibited little sign of interest.

Heci tried not to feel rotten about the excursion. She had been pushing Ralea, slyly testing her exactly when she shouldn't have. It was so easy to forget everything they'd just been through, to fall into the trap of acting like they were their past lively, active selves, powerful and unblemished in the eyes of the law. The old Ralea would have roared with laughter at the alien cheerleaders and demanded to see where they hid their lasers.

But it also frightened her that Ralea had trusted her with her fate.

Heci, if she were to be completely honest, didn't feel very much in control of anything at all.

In the next few weeks the two agents were introduced to a remarkable array of scientific equipment, procedures and outright magic, all of it with a laser focus on turning them into the healthiest human beings they could be.

Heci had been expecting a strong detox angle to the program, but was amazed to find that its initial phases were solely concerned with anti-senescence. The reasoning, she was told, was that a body in a bad state operated at an accelerated breakdown rate, a slippery slope that could cause even more damaging and less reversible breakdowns than the subject had suffered thus far. Before they could be made to rise again, the overly cheerful doctors explained, their plunge had to be slowed down.

The removal of senescent cells and extraneous cellular material, mutations and other abnormal growths all took a lot longer than Heci had expected, partly because it was a tedious process that required a lot of lying still and listening to the hum of machines. The treatments that followed, however, were a little more exciting, and looked far more exotic.

There was a trend among the Gallentean people for unorthodox medicine. Gallente medical authorities, adaptable and possessing a greater understanding of human nature than they cared to admit, had reacted to it by offering 'advanced' versions of traditional treatments. Moss covers over penicillin pills, effectively, these versions had reached great popularity among the Federation masses.

In one instance, Heci and Ralea went through a period of blood cleansing wherein they lay on the shielded patio of a very tall building and bathed in sunshine, while traditional healers, dressed in flowing historical garbs, placed little metal discs on their bodies. The discs, slightly oval in shape, looked entirely without harm or function.

Leeching was popular in many cultures of New Eden, not least among the Gallente. With miniscule grapplers these discs slowly traversed their occupants' backs until they sensed something beyond the skin – an improper flow, a disharmony in the energies, or a budding infection, depending on who you asked – that needed to be corrected. They injected a little local anaesthetic, then latched on to the skin and slowly began to draw out the tainted blood. To ameliorate the visual discomfort caused by the sight of the metal leeches, the bleeding caused their carapaces to change, unfurling petals reminiscent of beautiful, iridescent flowers. The petals served as status indicators, and once their colours had changed from white to a darkened orange they would be removed, the healers lifting them off with great ceremony. The patient was intended to feel their blood had given life to something; it was part of the subtle mental therapy of the sanatorium.

The combination of spas, rejuvenation therapies and blood extraction did wonders for the two agents. The physical therapy they underwent slowly gave them strength as the weeks went by, and it removed all physiological traces of Ralea's addiction, but there was nothing that could yet be done for her mind or the breakdown it had suffered.

After they'd been put through the wringer of rehabilitation, Heci started them on activities. They went slowly at first, but before long their renewed, detoxed bodies started craving more exertion. Heci loved using her body constructively – the rejuvenation had removed the exhaustion she felt after constant overwork and the recent emotional turmoil – but she took even greater pleasure in seeing Ralea free of the need for drugs and able to roar into action again. Ralea showed no initiative in choosing their activities but remained open to try anything Heci asked of her.

They took off for a fortnight in their hovercars, flying far beyond the layered cities and spending nights out in the openness of true nature. They used surfing capsules to plunge into the deep sea, cloaked and silent, their overhead views guiding them towards great shoals of shimmering fish, gliding like mercury through the blue ocean. The air was theirs, too; they discovered extreme hang gliding, hovering on rocket-propelled craft over gullies and mountains, even passing over an active volcano situated on a beautiful, uninhabited island. One of the more glorious moments of their time on Gallente Prime came when Heci, in total control of her glide, turned her skimmer, swiftly unzipped her pants and fastenings, and peed into the volcano; Ralea laughed so hard that she nearly plunged into the lava.

It was shortly after that Ralea started to talk.

They were lying underneath the stars, watching movies cast in the air by their microprojectors. It was mostly for something to drift off to; they had turned the sound to mute.

'I feel so much better,' Ralea said.

Heci turned to her and smiled. 'You look so much better.'

'Still a murderer, though.'

'Won't ever escape that, sweetie. Not even as an agent.'

The movie ran on, brightly lit players on a darkened planet.

'It's a freedom, this,' Ralea said. 'A new kind of freedom. I've almost gotten used to it.'

'You can go back for a little while,' Heci said. 'Even with your wanted status, you'll always have a day or two before they dare touch an agent.'

Ralea nodded. Then she added, 'But if I want to go back and *stay*, I'll need to change.'

Heci hesitated. This was not a subject she had wanted to broach.

Ralea continued, 'I've been thinking a lot about it. Facial remoulding. Fingerprint alteration, total restructuring of various body parts so they can't rely on volumetric image reconstruction from archival footage . . .'

Heci waited.

'I don't know if I can do it,' Ralea finally said, the sentence fading to nothing. 'I'm sorry, we've been here a while and it's all been so great, so wonderfully overwhelming, I just—'

'Hey. Hey. It's all right!' Heci said, laughing to mask her relief. 'I forgive you for not wanting to spend the rest of your life in the body of a different person. Relax!'

She watched the movie for a little while, allowing her friend to rethink the apology and argument she'd likely assumed were impending.

'But we're cool?' Ralea said.

'We, sweetheart, are definitely cool,' Heci said. She waited a moment, then said, 'You know, it's a pretty hectic life here, even aside from all our troubles. We might simply be best off finding a new home in a quieter part of the cluster. Somewhere totally different. Maybe even with the Amarr.'

'Seriously? To the empire of zealots and madmen?'

Heci took a deep breath, choosing her words carefully. 'I don't feel we have a responsibility to anything other than ourselves right now, and certainly not to our Gallentean home. I've needed a break for ages, truth be told. *You* are a murderer on the run from the law, even if the law hasn't thought to look in this direction yet, and you've been abusing yourself for years. I don't think that a quiet stay a long way away would do us any harm right now. And I . . . I think I've had enough of this place, of the Federation. I don't like what it does to people. What it did to you.'

Ralea said, 'Well, what's most important to me right now is feeling at home in my own body. Maybe I could pull off that identity change and stay in the Federation without losing my mind. New eyes, new face, new everything. And not go utterly crazy . . . I don't know.'

'Maybe,' Heci said. The tone of quiet desparation in her friend's voice had been unmistakable. 'In an ideal world I'd want to stay, I'd want *us* to stay, but . . . I don't know, either. What you'd have to do to yourself to avoid detection here in the Federation, it's not something people do lightly.'

Ralea nodded. 'And there's no guidance to be had. I can't rightly call up someone and go, hey, is this the support group for criminals who've had their bodies rebuilt from scratch? I don't even know what kind of problems I might have, mental and physical, if I do that to myself, and I haven't exactly been the most stable of persons so far.'

'So what are you planning to do?' Heci said.

'I've got no fucking clue,' Ralea said with such an exasperated smile that Heci had to laugh. 'I mean, it's a terrifying option, but I can't just discount it. Our people are good at remaking themselves, and there's got to be something out there that'll prove, one way or another, whether I can really go through this kind of change without completely losing my mind.'

'Let's sleep on it. This isn't something you decide on without a lot of thought,' Heci said. 'And the Amarr are always available.'

'Sure,' Ralea said but without much conviction. She switched off the movie and had the projectors scroll through a massive list of activities. 'I'm just going to look through this, see if there's anything that catches my eye. If I can't find it, hell, we'll probably go somewhere else like you've been saying, before they catch us. Be somebody else,' she added.

Ralea searched intently through the list. It went on for so long that when she finally spoke, her voice startled Heci out of a drifting half-sleep.

'I want to go there,' Ralea said. 'I need to see *him*, and I want to go there.'

Heci inspected her selection. Strange people with strange bodies hovered in front of a Gallentean station, and the superimposed description spoke of the largest, grandest, weirdest body modification expo in the entire Federation. A separate note mentioned a special guest: someone called the Upright Man, a famous but seldom-seen body-modder who supposedly embodied the epitome of the art. According to the details Heci looked up, he was the Federation's foremost expert on any and all manner of advanced body modifications and on the psychological implications these had for those who undertook them. Reading between the lines, Heci got the distinct impression that this person was renowned for procedures that were quite possibly illegal.

It was at once completely nonsensical and yet the only reasonable choice her friend could possibly make, if she was committed to this path. If you wanted to find out how comfortable you would be in your own new skin, this was the place you would go.

Ralea said, 'And, uh, Heci?'

'Yes?'

'I think I need to do this alone. Take the first steps into ... not independence, because that's not what we're after here, but self-reliance.'

'I know,' Heci said, with nothing but love. 'I wish you wouldn't do this, but it is your choice, not mine.'

'Thank you.'

They turned off the monitors and lay on their mats under the gentle night breeze. Heci listened for Ralea's breath until she fell asleep.

They didn't use scanners when she went through the doors. Every single attendee had already been checked, since all the implants, modifications and arcane equipment they carried would make local inspections both unpleasant and time-consuming. Ralea flashed her pass at the guards and at everyone she met on the other side, but nobody gave her even a second look.

She had bought her way into the VIP section of the body modification expo, and its floor was huge, crowded and strange. Electric banners flashed through the sky, their glowing letters shifting about, cutting through each other, writhing like a den of metallic snakes. Vidscreens the size of houses alternated between samples of inventive modding and ads for various services, a few of which showed physical procedures that even Ralea, who had seen a lot, didn't want to contemplate too heavily.

In the midst of the wave of attendees there was a volumetric figure that reached to the ceiling. It showed a woman in clingy skinwear who reminded Ralea of the ones she'd seen in the docking areas of some Gallente stations. The figure altered and shifted before her eyes, cycling through various modifications that would undoubtedly be on display in the flesh among the convention crowd. It was a striking display, but the image's greenish tint and the woman's perfect figure pushed her too near the uncanny valley of human realism for Ralea's liking, and as the creature morphed again and again she felt as if she were looking at a slideshow of evolution.

Everyone in this place, Ralea reasoned, would be a specialist in changing themselves from the inside out. They had embraced reinvention. If it could be done, it was done here, with more acceptance and vigour than anywhere else. Human creations passed her by on all sides.

She had an appointment with the Upright Man, but it wasn't for a while yet. She started to circulate and tried to socialize, in careful but assured steps. There was a definite love of the fantastic in this place, even if its precise definition seemed to elude most of those she talked with. Some worshipped the far future, as evidenced by the more extravagant mods on display. Others seemed attached to an alternate version of the near future, one where the social mores would allow them to fit in – except then, Ralea suspected, they would find new ways of modding themselves just enough to stand out yet again. She had the feeling that with some, their sole purpose in life was the pursuit of ideals that simply didn't exist.

As much as Ralea tried, the one subject that no one seemed willing to expound upon, oddly enough, was the Upright Man. They revered him, clearly, but it was an unquiet awe, for reasons that no one would divulge. She accepted this and listened as others talked about their own mods instead.

The range of human display was astounding. There were people whose bodies were canvasses for slow-motion plays, their skin displaying colourful vistas with moving actors in the foreground. The simpler versions, usually covering some minor part of the body and almost always involving starships, had tattoos that moved jerkily, like stop-motion imagery, and reminded Ralea of neon blinklights in scummy bars. As the tattoos got more complex, and covered more skin, their motion became progressively smoother. The subject matters changed drastically, too, turning away from space and toward flora and fauna instead, as if unaltered natural life held a nostalgic value – which, for someone so deeply mired in the modding world, it actually might. Ralea loved the idea that her unchanged body might seem exotic to the people around her.

Other mods went so much deeper, with implants that bulged and writhed under the skin. One was a series of small metal spikes, aligned in a straight line, poking out in rhythm through the flesh of that person's forearm, and after a few moments Ralea realized that they were tapping out the first lines of a Minmatar rebel anthem. Other mods would expand and extend feelers that looked quite menacing – often very sharp – and even rotated slowly on their bearers' skin.

There were cutaneous alterations whereby the skin had been turned scaly and silver, or given a multihued, oily patina, or had even been turned rough and coarse, often inset with tufts of shaggy hair. The people with the rough, hairy skin tended to have sharp teeth as well.

What brought Ralea to a total halt were the Replacers. Parts of their bodies – skin, hair, bits of muscle and so on – had been removed entirely. Some had foregone replacement, leaving the remains – open wounds and gaping maws – either bound with transparent sealant or left in glass-like tubing so that one got a disturbing look at their insides. She shook hands with one of these men and couldn't help but look at the way the muscles in his skinless hand pulled and gave, like an anatomy lesson. The idea that she could look like that, even if only for a few moments on a surgeon's table, gave her shivers.

Others had created unique replacements, often of weird, seemingly non-human designs; one of the modders had had his shoulder blades replaced with what looked like insect wings, while another had a good part of the sinews in his upper body changed to look very much like tree roots. Ralea looked around for more of these but found her gaze mercilessly drawn to the liquefied Replacers, the ones who'd had some inner body part, even an entire organ, replaced with a chemical soup that presumably served the same task, stored in an unbreakable glass-alloy display container that reached all the way to the surface of the body. Ralea found herself wondering what kind of future the Replacers foresaw.

She couldn't take watching someone's digestion happily at work, so she wandered back to the area centre, directing her gaze at the more pleasant form of the volumetric morphing figure. As she glanced at the figure's skin she noticed that even the time of day was morphing through her, its numbers bleeding through her skin like liquid arrows. It was nearing time to see the Upright Man, and Ralea gingerly started making her way through the crowd.

A large man with blades in his skin welcomed her, taking her down a corridor and into an empty, sizeable room. The atmosphere was more relaxed here. There was no furniture to speak of, only a series of large pillows strewn over a rug. The walls were in dark colours, the lights were slightly dimmed, and there was the smell of incense in the air. She waited a little while, enjoying the quiet, before she heard a door open and close and a man's voice say, 'Sorry to keep you waiting, Miss.'

'Not at all,' Ralea said, turning to the entrant. She was entirely aware that without her money and connections – the ones she could safely use as a fugitive, at least – there wouldn't have been a meeting at all. Her subject was sought after and reclusive. 'You're right on time, Mister . . . Man.'

He laughed. Like so many others at the expo he wasn't dressed in much, merely a loincloth and sandals. He was of average height, athletic and with well-defined muscles. Ralea gave him a quick look over but couldn't spot any modifications, and when her gaze again met the Upright Man's, the modder grinned at her. There was a strange look in his eyes, but then, that was nothing new at the expo.

'Sorry,' Ralea said. 'Couldn't help but be curious. You've quite a reputation.'

'Yes, so it seems.'

'In fact, your past interviews maintain that you're one of the most experienced bodymodders out there, though they're extremely short on details. You're certainly one of the more loquacious speakers on the subject of personal change and how it affects the individual.'

He nodded in polite acknowledgement. 'What would you like to know?' he asked, 'And what sparked your interest in our little hobby?'

Ralea decided not to go for any personal revelations right away – she was adamant not to share her own reasons for being at the expo – and instead started asking about body modifications. By the Upright Man's enlivened expression, she saw that she'd made the right choice.

They talked for a while about the Upright Man's impressions of the modding scene and of this expo, from its nascent planetside days to the current, massive incarnation. Interest in modding ebbed and flowed, the Man said, depending on what was happening in New Eden and how much civil discontent was present in each empire. Ralea asked technical questions about certain mods, ensuring she came off as well-informed rather than as a braggart, and the Upright Man responded in kind.

The conversation wore on, and Ralea was beginning to think she might start delving into her subject's own past history and ideas of modding and identity, when the Upright Man asked how she herself felt about all this.

She thought about it, and decided to give her honest impression. Choosing her words carefully, she explained her interest in reinvention, her fear of a resulting identity crisis, and her suspicion that bodymodders might hold the answers. When she mentioned her impression of the nebulous future visions everyone seemed to share, and the progression she'd witnessed from simple tattoos to liquid Replacers, the Upright Man smiled and said, 'Yeah, they do take it to extremes, don't they? Everyone is becoming a piece of art, or expressing themselves with a bullhorn, or whatever else. I'm amazed they even count me among their number.'

Ralea saw the bait and took it. 'I must admit, I'm puzzled. They say you've understood this art better than anyone else, but on the outside I'd say you hide it pretty well.'

The Upright Man seemed quite gratified at this. 'You can't spot anything? Be honest.'

'Well, your skin is a little pale, but given the mystery that surrounds you, I doubt you spend much time sunbathing on the station patio.' Ralea added, 'And there's something about your eyes, though that might just be the general look I've seen on most faces here.'

'Captivated?'

'Batshit crazy, I was going to say, but yeah, that too.'

The Upright Man laughed, and explained, 'It's all about being so different. Getting away from the present and running away to some indefinite future, like you were talking about. I don't see the point. Everything turns full circle; everyone goes back to where they began. The naturalist tattooers have the right idea, but they're merely painting themselves back to what they'd like to be.'

'So it's a journey-not-destination, kind of thing?' Ralea asked. She liked his thinking – it seemed to speak precisely to what she wanted, to find some kind of meaning in modification that was strictly personal rather than symbolic, but there was a vague darkness to it that set her on edge.

'Oh, absolutely. You do like the reptiles, and you shed your skin.

They do it every now and then, you know; moult, become something else while remaining entirely themselves.'

'I thought that was cocooning,' Ralea said.

The Upright Man waved a hand. 'That too. Point is, turning yourself into something greater is an ongoing process. My identity lies in my movement and the modding only plays a part in that. Everything I do now, every interaction with the outside world, becomes part of what I am, and thus part of this being that I'm in the process of creating. But I've had to leave some things behind, of course.'

'I remember reading somewhere that we shed all of ourselves every seven years,' Ralea said, feeling unnerved by that last comment of his. 'That the dust around my body is mostly dead skin, left around by someone who was me but no longer is.'

'It's all about transitions,' the Upright Man said. 'Leaving behind what is dead or useless.'

Ralea thought about this. Once more, while there was an edge to that comment it felt like exactly the kind of thing she'd been after. It wasn't until she looked closely at the Upright Man, and saw his quiet grin in the dim light of the room, that a horrified realization began to bloom in her mind.

'I see you're crossing over,' the Upright Man said, and grinned even wider. His teeth were very white.

Ralea, beginning to understand the true madness of making oneself anew, swallowed dryly and said, 'What did they leave in you?'

'They told me they would have to keep the brain, obviously, and the spinal cord. There's the blood and a small handful of sinews, but everything else is gone. For what it's worth, I had gone through a massive series of transformations first. I didn't quite turn into one of the Replacers, but I was right up there with them. And then I thought, why am I doing this? More importantly, where does it lead? I didn't want to be doomed to be constantly one-upping myself, to be nothing but a slave to my mods.'

'So you became them,' Ralea said.

The Upright Man picked up a pillow. 'I'm still getting used to everything that's inside of me. It all works, almost too well. I don't want to do this by accident.' He tore the pillow apart like wet paper. Shredded pieces of foam spilled all over the carpet. 'I want to complete the circle, which means not acting like a machine.'

The creature stood there, beaming at her. This was the Gallente ideal taken to its extreme. This was the remaking she had thought she wanted; a need so desperate for the fixed old patterns that she would gut herself simply to keep the slightest hold of them. Everything that was her; torn out, surrendered and placed on the altar of the lifestyle of destruction.

Whatever peace she needed would not come from this; not here, and not with them.

But before she left, wanting to scream so loud that the ceilings would shake and totter, Ralea had to ask one last question.

'How did they remove it all without utterly tearing your skin apart? Most of your orifices must've been too, uh, narrow, and I can't imagine they wanted to plunge down your throat to start with your stomach or your lungs. They would've had to destroy *something* to get in, and if your skin was this important I don't think you'd let them ravage that, not even for temporary lesions.'

The Upright Man smiled in the gloom. 'You're absolutely right. Even though they achieved a remarkable degree of liquefaction before extraction, it wasn't enough. There was only one place they could go through to achieve my rebirth, and even that was a little uncomfortable until they managed to clear out some space just below it. But it worked out fine. And I remained awake through the entire process. I didn't want to miss a thing.'

'Where was it?' Ralea asked. She would get on a shuttle, go to the Amarr Empire, find the retreat and stay there. Far away from the Gallente Federation. Far away from *this*.

'Where else?' the Upright Man said, and smiled. 'They went in through the eyes.'

10

Drem looked out the ship's bow. A tiny glinting mass in the distance hinted at the form of a stargate, which up close would be massive enough to dwarf their own vessel.

'I don't know if you should be here,' he said.

Yaman, sitting impassively in a chair across the room with Verena on one side and Ortag on the other, happily said, 'I don't even know what I'm doing here, and I'm fine with it.'

In the message Drem had received from Captain Kiel Rhan there had been a set of spatial coordinates to an unknown location, and an economically worded note explaining that what he'd asked for at the meeting with the man in white – how the hell he knew about that, Drem had no idea – existed but would not be made available to outsiders. It told him there was another way to acquire this information, and that someone with the power to give it to him – someone who had been keeping a close eye on his efforts – wanted to meet him at this location and have a long talk.

It also advised him to bring a space suit.

'I did say I was fine with going this alone,' he said without rancour, turning toward them and leaning against the port. 'For all I know it might be dangerous.'

'Not a chance,' Ortag told him. 'I think everyone needed some time off after that last mission. And not time off sitting in our quarters, staring at the ceiling. Proper time away.'

'It feels good to be out here, not having to rescue anyone,' Verena agreed. 'And besides, we're not letting you out of our hands.' She gave Drem a brief look that brought a flush to his cheeks.

'You guys don't even know what we're in for,' he protested feebly.

'Don't know. Don't care,' Yaman said. 'Someone wanted to meet you, gave you a marker, no goddamn way we're letting you go alone. Might be dangerous,' he said with a faint glimmer of hope.

'Well, yeah,' Drem said.

'And it gets us off the station, like Ortag said,' Yaman added. He rolled his eyes. 'Fuckin' Angels.'

'Yes, they've gotten ... a little more tiresome since my last time here,' Ortag said diplomatically.

'Biggest terror of red tape in the cluster, you mean,' Yaman said to him. 'It was never like this with the Guristas. *They* know you have a job to do and they bloody well let you get on with it. If I have to do one more mission where I spend three hours pulling Angels out of smoking wreckage and then another three being debriefed about *tech damage* back at base, I'm going to hit someone in the face.'

'What do you think?' Drem asked Verena. 'You changed your mind on wanting to leave?'

'The place certainly had its good moments,' she said with a little smile. 'But no. I don't belong here. What I missed has moved on, or I can no longer see it, and what remains is everything that bothered me the first time around. It's not my home any longer and I don't think it ever will be.'

'When we get back from this thing,' Ortag said, 'we'll want to think about rotation. We've done well and I know the Angels are happy to have us, but from you people it's clear we're losing patience with the Cartel. Lesser teams have been burned out in far shorter time. I don't want us to risk getting a distaste for the job.' He looked at Drem. 'That's assuming, of course, that this friend of yours doesn't tell you something that makes you have to stay here.'

'I'm hoping she won't,' Drem admitted.

'It's a she?' Yaman said in surprise. When Drem nodded, the big man added, 'Actually, I'm getting curious. What's this all about?'

Drem took a deep, slow breath.

'In my spare time I've been studying up on Angel Cartel history,' he said. This was not quite a lie. He had certainly come across the information before, during his datadive back at the Sisters colony, though he had been rather focused on other plans at the time. 'Have you guys ever heard of the Black Mountain case?' he asked.

Yaman's blank stare was an answer, as was Ortag's furrowed brow. Verena gave a knowing grin, though Drem wasn't sure whether it was because of the trip itself, or because of him.

Drem said, 'Long story short, Sisters lore has it that we once got involved in a hunt for something incredibly valuable. I don't know what it is, other than a code referring to something called the Book of Emptiness. At some point the Angels got involved, had the thing for a while and then lost it. They also lost some people in the process, so it's a sore point for them. Hona was one of the few survivors. Why are you grinning?'

This was directed at Verena, who said, 'I saw her name in the message.' She quickly added, 'When it was sent to me. And I forwarded it to you.'

'You know this woman?' Ortag asked her. To Drem's relief, he didn't seem to pick up on the secondary meaning of Verena's comments.

'I know of her. She's a bit of a legend among the Cartel, though we don't speak of her in public.'

Drem added, 'She was an Angel captain at the time. After the Black Mountain affair ended, most of those involved mysteriously dropped off the map, in the way that people do when someone drops a load of nanolysins into their drink. Hona, though, seems to have withdrawn from Angel life of her own free will. Supposedly the Book of Emptiness imbued her with special gifts of some sort.'

'Who believes that shit?' Yaman said.

Drem shrugged. 'She has followers. Not only that, but between them and whatever gifts Hona possesses, rumour has it she operates an extensive information network that lets her keep tabs on everything that's happening elsewhere in space, and grants her free access to all sorts of Angel resources. She is apparently seen as a wise woman.'

Ortag asked, 'So she actually exists?'

'Apparently so.'

'Why has she asked to see you?'

'I have no idea.' This was quite definitely a lie, and a blatant one. He found himself surprised to realize that even though what he was after seemed fairly innocuous – the name of another human being – the ways in which he'd attempted to acquire it were entirely unorthodox, and too grimly embarrassing for him to admit. These people had fully devoted their lives to rescue work; and to his shame, Drem, who had risked his own life with them countless times on crumbling and burning colonies, could not yet make the same claim. He hoped so dearly that hearing the man's name would help him let go.

'I'm so excited to meet her,' Verena said.

The ship hovered up to the stargate, looking like a pebble next to a mountain.

Stargates made it possible for vessels to cross immense distances in the blink of an eye, by shunting them between solar systems. If they were not quite magic, they were too complex for the general traveller, who assigned them to that great grey space that lies between science and mysticism.

The ship passed close, and the ship lit up, and the ship disappeared.

Inside, the crew closed their eyes and emptied their minds as best they could. It was entirely possible to stay aware of the outside surroundings during the jaunt, but it was certainly not recommended, lest the viewer wanted to suffer grey hair and dementia.

When they opened their eyes again, they were surrounded by red.

The system into which they'd jumped was traced all the way through by a nebula that writhed and contorted like a serpent, its cloudy body lit up by the aging sun in the distance and pierced by the eyes of a hundred glowing stars. Drem felt like he'd entered the head of a Blood Raider.

Everyone onboard took their time in enjoying the vista. Drem's coordinates would take them to somewhere deep within the system, at least another full day's flight, which meant there was little rush to get ready. It amazed Drem that he could close his eyes only to open them again in a new world; but then, he reasoned, he'd done exactly that twice over in this new life of his.

There hadn't even been a need to apply for an undocking licence: Sisters requests were fast-tracked as a rule, no matter the reason, and by now Drem's team had developed enough of a reputation that they could leave at will entirely uncontested, a luxury afforded to few in the area other than the high rollers, the top brass, and the capsuleers themselves.

They'd let the vessel's AI take care of the flight while they busied themselves with simple tasks, content at last to be out on a journey without life-or-death consequences. There was a delightful simplicity to be had in merely cleaning the bridge floor, checking the status on various AI subroutines, and sitting by large viewports in total quiet.

Along with the coordinates and a brief note on Hona, Rhan had supplied a long datakey for whatever use – Drem suspected the ship would have to pass through a secure hangar gate at some point – and a simple concluding exhortation, 'Don't be stupid again.'

Drem kept that thought in his mind throughout the day, busying himself with pleasantly idle tasks. The ship was open at all levels, and he spent most of the evening wandering the corridors of its bottom hull, watching the engine sections in operation and listening to the divine hum of the massive piece of machinery engaged in quiet action.

During the night he was visited by Verena, who said very little but let her actions speak for her, and the next morning he awoke to an empty bed and the sight of an amazing construct crackling in the distance.

Acceleration gates were ancient pieces of technology created by various space-faring societies of old as a way to quickly hurtle their vessels across vast distances. They were effectively warp initiators, devised in an age long before the idea of warp had even been realized. An acceleration gate wouldn't shift a ship between solar systems like a proper stargate would, but it could bring it to even stranger places.

Due to any number of natural phenomena, certain areas in New

Eden remained inaccessible to starships in warp. Assuming the phenomena weren't detrimental to vessel integrity, these areas – called 'deadspaces' – could still be explored, but at an immense cost of time and effort. Often they held nothing of value, and thus the explorers of days past and present tended to bypass them in favour of more interesting sectors of space. This made them excellent retreats for those who demanded secrecy, for whatever reason.

Acceleration gates were the key to entering these sealed places. They didn't require the ships to activate their own warp engines, merely that crew and pilot be willing to have themselves sling-shot into the unknown. The gates themselves were either refurbished versions of original constructions, or new ones built from scratch by forces with sufficient wealth. Each gate was built to be secure and thus could only be activated by those who had the rights to pass, in the form of access codes. Or a datakey.

When the team saw where Rhan's coordinates had brought them, at first they did not react. As the ship floated inertly beside the massive gate, blue arcs flickering on its hull and earthing themselves back on the gate's curved launch pathways, all four of the ship's inhabitants calmly proceeded to eat a full breakfast, run basic checks on their vitals and ensure that all the ship's processes were fully functional, before they convened in the pod room, each taking a seat on a small, synthetic-covered metal bench beside their respective emergency pods.

'What the hell are we in for?' Verena said. Her voice sounded too loud in the silence of everyone else's thoughts.

'I really don't know,' Drem said.

Yaman went over to Drem and put a hand on his shoulder. 'Don't look so goddamn glum. If I got to do this kind of shit on every vacation, I'd be a happy man.'

Drem nodded, and the team got ready for launch. While everyone else fitted into their hazard suits, Ortag ran final checks on the ship's facilities, ensuring the emergency pods were launchable and topped with oxygen and nutrients in case the mission went to the worst. Drem's mouth was dry as he put on the helmet, and his stomach kept knotting up as if it had just come out of warp.

When the group was ready, Drem fed Rhan's datakey into the ship's console and had it broadcast in a loop. Ortag had already called up a view of the acceleration gate, which lay inert apart from the electric currents that constantly arced between its nodes.

The ship's equilibrium systems could, with a bit of effort, hold its crew in place through the gate's massive acceleration process. The alternative was for everyone to seal themselves in their pods as if for a proper warp, but doing so would lessen their reaction speed to whatever they found on the other side. If they were to encounter opposition, those few seconds it took to activate evasive manoeuvres could spell the difference between survival and doom.

Everyone kept their gaze on the gate, staring at it through the visors in their helmets. Its electricity crackled and whipped the ship in ever-brighter arcs until the entire hull was enveloped in a ghostly blue halo.

The ship lurched toward the gate, pulled in by its electrical web until it was perfectly aligned on its path to the strange void. The ship's machines powered up to stabilize against the gargantuan forces about to impact it. All the members on the team instinctively rubbed their necks through their hazard suits, feeling for all the world like they were about to go into a proper warp. The vessel hovered over the acceleration gate's electrified ramp, all aglow with the surrounding power, and there was a single breath of utter stillness before the gate disappeared from view as the ship roared towards the unknown.

It took only a few seconds, but felt like hours. The ship decelerated from its mad speed and eventually came to a complete stop in front of some artefact. When Drem's brain, high on the oxygen he hadn't even realized he'd taken in from hyperventilating, finally managed to understand what he was looking at, he didn't know whether to laugh or cry.

In front of them was an asteroid the size of a moon. It was a greenish grey, empty of human structures and, all in all, the dullest thing one could imagine seeing among the mysteries of space. There was nothing else there; no colony, no immediate life signs, nothing at all.

*

Yaman, who had been trembling with excitement, tore off his helmet and let off a string of curses, then spat on the floor in anger. He stopped himself, looked at the others, blushed and murmured a 'sorry' before rubbing on it with his foot.

Verena kept her own helmet on. 'Since we're here, might as well explore the thing.' To Drem's surprise, she opened a secure channel between the two of them and whispered, 'I'm so sorry.'

It wasn't a public display of affection by any means, but it warmed his heart a little and stopped whatever ugly cycles of thought he'd been caught in. On an open channel, he said, 'At worst we can take a few samples, maybe laser out a rock that I can use to crack Rhan's skull.'

Yaman grinned at him. 'I'm up for that.' He put his helmet back on, sealed it, and walked over to the launch area.

A chute opened on the side of the ship, and the team slowly hovered into space. Carbon nanofibre threads connected them like flies in a glittering web. They manoeuvred the ship as close to the asteroid as they could, using the thruster units woven into the threads to control their progress.

Ortag took care of the flight and landing. The asteroid had enough pull that the team could retract the nanofibre threads and pack the thrusters away. Low-gravity missions were uncommon, but a regular asteroid rescue project could turn at a moment's notice into an oxygen-vacated nightmare, and the Sisters trained their people with vicious precision for those kinds of situations.

Drones were lifesavers on these kinds of rescue missions. They worked just as well in low- to zero-grav, and often used even less power than in oxygenated conditions. From the body of the drop drone that followed them, Drem fished out a bundle of seekers and set them loose. Through his overhead he tuned them not to hunt for people, but to seek out cracks in the surface. It was a vital talent for situations where an agent might be seeking a way out of a wreckage rather than in, and on this asteroid, large enough that even traversing its circumference might take more than a day's walk, it was the only way they would find anything of interest.

Most of the seekers reported nothing, but one disappeared from the radar altogether, raising Drem's worries that there might be dangerous or unstable areas on the asteroid. The seeker drone returned to the overhead view shortly after, reporting a hotspot in a small gully not far from the Sisters. The machine had found a way in.

When they arrived at the gully, they found the drone hovering outside a small cave mouth set a few steps up into one of the walls. It was impossible to see unless one was looking straight at it; and even from a distance, it looked like the drone was simply passing in and out of a solid wall. Drem noted with interest that if he loosened the drone's search parameters sufficiently to let it hover further into the opening, its signal weakened substantially. Whatever this rock was made of, it was capable of blocking signals designed to pass through some very dense materials. He wondered why the gravity wasn't much greater on the asteroid than it was.

With the help of Yaman he rigged a pulley system with a fibre basket, and one by one the team entered the cave.

'We're fuckin' lost,' Yaman said.

'I don't understand this,' Drem said, staring at the wall in front of him. Huge crystal shards stared back at him, dead and unseeing.

They had been wandering for hours. At first their progress had been linear, down slanting corridors that held few turns and no surprises. They were large enough for humans to comfortably pass, but there was no indication that the asteroid might be inhabited.

There were crystals inset in some of the walls, tiny signpost needles pointing the way in the absolute darkness. Yaman absent-mindedly stroked his hands over them as they passed, leaving silvery cascades in his wake.

As the team advanced further into the asteroid's core, their passage became increasingly complicated. They were untroubled at first by the altitude drops, most of which required only an easy climb and a moment's care; and any narrowing of tunnels held no challenge for them. But the drops became sharper, including a few that occurred at blind turns, and it took a brave agent to get on his knees and crawl into increasingly cramped passages in the airless darkness without feeling at least a twinge of claustrophobia. Verena had few problems making it through, but Drem had bulked up considerably in his work with the Sisters faction; and Yaman, who easily outweighed both of them and found the wriggling immensely uncomfortable, kept up a ceaseless muttering commentary on the similarities between narrow tunnels and tight arseholes.

It was the sudden unreliability of their overheads that gave the team pause.

A tunnel mouth that should have led to a much wider opening turned out to end in a small cul-de-sac. A drop that should have been only a small jump gave Drem a jaw-snapping shock when it turned out to be three times what he expected. In both cases the overheads' estimates, invaluable in the darkness, had veered off by considerable amounts.

It got no better when the tunnels began turning in on themselves. The team had been progressing down a corkscrew ramp, which Drem was convinced was leading them deeper into the asteroid, but at some point the ramp levelled out, and they eventually found themselves going through an opening that turned out to be a side tunnel they'd bypassed half an hour before. They went on to discount it, right until they had the same thing happen again, and twice more in quick succession, on each occasion exiting a tunnel only to find they'd been inadvertently backtracking the entire time.

The idea of getting lost in an airless maze wasn't appealing to anyone, and the team found their collective nerves starting to fray. Conversations became curt, then increasingly hostile, with blame on badly chosen routes being cast back and forth until Ortag chimed in and threatened to cut off comms, if not oxygen, for the next goddamn person who lashed out.

By then their overheads, which were supposed to mark the tunnel passages and build a progressive route, were displaying nothing but an incomprehensible jumble that looked more like a knot of intestines than a useable map.

They kept on walking. As the hours passed the first few pangs of hunger began making appearances, then thirst and finally the dreaded faint dizziness that they knew would eventually lead to asphyxiation. Their hazard suits contained emergency IV nourishment that could keep them going for a while, but the only air they had was the rapidly diminishing remains in their tanks. If they collapsed here, Drem thought with a churning panic, no one in the outside world would realize until far too late; and even if emergency signals from their suits managed to pierce this dark, underground world and make it to their ship for further broadcast, rescue vessels would never find them in time.

The floors appeared to be slanted, and so did the walls, though Drem didn't know whether the effect came from the landscape or merely his own head. They marched on and on and on.

And at some point, Yaman doomed the whole thing to mysticism when he stopped, slowly pointed to a wall and said in a drawl, 'Hey, are these drawings?'

The one constant in the team's passage had been the crystals, whose nebulaic forms snaked over the walls of every tunnel. They had quickly faded from everyone's consciousness, but Drem now saw that they had grown in size and area, covering well over half the surface of each wall in the current tunnel.

He looked over to where Yaman was pointing. The crystalline whorls on the walls did, in fact, look a little like identifiable shapes, though he wasn't sure what they were supposed to represent. Some reminded him of humans, others of faction logos – there was a particularly impressive series of narrowing curves that brought the Angel Cartel insignia to mind. Some were shapes that Drem would swear on his life he'd only seen in that infinite space between sleeping and waking, though whether they were really there or simply the product of his increasingly oxygen-deprived consciousness, he didn't know. The forms held a fascination that was comforting and terrifying all at once, like the rocking embrace of a monster. Here and there a piece of some metallic rock embedded in the wall would shine through in their helmets' night vision, and for a dizzying moment Drem felt he was looking out at deep space again.

To his side, Yaman stepped forward and stroked the walls. 'Weird,' he said. 'Dead sharp, too, at least on one side.'

Drem saw the glittering dust trickle to the floor from under the man's touch, and something about the destruction of those crystals compelled him to motion. 'Let's keep going,' he said. 'There's bound to be a way out of here, if not a way deeper in.'

Ortag, who seemed equally fascinated by the crystals, nodded to him and followed his lead.

They passed on through the dream-like architecture, which routed them in on their own paths so often now that Drem half expected to meet himself coming the other way. There was no panic in anyone's mind any longer, merely a quiet acceptance. Much as in any rescue mission, they had been caught by something beyond their understanding and needed a hyperfocus on survival. Anything else could wait.

They tried sending out seeker drones, which, to nobody's surprise, disappeared and were never found again. The explosives in their gear remained untouched as an option of last resort. Without reliable data they might still bring the team out, or simply cave the asteroid in on them.

They tried a spoke bomb, too. Yaman, with Drem's help, attached one to a ceiling they agreed showed the best chance of leading them to an exit tunnel. When it went off, the rocks collapsed with such force that the team had to run away fast, gulping up air they couldn't spare. They ended up with an impassable tunnel, and nothing more.

'This thing is bigger on the inside than out,' Ortag said, half to himself, as they wandered down yet another crystal corridor.

'Think so?' Drem asked him. The same thoughts had been circulating in his own mind.

'What I think is happening is something in these walls is mucking up our equipment. And I wouldn't be surprised if the crystals add to the effect, somehow.' Ortag kept on as if he were still talking to himself. 'They know we can't find our way around anymore, so they want us to get a little spooked now, a little superstitious. That's fine. Superstition's just another word for respect. I'll respect them and we'll get along all right.'

Drem allowed himself to drift over to the wall and stroke a hand over the crystals. They felt smooth under his gloved fingers – which were growing increasingly sweaty on the inside of his suit – and slanted, like algae being pushed to the side by a rushing river. He imagined them pointing the way, on this strange and deadly odyssey.

He stopped. The others noticed, and halted their progress as well.

Verena came in on a private channel. 'You OK?'

'What's up?' Yaman said over public comms.

Ortag regarded him, then said, again almost to himself, 'Our boy's found something.'

Slowly, daring himself not to think it, Drem stroked his hand backwards over the crystals. His glove could withstand their edges, but even through its protective material he could feel the sharpness.

'We're relying too much on equipment and technology,' he said. 'And it's not getting us anywhere. Plan's not working.'

'So you have a better plan?' Yaman asked hopefully.

'I don't have a plan at all. I've got instinct.'

He stroked a hand over the crystals again. Smooth one way, jagged the other. 'Listen to me. I think we're being shown the way. There's no wind here, no air or water, and definitely little in the way of organic materials. But there are crystals, and they all seem to be leaning in one direction. A blind man could find his way here.'

'You think they're signposts,' Ortag said. It was less a question than a confirmation.

Drem nodded. 'I think we should turn off the overhead completely. No map, no seekers, night vision at most but we won't rely on that. Let's see where the crystals take us.'

It was testament to their exhaustion that they did not even discuss it. One by one their overheads went off, and then they formed a line after Drem, walking beside the walls with hands outstretched; as though a procession of the blind, seeking sacrament.

When they came to forks in the road, the crystals would unfailingly be sharp down one way and smooth the other. It went on for a long while, the crystals getting larger and more widespread over the walls, until the crew had gone so deep that even the ceilings were covered by crystalline structures. Nobody complained, but Drem noticed how their progress became a little laboured with time; their steps a little more carefully chosen. He tried not to think that he had led his best friends, and a woman he was beginning to love, into a death trap. His own life did not matter, but theirs did, and he pleaded in silent thoughts that this procession of theirs would lead them home.

The crystals led the way and a stupid, warm hope had started to glow in Drem's heart when the team went past a bend and found itself standing in front of a rock-solid wall, high and whole and glittering.

They stood there, unbelieving, for a good long time. Eventually Ortag, Yaman and Verena leaned up against the wall and slowly slid down until they were all in a semi-crouch.

'Well, that's it,' Verena said. Her voice was carefully modulated, each word intoned with the proper amount of breath.

'I'm going to fucking cry,' Yaman said with a tiny sigh. He ran a finger through the dirt on the floor, tracing an inward spiral. 'Any other ideas before we die here?'

Drem walked up to the wall and ran his hands over the crystals. Yaman had already taken a few shuffling steps away when Drem said to him, 'Wait. We're tired and stupid, and on our last breath. Let's stop, let's think about what we're seeing.'

'You want to use the overhead?' Ortag asked him.

'Worth a shot,' Drem said and turned it on. After the recent darkness it was intensely uncomfortable, like looking into the blaze of a starship's engine. Reports fluttered up and told him there was nothing on the other side of the wall.

'Everyone else getting a dead reading?' he asked. The other three said they were.

'Guess that's it,' Ortag said. 'Let's walk while we still can. I don't want the darkness to take me just yet.'

Drem regarded the wall. There was something off about it. It was too whole, especially the way it was covered in crystals. It was an obvious endpoint; a cul-de-sac that looked not of natural design but of natural *intent*. If he had asked a child to draw a crystal maze that ended in a secret entrance, this was what he would have been given. It was so real it had to be fake.

'Ortag, hand me a spoke bomb, please,' he said, holding out a hand and not taking his eyes off the wall.

'I can't walk through rubble and dust, son,' Ortag said. 'Or ceilings that'll flatten my head.'

'There is a way here,' Drem said to him with false bravado. He could feel the others' trust in him ebbing, but the assurance in his voice seemed to have the desired effect. A spoke bomb was placed in his open palm. The others moved well away from the wall, and sat down again as exhaustion took its toll.

He said, 'I don't know if this'll work or not, but either way, guys, from the bottom of my heart, I'm sorry for leading you down this path.'

Ortag breathed in audibly, deep and slow, and said, 'The last person we had on our team walked into the cruiser exhaust. One before that stood and waited for falling girders to spear him to the ground.' He put a hand on Drem's shoulder. 'If your biggest muckup is traipsing around an empty asteroid where the only danger is a little shortage of air, well . . . I can think of worse ways to go. Toss the bomb.'

Drem nodded. He held the bomb in his hands. On a private channel, he whispered, 'I'm sorry,' to Verena. He heard her exhale. She said, 'No, I'm sorry.'

He thought for a moment to tell her that no, it was really his fault, that he had lied to her, but before he could say a word he threw the bomb at the crystal wall.

Materials in spoke bombs reacted to oxygen, but each bomb contained a small capsule of pressurized air that let them go off in vacuums. Drem prayed that this one would not cave in the ceiling on them.

The spoke bomb clacked soundlessly onto the pellucid surface before exploding, shattering the crystals, blowing the wall apart and revealing a waiting group of spacesuit-clad people on the other side, all of them holding guns aimed directly at the Sisters.

'Oh good,' Verena said in quiet gasps. 'I was hoping. This could get. Just a little more weird.'

The men carried them in silence down a gently curving hall that sloped sharply downwards. As they spiralled down, Drem, who was fading in and out of consciousness, fuzzily realized that all this time they had merely been walking in the outer layers of the asteroid.

He did not have the energy to fight or argue with these people. His last sight of Verena had been of her lying on the ground, dying with him. He wanted to call out her name but before he could say a word he faded out again.

Slowly, the four of them regained full consciousness. When Drem resurfaced, his first thought was how cold he was, and for a moment he thought he had died. His gloved hand went up to his face and touched bare skin, slick with sweat rapidly cooled by a breeze.

They had removed his helmet. And he was breathing.

He quickly sat up, nearly fainted, then lay down again as the darkness encroached on his vision. He turned so that he lay sideways, put his head on the ground and looked around for his friends.

A light flickered. Not much, but enough to see the three others near him, lying still on the ground. Their helmets were gone; he saw their faces, slack and still. He peered close, and when he saw Verena's lips move slightly, his heart felt as if it would burst out of his chest.

'Probably had a hidden door closed off and oxygenated the place some while back,' Yaman said as he brushed dust out of his hair, though he sounded no more convinced than Drem was. Torches dotted the walls, casting their deep orange light.

Their saviours – and captors – stood by patiently until the team was ready, then led them on a walk down the spiralling corridors. They appeared perfectly normal, all older than him and of varied origins. Some wore Angel hazard suits, while others were clad in gear Drem had never seen. They didn't say anything and no one on the team could yet think of a sensible question to ask them.

'I feel like I should be asking them where I'm going,' Ortag murmured as they followed the unknown men, 'but after getting lost in this place, following directions seems the best idea. I can handle that idea. I like that idea.' The others nodded in agreement.

They walked down to the core of the great rock, passed through a great opening, and came into a hall that dwarfed them like sand under a night-time sky.

'Oh my gods,' Verena said.

'I think maybe we died after all,' Yaman said in a tone of hushed reverence.

It was a massive natural cave, as large as a city. Stalactites the size of cathedrals hung from the distant ceiling. Hundreds of hollowed-out cave openings in the very sides of the walls shone with flickering torchlight, and by their illumination Drem could see that the walls themselves were covered with immense paintings of religious icons and faction sigils and all manner of scenes that looked old and deep. He realized the paintwork must have taken multiple teams of people, suspended from deadly heights, and he was awed at the Sisters-like dedication they must have brought to their task.

'Where are we going?' he heard Yaman ask one of them.

'To see the Lady,' the acolyte answered and left it at that.

Verena walked up to Drem and murmured, 'Did you hear that?'

'Hona,' he said. 'Has to be.'

Verena said, 'I'm amazed. I'd heard stories about a strange society that had foregone high tech, or somehow incorporated it into an Amarrian-like religious design, but I never believed it. Temples on a colony, paper in place of datapads, maybe. Nothing like this.'

'I wonder how they run the place. Look, these things are all over,' Drem said, pointing to the distance. The floor of the great cave was dotted with stalagmites of varying sizes. Some of them were little more than statues, and had clearly been carved out with more religious sigils. Others were taller, rising up to several storeys high and clearly occupied – though with what, Drem couldn't make out. The larger ones also had little nooks that had been hollowed out and filled with something that burned bright and sweet. The air was warm but not heavy, and there was even a light breeze.

'I can't believe we're actually going to see Hona. I've heard so much about her,' Verena said, staring in amazement at a painting that covered a wall to the east. 'How *big* is that one? I have no frame of reference anymore. It feels like it's the size of a starship.'

'I thought I'd lost you,' Drem said, quietly. 'I thought we were all going to die.'

She took his hand and squeezed it. 'We're here. We were meant to be here, and we're here. Everything's working out.'

He sighed, and shrugged, but he squeezed her hand back.

'Just so you know,' Yaman said, coming up from behind and clapping a hand on his shoulder, 'I never doubted you, man.'

'Liar,' Drem said, and the two men grinned at each other.

'How many people they got here, anyway?' he said.

Drem peered down the walkway. Their guides had led them to the mouth of what appeared to be one of the main throughways in this section of the cave. It was hard to make out every little detail – the light was fickle, and beyond it the darkness seemed to extend forever – but Drem could still see hundreds, if not thousands, of people passing every which way, most of them dressed in thin, dark robes. The larger of the stalagmites seemed to function as buildings, and Drem saw the crowd pass in and out of them like ants.

His steps reverberated as the group marched down the arcade. All around them there was the murmured susurrus of people busy with their quiet business, gathering briefly in small groups before passing on their way to somewhere else. There was too little light for Drem to see what they were up to, but he was amazed to find that there seemed to be practically no advanced technology about. Whatever these people were engaged in, if it was information gathering it was like nothing Drem had ever seen.

'You think it's a cult?' Yaman asked them.

'Not sure,' Ortag said from a little further back. He had been taking in his surroundings just as intently as the rest of them. 'It seems like a society, in much the same way as Drem's own Sani Sabik run their faction. These are people going about their daily lives.'

But everyone prayed to someone, Drem thought, and they were going to see the Lady.

The acolytes brought them through the arcade and marched onward. After a further extended walk, past stone and fire and the darkness all around, they eventually made it to the other end of the cavern. Nobody paid them much mind.

'There's far less people here,' Verena whispered to him. It was true: the crowds had thinned out noticeably. 'Should we be worried?'

Drem shook his head. 'They're not bringing us to some run-down section of the cave. This place looks like it gets even better care, if anything.' The streets were clean, and the torches that lined the little stalagmites were all fresh and burning bright. The lack of soot on the rocks behind them spoke to a detailed attention by the unseen caretakers.

They eventually came to a hollowed-out stalagmite that reached to the skies. Drem was amazed it existed at all, and wondered how long this asteroid had taken to form the structures before it was finally settled by these people. The stalagmite could well predate his own civilization.

They entered, beckoned on by the acolytes. The inside was a great circular space, covered with stone benches hewn out of the asteroid's own rock, and interspersed with support pillars that also seemed to merge seamlessly with the housing itself.

Drem had expected the temperature to fall inside, but the crackling sounds that greeted his amazed ears eventually resolved into massive fires, hanging from stone and metal baskets suspended from the ceilings. Oxygen was one thing, easily enough generated with the proper equipment, but where these people were getting combustible materials Drem had no idea. Certain metals would burn under the proper conditions, but they were rare and hard to procure. He hoped that whatever kind of information network this Hona had would be equivalent to her supply network. He also wondered if she would ask him to reveal his request in front of his team. The fact that Kiel Rhan had seen fit to pass on her offer gave credence to his hope that she would know to be cautious.

The floor slanted enough that each stone circle could see past the next one, while in the far distance the room ended in a flat, circular pit. The acolytes led the four Sisters onward annd directed them to sit on a bench within shouting distance of the pit, then left the stone cathedral, retreating until there was nothing but the burning sound of the fires above.

Verena sighed and ran her palms over her face.

'Tired?' Drem asked.

'Exhausted. I want to meet this woman more than I can say, but I'm reaching my maximum tolerance for this eldritch weirdness.

The heat and the fires are putting me to sleep. I half expect this to turn into a nightmare and the walls to start talking to me.'

From the air a voice said, 'I know why you're here.'

Verena's mouth issued a stifled, tremulous, '... gahaargh'. She buried her head in her hands.

The others looked around. The shadowy fires flickered over the landscape, and eventually resolved into the sight of a woman sitting on the other side of the pit.

She was dressed the same as everyone else they'd passed, in a robe of darkened colours. Her hands had the worn, leathery skin of someone who carries rather than is carried, and her face, of an age not that far from Drem's, was bare and heavily lined.

What stopped Drem short were her eyes, as they fairly glowed in the dusky light. He had looked into the eyes of people who had suffered so terribly, whose minds had witnessed such utter destruction, that they'd gone right through the wall of sanity and out the other side. He'd been close to it himself, but there had remained enough fight in him to claw his way back.

These eyes held no resistance. In them Drem saw a full and serene acceptance, and the mad power that it brought.

'Throw that harlot out,' she said.

The team was silent. Verena raised her head from her hands and stared unbelievingly at the woman. 'Excuse me?'

Hona said, 'The three of you can stay, but the woman does not belong within these walls.' To Verena she added, 'I knew someone in your position once, and she made very different choices. You'll want to think about that in times to come.'

Drem, trembling with indignation and nerves, said, 'If she leaves—'

'Then the rest of you stay. Save your grand exits for those they'll work on,' Hona said, quite calmly.

Drem was ashamed at the relief he felt at hearing that. He hated the woman for what she'd said to Verena, but he truly did not know whether he could have brought himself to walk out in protest.

Verena got up. 'It's OK. I'll go.'

Yaman protested, 'Hey, listen, you didn't come all this way—'

'It's fine!' she cut in. 'I'm tired and worn out. I want out of Angel space. Some old hag out of some old myth isn't going to change things, one way or another.' She put a hand on Drem's shoulder, muttered a '*fuck her*' that he was pretty sure only he had heard, and walked out.

The rest of them sat there in silence, their surprise slowly giving way to a worn anger.

'I know what you want,' Hona said to Drem. 'And tell that angry young man beside you that if he does what he's thinking of doing, he'll be leaving this place through separate exits.'

'I wasn't going to do shit,' Yaman said, but subtly removed one hand from a pocket.

Hona looked at them. 'One of you is a traitor, two of you are murderers, and all of you are liars. A sorry gathering, the lot of you.'

Yaman said, 'You called us here, you fuckin' witch.'

Hona looked at him, then back to Drem, who prayed she wouldn't give him up. The team still thought they were here on her orders, and not his own stupid search for a piece of information he wasn't supposed to have.

After a moment she said to Drem, 'You and I, we need to have a talk by ourselves.'

'I'm not sure I want to leave my friends here,' Drem said, hoping he was playing it right.

'We'll be fine,' Ortag told him. 'You go on and hear her out. Then you come back here, and we leave this mad, twisted rock.'

Drem nodded, gave a silent thanks, stood up and walked down the aisle and into the pit, then up out of it and towards Hona. Close up she looked even more worn, as if an aged soul had been transplanted into a young body not quite capable of handling its wisdom. Those unblinking eyes, though, kept him on his feet.

'Walk with me,' she said, and set off into the dark. He followed.

Once they were out of earshot Drem, keeping his voice level, said, 'I want—'

'I know what you want, young man. I am not sure that you should have it.'

Drem was not sure what to say to that. 'You ... know what happened to me, I presume.'

She looked out into the dark. 'That was terrible business. Little wonder it drove you down those strange roads. But you're an intelligent young man, if not, perhaps, as insightful as you think.'

Drem felt the pressure inside him build and build, and he couldn't help but vent. 'Why did you call me all this way if you weren't intending to give me the one small thing I wanted? Do you even have it? Who *are* you?'

She turned on him with a sad smile, entirely unruffled by his outburst. 'My dear boy. My precious, dear boy. You've done such wonderful things since you found your way again. All those people you saved, all those lives you brought back from the brink. And now you want to destroy it.'

'I'm not destroying anyone. Or anything. All I want is a name to pin on to the worst memory of my life.'

'That is only the start of what you want, even if you don't yet know it,' she said with a sigh, then added, 'I knew someone like you once. A good man. Righteous of purpose. He thought he was making the right decision, every time. All those little choices.' To his stunned surprise, she took his head in her hands, leaned close and kissed him on the forehead. 'Don't end up like him.'

'So that's it,' he said. 'You have nothing for me.'

She stood there, silent. The torchlight flickered over her face like thoughts through a mind.

'Come with me,' she said at last and walked deeper into the darkness of the stalagmite cathedral. Drem followed.

They flickering torchlight faded, and after a while he could no longer see where the walls were. It seemed to him that they were walking through a tunnel; the air felt too stirred by his motion, too constricted for the vastness of the hall he had left behind.

'Some say the Angels acquired their power from Jovian technology, left here for us like poisonous little candies,' he heard Hona say.

They kept marching down the tunnel of darkness.

'They were right,' she said.

The light increased a little. They were in another hall now, empty, with raw rocks on every side. Drem had no idea where the illumination came from; it was so faint that the gloom turned everything unreal.

Hona stood in front of him. She turned so her gaze met his own, and her eyes glowed in the darkness.

The eerie atmosphere was too much for Drem. He broke the silence. 'If you found Jove tech, you must've become rich.'

Her look did not change, not in the slightest, and nonetheless became even more terrifying. 'Oh yes,' she said in a dead voice. 'I am all the richer for it.'

She raised a hand to the walls in the distance. 'There is technology so vast that it cannot be separated from the world around us. It becomes who we are, and what we breathe.'

'And lets you see farther than most,' Drem said quietly.

'I can see for a thousand years,' the woman said in a voice that barely sounded human.

Trying to shake off the chill that had run down his back, Drem said, 'So where is it? In this low-tech rock in the dead of space, with burning fires and your acolytes in robes . . . are the Jovians here? You clearly have power. Where have you hidden what they gave you?'

'In plain sight, dear child,' she said. Her hand, pointing at the walls, had not yet lowered.

And Drem understood.

No wonder the rock was so dense on the asteroid. It wasn't just rock.

He managed, 'The entire colony . . .' before his voice trailed off.

'Is more alive than you can imagine. It listens, remembers and contains. It gives life. It breathes, and its exhalations are pure air.'

'How was this place made?'

She gave a very human shrug. 'Why made? Who says it wasn't grown?'

Before Drem could think of anything to say, the woman added, 'Leave now. Make your choices. Try to make the right ones. There will be more than you think.'

Drem turned and slowly walked away.

In the air, her quiet voice said to him, 'Some day, if you ever find the right road, talk to me again. And I will give you what you ask, so that you can do what really needs to be done.'

Once they'd finally made it to their cruiser and were headed for home base, Drem received a small datapackage, encrypted and coded to his bioID, from an anonymous and untraceable sender. The package contained some classified station schematics, brief information on various key personnel in that station, and an abbreviated list of high-level inhabitants.

It told him two things.

First, that this woman, however crazy she might be, truly did have access to a vast repository of information, some of which might be his if he needed it.

And second, on this list, on this dead little list of letters and digits and diagrams, a single name had been highlighted. The name of a capsuleer, living his untouchable life of safety and money and power. The name of the man who had destroyed Drem's colony.

11

When the two women left the shuttle the air outside was warm and the scorching ground undulated before their eyes. The heat's haze made everything seem so much closer. Ralea reached her hand out to shield her face from the sun and instinctively cupped her fingers over some buildings she saw on the far horizon. They felt like they were right there with her, perfectly present so long as she didn't try to touch them.

Everything was so natural, as if they'd landed in the times of Reclamation. Beyond the tarmac of the landing area there were fields in which groups of workers gathered the harvest, their sweaty bodies glistening among the wheat and barley. There were hills, possibly mountains, waiting for sandal-clad feet to traverse them. Everything was golden; everything was bright.

The journey here had not taken them long. Enough time to pack, enough to set up the retreat and to make sure they weren't being followed by the law. For Ralea it was a nice change from the recent horrors of Gallente madness. If she was to be remade, it had to be from the inside out; but more than that, it needed to be spiritual: a true internal change whose origins lay not in the machinery of flesh but the function of the soul.

They were at a religious retreat in Amarr space with a group of other offworld attendees. All of them had, for whatever reason, grown weary of the values and rhythms of their old lives, and had signed on for a long stay. The planet was close enough to the empire's centre to be safe from attack but far enough away that the endless struggles and bickering between the royal heirs wouldn't have saturated local culture. They would engage in faithful study here, and work for their upkeep in the golden fields.

Before the group had walked long they were met on the path by the head minister, an older man with a wrinkled, amiable countenance. He was dressed in a robe of light fabric, maroon and golden in colour, and sandals that looked like they'd walked with him since birth.

'Welcome, everyone,' he said. 'My name is Sandan. Please pick up your bags and follow me.'

Ralea and Heci obeyed, as did most of the people around them, although they heard a man nearby mutter, 'Don't know what kind of place this is, goddamn slaves all around us and we still have to drag around our own damn luggage. I might have a heart attack.' The man was dragging along two suitcases with assistant motors that wheezed and trembled under the weight they bore. His hair, bright red, glinted like fire in the burning sun.

'Shame. He was good-looking, too,' Heci whispered to Ralea, who snorted in laughter. Behind her, Ralea heard someone say, 'Man just travelled countless AUs for this very thing, only to bitch about walking through dirt.' Another voice responded, 'We had someone like that, back when I first started playing Mind Clash. Came to the first day of training, moaned about the heat and equipment and finally left halfway through, telling us we'd all be sorry for how mean we'd been to him.'

'Were you?'

'Oh yeah. If he'd only stayed till the end of the day, I could have pissed in his gym bag.'

Ralea smiled at the two men – a Minmatar likely a decade older than her, and a Caldari whose fine-cut face and intent eyes belied his age – in unspoken fellowship. They smiled back.

'Asthonen Kasmon,' the Caldari introduced himself. 'Or just Ash. Play Mind Clash, need time off from the grind, and don't mind carrying my own damn bags.'

'Serious? That's awesome, what team?' Heci said.

Ralea was surprised. 'I didn't know you were a sports fan,' she said to her friend.

'I'm really not. But Mind Clash is different,' Heci told her. 'It's the best thing to come out of the State – sorry, no offence meant, Ash.'

'Hey, none taken,' he said, looking amused.

'Two guys get up on a podium, put on helmets, and they think up all these freaky virtual things that fight each other,' Heci said. 'It's amazing what comes out out of their minds. Anything's allowed.'

Ralea, who had heard of the sport but knew next to nothing of it, felt at a loss in the conversation. Thankfully Heci didn't pursue it, and instead said to Ash, 'We'll have to talk more about this later, when we've gotten settled in.' She smiled at the Minmatar walking next to him.

'Neko Asgulf,' the man said, stepping forward. 'Do this and that, some of it nicer than the other. Needed to lay low for a while.' He said it in such an innocent way that Ralea decided it was primarily a harmless joke, whatever else it might have meant. The two men shook hands with Ralea and Heci without missing a step on the path.

Sandan seemed to sense the collective mood. 'The walk to the ministry is not a long one, children. But everyone is expected to make it.'

As if to forestall arguments from the red-headed man, the minister went on, 'This brief ambulation is considered your first test of faith and devotion, of willingness to walk and work the earth. And really,' he added wryly, 'if your health won't let you walk a few miles under sunny skies, you're too close to God already to be of much use on this plane.'

They marched on, walking down a wide dirt road that led through the high grass. Ralea and Heci quickly found themselves in the lead, excited to move on while eager to take in everything they saw. It was a marvel, after all this time onboard a station with all the synthetic sights that kind of life entailed, to see the stalks of barley that swayed gently into the road. Ralea let herself drift to the edges and stroked her hand over their bowed heads. The slaves working the fields did not seem to notice the group's passage; or if they did, they did not care.

Eventually they crested a hill and saw in the distance a glinting house that quickly grew to a mansion, several storeys high and wide enough to house a battlecruiser. It was clearly of Amarrian design, with its ornate curves and majestic terraces, but it was far from the impressive creations that could be seen in the core of the empire. The typical golden sheen of Amarrian design was entirely absent, for which Ralea was thankful, as it would have been blinding in this sunny weather. Its surface was a stucco finish into which were subtly carved the converging curves of the Amarrian sigil.

As the group drew up, the doors, high and old, slowly creaked and clanked open. The minister stopped at the entrance, and so did the group. Now that she was closer Ralea could see him better. His forehead was adorned with a minor deco: two slanted, parallel lines that rose up either side, along with a small dot hovering right in the middle; as if a four-handed man were raising his arms to the sky. It gave him a look of eternal, benevolent surprise, while the wrinkles around his eyes and the smile that hovered around his mouth implied that he was not at all averse to such an appearance.

'Welcome to the house of Scriptures,' he said to them. 'I'm glad to have you here.'

He indicated a slave who stood to his right, also clad in a maroon robe but otherwise unadorned. 'Jorek and I will show you around while we wait to receive your luggage. You have each been assigned a chamber, which you will find to be spacious but sparse. We encourage you not to decorate it too heavily. The ties to this life are many and persistent, and the more of them you cast off when commencing your stay here, the happier you will be. It's a simple life you'll lead here, in the way that the sun and the seasons and the harvest are simple, but you will find more than enough to occupy your every waking hour, and what you reap will likely prove what you want to have around you in your private time.'

He walked into the cool space of the ministry, followed by the group and tailed by Jorek the slave.

The inside felt dark the way a space always does when one has been out in bright sunlight, but Ralea marvelled at how welcoming and pleasant it was nonetheless. Strategically spaced windows let in little spears of sunlight that lit up the myriad banners, icons and religious objects all present in the ministry's main hall. The sight reminded Ralea of a museum, but the items were not on display; there were no glass cabinets nor cordoned walks here, and she had to hide her delighted surprise when one of the acolytes – whether freeman or slave, she had no idea – went up to one of the cracked old leather-bound books that lay on shelves of stone, picked it up and nonchalantly thumbed through its pages. There were little clusters of people everywhere, some in quiet discussion, others carrying books or even relics, and a few holding pieces of dismantled farm equipment.

'We don't stand on ceremony here,' the minister said. 'We're beholden to God but we rely on each other, and what was made by man will be used by man.'

They settled in their quarters, and breathed.

Dinner was held in early evening. Conversation was quiet but pleasant. The new inhabitants were all well-off to some degree, but any attempts to direct the talk towards material experiences petered out under stoic silence from the acolytes. Ralea and Heci sat next to Ash and Neko and talked among themselves; Ash shared stories about his career in the sport.

'It's played one-on-one, and you never touch your opponent. You sit on a podium or wherever, depends on the arena, and you put on a helmet that plugs pretty much directly into your brain.'

'Ouch,' Heci said with a grimace.

'It's really not that bad. It just . . . takes you somewhere else. It's like meditation, a higher space where you don't need to intellectualize the existence of anything around you. You accept it, and you react. Once your opponent joins that space, you square off and fight to push each other.'

'I thought you guys visualized animals and starships,' Neko said. 'Puppeteers, like.'

'Yeah, that's what broke the sport, made it so popular,' Ash said, then added excitedly, 'But in our level, it's not like that. The actual fight is so deep inside your head, nothing concrete like that even exists there. It's like . . . like . . .' He waved a hand. 'It's like trying to win an argument without using words. There are understandings, and emotions, and feelings that absolutely transcend language. The tech to do this was around for a good long while before the sport even existed.'

'So you guys figured out how to put it into pictures,' said Ralea.

'Exactly. Most of the tech deployed in matches is not to help us conduct the fights, but to translate them into forms that the audience will understand and appreciate. Which is good, I suppose. It brings in the crowds.'

'Doesn't sound like you approve,' Neko said, taking a slow sip from his glass.

Ash shrugged. 'To me, what I experience feels much more pure. The further outside my head that I get when I look at Mind Clash, the dirtier it feels. The matches themselves, the sports leagues and the problems they have, the whole system that supports it . . .' He shrugged again. 'I just like to put on that helmet and feel it all go away.'

'What problems do the sports leagues have?' Ralea asked him.

Ash seemed to choose his words carefully. 'Mind Clash is an incredibly popular sport. Incredibly popular. So we don't need more players. What we need is good managers who can keep the sport clean. People who can run things the way the teams need them to be run.'

'You mean the way the State needs them to be run, don't you?' Heci needled.

He gave her a look that was hard to decipher. 'No, I'd say the teams. State comes second.'

'Not a very Caldari attitude, there,' Neko said.

'Which explains why I'm here,' Ash said and smiled at Ralea and Heci, who both knew he was telling only half a truth.

'How about you?' he asked Neko. 'I don't know if they get many of your kind here.'

The Minmatar took another long sip. 'My people are having a

renaissance right now. Re-evaluating what we stand for.'

'And you wanted to get to know the enemy?' Heci asked.

'Something like that. This empire, all everyone used to talk about back home was how they'd ruined us and how we'd make them pay. Now we're looking towards our own culture at last, starting to rebuild a little, but I don't know if we realize just how much the Amarr Empire affected us through the years. I want to see how they think. What right and wrong is to them.'

'The slaves outside don't bother you?' Ralea asked.

'Of course they do,' Neko said. 'That's why I'm here.' He emptied his glass, leaned back in his chair and stared at the ceiling. 'It might also have something to do with a few deals that went wrong and with some people who'd very much like to have a word with me back home. Even those idiots, crazy as they are, wouldn't dare cross over into the Empire,' he said with a grin.

They kept on the chatter amongst themselves, while every now and then the minister joined in with polite, incisive and, to Ralea, surprisingly witty comments about whatever the group was discussing. His was an easy laughter, which she liked. It had none of that arrogant, overcontented happiness she'd often encountered in the faithful.

Nobody knew how long the attendees would be here, nor were they expected to decide. It was understood that some might leave in the near future, without rancour on either side, while others might never leave.

After dinner, in the waning hours of the land's setting sun, the group was brought a nice dessert and a new guest. He was a middle-aged man, a little rotund in the manner of those who've lived off the land most of their lives, with big, worn hands and a large beard the colour of whetstone. He introduced himself as Karel Morn, an overseer on the plantation.

'I apologize for being late,' he said, taking a seat near Ralea. 'The minister had graciously invited me to dinner, but there was plenty of work to be done. Sometimes an extra effort is needed.'

No one seemed to mind in the slightest, and Karel joined in with the dessert.

As they ate, Ralea asked, 'Is an overseer in charge of the … workers here?'

'The slaves, yes,' Karel said, cutting from his cake a piece that seemed entirely too big, and readying to stuff into his mouth. 'We call them that, as they do themselves.' Neko's own hand stopped halfway to his mouth, and he turned to listen intently.

Annoyed that she'd had her attempt at cultural courtesy shot down, Ralea let herself say, 'Not that they have much of a choice.' She felt the words fall like weights as soon as she let them go, and in the vacuum of silence added, 'I'm sorry. That was rude, I shouldn't have said it.'

'Nonsense!' Karel said, and laughed heartily in the face of Ralea's utter surprise. He brushed crumbs off his chest, took a drink and said, 'Look, dear, people need to be forthright. Nobody's going to reach any inner truth here if they lie to themselves and to others about what they think of the world. And for outsiders like yourselves—,' he indicated the whole group, '—you're carrying a lifetime's worth of misconceptions. That's *all right*. I don't take offence, slaves keep working the fields, life ticks on nonetheless.'

'So what are these misconceptions?' Ralea said, trying to make up for her gaffe. 'Educate me.'

'Well,' the overseer said, taking another bite from his creamy cake before continuing, 'we come in with overwhelming forces, kidnap them and their families and children, take them off to a distant part of the cluster and put them to work for the remainder of their lives. Some of them we hook on a drug called Vitoc and leave at the mercy of a continued supply.'

A croaky sound that might have been an astonished little laugh escaped from Neko's throat.

Vitoc was a highly addictive chemical developed by the Amarr Empire to keep its slaves docile. They'd be slack-jawed and shuffling, with dead eyes inside dying bodies, but it would make their days bearable so long as it was provided. When cut off, the result was an agonizing death. Vitoc addiction was manageable, but irreversible.

'Are you kidding? That's awful,' Ralea said.

'It's goddam atrocious is what it is, excuse my language,' Karel said, nodding to the minister, who smiled and shrugged.

Karel continued, 'That's one side of the coin. Other one is that we take them from places so horribly downtrodden you can barely call them civilizations. Seeing how these people live, you'd think we were still in the dark ages. Their life expectancy is low, their quality of life is miserable, and their distant leaders seem more interested in fighting us than in taking care of their own people. We bring them here, clean them up, and give them a life worth living.'

'Sounds like my old drill instructor,' Ash whispered to his companions.

'Then I presume you give them the same rights as you enjoy?' Heci piped in.

'Almost,' Karel said. 'It depends which House they belong to and what planet they live on. There's places out there that treat them like shit, excuse me again, and think the best of them are good for little more than Amarrian chattel.'

'Thankfully we've seen a change in that kind of attitude,' the minister said.

'Absolutely,' Karel added. 'Even more so after her Holiness took the throne. Now honestly, I won't deny that some Holders really burn up the Vitoc in keeping their people docile. I've seen places that looked like Sansha colonies, zombies all walking around. But that's no way to run a farm and I won't have them treated in that manner while I'm around, not on this planet and not under my command.'

'They were also taken from their homes,' Heci said.

'And raised in ours. There's cases to be made for the superiority of either, but I fear it's not an argument anyone's ever likely to win.'

'So, Vitoc aside, no slaves here are mistreated,' Ralea said as she leaned down to innocuously take a bite of her dessert. She snuck a look at Jorek, who was standing nearby. His utterly impassive face was all the answer she needed.

'Not in my judgement, they're not,' Karel said.

Others led the conversation away from the slaves, and Ralea let them. Ash joined eagerly in the patter, while Neko ate in slow, quiet thoughtfulness.

Afterward they split into smaller groups, roaming the dark halls, most too tired to talk at any length but still far too buzzed about their arrival to get any sleep. Their brownian motion eventually led them towards their personal quarters. Ralea was looking forward to getting a little shut-eye, and expected it would be the most restful one she'd enjoyed in a while. Her quarters, which she'd seen earlier in the day, were spare and would be kept spare, in the hope that whatever vestiges of her past life still clung to the hem of her present would not assert themselves.

The redhead who'd grumbled at their first arrival – whose name was Theban, and whose local-style clothing so fitted the setting it was like a *tourist* sign hung around his neck – suggested they visit his quarters, with the implication that it would be a sight worth seeing.

It was. Train wrecks generally are.

Theban had not wanted to let go; that much was certain. His quarters might have been more spacious than Ralea's but felt more cramped for reasons that were blindingly, glitteringly, loudly obvious. There was entirely too much crammed into the space, too much technology that would be a useless distraction in this new life. It all spoke of a life as yet unsatisfied; as if the man's aim when looking into the quiet pit of his own soul had been to scour it for any remaining vestiges of material possession. Items buzzed, hummed and squealed.

The central display piece truly shocked them all. It was unobtrusive in this room of miniature drones, volumetric displays and long-reach radio receivers, so when it drifted into focus at last, its quiet presence carved itself indelibly into reality like a knife cut on flesh.

It was a Khuumak.

A long time ago, a slave had used a life-sized one of these – back then a sceptre used in Amarrian trial and judgement – to murder an heir of the royal family, precipitating a retribution so monstrous and bloody it culminated in the near-extinction of an entire bloodline of Minmatar slaves.

The replica stood on a pedestal, and was the height of a

man's forearm. It looked like it was made of some rather valuable alloy, the kind swiftly mined in lowsec by someone with a small cargohold and large afterburners.

'Doubt it's good for the spirit to have that,' Ralea murmured.

'Doubt it's good for the wallet,' Heci said. 'A thing like that is offensive on a hundred levels. Might end up destroyed or gone.'

'My team gets half its budget cut and has to do who-knows-what to stay afloat,' Ash said, 'and this asshole could probably pay for our entire next season instead of throwing away his money on things like this.'

'Bad times,' Neko said.

They wandered away from Theban, the crowd and the noise, headed back to their rooms of solitude, and fell asleep, each in their own cot, in the blissful silence of their restful heads.

Reveille was always at sunup. Ralea's body reacted to this new tradition as a person would to a fresh new breath. She would roll out of bed and tiptoe across the chilly stone floor to the small fur mat in the other corner of her bedroom, over which hung her underwear, robe and belt. On the other side of her S-shaped quarters was the small living room, dark now while the bedroom was bright with the morning's golden light.

She tilled the land with all the others, freemen and slaves both. There did not exist any more social equality in the fields than elsewhere in New Eden, but there was a definite lack of social distinction. You were the person who held the microblade scythe; you were the person who ran the twine on the bales; you were the person who operated the transport boards. The rain alone would judge you.

Yes, she thought, this could be done by machines, but those machines would bring with them problems of all sorts; and moreover, Ralea suspected that this was all part of a lifestyle that needed to proceed in this manner. Little point to prayer if the harvest was left fallow.

Each morning turned to afternoon and bled into prayer time. The hours were not measured by meals, but by the shifting focus from duty to the land to a duty to the spirit.

Ralea enjoyed the day's mindless work, and she liked coming inside the cool temple – it might have been a mansion, but to her it was a temple – at the very end, where she would take off her dusty, muddy robe and throw it into the laundry, then head to the showers and wash off all the day's soil that clung to her skin.

In the evenings the light spilled orange and deep into her living room, illuminating the texts in her hands. They were printed on real paper, pulped and pressed in this very region, and bound in books of leather taken from animals of these fields. Sometimes Ralea would hold the books to her chest for a while, smelling the worn leather while her fingers traced over their cracked surfaces.

As she read she decided there was nothing wrong with faith, nor with believing in whatever gods one wished, and there was also nothing that said one could not do this and yet accept the real world on its own, secular terms. Faith by its very nature transcended logic and sense, and to Ralea was a deeply personal thing. The problems everyone – particularly the Gallente – had with the idea of belief arose only when people with personal convictions started expecting others to adhere to and follow the same.

Besides, she had watched plenty of holovids back in her life on the station. She did not know anyone who failed to indulge their sense of the unreal, in dreams if nothing else.

She read on and on, the golden light of the setting sun falling on their texts, and thought of the barley falling under her microblade scythe.

'I'd never have picked you for the faithful type,' Ralea told Heci on one of their walks. They had been aimlessly ambling down a dirt road, but had left it when they got to wherever it led, and ventured into the fields instead. There was a lake not too far from the ministry, a shallow muddy thing that lay flat on the ground, and a little further were the woods that held some of the larger domestic animals.

They had days off; sometimes one, sometimes more, depending on the harvest. Ralea used to hate spare time and held genuine loathing for any vacation that went on for more than a single day without some kind of activity to keep her busy.

It was different now. She spent her quiet hours in contemplation: reading the Scriptures, staring out the window, or exploring the surrounding area, roaming beyond the fields for endless hours while thinking about God and this place.

Heci joined her on some of these. To Ralea's amazement, her friend had taken to this life with the same quiet joy.

'I needed this, truth be told,' Heci said. 'That Gallentean land of temptation was just not healthy for me to be in,' she added with a grin.

'You're looking better. I know, it's *me* saying that, but still.'

'No, I really like what this life is doing to my body. And you're not looking so bad yourself,' Heci said.

Ralea nodded. Each day she felt much more alive and at peace than before. She could see new lines of muscle, particularly in her thighs and upper arms – and she could walk practically forever.

Heci said, 'Really, I'm quite enjoying my vow of celibacy,' and Ralea snorted with laughter.

She looked around at the fields and the woods. The constructs she'd seen on the horizon, in a grey and dusty vision, remained somewhere in the back of her mind, though for some reason she hadn't walked in that direction for the longest time, preferring instead the calm of the lake and the quiet whisper of the woods. It wasn't until she'd been in the ministry for a good few weeks that she had even begun to notice them again, but they itched at her consciousness.

A few weeks into her stay on the colony of the faithful, when she had the entire day off, she set off alone on a walk.

There were no dirt roads leading to the grey buildings, no signposts, nor even any downtrodden paths, and when she got to ditches and streams there were no bridges to be found. She passed them nonetheless, her robe taking on the dirt and water of the earth.

The smoke was abundant. Big, grey plumes wove their way into the blue sky.

She stopped on the edge – and it was an edge, with a drop that would break legs – to gaze in stunned disbelief at what lay beyond it.

The pit's circumference extended beyond her vision, obscured by the dust that constantly hovered in the air from the mines and the grinding equipment and the thousands of people all walking around on the grey loam, dragging pickaxes and shovels, pulling carts full of metals, shuffling toward the shade or the water pumps.

They dragged their feet, stumbling and falling.

There were thousands of people.

Some of the workers were children.

She found her way down and she wandered among them. Nobody met her gaze; she was a ghost among ghosts. Their jaws were slack and their eyes looked at something that was no longer there. Those who were not stumbling about stood stock still, pickaxes in hand, hewing out the grimy rocks from the wounds in the ground.

They were all slaves. She knew this. They were slaves and children of slaves, taken from their homes – their filthy homes, on their unprotected planets, living their malnourished lives – and brought here, where they were fed and clothed and given medicine when they needed it, and they were taught the ways of the Lord.

Ralea walked because she could not bear to stop moving, as the sun passed over all their heads. When it set at last, and the people in the mine began to pack up, she walked back home to the ministry, not having spoken to anyone at all.

The knock on her door was soft, which meant it was not Heci.

She fidgeted with her nightwear, a thin robe, white and pristine. Her day robe still hung unwashed on the hook. She didn't usually wear much in the evenings, but she felt the need for something to cover her.

The door opened. Sandan the minister stepped in on quiet feet.

'May I take a seat?' he asked.

She nodded three times in quick succession. She faced the living room window, looking out at the fields. Those beautiful fields, where they all worked together without any distinction or division of class. In this empire of the spirit.

Motes of dust danced quietly in the gloomy dusk.

'You had a long walk today,' Sandan said, sitting on a chair beside her. 'Long walk.'

She nodded.

'Saw some things you weren't ready for, I'll venture,' he added. 'I won't say you weren't expecting them, because everyone goes to the mines for a reason, but not many people can take in what they see and remain untouched.'

'There were so many people,' she said in a whisper.

'This planet has thousands of slave colonies. Most of them are layered, meaning that a lot of the slaves work hard labour and a smaller portion get to undertake more complicated tasks.' He held the book of Scriptures in his hand, looked at it without opening it. 'We let people see this, Ralea.'

'It's unfair.'

'It's absolutely miserable. I consider myself lucky, and nothing else, to have been born a little closer to God than those poor people in the mines, in the same way that you're lucky to have been born into wealth and prosperity. But luck isn't enough for salvation; everyone has to work.'

'What chance do those people have?'

'Some of them won't make it. There's no getting around that. They're born and they die in the dust pits. Others work hard, attend their Scripture class and pray, and they or their children will be lifted out by God's hand, to till the soil or serve the ministry. It's about the same elsewhere. The local overseer keeps an eye on his prospects, and so do the guards, and so do the slaves themselves. Whoever's judged to be worthy is let out of the dust and allowed to work in a field or a factory, or a school, church or even administration. There are limits, of course there are, but there are limits on everything in this world.'

'And you are happy with this?' Ralea asked, in a tone as flat as the muddy lake next to the forest on the other side of the fields.

'I think it's ... a marvellous thing. A terrible and marvellous thing.' He saw her expression and quickly added, 'I am in charge of a grand building that appeases the Lord – and the Holders, really –

where I can educate the slaves, keep them healthy, and bring them into the fold as people of the empire. If some of those you saw won't ever come to the ministry, their children will, encouraged or prodded by their parents. We think of more than just one life's worth and advancement here.'

'Those aren't lives, what I saw down there. Those people are barely surviving,' Ralea said.

Sandan gave a stern look. 'You knew about this. The slaves of the empire, the ways of our world. It's a shock to see, but it's not ours to sit in judgement.'

'Knowing isn't the same as *knowing*.'

Sandan sighed. 'Yes. You can know without understanding, and understand without accepting.' He patted Ralea lightly on the shoulder, and stood up. 'You're welcome to go out there as often as you like. Come back here after, spend some time thinking about faith and how it works in practicality. We have thought of it too. We are not monsters, Ralea.'

'Is there Vitoc?' she asked

'I'm sorry?'

'*Is there?*' she asked.

The minister looked at her for a long time.

'Yes,' he said at last. 'There is Vitoc there.'

'Where is it?' she asked.

He started to walk out of the room.

'*Where is it?*' she asked again.

Sandan stopped at the door.

'In the water,' he said. 'It's in the water.'

'You need to find this goddamn thief,' Theban said. 'I don't care how you do it.'

'We are looking as best we can,' Sandan told him. He added, perhaps unwisely, 'But there is also a harvest to be brought in.' The two men were standing in the ministry's main archway, within earshot of Ralea.

Someone had stolen the expensive Khuumak display piece, and

of course Theban had raised the roof. And of course he loudly blamed the slaves at first.

Rooms had been searched, usually with permission, but nothing found. The fields were scoured, the forests combed. The lake, at last, was dredged, though the idea that anyone – Amarr or Minmatar – could have thrown a Khuumak into its muddy depths was unimaginable.

'I don't give a shit about your harvest. I could buy this place outright. And I tell you another thing,' he said, pointing a finger at Sandan, 'with the kind of people you let into this place, I wouldn't be surprised if some of them had a hand in it. They had access. They knew it was there. Some poxy slave couldn't have made it disappear without inside help.'

Ralea, who had sometimes spied Jorek staring longingly in the direction of the salt mines, said nothing.

'I'm not sure that's the kind of accusation you should be levelling at anyone without proof,' Sandan said sternly.

'I'm working on that,' Theban said with bristling pride. 'I'm having background checks run on every member of this community.'

'Hey now—'

'Every one! And once I find out what kind of lowlifes and criminals surround me, you can just bet that there'll be bells ringing in this tower. Don't you try to threaten me, either. I'm having copies of the checks sent to the authorities in all four empires.'

Ralea cursed silently and rushed to Heci's quarters. She knocked on the door, then knocked again. There was a muffled, 'Coming!' and a little while later Heci opened it. 'What's up? Hey, are you all right?' she asked.

'Serious trouble,' Ralea said. 'Can I come in, please?'

'Yeah, of course.' Heci let her in and closed the door behind them. When Ralea walked into the living room, she found Ash and Neko there, lounging on a sofa. 'Uh, hey guys.'

The two men waved. 'It's that red-headed idiot again,' Neko said, in what was barely a question.

Ralea sighed and nodded.

'What's the problem?' Heci said.

Ralea hesitated. 'I think it might be best if just the two of us talked. Sorry, guys,' she said, smiling awkwardly at Ash and Neko.

'No problem.' Ash started to get up off the couch, but Heci stopped him.

'Hang on. Tell me first what the guy's up to. I think we might all want to hear it.'

Ralea frowned, but decided to trust her friend. 'He's started background checks on all of us. And he's going to have them shared with the authorities in each empire.'

The rest of the room's inhabitants shared silent looks.

'I take it – and I say this as someone whose own past really doesn't bear looking at too deeply – that you'll get in trouble when this happens,' Ash said carefully.

'Yes,' Ralea said.

'Serious trouble?' Neko asked.

'Yes,' she said.

He nodded. 'Me too,' he said, closing his eyes and rubbing them tiredly.

'I'm not going to tell you two any details,' Ralea said, more petulantly than she'd have liked.

'We don't particularly want to hear them,' Ash said. 'Got enough damn trouble of my own right now, if what you're saying is true. I'm going to have to leave before those checks come through.'

'Same here,' Neko said.

'Where are you guys gonna go?' Heci asked them.

'Anywhere except my own nation,' Ash said, and Neko nodded.

'Us, too,' Heci said.

'You're wanted in the Federation?' Ash asked them.

Ralea hesitated. Heci said, 'Yes.' Ralea hissed at her, but Heci shrugged and said, 'What? We can trust them. And if we don't figure this out, we're all going to be in trouble.'

Ralea said, 'I have an idea who stole the Khuumak. Or not – I don't know yet. But even if we do find it, those checks have already been started. So either way we're going to have to run.'

Neko said, 'You guys want, I can pull strings. There's a huge

Minmatar exodus ongoing, into deepest space, on some big project nobody knows much about. Everyone's welcome there. I think I'll go myself.'

Ralea looked at Heci, then down at the ground, in dark thought. 'I didn't want my stay here to turn out like this,' she said.

'Me neither,' said Neko. 'But I'd rather follow the Minmatar than have them find us here.'

'I suppose.' She looked at Heci, who said, 'If you're not ready to go there, we'll find someplace else.'

'I just . . . I think I need something more concrete. Going on that trip – and I'm sorry, Neko – but it'd feel like running away. I need to end up somewhere I *belong*, or at least know where I'm going to end up at all.' She looked around, at the small room, and at the windows that showed them the dusk falling on the fields.

Ash broke in. 'You both have money, and at least one of you loves Mind Clash. My old team desperately needs backers. They're starved and they won't be picky, so it'd be fairly easy to enter through a corporate backdoor and take charge. If you want to improve people's lives then you'll certainly have sufficient opportunity – and the Caldari State, perverse as the thought may be to Gallenteans like yourselves, is the last place the Federation would look for its people.'

'Would we even be allowed in?' Ralea asked.

Ash said, 'Not if you wanted to work in the regular corporate world. But sports is a place unto itself, where money counts more than nationality. We get shadow backers of all kinds there, and they can hide themselves pretty thoroughly in the paperwork jungle.'

Ralea looked at Heci, who shrugged and said, 'We do have money. And it wouldn't be any crazier than what we've been doing so far.'

'All right,' Ralea said. 'Ah hell . . . all right. We'll go. But I think we can buy us a little time . . .'

She didn't know whether to say it, but the silence of the group spurred her on. 'Slaves are property, and property is a matter of record. So if I'm right, and with all the furore over this theft raging on, one of us could probably ask for and be given access to the ministry's books without anyone asking questions. We could say we just want to get more involved in the ministry's daily operations. Sandan's got other things on his mind, so I don't see how he would refuse.'

'So you think a slave did this?' Neko said.

She nodded. 'Someone here at the ministry. But I don't think he did it just for himself. Other people are going to be involved. Other slaves.'

'Who was it?' Neko asked her.

'I think it was Jorek, Sandan's assistant.'

It didn't take them long to dig up the information, and Ralea's hunch proved entirely correct. Jorek had family on the planet. They were trapped in the mines.

She had merely wanted to retaliate against whoever had stolen the Khuumak. At some level she also wanted to hit back against the Amarr Empire, proving to them that one of their spiritual own was entirely capable of base deeds. Any misgivings she had, she managed to keep subdued, though she felt increasingly uncomfortable even as she returned to that charred, blasted place. When she called over one of the guards to inspect the particular home of a particular family, the looks on their faces told her everything she needed to know and nothing she would ever want to remember.

They hadn't been keeping it for themselves. They were keeping it for Jorek's loved one, also a mineworker, whom Jorek had wanted to run away and sell the Khuumak on the black market – for there would always be someone who desired a thing like this – and make a new life for herself elsewhere, never to return to the mines, or to him.

It broke Ralea's heart.

It was too late for her to take back the revelation. Theban found out immediately, and Sandan shortly after. The overseer came to the ministry the next night, with a quiet face and an electric whip.

They held it in the courtyard, so everyone could see. Ralea's team was ready to leave, all of them packed and waiting for the shuttle to take them off planet, but she refused to board right away. Instead, she stayed for the punishment, and she made herself watch it, remembering throughout that yet again she had held in her hands someone else's life, and she had let it fall to pieces.

This life of mind and spirit, it was nothing without equality. Nothing at all. And she would find no home nor solace here, not after what she had done. Only people mattered; and there were consequences to every action.

When it was over she left the planet and headed for the Caldari State.

12

'I'd like to know what this old bitch wanted from you,' Yaman said.

They were back onboard their ship, catching their breaths.

A lie came easily this time. 'She was worried about safety on her colony.'

'As well she should be,' Verena muttered, 'with her at the helm.'

'She wanted to recruit me as a special agent. Have me oversee a rescue squad on the asteroid.'

'That woman,' Ortag said, 'has a strange way of asking favours.'

'Again, I'm really sorry. I had no idea it'd be like this.' That, in fact, was very true.

The team shrugged. Ortag said, 'A wander through strange places, a lack of breathable air, and encounters with people who don't entirely seem as grateful as you think they should be.'

'Sounds about right for any rescue mission you care to mention,' Verena added.

'Won't leave any scars I'll notice beyond the rest of 'em,' Ortag said. He smiled at Drem. 'I think we have more important things to consider now.'

Drem was still reeling from the darkened meeting he'd had with Hona deep in the stone cathedral, and he thought for a panicked moment that they had discovered his lying and were about to boot him off the team. 'Guristas,' Yaman said with a big, dumb grin. 'Guristas all the way.'

Ortag nodded. 'I think the consensus, even before we went on this little sojourn, was that we've had enough of the Angel Cartel. I know I have, and I also know we've earned more than enough karma for rotation anywhere we like. Anyone change their minds about this since the last time we talked?'

'Nope,' Yaman said.

'I want to leave. I want out of this place,' Verena said. Drem felt for her. It was bad enough going back to a place of memory only to find it was no longer a suitable home, but there was nothing like discovering the ugly truth about an idolized local figure to put one off the place for good.

'Drem?' Ortag asked.

'Hm? Oh. Yeah. I think it's time we leave this all behind,' he said. He looked at Verena, and she looked quietly at him.

'All right. I'll send off the request. Let's take it easy on the way back, people,' Ortag said and headed off, followed by Yaman.

Only Verena was left in the room with him. 'You've been strange since we left. Was there something else on that asteroid you were expecting?'

Drem thought it over. 'I had . . . certain hopes. I'm slowly coming to terms with the idea that something I was looking for may actually not have been meant for me at all.'

She frowned, walked over and stroked him on the cheek. 'I hope it wasn't something crucial,' she added.

'It might have been. I'm not so sure any longer.' He looked at her for a while. 'I think I need to seriously reconsider what's important to me.'

She nodded, and ran her hand over his face one last time, a little sadly, before leaving the room.

He stood there for a long time, looking out the bow, watching the stars go by.

They continued working for the Angels, saving the lives that needed to be saved, but with a sense of renewed urgency that had threatened to fade from them in the muddy length of time. Their request for transfer was being processed. Everyone on the team had to deal with the sense of guilt that came with the idea of leaving their posts with the Angels. Each time Drem held an injured man, marking him for the oncoming rescue teams, he thought, *I might not have found you. I might have been gone.* He was surprised by his reticence to move on, even though the Cartel had nothing more to offer him.

Drem was also amazed at his team's continued support, even after he'd nearly led them to their deaths. It was, he suspected, not all out of friendship and loyalty. Firstly, the team increasingly acknowledged Drem's tactical abilities as the primary cause of the ever-increasing number of lives saved. They needed him now.

And second, they really didn't mind the risk. At the back of the mind of every Sisters agent, lurking somewhere behind the blanket acceptance of possible death, was the idea, the quiet longing, of having death actually come. Of no longer waiting. Having the burning life extinguished at last, the drifting ashes given to the winds.

They kept working, searching for the dying and the dead, saving all they could before time ran out.

Drem and Verena kept up their celebration; either of life or living – Drem wasn't entirely sure. They kept their liaison a secret, to his carefully tempered annoyance. Though he was growing increasingly sure that he loved her, he could not be sure that he would have ended up with her in circumstances less suffused with death and despair. Love aside, he had to acknowledge that he needed her. Whether it was her warmth, her presence, or simply an intimate moment with one of the few who *understood*, it had enough of a hold on him that he couldn't walk away. It felt like a connection to something new, or, even more, the beginning of a break from the old.

One night when returning from her quarters, he found a message was waiting on his e-tag. It was from Rhan, whom he hadn't seen since that visit to the asteroid sanctum, and it informed him and the rest of the team that their request had been approved by Sisters HQ. They would be transferred to the Sisters' Gurista base at their leisure. It had been an open request, so the Angels had provided references on the team's work, and the note implied quite heavily that a promotion would be imminent as soon as they arrived in Gurista space. Rhan did not mention Drem's meeting with the man in white, nor did it seem to have affected the team's high standing with the faction. They were appreciated, the note simply said, and they would be missed.

Drem appreciated that small sentiment more than he could say, as well as the fact that a pirate faction, their deals with the Sisters notwithstanding, was willing to let him work for its effective rivals. Sometimes the saving of lives could take precedence over politics.

He suspected the others would be happy to move on. It was important to keep moving. Stagnation was death.

'I am so glad you joined us,' the Gurista overseer said to Drem. 'Your reputation preceded you.'

They were walking towards the residential area of the Gurista colony. There had been a small reception where the Sisters were welcomed, to their surprised pleasure, and lauded, much to their embarrassment.

After the reception the group split up and each member was shown to their quarters. Drem was escorted by the Gurista colony's overseer, a genial man in middle age who seemed entirely uninterested in standing on ceremony.

'I can't emphasize enough how important it is to have an experienced rescue team on hand. It's a good life here, but it's a dangerous one. I'm sure your team will be a great boon to our work,' the overseer added.

'I hope so,' Drem said. 'It'll take us a while to get into gear, though. There's going to be a lot of procedures and processes in your faction that we're not used to.'

'Don't worry about that. Everything can be worked out,' the overseer said, waving a hand. 'Ah, here we are.'

The building seemed entirely too tall, so clean it was virtually spotless. The reception was expansive and replete with golden metals. 'You have a separate exit,' the overseer told Drem. 'This one is locked at night, so it might slow you down. Though it'll open without question for you.'

The elevator, to Drem's open-mouthed surprise, was also set to override on his ID. It would follow his projected trajectory no matter who else might be waiting.

'This is not the best apartment we have to offer on the colony,' the overseer said as they stepped out of the elevator and into the only flat on that particular floor, 'but we believe it is the best for your particular needs. That said, if you ever find that you are no longer comfortable here, for whatever reason, please tell me about it and we'll find you a new place. No questions, no bother.'

Drem looked around in astonishment. These private quarters were well over twice the size of what they'd had with the Angels, and equipped with every modern comfort he could dream of. He also had a great view over the more stylish part of the section, with human traffic far below and the rolling hills of carefully cultivated nature in the distance. The windows had ad-filters, leaving Drem's view entirely unobstructed. It was a perfect location: right in the thick of things, for those times when he wanted either company or simply to be a presence in the cavalcade of humanity, and yet high up above them, for when he wanted nothing but quiet isolation and the sights of life quietly creating itself. The ability to choose the amount of immersion in human life was important to the Sisters.

Even with their immense successes, they had been kept aside on the Angel station, uncomfortable reminders that the faction's humming machine could occasionally spring a cog. Here they were venerated.

'There is one last thing I should add before I leave you to settle in,' the overseer said. 'I have a message from your commander back at the Sisters' base.'

For a panicked moment Drem thought his excursion to Hona's place and all his datasnooping had been discovered, but he remained calm. 'Really? What did he say?'

'He offered his congratulations on your team's promotion to squad leaders.'

As Drem blinked and stammered, the amused overseer went on, 'From what he says, you are all still expected to engage in rescue operations, but you will have more control over Sisters activity in this sector of space, and you will command any other teams in active operation. And on a private note, I should add that while I had wind of this promotion before we approved your transferral into the Guristas, it made not a lick of difference to my attitude towards that request. I would have accepted you into our fold no matter what.'

'I … don't know what to say,' Drem said. He was immensely gratified by this, not least for the opportunity it provided him for tailoring the Sisters' efforts to each rescue operation. He had not associated much with agents other than those on his own team, but he kept tabs on mission reports and already had people in mind for certain tasks in the field.

All of which ran through his head in half-formed wordless thoughts, so he settled for uttering, 'Thank you.' The overseer nodded amiably, shook his hand and left him to the new life.

Not long after, the doorbell sounded. It was Verena.

He let her in. As soon as she'd stepped through the door, she looked around in astonishment and said, 'Yours too? Wow.'

'I know,' he said. 'It's the same old us, except somehow we've turned into celebrities. It's like a new life.'

She sat down on a couch that moulded itself around her shapely form. 'I've been meaning to ask you about that. Back on the ship, you mentioned something about letting go. Have you been having a rough time?'

Drem walked over to the window and looked out while he thought this over. The people on the ground went about their own lives, oblivious to rescues and dangers. 'I had,' he eventually said. 'It's fine now.'

'What changed it?' she said.

He thought this over, too. Eventually he turned to her and said, simply, 'You.'

As she gave him a brittle smile, he continued, 'The team is what keeps me going. There's all sorts of darkness I've been dealing with since what happened at my home colony, darkness and the thoughts and plans it leads to. I was pretty committed to something. But after I got to know you guys, I started seeing there was more to life than my own stupid ideas. And after … you and I started, I began to let go of those ideas for good. I am content with this life now. This life with you. At last.'

She stood up, walked over and hugged him tight.

He said, 'You're my anchor. I'd be lost without you,' and felt her nod on his shoulder.

She eventually broke the hug and said, 'I have to go. My apartment is perfect and beautiful and there's only about five million things in it that I want to rearrange.'

He laughed, and nodded.

She walked away, stopping at the outside door to blow him a kiss. She looked immeasurably sad, and he wondered if she, too, had her own darkness that interfered with happiness. He hoped that together they could bring in a little light.

'We're all happy with this setup? No second thoughts?' Drem asked the team.

Each member looked to the other, then back to him and nodded acquiescence. It was late evening. They were sitting in the ops room, a secured and secret part of the Sisters' presence on the station. Tactics was part of fieldwork, but here, in this room, they decided on strategy. And not only for their own team.

'All right,' Drem said. 'The four new backup teams all go into rotation, each working with their own sector: refining, production, training and social.'

'Pleasure hubs,' Yaman said. 'I still think I should be overseeing operations in that one.'

'You'd die of dehydration,' Drem said.

'And shock,' Verena deadpanned. Drem grinned, but she kept her face impassive.

Drem went on, 'Better to keep them in rotation than have each team be attached to another one for too long, and pick up too many of its quirks. It might have worked with the Angels, where every place is run the same, but the Guristas' situations are way too unique for any kind of single team's tactical approach to work in all cases. Best get people used to it, used to having to grasp new situations all the time, and to learn how to work with fresh faces instead of acting like they're superior.'

'You're getting a commendable grasp of the Sisters' way of thinking,' Ortag said, in apparent honesty.

Drem felt a little burning flush in his ears. 'I guess. Can hardly believe they gave us this authority, really.'

They'd clearly developed a good reputation. With the promotion, his team had been given almost total strategic command over operations in this sector. It did mean that they stayed out of constant rotation – not that they wouldn't risk themselves when needed, but the work in organizing Sisters rescue teams, and sometimes jumping in on remote tactical advisement, was enough to keep them all in full operation, with Drem unquestionably at the helm. He was humble and proud at this, at the same time.

But the lack of action nagged at them, and they made sure they still joined the fray whenever possible. For this kind of work, it was unwise to let oneself drift too far away from the action. The more time that passed, the harder it would be to get back into the game; and all the more tempting instead to sit and watch, letting people – real human people – turn into numbers on a screen; or worse, statistics in reports.

'I'd no idea that life would be so busy at the top,' Yaman said and rubbed his eyes.

'We do have far more missions to run here than we did back at the Angels,' Drem said. 'I suppose by extension the Guristas are more inclined, or at least less averse, to danger than the heavily organized Cartel dares to be.'

That was all right with him. The Guristas had a deserved reputation for cackling madness and operated on instinct as much as they did on cold planning. He, in this mad new life of his own, could very much relate.

They had been so busy that he and Verena weren't spending as much time together as he'd have liked. She was starting to feel a little more distant, which, given everything they'd gone through, was no real surprise to Drem.

'They know our names, too,' Verena said. 'I've started to get recognized in the street. It's weird. I'm honoured, every time, but a little embarrassed. I know we don't save everyone, and I wonder how many people are standing at the sidelines, thinking that we've become these distant superstars.'

Drem and the others nodded.

Ortag said, 'A reputation and a few grinning nods. It could be worse, and if we mess up, it *will* be.' He turned to Drem and said, 'Especially for you, I reckon?'

'How's that?'

'I've done a few more rescue missions than you in my time. I know the faces of relief. And when people see that it's you, behind that helmet of yours, they light up.'

'Aah, I'm not sure . . .' Drem said embarrassedly.

'He's right,' Verena said. 'People respond to you. They know who you are, and their faces show unmistakable relief when you arrive. Not just the victims, either, but other Sisters when we're called in to assist. You can see it on their faces. Drem is here. Everything's going to be all right.'

Drem looked at her for a moment. It was almost as if she disapproved. He pushed the thought out of his mind and turned back to the evening's plans, which hovered still on a vidcast in front of them.

'So the four teams—' he managed, before a large red icon cropped up on the cast. It was echoed in all their own datapads.

Without a word they all stood up and rushed out the door. Something had happened, somewhere in their domain, and they were needed. Everything else could wait.

A group of off-duty operatives had been trapped during an assault on a social hub. As soon as Drem inspected the call he knew it was a capsuleer attack. The realization made his skin crawl with hatred, but he pushed the feeling far down and kept his head cool. Anger was tempting but wouldn't help anyone.

The hubs were effectively a bundle of personal quarters interspersed with casinos, bars and whorehouses. The social refuges were structurally sound, far more so than the asteroid colonies and hi-tech research facilities, which tended to respectively mine their base out from under their own feet, or melt, char and explode it without notice. A social hub would not collapse without intense structural damage inflicted from an outside force.

Drem and his team travelled swiftly. The routine was so familiar that Drem's body responded almost pre-emptively: pre-flight thirst and speed of digestion heightened immensely, lest he be caught in a long-term crisis situation while dehydrated and needing to shit; need for oxygen increased sharply right after warp to keep away the fainting, while ambulation reverted to a slow-moving slouch lest a stiffened body cramp up and vomit; and the eyes unfocused at the first sight of the calamity on-site, so that it could be taken in in layers and evaluated without emotions and memories all crowding in.

After Drem had oriented himself, he consulted briefly with the operating Gurista rep on the kinds of crowds that had been in the hub, then had his teams fan out according to his projections on where the biggest concentrations of injured would be found.

Drem brought his own team and a small group of Guristas to the nearest casino, an eight-storey building turned to a one-storey pile. Overhead projections indicated that a surprising amount of structural integrity had been preserved in the building's core, but the rubble that surrounded it from all sides was proof that nearby structures – none of them inhabited, thankfully – had not had the same luck. Meanwhile, colony data – what they had managed to extract so far – indicated that a host of people were trapped inside that building.

Drem entered it alone on an initial scout, and had not been in there more than a minute before he heard that familiar and terrible sound: the soft, crying creak of metal giving way under pressure.

There was suddenly an immense amount of noise, and then there was darkness and pressure, and then there was nothing at all.

He woke up to the sound of grinding and trembling, as if it were originating from all around, both outside and inside his own body.

There was a little light. Not much, but enough to make him feel very cramped.

'—k to me, son. Say a line, say a word. Let me hear you're all right.' That was Ortag's voice, speaking into his helmet.

'Hey,' he said. 'What happened?'

He heard a sigh of relief. 'Foyer crashed down on you, pushed down by a superstructure collapse higher up. We're trying to get you out, but some of the materials mixed in with the rubble weren't meant to be cut through with normal equipment.'

Drem blinked a few times, then had his overhead light up the darkness. He was lying in a small cavity with a tiny exit hole close by. There wasn't room for him to stand up, but at least he didn't seem to be pinned down. He shrugged carefully and pulled his knees closer. No pain. Nothing broken. He sighed with relief.

The grinding sound started again. He spoke loudly into his helmet, 'Any luck with that?'

'None, really!' Ortag yelled back. 'But we'll keep trying!'

Drem crawled close to that exit hole and peered out. There was plenty of rubble beyond, but he thought he could spy his team standing beside a group of Guristas. Some of the latter were hard at work, but Drem could see they weren't getting through.

'This isn't working!' he said. 'We need to get on with the mission!'

Yaman piped in, 'We're not leaving you here, you idiot!'

The Gurista crew stopped working, and an unknown voice said, 'If I may. My name is Jeren Khal, I'm the lead of the local team, and as you can tell we're having a hard time getting you out.'

'Pleased to meet you, Jeren,' Drem said into his helmet in the most jovial tone he could manage. 'You have a Plan B for us?'

'As a matter of fact, I do. I called over an expert who was working in another sector of our station, and I can see him arriving now. His name is also Jeren, but he'll answer to Demo.'

'As in "Demolition",' Drem said.

'Precisely. I'd trust the man with my life, and I'm hoping you can do the same.'

Demo came up and introduced himself. Drem saw his approaching form through the peephole: a large man, age somewhere between Drem and Ortag, walking with intent and care, and followed by a younger trio of assistant crew.

'You can get me out of here, Demo?' Drem asked.

'Well, sir—'

Yaman interrupted them. 'Dude, I don't like this. No offence to anyone, but it's obvious we need special equipment to get you out, and to prop up the rest of the rubble so it won't fall back down while we're at it. I don't think blowing shit up is going to help.'

'Demo, what's your call on that?' Drem said.

'Well, sir, we can go that way. It'll take you a good long while, since there's nothing like that on hand at the colony.'

'Or . . . ?'

'Or I can do it in far shorter time, and not have anything collapse.'

Drem shrugged, and realized he did in fact ache quite a bit. Adrenaline had carried him, and it still ebbed in his bloodstream, but in not too long he'd start feeling like a man who'd had half a colony dropped on his head.

'Do it,' he said.

Yaman said, 'Dude, are you really sure—'

'Do it!' he yelled. 'There could be people dying in there!'

Yaman stared at him for a sec, through the barrier of rubble, then threw up his hands and said, 'Fine! The madman has spoken! Blow him up if he wants it so bad!'

Demo got into place and started laying down wires. His team, meanwhile, cast repeated stares in Drem's direction, and as they whispered among themselves Drem realized with a start that they knew him, even though he was almost certain he had never met these people. He opened a private channel to the older man, who had moved on to wiring the explosives, and asked in a low tone whether he'd met this team before.

'We all know you, sir,' the demolition man said quietly, and gave him a respectful look Drem was not at all expecting from a man with a deep gaze and burn scars on his hands.

Drem hadn't heard Verena speak to him since the collapse. He felt a sense of panic-streaked depression rising in his mind, as he watched Demo hook things up with hand motions that seemed entirely too swift and haphazard for someone rigging high explosives.

Drem couldn't help but ask, 'Are you sure you know what you're doing?'

The man grinned at him, his hands not stopping for a second. 'Used to work for the Caldari. Demolitions, ten years. You won't find that kind of job experience many places in New Eden.'

'What happened?'

'Guristas pay better. Also, boss slept with my wife.'

'Really?'

'Yeah.'

'Where is he now?'

The man inspected an arrangement of wires and screens he'd hooked up. 'Oh, in about ten different places.'

Even inside the privacy of his helmet, Drem kept his face carefully inexpressive. 'And the wife?'

Demo nodded his head towards the crew. One of the assistants, a very attractive woman clearly a few years younger than the explosives expert, was smiling shyly. 'Hi there,' she said.

Drem, unnerved, smiled back. He addressed the group, 'Look, once we sort this out, you all should hang back. There may be things you don't want to see.' He hoped one of those things wouldn't be his mangled body.

'Here we go, sir,' Demo said.

'Are you su—' Drem managed before there was another stifling onset of pressurized silence, followed by swiftly encroaching darkness.

This time, he dreamed a little before the voices called him up from the deeps. There were people he'd known, and old places long gone; and strange voices that called to him through the haze.

'Come on. Let's see a bit of movement, son.'

Drem raised his head. Everything was much brighter now. He was lying on his stomach, and he was surrounded by feet. He rolled on to his back – his muscles let him know that this would go on their bill later on – and looked up. Half a dozen faces stared anxiously down at him.

'God, you people are beautiful. Except you, Yaman.'

'Fuck you too, man.'

The people helped him up, and after he noticed the casino behind them, still standing and open, the first thing he said was, 'I'm going back in and anyone who opens their mouth to the contrary, Yaman, had better have a good reason for wasting the last of other people's lives.'

Yaman shrugged and grinned. 'I knew you were crazy.'

He looked at Verena, who smiled but said nothing. 'You taking point with me?' he asked.

'You get this one,' she said. 'I'll be along.'

He frowned, then shrugged and turned to Demo. 'I don't think I can thank you enough.'

The man nodded curtly and said, 'You just got buried and now you're going back in for our people. Man, I'd say you've repaid in full.'

Drem smiled, and quietly said to him and his team, 'By the way, I meant it about not following us. Stay out here. These things leave scars.'

They acquiesced but Drem knew they didn't believe him.

The team did its work and eventually got in, safe and sound – only to find a pool of humanity waiting in dead silence.

There were dozens of them. The air was warm and fetid. A single remaining light flickered in the ceiling, slanting awkwardly on to one of the ruined walls.

Their bodies occupied a space that now seemed entirely too big for them, as if the passage of their lives had deflated their physical remains. Or it might have been the flies, now too engorged to move off their flesh.

Drem and his team kept it steady. He and Verena swiftly ran scans on life and launched seeker drones to check in the crevices, while Yaman and Ortag did the best they could to keep the Guristas well away from their destroyed faction mates.

As soon as the scans came up dark they ushered everyone out, but they couldn't stop some of the attending crew from crowding in and seeing the carnage. The last Drem saw of the demolition man, he and his people were stalking away, their faces white, Demo himself cursing and spitting in shock.

Thankfully the rest of the mission went better, and lives were saved in multitudes. During those moments when Drem couldn't keep idle thoughts at bay, he found that he was wondering more about Demo and his crew's welfare – not to mention the way they'd all seemed to recognize him – than the carnage they'd all seen at the casino. He liked that. The living deserved a higher place in his mind than the dead, he felt.

When they were done and the last life noted, Drem and his team returned to base for debriefing, only to find that the arrived survivors – those who were mobile and conscious, at any rate – had pulled themselves out of their cots and begun to celebrate. The team barely had time to change into normal clothes when a procession of Guristas swept them up, carrying them all the way down through the civilian section and into the recreational areas. They moved down streets Drem had never visited, into buildings with far too many lights and loud noises, up on a pedestal of roaring life and into the madness of the bright night.

Drinks and other substances were being passed around in frightening quantities. Drem had seen it before – this crowd wanted to prove to itself that it was alive – and as much as he really wasn't in the mood to party, he saw everyone else on his team getting sucked into the festive atmosphere. Maybe it was time to let go a little.

He shrugged and accepted a drink someone handed him. It wasn't so much a liquid as a chemical reaction, slowly changing its hues and taste, and, he was told with a grin, its potency. Its purple colour reminded him of deep space.

Life slowly took on the disjointed quality it always did when those locked in their own alcoholic cycles of logic felt the overwhelming need to explain themselves to everyone else. Drem had conversations with people whose names he'd forgotten long before they finished saying whatever was on their minds. Most of them, apparently, loved him.

He finished his blue drink. Someone refilled it.

In one corner he spotted Ortag, surrounded by admirers and looking even more sedate than usual. He approached the man, seeking him out like an anchor in an unquiet sea. Ortag leaned forward at his approach and smiled, eyes half-closed.

'This is all thanks to you,' he said to Drem, who lip-read half of it over the noise. The bar was so large and dark they couldn't see where it ended.

He began to compliment Ortag in return, but the old man wouldn't have it. 'Listen to me. Listen. This is all thanks to you. Don't fuckin' deny it. You pulled the team together from the very start, and I've never in my *life* seen anyone so, so tactically aware, so focused, as you are. I wish we could be better partners to you.'

Drem started to reply but was interrupted by someone taking his empty glass out of his hand – he couldn't even recall drinking it – and filling it to the brim with more greenish liquid.

'You'll be a god's grace to us all,' Ortag said, then slapped his own knee and leaned back in his seat, looking as if he'd delivered the crushing blow in a debate. Drem mouthed a thanks.

Yaman drifted over with a group of his own, mostly big, tough guys who made him look like he had an entourage. He put his arm around Drem's shoulder and sedately said, 'Yeah.'

Drem waited patiently.

'Yeah, man. We've been waiting for you for longer than you know,' Yaman added. He thought this over. 'Yeah. You're it.'

It was an odd thing to hear, particularly after the exchange with Ortag. For the first time since they'd started working as a team, the two men felt like total strangers to Drem: people whose thoughts he could no longer read, as he could practically do when they were in the field; outsiders, whose minds were alien and entirely closed to him.

It became apparent the conversation had stalled. Yaman's arm remained firmly on Drem's shoulder, his face registering intense concentration. While waiting for him to talk, Drem turned his head and started subtly looking around for Verena.

'She's not here, man,' Yaman said. Ortag hissed at him.

Drem was about to ask when he noticed that Yaman's gaze was only half on him. He turned, although Yaman tried to turn him back, and at a distance down the bar he saw Verena sitting in the lap of some Gurista guy, her chest facing his, her hands stroking his head, her hips slowly grinding on him. Drem felt an acid pit in his stomach and drained his poison-yellow drink, which was instantly replaced.

Someone he didn't know, a man Ortag's age who appeared entirely sober, inserted himself in the group and said, 'Excuse me, I'd just like to thank you for the wonderful work you've been doing for us.' He held out a card for Drem.

Drem kept his eye on Verena, who'd unbuttoned the man's shirt. 'Thanks,' he said, accepting the card and putting it in his pocket. 'Anytime.'

The man went on, unabashed. 'I have contacts,' he said. 'With people the Rabbit doesn't even know about. They have a *lot* of money to work with. A lot of money. They like you, and could give you anything you want. Shower you with riches.'

Yaman said, 'Hell, yes!' and made to shake the man's hand, but Ortag pulled him back.

'What?' Yaman said to him, stumbling.

'This offer isn't for you to take,' Ortag said. 'We have our purpose already.'

Drem, who till now had not taken his eyes off Verena and her interest, turned to the man. Whatever was in his expression, it pushed his willing benefactor back.

'Do you want me to answer that?' Drem asked in a voice of stone.

The nameless man shook his head and faded into the crowd. He said, 'We'll see you later, dead man's brother,' but Drem was too angry to listen.

When he looked back to where Verena had been, she was gone. So was the Gurista she'd been seducing.

Somewhere in that deep, dark pit of his heart, an old and evil flame started to burn brighter.

Someone refilled his empty glass with a dark red drink, and someone else put an arm around his waist and in a tone as smooth as the setting sun said, 'I'll be her, beautiful.'

He looked into the unknown woman's face. The world felt askew, slippery, making him slide off the edge.

Before he could think it over he leaned in and kissed her, and she slid her warm tongue into his mouth. Whatever she'd been drinking tasted almost too sweet. She pulled him closer, rubbing herself against him as the crowd around them cheered and hooted.

Someone, possibly Yaman, clapped him on the shoulder and left.

He broke off the kiss and drained his glass in one gulp, dropped it on the floor before it could be refilled for the millionth time, grabbed the girl's hand and said, 'We're going.'

He didn't say where. She knew.

The day after – late in the day after – Drem found himself sitting in the soft, felt-covered chair of the overseer's office, staring blearily out the windows at the hovercars in the distance, the little birds in the sky.

The overseer, a calm man with the quietly amused demeanour of a custodian in a madhouse, handed him a cup of hot tea. Drem accepted it gratefully.

'I see you're adapting to our ways,' the overseer said, not quite disguising his amusement.

Drem sipped the tea, winced as it burned his lips, sipped a little more. 'I wish they'd adapt to me,' he said.

'I take it the regular hangover cures didn't work.'

'Someone, at some point, filled my glass with something that now feels like lead bearings rattling around in my skull. Your people can mix their drinks, I'll give you that.'

The overseer leaned against his desk. 'If I'd known you were in this bad a shape after yesterday's festivities, I would've given you more time off before calling you in. We can always meet again later.'

Drem waved a hand in the air. 'No, it's fine. I do prefer having some reason to get my sorry head out of my quarters, and a call from you is just the thing. Just don't ask me to warp anywhere, or do low-grav work. Or have strangers approach me with money.'

'Nothing of the sort, I assure you,' the overseer said. 'We can sort it all out right here in this office. What strangers, incidentally?'

Drem closed his eyes, waited for the headache to ebb, then called up the image of the man who'd approached him at the club. He described this man to the overseer. 'Gave me a card, too,' he added, and handed it to the overseer, who accepted it and ran it over a scanner.

'Hmm,' the man said, and frowned.

'What's up?'

'Probably a good thing you didn't give him more of your time. This man has ties to the Blood Raiders. Probably a scout.'

Drem's blood turned cold.

'I wouldn't worry about it,' the overseer said. 'They find their way here from time to time. And whatever your past, no one is going to take our best Sisters agent away. I guarantee you that.'

A whistling sound caught Drem's attention. In one corner of the big room, fitted in between the door to the holochamber and the wall of Amarrian drapes that had undoubtedly been stolen, was a large tree, the height of a man and a half, set in a wide circular base, moulded directly out of the metal floor like a volcano cut off at the base. He had noticed it from the corner of his eye but couldn't see beyond its heavily foliated branches.

The overseer walked over to the tree, hands in pockets. 'Things can hide their purpose.' He reached out for a branch, took firm hold of the stem of a leaf, and picked it off the tree.

To Drem's astonishment the rest of the tree's leaves immediately folded in on themselves, curling up and flattening against the base of their branches. Within the tree's formerly green sphere there now stood revealed a dozen brightly coloured birds. Their plumage shone so clearly through the bare branches, it was a wonder he hadn't noticed them before.

They were apparently well-trained. None stirred at the exposure. The overseer reached a hand into a small metal container that stood on a pedestal beside the tree, and pulled out a handful of seeds and dried fruit. He raised them to the nearest branch, palm open. One by one the birds hopped and fluttered their way to him, picking the bounty out of the man's hand. They sang to him, in beautiful tones.

'I don't do this all the time,' the overseer said. 'The birds deserve their privacy. Plus, it would cheapen the moment.'

He brushed the shells off his hand and turned to Drem. 'Understand,' he said. 'What I am about to offer you isn't to sell your soul.

It isn't you giving up your identity, or joining the dark side, if there even is such a thing. I won't be calling in any favours from you.'

'But you're going to make me some kind of offer,' Drem said. His head felt clearer after the tea, and less like a mining colony in full blast. The Blood Raiders were back on his tail, an old and familiar anger that mixed in with a brand new one. He remembered last night. It hurt.

'Your reputation is now legend, both here and with the Angels.' The overseer laughed at Drem's surprise. 'Oh yes. We keep an eye on things. Your modesty notwithstanding, we are very careful in picking those we work with. With all the madness inherent in Gurista life, we need solid people with good minds. You've proven to have quite a good mind, and the bravery to back it up.'

The birds tweeted at him, as if in emphasis. The overseer reached into the metal feedbox and brought out more for them. 'A familiar name came up when we ran checks on you. Dakren,' he said.

Drem was nonplussed. 'Dakren? You knew him?'

'Knew, and knew of him. He worked with the faction a number of times. I greatly respected his ability to get things done while retaining some semblance of ethics; a not inconsiderable feat in this world we inhabit. He would go over and beyond the call of duty to do what he felt was right. I see you doing the same.' He walked back over to the seated Drem, looked him directly in the eyes. 'I want to do well for you, because you and yours have done well for us. You have saved lives.'

'What do you want me to do?' Drem asked. Something about the birds bothered him, but he couldn't see clearly from where he sat.

'I want you to accept the money I am planning to give you.'

The room was entirely quiet, save for the sound of small birds.

'There are no conditions,' the overseer added, speaking swiftly. 'We want you to do the same great work you've always done so far. This is merely an added bonus, one that we plan to provide on further occasions.'

Drem regarded him from the chair. 'You want me to start taking money from the Guristas.'

'We want to help you on whatever path you've chosen. The gifts can be for the Sisters, or they can be for you. If money's unsuitable, we will find something else. We want to help fulfil whatever dreams you have. They can be for your own purposes, or for any kind of philanthropy you care to support.' The overseer smiled and waved a lazy arm over the floor, as if presenting it to Drem. 'To keep changing these dead asteroids we happen to call home, these dead rocks in space, into food and life for the people who need it the most.'

'That's admirable, sir,' Drem said. 'The kind of sentiment that propels a man to join the Sisters in the first place.'

The overseer ignored the sarcasm. 'It's an offer in good heart. I don't blame you for being hesitant, but I can't imagine anyone would blame you for considering it, either.'

'And you're making this offer on your own, sole authority?'

The overseer frowned, as if thinking it over. 'Not entirely. I fully support it, but I'll admit that I've been ... encouraged by other people. We all have your best interests at heart.'

'You know what I've noticed about the Guristas?' Drem said, getting up and walking over to the tree. 'They're your best friends. I mean it. They will go above and beyond to help you with whatever it is you need to do. You've just made me a generous offer, and I think you did it in the exact same spirit as a demolitions man did yesterday.'

Drem reached into the metal box and picked out a few seeds, then held them up to the birds. They ate unhesitantly from his hand.

He could see now what had been bothering him: the birds were attached to the tree, tiny strings dangling from their bodies like mammalian umbilical cords and sneaking into an open leaf stem at the other end. When the birds moved, the strings stretched to accommodate. Drem imagined it didn't make flying an easy matter.

'It's the results that matter to the Guristas, not whatever motivation or rules form the framework,' he continued. 'They'll give of themselves even when it might not be wise. This demolitions expert, he did that. And it cost him.'

The overseer frowned. 'What do you mean?'

'He was in bad shape when I last left him, so this morning, after

I'd pried my eyes open, I ran some intra-station checks on him. Turned out he couldn't stop talking about what he'd seen, and it got him into trouble.'

Drem reached for another handful of seeds and fed it to the grateful birds. 'He is no longer on your station.'

'I had nothing to do with this,' the overseer said in a quiet tone.

'I'm sure you didn't. Guristas will happily resolve their problems without getting caught up in protocol. And they're not going to let some rogue voice frighten their people into thinking maybe their faction's signature recklessness might sometimes be a bad idea.' He brushed the rest of the seeds off his hands. 'The Guristas make wonderful offers, but they demand a lot in return. Probably more than even they themselves will ever realize.'

'Your Uncle Dakren would have considered my offer.'

'My Uncle Dakren is fucking dead,' Drem said.

He stood there, stock still, staring at nothing very much, feeling the anger rise to the surface yet again. This time he couldn't bring himself to stop it.

All those people he'd saved, he now realized, would not bring his family back to life no matter how much he tried to will it into being. They were the one thing that had been unconditionally his; a family and a sense of home. He had accomplished nothing to avenge them. Anything else – anyone else – had been good only, in truth, for a transient, fleeting joy.

And now, with the Raiders suddenly on his tail again, he had been given a reminder.

His time was running out. Once they caught up with him – and they would, there was no doubt of that; the only delays in their path were their current inability to take him without undue fuss from other factions – once they caught him, he was a dead man. There would not be a long career of rescue work, and there certainly would not be a long life spent building something new with a traitorous lover.

He had a name. He wanted more – he could admit this to himself now – but he had a name, and there were people out there who had even more information. That name was emblematic of an emotion he'd tried to deny for so long, one that had never quite been extinguished: a pure, thorough *hatred*.

He had a name, and he had an ability to plan ahead, to see where all those lines came together and to put his finger on their intersection. It had served him well in his career with the Sisters. And now he knew that the Angels – or someone related to them, at least – had a lot of information on capsuleers, and that the Guristas had more money than they knew what to do with.

A part of him felt guilty. It felt that even though his life was probably at risk, and even if he had something coming together in his head – he could feel the intersections of all those little lines, and he *knew* there was something to what he was thinking – that still did not justify betraying the cause. Letting down the people who trusted him.

Another part of him thought of last night, of what he'd seen and felt, and he winced in pain. Whatever trust there had been, if it ever had been real, it was gone now; replaced by empty faces.

And there was that memory now, rushing into his mind, of what the Blood Raider had said to him last night. Dead man's brother. Leip was still frozen in his cold coffin, still kept unburied and unacknowledged by the world. Nothing Drem had done, no life he'd saved, had changed this condition one bit, and it simply never would. If he spent the remainder of his time running after strangers in ruins, the one that mattered the most to him would still be lost. None of the rescues would save his brother. But there might still be a way.

Time was running out, was running out fast, and he could do something meaningful with the little he had left, or he could weaken and let it be extinguished without so much as a ripple. Just him, and Verena, and all the lies that were his life, buried with the dead man's dying brother.

He took a deep breath and said to the overseer, 'I will take the money.' As the man was about to speak, he added, 'But not from you.'

On the otherwise lush and green planet, the waterfall city was made of crystal and synthetics, its walls altering their translucency for optimal brightness at every moment of the day. The river that bordered it was the widest moving body of water on the continent, and the city perched on its banks like a hunter. At the horizon just a few miles downriver the ground disappeared entirely, plunging down a waterfall many miles high.

There were few metals here, but it was not all pale whiteness and glass. Drem walked at a slow pace, shooting the occasional glance at his companion. He was a notorious and feared man, the one surviving faction leader of the Guristas. Koroko Korasami. The Rabbit.

They walked through a central garden. The edges of its floor morphed from clear crystal to red brickwork paths, buffeting small fields of grass and woodland. The path they walked radiated warmth, picked up from the sun's shine through the crystal roof.

'You had no problems getting here?' Koroko asked. 'Some people, I'm told, find the ride down to be quite hellish.'

He was a tall man, angular and narrow in face as the Caldari could sometimes be, but with a relaxation of movement that indicated a supple ability to adapt and, Drem suspected, an unhesitant willingness to follow any action through to its very end. This was not a man to make an enemy of.

'No, I'm . . . used to rushing heedlessly into hell on my own,' Drem said, bringing out a brief burst of laughter in the man. 'And I trusted that your shuttle pilot knew what he was doing.'

Despite the gravitas of his presence, Koroko found this amusing. 'Trust is good,' he said, in a tone with an edge of darkness to it. 'And so is a willingness to visit strange places, do strange things.'

He stopped and looked around him, at the city's crystal spires high up in the air, and the planetary shielding beyond it. 'We built this city of strangeness together, my partner and I,' Koroko said. 'Those were better times.'

It had taken Drem some effort, but eventually he had convinced the colony overseer to request on his behalf an audience with the most powerful man of the Gurista.

'I'm informed you do excellent work,' Koroko said to him.

'So they tell me. It's hard for me to evaluate objectively,' Drem replied. Despite the Rabbit's nonchalant tone, Drem had no doubt the man had carefully studied the reports on his performance. Koroko made a point of being accessible to his people – at least more so than the Angel Cartel high command were, or the Blood Raiders for that matter – but gaining his audience had nonetheless been an honour that Drem took very seriously. He was a man of vicious intellect, and wasting his time would not be appreciated.

'I can understand that. As can I understand your reticence to accept what I'm informed was a generous offer on our behalf. Straddling two worlds isn't healthy in the long run. One commits, and one follows through.'

They passed a tall fountain shaped like a miniature version of the waterfall outside the city. Water cascaded over it, tumbling endlessly down. The entire place was quite modest, stamped with a simplicity of nature and order that seemed at odds with the Gurista lifestyle.

Koroko stepped off the brickwork path and on to the grass. He walked over to the fountain and extended a hand, filling his cupped palm with water that he drank with apparent relish. 'It's so unbearably clean. When we settled this place, the first thing we did was install a planetwide water purification network.'

'It didn't have the same vistas it does now, I suppose,' Drem said. He'd had a chance to see the planetary surface from the elevators. It was a gorgeous place, abundant in natural beauty; one of those miracles that revealed ever more of itself the closer one looked.

'It was barren. The whole thing was a toxic lump.'

Something about his tone of voice stopped Drem short. 'The whole planet?'

Koroko nodded.

Those lush forests, those great vistas of nature, all swam before Drem's eyes. 'You terraformed it,' he said in dawning amazement. 'From scratch.'

'We made it into what we wanted,' Koroko confirmed.

'Everything? Everything on the planet?'

'Not a tree grows here that we don't know about or expressly desire,' Koroko said, taking another sip of cool, clear water.

'You could have simply sectioned off this mass of land, cleaned it up,' Drem observed, less in challenge than to simply try to encompass the magnitude of what he was seeing.

'We could.'

'But you don't believe in half measures.'

'Never have.'

Everything in this place was ordered. Drem had spent a lot of time around man-made environments and recognized the patterns. It was amazing, such an opulence that it encapsulated everything there was around them. This man he had met did not need to decorate his world with baubles; he had made the world itself.

Drem took a deep breath and stepped on to the grass. 'I have a request to make.'

'I know,' Koroko said. 'And we can fulfil it. We may not, but it is a possibility.' He took another sip of the crystal water. 'So the Sisters aren't giving you all you need. You have ambition. That's good. I like ambition.'

'That's good to hear,' Drem said, wondering what devil's bargain this maker of worlds would offer him.

'I'll give you exactly what you want,' Koroko said. 'But I would like you to take an active role in Guristas tactical development. Help decide where we situate our people. How we perform certain operations. In its own way, it's not dissimilar to what you do for the Sisters.'

Drem listened, and thought carefully about his response. 'You know that we cannot affiliate ourselves with individual factions,' he said. 'Our relationship with you, as with all the others, has been carefully structured to preserve our integrity.'

'Which is why I am not asking the Sisters to come in and help save the lives of our men,' the Rabbit said. 'I am asking you.' He spoke in that same calm voice, that dulcet hum which slid through the ear and into the brain and coaxed it into believing that everything was safe and good and true.

'You want me to leave the Sisters?'

'Yes.'

'I don't think I can do that,' Drem said.

'Your mission with us would be to save every life you can. Since you have no affiliations, one pirate is the same as any other.' Koroko added, 'I would not make this offer to just anyone, but I have, in fact, made it to far more people than you may think. I am still intimately involved with the operation of my organization, and it's a foolish leader who can't talk to his own people.'

'Among which you'd like to count me,' Drem said.

'You have immense value, as you well know. It's called fulfilling one's potential, and I suppose it is. I see it as having a purpose and going for it. Not languishing in the mire of uncertainty and half-dreamt dreams. Allowing yourself to jump off the cliff with the knowledge that your fire will carry you on.' The man took another drink. 'You have drive. I recognize that, better than you can imagine.'

'I do,' Drem says. He realized he was getting thirsty.

'What do you say?'

This was the moment of truth, Drem realized. He could accept what this man wanted to give him, possibly even deal with the Blood Raider threat, maybe try to rebuild things with Verena, and . . . No. He could not. The time for temptations and distraction was over.

'I think,' he said, feeling like the river rushing headlong, 'I had better explain to you what truly drives me.'

The weeks he'd had to wait for this audience, he had spent wisely. He had thought over everything he'd learned, over and over again, revolving the facts in his mind as if they were sharp little diamonds.

His quest had been simple: to rid the world of capsuleers. Not merely the one he'd encountered all those ages ago, but every one of them. A purge of evil.

He had a good memory. He recalled not only the vast amounts of data he'd unearthed on the lives of capsuleers, but also what had been told to him back in the Sisters' training camp. About Angels, and Guristas. About Sansha's Nation. With the power he now held, it had been the work of only a few evenings to confirm those memories, and to dig a little deeper still.

To fulfil his goal, what he needed was enough tactical information for him to gain access to the capsuleers, sufficient funds to fuel whatever plan he came up with, and some piece or collection of technology that would allow him to eliminate them. It could have been simply a series of explosives set at strategic points, or a force of like-minded people armed with guns and a deadly, singular purpose, but the likelihood of being able to go after even a fraction of the total number of capsuleers before having the plan exposed rendered that kind of approach unworkable. He needed some piece of technology that wouldn't attract attention and could be made to work on all capsuleers, everywhere, simultaneously.

He believed he knew just the thing.

One series of searches on the well-documented field of capsuleers and capsuleering equipment revealed to Drem that while cloning facilities were practically impossible to infiltrate, they were not the sole location where capsuleers interfaced with non-capsule equipment that had direct access to their bloodstream. The disengagement chambers, where the pilots' capsules were brought for automated breaching after they'd docked at space stations, had all manner of monitoring equipment that ensured the capsuleers' safety during the process by plugging into the capsules and by extension into the capsuleers themselves. The sudden shock of disengagement from capsule systems required the pilot to have his basic physical processes under close monitoring, lest he suffer cardiac arrest or organ failure when spewed out of his pod, but the systems did not appear to conduct any kind of detailed analysis. Whether it was due to the capsuleers' possible drug use – a constant myth – or whatever else, these systems were a gateway into the pilots' bodies, but did not inspect them further than absolutely necessary.

In his conversation with the great man of the Guristas, Drem told him this fact. He also spoke of the Angel Cartel, whose vast information repositories would hold all manner of details on space stations, their inhabitants, security systems, designs and vulnerabilities; and of the Guristas, whose boundless wealth might be used to manufacture all manner of advanced hardware, not to mention buy, cheat and bribe a person's access through the myriad security layers of a space station, all the way from ground level to the top of the famous, the agents, the cream and the capsuleers. He told of his conversation with Terden, the lapsed agent of Sansha's Nation, whose technology was capable of spurring into action the greatest, most cataclysmic strike against capsuleers the world had ever known.

People could, in theory, be brainwashed through injections; and the capsuleers routinely found themselves at the mercy of a system that might do exactly this.

All it took was a test case. A single occurrence to be tried out, by Drem and potentially some trusted parties, to see if this could be made to work on a grand scale. One man, whose quarters they would sneak into and whose equipment they would alter, to hang back and watch as he started to follow their commands. One capsuleer, whom Drem would likely never meet in the flesh.

And if the test case worked . . .

A mental image took shape in both their minds. It included scores of people, hired or recruited, all positioned as repair workers at those top levels, entering the detachment chambers to quietly install the machinery under the auspices of general equipment checks.

And it concluded with the vision of tens, hundreds of thousands of pilots all coming out of their eggs, time and again, each time being injected with the usual cocktails of nutritional elements and adrenaline solutions, but now also with undetectable nanoagents that went to work on the very elements that dominated all their decisions; and each time being brought closer to the moment where at one command, every single one of them would get into their ship at last, fly it to some dark part of space, and in unison, like leaves on a tree in fall, quietly be extinguished for good and all.

After the test case. After the initial run. One man, selected by Drem, to be flown to his death.

He would find the one who had destroyed his colony, and he would make this man the catalyst for the greatest murders in recorded history.

They stood by the waterfall for a long time; Drem talking, Koroko asking the occasional question. He did drink, but it was in communion, not in obeisance.

At the end, the Rabbit said, 'You're being offered a safe haven, one where you can do your part in fighting against the very people who destroyed your family, and instead you're going ahead with a madman's plan.'

'That's the gist of it,' Drem said.

'What makes you think it hasn't been tried before?'

'You would have heard of it, for one. But basically, it's just too much data for anyone to even have thought of putting together. In my time with the Blood Raiders and then the Sisters of EVE, I've pored over thousands of records and reports that give up practically nothing to the casual observer. I have the trust of the people around me, including, hopefully, yourself. And the components are hard to line up. I don't see the pirate factions cooperating on something like this, least of all Sansha's Nation, with its armies of the mindless and the mad.'

'Speaking of components. You don't have the data you need, but you believe you can scrounge it up?'

'If you guarantee the funds I need, it can all be had. If not from the source that promised it, then from others who will take the money without question.' He thought of Hona, and those ghostly eyes in the living rock.

'And you haven't yet acquired this technology you described, though I've no doubt it exists. Do you intend to march into Sansha's open arms and ask him for it?'

Drem shrugged. If neither his reasoning nor his track record would work on this man, then there was nothing left to add. 'Yes,' he said.

For the first time, the leader of the Guristas seemed entirely amazed.

'I knew someone like you,' he said at last, in the quietness of the water and the rustle of trees.

Drem nodded.

'Guristas have money, from our idiot bravery. It costs us lives, but it brings more wealth than we know what to do with,' Koroko said, with a level of honesty Drem had not expected.

He returned it, and said, 'That's why I came here.'

Koroko nodded. He stared at the fountain for a while.

'There were two of us once,' he said. 'Idiot bravery, indeed. We broke free of a terrible place, weighed down with too much knowledge and injustice. Nobody should have been able to do what we did. Build a faction on a base of instinct, daring and fury. Take to the skies and beat the damn empires at their own game. It worked. It worked for a while.'

He sighed. 'Until the capsuleers ruined it all. The great unknown in any plan. The gods of terror and whim. We live in a world now that they have created, and it's a darker, colder, more dangerous place than I could ever have imagined. My people go up against them every hour of every day, and our losses are beyond description. Even with rescue pods and safety measures and whatnot, there's not a man in this faction who hasn't lost someone to a capsuleer. Including me.'

He turned to Drem, and in the calm of his voice and the infinite stare of his eyes, Drem saw something he recognized; a rage that, like Hona's, had brought this man through the wall of madness and out the other side. He did not appear calm because he was at peace; he appeared calm only because the eye could not bring into focus the grand and furious churning of his anger.

As if acknowledging a fellowship, Koroko nodded. 'You will have the funds when you need them. And whatever guarantees you require. There is one thing I want in return.'

'What is that?' Drem asked.

'Seal this deal by allowing me to shake the hand of the madman.'

Drem grinned. They grasped hands by the waterfall. Koroko's was still wet from the last drink he'd taken. 'And if, by some chance, you live through this, you will tell me how it all went.'

'I promise,' Drem said, before they left the garden of the Guristas.

13

The peaceable garden had sand, and water, and an arrangement of precious translucent stones whose inner crystallization reflected the light back and forth between them. There were benches also, set on little rises of grass.

A man sat on one of those benches. He was dressed in comfortable clothing, and his neck glistened with sweat. A cool breeze gently blew into the garden and the man leaned his head into it, eyes closed, a tremulous little smile on his face. A single drop of blood wove its way out of his nose and plunged silently into the ground below.

There was a crunch on gravel. The man kept his eyes shut, and his smile faded.

There was more crunching on gravel, from deeper into the garden. The man opened his eyes.

Two Gallentean women approached him. The one further away had a tight look, as if she were armouring herself against the peace in the garden, wanting to engage with it rather than absorb it. The one closer to him, however, looked much more at ease, and even had a faint smile on her lips. He did not know whether the smile was real, but then, he didn't know much at all about what was real any longer, except the choices he had made.

The one closer to him sat down on the bench beside him, at a distance just sufficient to respect his personal sphere. She said, 'I am Ralea.'

'Hello Ralea. I'm Tarn,' he said. His voice came out as a whisper, and he cleared his throat.

The other one, the one with the tight face, sat down on the grass in front of him, pulled her knees half to her chest and crossed her arms over it. 'I'm Heci,' she said.

'Hello Heci,' he replied.

'You fucked up,' Heci said.

'I know,' he said.

'I haven't grown up with Mind Clash the way you natives have, but I've watched plenty of matches on holovid, and even I could see that you fucked up.'

He nodded. There was little else to say.

'What happened?' Ralea said. The breeze blew her scent to him, and he felt suddenly self-conscious of his sweat, as if its reek might give away how he felt.

He looked up at the sky, which was a fading icy blue. 'You should not be here,' he said, without rancour. 'This is the peaceable yard, where players can retreat to empty their minds before matches, and meditate afterwards on our losses.' Guilt passed over his face, then was hidden away. 'It's a sanctum. No Caldari would stalk in here like you two did.'

'These are strange times,' Heci said to him. She was rocking a little back and forth on the grass, he noticed. 'Do you know who we are?'

'I've heard your names mentioned once or twice. You're the team backers.'

Ralea said, gently, 'You do know that the loss back there, the one you suffered quite to everyone's surprise, has cost us dearly.'

'Yes.'

'Us and the rest of your team,' she said.

'Yes.'

'What the hell happened?' Heci asked.

He leaned his head down. The breeze stroked his hair.

'I lost,' he said.

'Why?' Ralea asked. He looked at her entirely too quickly, then looked away, trying to make it seem like he'd been planning to look elsewhere all along.

'I don't know,' he said.

'Gods,' Heci said. She looked at Ralea. 'He's like you were, back when we started.'

He didn't like the tone of that.

Ralea looked directly into his eyes. He found himself hoping she would see something in there, so he could justify telling the truth.

Ralea said, 'The coach'll be ready for you when you leave the haven. However long it takes. You two will need to talk.'

He nodded. 'I'm . . . sorry.'

Heci said, 'We've been in charge of this team for, what . . . how long, Ralea?'

'We've been effective owners for the good part of a season,' Ralea said. 'I wouldn't say we're in charge.'

'It's funny . . . I don't recall ever seeing you,' he ventured.

Ralea told him, 'You wouldn't have. Getting into the State, setting up the deal, establishing ourselves as your secret backers . . . it's been a lot of quiet, careful business. You're one of the few Caldari we've spoken to who wasn't covered by a nondisclosure agreement. Most of your teammates probably don't even believe we exist.'

'But we call the shots,' Heci said, looking at him again. 'I know this game pretty well. And the State. You people are a marvel, I have to hand that to you.'

She glared at him. 'You fucked up,' she repeated.

'I don't know what to tell you,' he said, which was true. 'If I collect my thoughts a bit, talk to the coach, I may be able to piece it together. Right now all I can see is that form he called up, bearing down on me.' *And the blood spurting out of my nose*, he thought.

'Tarn, do you know what we did in our old lives?' Ralea asked him.

He thought that was an odd way to put it, but assumed they meant they were acclimatizing to Caldari life. For a couple of foreigners who'd just barged into the peaceable garden, they weren't doing too good a job.

She said to him, 'We were mission agents. We worked with capsuleers.'

That raised the hairs on his neck. 'You what?'

'We spent a long time dealing with people whose wealth and power rivals that of the empires, whose armies span thousands, and who *can't ever die*. So we're used to bluffing with the best. And you,' Ralea said, laying a hand unhesitantly on his sweaty shoulder, 'are trying to bluff through the fact that you went in there and threw the game.'

He stiffened up, and tried to hide it. 'That is not an accusation you make to a Caldari.'

'You're right,' Ralea went on, in the same calm tone. 'It's an accusation we make to a Mind Clash player on our payroll who just played what should have been an easy win in an important match—'

'—and fucked it up colossally at the last second,' Heci finished.

'I don't know why you think I'd betray my teammates, but that's not how life works in the State. I've worked hard to get here. I stand by what I believe and who I am.'

'Liar,' Heci said.

'Hey, look—'

'We just want to know,' Ralea said, shooting her friend a quick look, 'if there's anything we can do for you. No more accusations, and nothing that leaves this garden.'

He didn't tell her. He *could* have told her – which unnerved him no end – but he didn't say a word. He knew they couldn't prove a thing.

They sat there for a while, then got up and thanked him for his time.

The Caldari State was composed solely of corporate factions, run by a man who'd instigated a worker's revolt to effectively *improve* those factions. In Caldari, as anyone there would gladly admit, the State was not the people; the people were the State.

Ash had spoken true. His directions had led the two women to an ailing team that possessed good players but was in desperate need of backers. Through intermediaries, Ralea and Heci had offered them funding in exchange for various complicated rights that were not quite ownership – perish the thought that a Gallentean could get so involved in a Caldari business – but nonetheless, once the influx of money helped the team get back on track, evolved into a secret dominance. For all intents and purposes, they now owned and ran a Mind Clash team. As Gallenteans they would not have found themselves welcome in the Caldari State – the two nations had been at war, one way or another, for most of recorded history – but as faceless, expatriate entities whose identity was measured in money and red tape, they fitted right in.

Mind Clash was another reflection of the State. Competition was a way of life with the Caldari, a direct reflection of State philosophy and a convenient, non-militaristic outlet for the aggression it engendered among its people. While Clashes could be vicious, the competitors never came into physical contact. Matches consisted of two opponents sitting across from one another in an amphitheatre, both of them enveloped in monitoring chambers that pierced their heads and monitored various sections of their brain activity. Their very minds would battle it out overhead, struggling for dominance in ways too complex for the layman to understand. Translation algorithms monitored this activity and rendered it into understandable, if intangible shapes, which subtle light equipment then projected in massive forms overhead, fighting like gods taken form.

The game was not who you were but what you could represent. A clashing of images. It was quintessential Caldari. If there was any way to get into their mindset, and to start getting the feel of working for a cause, Ralea had been certain it was here.

Of course, as it turned out, it hadn't all been abstract ideals. Ralea and Heci had managed to stay faceless and silent for a while, but eventually there came along dangers whose effects could not be ignored. Like cheating, or drug use; or that other Caldari staple, the one that came along with sports as certainly as victory and loss: gambling.

The city was a beehive, locked and structured into compartments that themselves resolved into smaller sections, all with sublevelled chambers that made the outsider feel as if the smallest unit might hold a city of its own.

Not all parts of the metropolis were like this. Some areas were almost blank: covered over with a transparent shield that looked down on nothing but rocks, sand, stone and the odd circle of grass. As for the rest there seemed, to Ralea's outsider eyes, no difference between a business district and a leisure one, just as she would be hard-pressed to judge the function of individual buildings from their construction alone. It was clear that just as much thought had gone into the aesthetics of buildings as into the peaceable gardens.

Ralea and Heci angled their way past right corners, walked down streets straight as lines, and eventually found themselves in front of a building indistinguishable from its neighbours. It had shaded glass walls mounted on metal scaffolding, and rose at least thirty storeys high.

Once they'd gone inside and travelled thirteen floors up, they found the corridors were all of metal and glass. The cubicle walls glimpsed in the distance had felt shading not unlike the grey windows of buildings. Even at this level, Ralea felt she was walking through, if not the streets below, then a replica in miniature. Conformity and equality were hand in hand, all the way down.

They wove their way through the angular maze, following little plaques tactfully fitted into the walls.

Their subject sat at his desk in an office walled with glass, several vidcasts hovering in front of him. Ralea knocked and entered, Heci following.

'The two Gallenteans,' he said to them with a smile that looked entirely genuine. 'You humble me. Welcome.'

'Thanks for having us,' Ralea said as they took their seats.

Heci looked around and said, 'What is it you do in this building?'

He waved a hand. 'Administration.'

'Big business,' Heci said.

'The Caldari State *is* big business.'

'That's a lot of vids you have,' Ralea said. 'I peeked into a few offices on my way here. Didn't see that many vidcasts. Not on the thirteenth floor.'

The man gave her the bashful shrug of those with greater fortune than they would ever care to admit.

She continued, 'I know we didn't state our purpose when asking for this appointment, so we're grateful you were willing to see us.'

'It's my pleasure to serve,' the man said. His tone was calm and confident; free of obsequiousness or arrogance, and shorn of any emotion that might commit his words to an interpreted meaning. 'Though I'm not sure what I can do for you.'

Ralea said, 'We are shadow backers of a Mind Clash team. We've been in charge of this team for a while now.' She leaned in, spoke in a more serious tone, 'We keep our eyes open, sir. Took over as investors after the team got into financial straits, so we're used to keeping an eye on the money. We know how the business works – and it *is* a business. That's why we're here.'

'I don't follow,' he said, with the same open, expressionless face.

'One of our players threw a match, a couple weeks back,' Heci said. 'We looked into his finances, which were clean on the surface but turned out to be a little grubby underneath. Payments that shouldn't have been made. Which led us to you.'

The man stood up swiftly, walked away from them and faced the window of his office. Had it been on the top floor they might have overlooked one of the peaceable yards, but all that could be seen here was the mirroring windows of the skyscraper across the street.

'I had nothing to do with this,' he said. He put his hands in his pockets and gently rolled back and forth on his feet.

Ralea and Heci shared a look. So that was how it was. He needed to be drawn.

Heci said, 'Is that why you're only on the thirteenth floor, then? Stuck in the middle, looking at other people's windows.'

He stopped rolling.

'No extra-curricular income, and clearly a stalled rise in the corporate ladder,' Ralea said.

He turned to them, and there was a glint in his eyes.

When Heci added, 'Also, your hair's going grey,' he let out an explosive laughter.

'All right,' he said, taking a seat. 'All right. Yes. I know who you are, and I know who you're talking about.'

'Name him, please,' Ralea said.

'His name is Tarn, and he's in a lot of trouble.'

'How can we help out?'

'You can't,' the broker said. The women began to speak, but he raised his hands, palms outward. 'I wish you could. I do. But that's not how it works in the State. Gambling is as much a part of our life here as competition is, and competition is *very* much part and parcel of the State. But one's allowed and the other is not, at least in Tarn's own case. If you make any attempts to help this player you will have to reveal what he did. You do that, you'll ruin his honour and reputation.'

'I thought you had changed after the revolution,' Heci said.

'We have, in countless ways. Everything was turned upside down. But we're still Caldari, and our values are the same.'

'So we'll just sit back and watch him torpedo his games, is that it?' Heci said.

'Nobody said he'd thrown a game,' the broker replied.

'We saw him take a dive that—'

'I can't tell you if he threw it or not,' he interjected. 'I am not the person who decides these things. I am an intermediary. If people want to gamble, they come to me. If they owe money and need to work out a deal, they also come to me. Most of the time I don't know what they're asked to do in return, and I'm happy to keep it that way. I relay commands to them, sight unseen, and leave it at that.'

He looked at their angry expressions and added, 'What I *can* tell you is that asking someone to throw a game in the Caldari State is a serious, serious request. It was that way under the old guard and has remained so after Heth took power. If my contact had told your man to do it, they wouldn't do it often, and it would not be intended to ruin your team. Our angle is the sea of money that flows past the game, and not the sport itself.'

Heci attemped to ask something, but Ralea briefly laid a hand on her shoulder and said, 'How can we be assured he won't throw any more games?' Before the answer could be provided, Heci shot her a glance of surprise – the question was obviously meaningless – but Ralea had decided that they were done here. There was something very wrong about the whole setup, and it reached further than the amiable face in front of them.

The man fixed them with his most meaningless Caldari smile and said, 'You can't. Nor will you ever know if it was by our request.'

They had good seats, high over the arena. As team managers they could have placed themselves closer to the fight, but non-Caldari in the front rows would attract too much attention, particularly during this match.

The susurrus of the place belied a throbbing excitement. The Caldari rarely went overboard in expressing their emotions – not unless they were invading sovereign planets, Ralea thought with a little grimace – but someone attuned to their ways could nonetheless sense those emotions churning beneath the surface.

The auditorium was an amphitheatre, its seats arranged in concentric circles that surrounded a central platform. Around the theatre, on massive screens that blocked out a good deal of the sky, corporate recruitment ads rolled in an infinite loop. Every now and then they were replaced by the image of Tibus Heth and his consorts, under an advertising banner that called on the citizenry to join the Caldari Navy.

In one part of the auditorium, near the stage, a particular section of seats stood empty. Ralea enjoyed watching those seats, which merely looked like they were waiting for some unorganized latecomers bearing food and overflowing drinks. They had no protection, but none should be needed: every attendee at this exhibition match had been carefully vetted, weapons-checked and bioscanned.

The ads cycled overhead. 'Amazing how they're willing to commit themselves,' Ralea murmured to Heci.

Her friend nodded. 'Not like they have other options. If you don't go full-out, turn to a cell in the body of a corporation, then you're not a Caldari.'

'Makes you wonder what they're missing by not having other perspectives.'

'Nothing they'd want to . . . oh, here we go.'

The authority was arriving. Not the fighters themselves, for whom a special entrance ceremony awaited, but the highest-ranking members of the audience. The government of Tibus Heth.

Several leaders of his consortium approached their seats, as did representatives of various megacorps. The last entry was the man himself, Heth – tall, fit and grey-haired, walking to his seat with a confident gait. They sat in unison.

Ralea brought out her quick-zoom binocs, grateful to be Gallentean. The other Caldari were giving their leader passing glances, but did not dare to look at him directly, lest their stares be judged uncouth.

Heth looked alert but entirely at ease, as befitted a warlord secure in his position. His grey hair was neatly cropped and his beard well-trimmed. The suit he wore, a traditional military garb, fitted him well. Not once did he betray an expression other than intense, restrained interest in whatever was occurring in that moment. Ralea, who had looked into the eyes of countless madmen, could not imagine sitting across the table from this man.

She shifted focus to his companions. There were no megacorp CEOs that she could recognize, though this was likely not intended as an insult to Heth, but rather so they wouldn't be drawing the limelight from him. They had clearly sent their representatives, in pairs or triads, each small group dressed in the same exact fashion according to corporate standards.

One pair was notable if only for their difference: a short man who kept looking in different directions, as if taking in his surroundings; and a tall, slightly pudgy man, with scars on his shaven head, who sat entirely still. Now and then the short man shot a word to the tall one. Ralea wondered whether he was saying anything funny. Humour – overt humour, at least – didn't seem a big part of State life.

There was a hush in the hall. An utter hush. In the Federation there'd be deafening noise, and she imagined that in the Amarr Empire and Minmatar Republic there'd at least be some shouting and catcalling from opposing team supporters across the halls.

She removed the binocs and stared at the empty stage. A little knot in her stomach reminded her that this was Tarn's first fight after his recent loss.

There was something wrong about the whole thing, the dive and the aftermath both. It was like that little man's whisper to his friend: unsubtle. In this world of quiet, careful consideration – not concern, but forethought and analysis – where everyone had their place and their rules and their retentive little goals, that kind of emerging pattern unsettled her.

The hush turned to a dead quiet. The players walked on to the stage.

They took their places on each side of a dais, their chambers a stone's throw from one another. Above their heads a cloud formed; not precipitation but interference, as if from a broken hologram.

Lights dimmed in the hall, leaving only the two Mind Clash participants. A voice boomed from loudspeakers, saying, 'Fight true and strong.' That was it; not even an acknowledgement of Tibus Heth's presence.

The game began.

The clouds remained amorphous but took on a solidified essence, as if they were congealing. The monitors overhead – vast, dark things – showed them in much greater detail, highlighting the neon-lit lines that had started to form inside their bodies like veins in a developing embryo.

Tarn's cloud suddenly changed, its tendrilled curves straightening, its corners forming right angles. It morphed into an MTAC with huge – Ralea peered at the monitors – *gigantic* autocannons that by rights should be fitted on a frigate. The opponent's cloud did the same, changing to an attack hovercraft mounted with lasers. They hovered towards each other in an elongated slow motion, as if they were travelling great distances.

Once the MTAC was close enough, its guns began to fire. Great neon bursts tore from its weapons and hit the hovercraft, which swerved around to try and avoid the assault. The craft's own laser guns fired, red and blue mottled rays that sliced into the MTAC's hulk and nearly brought it to its knees.

The MTAC morphed again, into a gigantic bird in flight. It rose up, high above Tarn's head, in clear preparation for a dive on to the other player's figure, which had lost its outlines and was taking on a new form.

Ralea blinked, rubbed her eyes. The halogen lines from the monitors were giving her a headache. She looked into the darkness instead, letting her eyes rest on the audience's ghostly outlines. The fight wouldn't be done for a while, and she wanted to give more thought to the issues Tarn was facing.

They had spoken far too freely with her, all of them. Someone was in debt, certainly – the broker they'd interviewed was clearly involved – but she had a feeling it wasn't Tarn. He'd been reluctant to talk, and clearly held something back, but it didn't seem to be anything that was eating him from inside. Tiring and worrying him, absolutely, but Ralea had met people consumed by guilt, and Tarn didn't have that faraway look they did: the one that said whatever hells existed in the afterlife, they had created their own on this plane, behind those glassy eyes.

The gambling was just too obvious, she thought. The intermediary they'd met had been entirely too confident, which could mean he really did not know anything about his shadow employers, or that he knew he had no identifiable ties to them. Which, in turn, meant they were big. A little too big to have a Mind Clash player throw his game solely to recoup money. It lacked finesse. There was that word again, cropping up in her mind. *Unsubtle.*

The winged monsters changed again, Tarn on the initiative as usual. His animal had been attacked viciously by the other player's, but he'd let it go to pieces, its individual parts all morphing into an army of small ant-like insects. It took a remarkable amount of control to maintain a swarm like that, and Ralea wondered again why this man had thrown his last fight so sloppily.

She turned on the binocs' infrared and scanned the crowd. They were enraptured, either craning their necks up to stare unblinking at the monitors, or peering at the players down below. Heth's crowd was watching intently; or most of them, at least.

Ralea blinked. She refocused on Heth's people, drew a bead on the short and tall guys she'd seen earlier. The talker and the bald, scarred head. The tall guy seemed fairly interested, but the short one had an odd look on his face. It seemed insufferably smug to Ralea – an anomaly with the Caldari – but tense nonetheless. He was worried about something.

She passed the binocs to Heci and told her where to look.

'Now there's someone hoping he won't eat shit,' she said, passing the binocs back.

Tarn had gained a clear upper hand with the swarm, and now pulled them all back into a massive bullish figure, some animal that seemed to be moulded out of pure muscle and sinew. He drew back, giving the other player scant time to refocus before charging the bull at him.

When they clashed a sigh arose from the audience, and Ralea realized that the tremor she was feeling in the floor came from everyone around her quietly tapping their feet in excitement.

Surprisingly, the opponent's figure, while dazed, didn't seem as exhausted as it should have been from that kind of impact. It got up and rushed Tarn, nearly goring his bull with the first swipe of its horns. Tarn gracefully avoided its attack and had his bull do a swift, close-contact attack to the enemy's flank, tearing out a piece that did not bleed but *scattered*, as if the animal were made of phosphorescent confetti.

This was the endgame. Tarn should have it; but his initial attack had been too weak, and his reaction to the opponent's counter hadn't provided the finishing blow. Strength had failed; so endurance would now carry the victor.

Tarn's own creature was too slow to prevent the opponent from goring an even larger piece from its backside, and it lost a leg in the process. While Tarn swiftly tried to morph a replacement, the enemy attacked his creature head-on and nearly knocked it over. Down on the stage Tarn himself visibly reeled from the assault. The crowd gasped.

Ralea stole a glance at the short man. Same smug look, but he seemed a little more relaxed now.

Tarn pulled himself together, on stage and in the Clash. The next time his opponent charged he stepped away again, but this time he morphed, the bull's mass springing into the air and turning into a wave of spikes, like a carpet inset with arrowheads, which engulfed the charging mass and instantly tightened around him. In the silence of the hall the other player's choked reaction could be heard to the rafters, and as he scrambled to change his form, Tarn tightened his own, squeezing hard and adding more mass to his carpet as it shrunk in diameter. There was the soundless crunch of bone as the carpet clearly enveloped the other animal's legs and snapped them to pieces, then its back, and finally, after an endless moment, its neck.

The other player fell to his knees, shaking his head viciously as if to dislodge a splinter. Tarn removed his own sensory helmet and waved to the crowd, which was still immobile in amazement.

Before the lights could be turned on, Ralea took one last look through the binocs. The short man was staring at the competitors, gaping in wide-eyed shock. He looked like he was going to vomit.

And then the lights came on, and the mass of people stood up to clap and roar in restrained but enthusiastic approval, and the short man clapped harder than anyone in the hall, and Ralea knew they had their man.

'I don't think I'm going to last in this place,' Heci said.

They were in their own peaceable garden. There was no breeze here, only sunlight shining through the transparent dome above.

Ralea, sitting barefoot on a bench, stroked a toe through the sand, leaving a trail, then let the sole of her foot swing back over, erasing it. 'I'm not sure I will, either.'

'I don't begrudge any of the time we've spent on the road. I hadn't taken leave in years, and you and I both were on the verge of self-destruction. I'm glad we did this.'

'So am I.' Ralea stroked her toe through the sand again. 'But it's not a permanent leave for you. Is it?'

Heci blushed. 'No,' she said in a low tone. 'I don't think it is.'

'You really still want to continue being an agent?'

'I don't know. But I haven't found anything else that suits me. I know that if I go back I won't get into too much trouble. You're locked out, but my track record is pretty spotless aside from having been on the run with you, and there's ways to get around that if you've got the money and connections I have. I can go back mostly without repercussions.'

The sun cast shadows through the branches of trees, and they stretched their sinewy tendrils out over the ground.

'Do you want to stay here?' Heci asked.

She thought this over.

'I don't know. Probably not. But I haven't found what I'm looking for.'

'Do you think it exists?'

Ralea sighed. 'I'm honestly not sure. I feel like ... I have this set of talents. And a drug-free head at last. I would have thought there'd be somewhere in New Eden that I could start anew, but there really doesn't seem to be anywhere I fit in. All I see is the cracks. Half our players here are using drugs, one of our stars is involved in some bizarre gambling scheme, and I'll be damned if Heth's man isn't a part of this whole mess as well.'

She took a deep breath. 'They're a driven people, but I don't think they have any idea where they're going. They just need to be better than anyone else. I let go of that attitude when I left the agency.'

'We all need a cause. A proper one, with meaning outside ourselves,' Heci said.

'Maybe. Seems when they find one, they invade planets.'

'There is that.'

'This isn't what I was looking for,' Ralea said. 'I want to run *to*, not run from. I want to help people, somehow.'

She put a hand on Heci's shoulder. 'And I'd like you to be with me. But I won't force you to.'

Heci traced her own line in the sand. 'We're going to stay together for a little while longer. I'm not quite ready yet. But it's getting, slowly, to be good and done.'

The sun shone on them now, bright but not too warm. The stone bench felt cool against the touch.

'There's something else,' Heci said. 'We're beginning to get noticed here, too. Getting involved with Caldari politics is serious stuff. If it goes wrong, it will get some people back home very agitated, and you can believe they'll come gunning for us. For you, mostly.'

'I can't go back. They'll lock me up,' Ralea said.

'We'll figure it out,' Heci said, and put an arm around her friend's shoulder. 'Anyway. Fuck it! More pressing problems right now. What're we going to do about the team?' she said. 'If I'm going to enjoy my time here properly, I want to get some decent use out of them.'

Ralea eyed her. 'Meaning?'

'Oh, you know. They're nice, big boys. Have you been in the locker rooms?'

'Oh my god . . .'

'Hey, just because I have needs—'

'You can't sleep with our players!'

'Not even the fallback Clasher?'

'Not even the fallback Clasher.'

'Have you *seen* his hands?'

Ralea gave her a look of disgust that didn't quite disguise her amusement. 'Let me be absolutely clear with you on – Heci, look at me. Stop grinning and look at me. Thank you. Let me be clear on this. You are not – emphatically not – sleeping with our sports team. All right? I know more about you than they do. This is a rigid culture. You will break those people.'

'Oh, I won't go that hard—'

'*No.*'

They snickered, and fell silent, letting the sun warm their bare feet.

'So, the Caldari,' Heci continued. 'What do you really think about this place?'

Ralea sighed, leaned back on the bench and stared out at the sand and the stone and the grass. 'They have a meritocracy now. Tibus Heth gave them that. Organization. A drive to do something good in this life.'

'But.'

'But the individual simply disappears. No one person makes a difference; it's all collective work. So they're constantly unwilling to risk themselves for a cause that's important to them as human beings, as persons, rather than something that they were taught should matter. People use others here, playing on their ideals and the ban on questioning them.'

'Is that what Tarn did? Get played?'

Ralea shook her head. 'I don't think so. Or if he did, it's at a far different level than we thought at first.'

'You think he's going to come out of it OK?'

Ralea thought about it for a while.

'No,' she said at last. 'I don't think he will.'

Tarn did not show up for the next practice, nor the one after that. Turned out that nobody had seen or heard of him after the exhibition match.

And then the two women were summoned to Heth's court.

A personal hovercar, tinted and unmarked, picked them up at their homes. The route took them to the other side of the city, but the journey didn't take long. The car's driver – a real one, not an AI entity – seemed to have preferential lane access. This annoyed Ralea. Heci was completely fine with it.

'About time we get a little special treatment,' Heci said. She leaned over from her soft leather seat and pinched Ralea in the side. 'Let go of equality just for once, all right? And don't think about how horribly this will fuck us with the Federation.'

The car stopped in front of a tall building surrounded by guards and automated security equipment. One of those guards escorted them in and directed them to the elevators, where another pair of guards waited. The elevator went to the top.

The room was large with an amazing view of the mountains in the distance.

Tibus Heth stood there to greet them.

'Genuine pleasure to meet the people behind one of our most promising Mind Clash teams,' he said, and they knew he was lying. Intensity came off the man in waves, as did a militaristic guile that immediately put the women on their guard.

'It's an honour to meet you, sir,' Heci said, in the absence of a comment from Ralea. 'What can we do for you?'

'Your player, Tarn. What's he been up to?'

Ralea hesitated before speaking. The mere fact that the leader of the Caldari State was taking time off for a couple of Gallentean ex-agents meant that this was serious business, and his knowledge of Tarn's name did not bode well for the player.

'He's been one of our best guys, for the most part,' Heci said. 'Though he's fallen off the radar for some reason, so perhaps you could tell us more about his most recent activities. Sir.'

Heth regarded her with impassive distaste. He was clearly not a man who suffered sarcasm lightly.

Ralea reminded herself that despite her growing distaste for all things Caldari, it was a personal one, coloured by a very subjective view, and under the circumstances it could possibly get her killed. She decided to try some subtle flattery. 'I'm worried about him,' she said to Heth. 'I think he's in trouble, and the fact that we're in the office of one of the most powerful men in the universe doesn't help my nerves. If you do know something about him, sir, please share it. If we can help him in any way, we will.'

Heth gave a tight little smile. 'I'd like your opinions on the game I watched, the exhibition match. Do you believe it was rigged?'

Ralea blinked, and locked gazes with Heci, who seemed equally confused by the turn in conversation. She said, 'For Tarn to win? No, sir. He fought fiercely.'

'That he did,' Heth said. 'Though he did flag a little, near the fight's end. You don't think he was exhausted?'

Heci weighed in. 'I think he was roping the other player in. Giving him a false sense of confidence.'

'Is he good at that?' Heth asked in some apparent sly amusement. 'Roping people in?'

'He doesn't do it often, but yes, someone at his level is perfectly capable of bluffing.'

'Good. Good. That's good to hear.'

Ralea had to ask. 'Sir, what—'

'Observe.' Heth nodded towards a large monitor, which

automatically turned on. Ralea realized this room, which seemed empty, must be under constant surveillance.

The monitor showed a man. Not Tarn, to Ralea's immediate relief. It was the short guy from the exhibition match, the one whose reactions had swerved from glee to mortal shock.

'Your man threw a match, not too long ago. This person—,' Heth indicated the figure on the screen, '—profited greatly from that loss. Do you know him?'

'He's on your staff. I remember him,' Ralea said.

Heth nodded. 'He was one of my trusted advisers. Still is.' He let his gaze linger on the image for a second, then turned to them. 'Seems Tarn got himself into trouble, found it necessary to throw a match. My adviser, who is an inveterate gambler, found out about this before the fact and decided to place a sizeable bet, one from which he profited nicely. When he was told, by the same sources who controlled the first fight, that Tarn was also going to throw the exhibition match – in full view of the State leader, no less – he made another bet, this one much too grand. He is having the hardest time hiding the loss from me.'

Ralea looked at those steely eyes. It was as if she could see the gears slowly turning behind them. She heard herself say, 'You knew. You were in on this all along.'

Heth said, 'As an outside party. Do you know much about Tarn, beyond his ascent in the sport?'

Ralea looked at Heci, who shook her head. 'Can't say we do. Caldari keep very much to themselves.'

Heth smiled at this, another thin line. 'Yes, we do, don't we? Tarn, for instance, is not very sympathetic to my rule. In fact, you might even call him a rebel. He disapproves of my efforts to improve the State from the inside out, and has allied himself with like-minded people. Apparently they believed that getting a financial chokehold on one of my advisers would prove beneficial to them, as if I didn't pay attention to the lives of the people I supposedly trust.'

Ralea, reeling from this, could only think to say, 'What if Tarn had lost? At the exhibition match.'

'There are other matches. I'm sure my man would have been

induced to keep betting. Once you start the avalanche,' he said, his eyes masking whatever was behind them, 'there really is no going back.'

'What do you want from us?' Heci said. Ralea heard the terror in her voice.

'If you were Caldari citizens, I would simply have you interrogated. As you're not, I would like you to consent to a short debriefing, coupled with a lie-detecting test. You will be asked questions related solely to this matter, and your answers will help determine the eventual fate of your friend.' Heth seemed to note the disgust on their faces. 'Merits count in my State. People are expected to take responsibility for their failures.'

'What's going to become of Tarn?' Ralea asked.

'I don't know. First we have to find him,' Heth answered.

She stared at him. 'You don't know where he is either?'

'No. But we are going to find out.'

She had to say it. 'And your adviser, what happens to him? How does he take responsibility for his actions?'

'Oh, I'm keeping him on, of course,' Heth said, and this time his smile was genuine. 'They've only just sunk their claws into him. A ruler must have a source to one's enemies, if only to feed them the right lies.'

The two women were speechless. Ralea took a deep, slow breath, tried to think of something to say, and felt something tiny and fragile break apart inside her. This was how life was here. There was no fighting it. She could only resolve to get out as soon as she could with a minimum of damage.

In a deceptively casual and perfectly amiable tone, Heth added, 'As for you two, once you walk out this door and complete the debriefing, you are relieved of your command. The shadow backing to your team will be up for bid in the private sector. If a bid fails, the government will take it over. The team will be taken care of. And you two will be transported back to the Gallente Federation, where I believe some people will want to question you over a murder.'

*

After the interrogation, which was quiet and painless, the two women were returned to their quarters. They were given a little time to pack, to make a few calls and sign off on their business. They did not panic. Their sole alternative to returning home was tenuous and risky, and panic was not going to help.

During her preparations, Ralea found a note in the team's peaceable garden. It was addressed to her and Heci.

Tarn hadn't been located. His home was empty, his accounts untouched. He'd disappeared completely.

The note, unsigned, simply said, *can't ever die*. Whether he'd escaped or died, she would never know.

Everyone was equal here, or at least had the opportunity to be at the cost of everything they were. And at the apex of this kingdom of equality sat a man who made it all work, planning which souls to grind in the blackened gears of this great and terrible machine.

Ralea tore apart the note and placed each piece under a separate stone. Then she made a few more calls, including an encrypted one to a trusted friend.

After they were done, Heth's men escorted them out of the premises, to the interstellar airport and eventually up to the orbiting station in the skies above. The journey took some time, but once they made it to the station, into the hangars, and through the final security checks, they were left to their own devices, armed only with directives to a Federation flight. One of the men warned them that any attempts to book different flights under their given names, or to make any large transactions while en route, would be caught and dealt with accordingly.

Federation agents would be waiting for them at home. Not for arrests, not right away – agents were holy beasts – but for direct and definite questioning, and the eventual due process of law.

Ralea stood alone in the great hall of the station hangars. She kept an eye on the viewports in the distance, watching great ships slowly hovering in to dock. Built into the floor right next to her was a great tree that stretched its limbs narrow and high, as if it had been an arrow shot into the ground by a giant. It was the only tree of its kind in this part of the hangar. She gently stroked a hand over its rough bark.

A man stopped by and checked his datapad. 'You a friend of Neko?' he said to himself, keeping his eye on the datapad's screen.

Ralea kept looking out the viewports. 'Yeah,' she said. 'Heading for the Minmatar exodus.'

The man scratched his chin, looked towards the sky for a moment as if trying to remember something, then consulted his datapad again. 'Gate four eighty-seven, ten minutes. You're sisters, Hera and Karleena Detkow.'

Ralea kept a straight face at this, but her eyes gave away a little smile. 'Thank you.'

'Be safe,' the man said, and slowly walked away.

Ten minutes later, as they boarded the shuttle, Ralea murmured to Heci, 'I wonder why Heth's guys didn't follow this through.'

Heci replied, 'We're out of his jurisdiction now, but the Federation wouldn't have sent people all the way here just to pick us up. It's no concern of his if we get lost on the way. It'll be egg on the Federation's face. I don't think he'd mind.'

'I wonder if I should feel thankful,' Ralea said, taking her seat on the shuttle.

'Generally grateful, maybe. But not to him,' Heci told her. 'Let's hope things go better in the Minmatar Republic. Because the stakes just got higher.'

14

The cracks showed in the dusty, soot-streaked floor, all of them covered with the glittering sealant. Asber idly kicked at one, felt his toe bounce off the translucent cement. That was all they did here when something tore open: pour sealant over it until it stuck fast.

Asber had lived most his life on this moon, breathing its dust and working on the banks of its molten rivers. The moon circled an uninhabitable, useless planet that was not even good for the lowest level of terraform, and was itself in slow elliptical orbit around the burning sun. Winters were hard here, taking away even the heat of the sky and turning the mercury from liquid to sludge. It was winter now. Asber felt cold, but he always felt cold.

In his hands he held repair equipment, and in front of him was a sifting unit supposedly capable of taking in liquid mercury and asteroid ore and turning it into something valuable. Asber understood how the machine worked, as a man would after having worked with machines like this for decades. Fixing it was a process that demanded patience, skill, and the ability to withstand the touch of hot metal skittering over worn skin.

He needed to do this uninterrupted, so he had brought the thing over to the landing area. It was empty and vast there, with nothing but a scattering of low buildings surrounding the berths where ships would be drydocked on arrival. If he dropped a wrench, it would land with a clang that would fade out before it could echo.

At the back of his mind was the pleasant, false hope that he'd see a ship coming in, full of salvage or ore that was ready to be worked on. He wouldn't be the first to spot it – sensors would bring the harvesting crowds long before the landing ship could arrive – but he would have a good seat, if it landed in any of the docks next to where he had put down his gear.

In truth it wasn't so much the expectation of a landing that had drawn him to this place, but the quiet, bittersweet pleasure of the expectancy itself. Sitting by the docks Asber felt connected to the invisible waves beyond them, and through them to the worlds they contained. Whether or not they washed anything up on these dusty shores was not important – a lie, but the mind, given time, was remarkably good at reducing anything so utterly vital to a forgettable detail – merely that they held, in their potential, everything there could be. It was a religion of nothingness; of the liquid river and the dust in the air and the broken machine.

He pulled out a few pieces of the sifting unit, inspected them, then used a cleaning cloth to dislodge some of the grime. The cloth, almost as grey as the dusty floor, was supposed to absorb and extrude the crud, but had long since given up and merely took it in. There was nowhere else for the grime to be put. Everything turned grimy here, in the end.

A faint rumble caught his attention.

Lights started flashing in one of the docking bays. Through the immense nanoalloy windows he saw a frigate hauled in, its bulk dwarfed by a bay usually reserved for industrial vessels carrying untold tons of heavy metals. A landing ramp was extruded, and shortly after a group of four people walked into the arrivals area. They did not speak to each other, but fanned out in a manner that implied they knew each other's thoughts, for better or worse.

Asber stood up but did not move toward them. A young man noticed him and walked over. Asber, unsure how to react, waited silently. The ship's arrival clearly hadn't been announced, but these people did not look like pirates.

'I need guidance,' the man said to him.

Asber did not know quite what to say. He was a hard worker and as quietly proud a man as his life would allow, but he did not feel his opinion would be worth a great deal, inasmuch as all he could advise anyone on this moon would be to leave as fast as they could.

'What is your name?' the young man asked.

'Asber Krestans,' he replied. 'And yours?'

'Drem Valate.'

Asber thought this over. 'I've heard of you.'

To his surprise the man sighed quietly and said, 'You wouldn't be the first.'

The two of them stood there, in the cold landing bay. Asber pulled out the cloth and wiped some of the oil off his hands.

'What can I do for you, Drem?' he asked.

'I need to speak with the overseer of this colony. But first, if it's all right with you, I'd like to ask you a few questions.'

Asber turned, pointed toward the core. 'Overseer's over there, by the towers. Or, well, the three houses taller than the rest of 'em. As for questions . . . I saw that logo on your ship. Sisters.'

'That we are,' the oldest member of the group said to him with an audible pride.

'Then I believe I got time for questions,' Asber said.

Drem nodded. There was a sadness about him; that, or simply prolonged exhaustion. 'These are my associates: Ortag, Yaman and Verena. We've been working in this area for a while now. We need to find out some things about your colony that we may not get to hear from the overseer himself.'

'Where were you, before you came here?' Asber asked out of curiosity.

'Gurista space.'

The two other men looked alternately at him and at the station, while the woman looked at Drem's back, or at nothing at all. Yet Drem stood almost directly in front of her, so that she couldn't even be in his peripheral vision.

Asber was sure these people worked hard. Work could distract from many things. He rubbed some more grime off his hands and waited for the questions to come.

'The machine you're working on,' Drem said. 'It's . . .' He floundered a bit.

'. . . shit?' Asber said innocently. He saw Drem's relieved smile, and found himself liking the boy. 'I'll tell you the truth if you need it, son.'

Drem grinned. 'Well, I'm wondering if it's indicative of the level of technology you're working with here at the colony.'

'Pretty much,' Asber said. 'There's some better equipment dotted around the area, and a few pieces kept safe at the centre, but mostly we use whatever does the job.'

'You're not at the centre,' Ortag said.

'No, I'm not,' Asber acknowledged. 'I don't dislike the people, but I don't want to be reminded that every one of us is far too old to live in a place like this.'

'There are no young people here?' Yaman asked, with the faintest tone of horror that Asber found both amusing and a little irritating.

He said, 'The young people left long ago, at least the ones with any sense. As you can probably see, those of us who remained were too tired and worn to make anything of the life here.' He nodded his head towards the centre. 'Everything is dirty and all the buildings are small.' It felt pleasant, in an odd and not entirely traitorous sort of way, to not for once have to sell the place to prospectors and ore miners.

'You don't sound too proud of what you've created,' Verena said in an odd tone.

'I'm an old man, dearest. Pride's too much work to keep up.'

'Why're the buildings small, though?' Yaman asked. 'Wouldn't you feel better if you had a higher view?'

'So I can see even more of this wonderland out my window, you mean?' he couldn't resist asking. Yaman grinned embarrassedly.

Asber went on, 'The official reason why we have these tiny hovels is because of the moon's instability. It trembles every now and then, when the molten rivers slowly dig at its core. But everyone knows that anything put in place on this wretched rock will collapse soon enough under the weight of its own decay and the lack of repairs.' He nodded towards the cracks in the floor. 'Sealant only goes so far, you know.'

'So you have no modern equipment, and no solid structures for storage or safety,' Drem said, in a tone devoid of both judgement and sympathy. 'How about trade? Are you in a network of any sort?'

Asber shook his head. 'We depend on shipments from harvesters. But we have no fixed contracts, so we have to be prepared at all times, lest they go elsewhere with their cargo.'

'And your refining base?' Ortag said.

'When we process those shipments, we use metals and materials from the moon itself.'

'Those won't last forever,' Verena said.

Asber nodded. Eventually the core would be gone, and with a single shrug the dead rock would rearrange itself, the rivers and hills, leaving behind nothing but still-dead rock and a bunch of broken old bones.

'No thoughts about updating?' Yaman asked him, as if this were the simplest thing in the world. 'Hi-tech industries are on the rise.'

Hi-tech industries were certainly on the rise, as they had been for much longer than Asber cared to remember. That was the thing about hi-tech. It was always on the rise. If you weren't rising with it, you were simply left behind, at the bottom of the world.

'No money. We're stuck here with what we got.'

'Are there many of you here?' Drem asked.

'Few thousand in the core. Maybe few hundred more, working round the edges. It's a small community.'

'And sole access is through the hangar where we landed.'

'Yes.' Asber looked to the distance, at sifters and production lines that stood empty.

Yaman's innocent face opened its innocent mouth, and Asber just knew what was coming out. 'Why—'

'Got someone pregnant when we were young. That answer your question?'

The mouth snapped shut. The face nodded, and blushed.

Asber sighed. He hardly knew her now, in this small shack they called home. They didn't have the energy to talk, even if they'd had anything left they wanted to talk about.

He was always so tired when he woke, these days. If he'd had a good shift, his hands would still be trembling from the effort. If he hadn't, he would rub them, waiting for them to have something to hold, bend or break. There was no thinking of going away, living in other places. He was too old, too frail; too broke and too broken. He spent his time waiting.

'Look,' he said to Yaman and the rest of the group. 'I'm not a religious man. There's no room for that here. There is a faith I follow, of sorts, but it's a belief in my children; that some of my spirit will live in them after I'm gone. I understand people who persist in thinking of another life than this. I don't want another life. I merely want to rest.' Rest, and not drink too much, and be paid on time, and not be coated in that bitter, tangy smell of unprocessed metals and dust.

Drem nodded, not in fellowship, but in the cold understanding of someone who's forged his own faith out of scrap metal and desperation.

Asber looked him in the eyes and said, 'It's the Sansha, isn't it?'

They all looked at him in surprise.

'Thought so,' Asber said.

'Is it commonly known,' Drem said, 'that they'll be coming for this colony?'

'They're said to be in the area, at least.' Asber shrugged. 'Those kinds of rumours, they surface every now and then. They're especially common in wintertime, like now, when people really start wanting to get out. Winter brings the cold to people's minds. Some of the worst cases will eventually throw themselves into the mercury rivers, while the rest of us who lack the desperation, or the fortitude, will just talk about the coming onslaught of zombies.'

'People have experience of this?' Ortag asked.

'Ah, there's always someone with stories of old colonies and how they were cleaned off by the Sansha.' In truth, he'd wondered what it would be like to be taken by the True Slaves. Much as it was right now, his gut told him, except he wouldn't have that feeling at the back of his head that reminded him what a mistake it had been to stay.

'And you just sit here, waiting?' Yaman asked in horror.

'There's rivers of mercury flowing through this place,' Asber said conversationally. 'Lungs need filtering every six months to avoid the cancer. They'll dope you up a bit, though not so much as you'd miss a full working day, and then they put you under. It's fucking hard. It's like drowning and having the air all sucked out of you at once, except the air is made of cold metal pellets tearing their way through your insides.' He took a breath. 'I haven't seen my son in thirty years. Industrials come here so infrequently, it's practically an event. We've got no money to leave this place, much less keep it in proper working order. No defences at all. You know as much, because that's the real question you've been asking. So you tell me.' He looked at the little group of Sisters, standing there in the great, big, dark hangar. 'What else is there to do?'

While they searched for words, he stood up and said, not unkindly, 'Come on. I'll take you to the overseer.'

He set off, Drem keeping pace by his side, and the others following.

'Do you think everyone feels the same as you do?' Drem asked.

'Nah. If it comes to that, they'll run. Them that can, will fight. Don't listen to an old man.'

They glimpsed the end of the industrial area. To the right, even further away, the river flowed.

'Are you going to get us out?' Asber asked.

Drem nodded. 'If it happens, I'll be overseeing it. The Sisters have teams of agents who'll engage in the evacuation. We pay for everything; transport, new housing, re-education if necessary, whatever medical treatment you need to do a decent day's job in the new world.'

Asber nodded. 'But you do this only for places where the Sansha might come.'

'We do.'

'And everyone else who isn't a potential target for a harvest ...'

'Is up the same shit creek they've always been,' Drem said. 'I grew up with the Blood Raiders, Asber. I know what life is like in the darker end, and how easy it is to prey on places like this. We can't save everyone. There's always someone else out there who has it almost as bad. All we can do is help those who we know for absolute certain are otherwise going to get eaten up.'

'I told you we were expecting it, but that was the usual fear-mongering and desperation. How do *you* know?' Asber asked. 'Really, why us? Why not the three other colonies in the constellation?'

'It's going to be you,' Ortag said from behind them. 'He's always right.'

'And you know this how?'

'I ... see patterns. Apparently I'm good at it,' Drem said, uncomfortably.

'You've worked with other pirates, you said.'

Drem nodded. 'We ran rescue for the Angels for some time, working front lines of emergencies. Eventually moved to the Guristas, doing oversight work; strategic planning of encounters, hotseat rescue operations. Now we're in charge of Sansha operations in this area.'

'And you all are here to convince my overseer that the people on this moon should be put into your care.'

'Got it in one,' Ortag interjected.

'But you stopped to talk to an old man first.'

Drem gave a small smile. 'Overseer business is all deals and politics. Figured we might first get a few honest answers from someone who knows this place.'

Asber, still reeling from the potential of the visitation, said, 'Why are you doing this?'

'People need to be saved,' Drem said, and the old man knew it was a lie.

Some time after that, when Asber had returned to his repairs, the unthinkable happened: another ship docked. Another passenger ship, its plates vermilion gold, and not a piece of ore in sight.

Two men got off. They were dressed in grey clothes, entirely forgettable except for the faint, dark shine of golden red, as if from rivers of lava coursing beneath an asteroid's brittle crust.

They seemed to know about the earlier ship, for they asked Asber several questions about the Sisters team. He answered to the best of his ability. Something in their eyes told him they would know when he lied, that the truth of his answers mattered more to him than the life in his body.

Eventually they left, returning to their ship without a word. He watched them pass away and felt his blood run cold.

This was not a moon-mining colony. The people in this dimly lit place were hard workers, undoubtedly, but of the sort who preferred their tasks not to reach the public eye.

Privacy shields covered every booth, turning their silenced inhabitants into silhouettes.

Drem, sitting inside one of the booths, casually regarded his opponent. It was a man his own age, dressed in stylishly designed clothes that almost managed to hide his fading figure. He was so thin as to approach being gaunt. His chin was shaved clean; and the dark hair that had once been overgrown like a forest was now finely cropped. Drem thought his ears stuck out, but kept that observation to himself.

This was not a meeting that a Sisters operative should ever have, and Drem realized that his light mood – and the temptation to reach out and tweak the man's ears – was a nervous reaction. He was doing something that was precisely right for himself and utterly wrong for everything he had come to represent in this new life. 'How do I get you to stop this shit?' the man said. His leather gloves drummed a tattoo on the tabletop. His name was Terden and he had once been a recruit for the Sisters of EVE, before which he had been an agent for the Sansha. He had made it into the Sisters, but eventually lapsed and returned to the Nation. He would never know it, but Drem had chosen this area partially because of his presence.

'Ten harvests foiled in the space of a month, a full dozen if you count those two mining vessels we rerouted,' Drem said. 'Following on the heels of a winter's cold season where we cut you off in the same manner for months on end. Your quota must be hurting.'

Fingers drummed on the table. 'Man ... if I'd known you would pop up like this, I would've found a way to kill you in your sleep back at the base,' Terden said in that old, familiar snake whisper of his.

Drem gave a tiny smile. Despite the apparent animosity, Terden was clearly just as amused by the meeting as Drem. They were two men of evil purpose, weaving their way down a dark path. A fellowship like that allowed for a lot of unstated acceptance, if not forgiveness.

Drem said, 'You should be glad I'm here at all.'

'Someone would have come, eventually. Nation has been sending out feelers to you for a while, you know.'

'Yeah. Untargeted ones, aimed half at making a deal and half at luring us into a trap,' Drem said. 'And all you'd have gotten would have been a half-hour argument about ethics, and maybe one more unwilling recruit at the end of it. Nothing of any real value.'

He slid a datapad over to Terden, who picked it up and activated it without taking off his gloves. 'This should mean something to you,' he said to the headhunter.

Terden inspected it. The screen lit up with information about rumoured Sansha technology. 'I'm . . . not sure,' he said, put the pad on the table and slid it back.

In a monotone, Drem said, 'You have three likely harvests coming up,' and named the location of each. He saw the headhunter keep his face carefully blank, all the confirmation Drem needed. 'This is not going to be a meeting where we bluff and double-bluff, and that datapad is not a jab for you to parry. We're going to be honest. You give me what I need, and I will stop ruining your harvests. The Sisters will stop acting, and start reacting again. I need what's on that datapad.'

Terden's eyes narrowed. He leaned back in his chair, sat silent for a while.

Eventually he said, 'I cannot give it to you because I don't have the rights or the in-house collateral, but I can put you in contact with someone who can.'

Drem nodded. He knew this was true. If the headhunter had been planning to trick him, he would have offered Drem the tech on the spot, contingent on Drem's appearance at some location sure to be a deathtrap.

'I'll grant you the safety of passage that I can, that I promise, but nonetheless . . . accidents can happen,' Terden continued. 'It'll be in Sansha space and you're a Sisters agent, so you presumably know how it goes.'

'That's all right,' Drem said. 'Your people's attacks are hard to pattern, but not impossible. I developed an algorithm that predicts with a fair certainty where you're going to strike next, and it's couched in a self-modifying program by now. Nobody knows it exists yet – they think it's all my intuition – and nobody ever needs to know. But if I go on this journey and disappear, that program will send itself to every Sisters team leader in the constellation. Of course it'll only work so long as the same Sansha head is running your operations, but since he's the one I want to meet, I imagine he'll go to considerable effort to keep me safe.'

Terden nodded amiably, as if he found this safeguard entirely understandable.

'It must be hard for them to get committed agents like you,' Drem said.

'It's not hard for them to get people who'll . . . work independently. As you probably remember, there are many who welcome us, even seek us out, in worship or desperation to escape from themselves. An abundance of slaves willing to be taken,' Terden said with an undisguised tone of disgust.

'But headhunters don't come easily.'

'No. Headhunters don't come easily at all.'

'What do you think of being worshipped?' he asked, not quite knowing why.

Terden shrugged. 'What would you think of it?' he answered, in the faintly revolted tone of a man who has held the fates of thousands in his hands, quite against his own deepest wishes.

Drem felt a rising level of understanding, however fleeting, that he had not expected.

'You're sure you want to do this?' Terden asked.

Drem nodded.

'Well, whatever your plans, you've got my people in lockdown so you'll get their go-ahead, and you don't seem to have lost any more of your mind than you had back at the colony, so now you have mine.' He rose and extended his gloved hand.

To Drem it felt like the last opportunity to back out before the fall. He bit back any number of destructive comments and consoled himself by shaking hands with the headhunter and saying in a jocular tone, 'The gloves, they're to cover the sweat?'

Terden gave him a long look and eventually said, 'A piece of advice for you . . . If the Sansha do end up overwhelming you at any point, which they won't do on my accord, make sure you have a suicide plan ready. It's not a world you'd want to live in. And yes, they are.'

'Last call before brainwash,' Yaman said, as he wandered off to take a leak.

They were headed for a colony owned and run – quite possibly created from scratch – by Sansha's Nation.

'I still can't believe we're doing this,' Ortag said quietly and scratched his beard.

'You know, you didn't have to come along,' Drem said. It was not merely a question of their safety: ever since the Guristas, he'd started to feel more and more uneasy about their loyalty. Not only Verena's, but the others' as well.

'We wouldn't leave you.' Verena tried to get eye contact, but he ignored her and went back to checking his hazard suit.

They had barely spoken since that ugly evening with the Guristas. Even rescue mission conversations were reduced to bare facts. There had never been an official split, just as there had never been an official relationship. The pendulum of the obvious had merely swung in the other direction.

This did not stop them from sleeping together, which had happened – from various combinations of intention and coincidence – a number of times since the unspoken breakup. The sex was raw and necessary, even as it ate Drem up. Whatever it was she gave him now, she took just as much, and he had no doubt that the twisted hunger that drove her was equal to his own. But the trust was gone for good. So was his energy to rebuild it.

If there were others, he didn't want to know, in the way one doesn't want to utter a question just to hear an answer that's not going to be any kind of surprise. He had slept with other women himself, and sometimes he could look at them and not see her face.

'Question is, are you yourself sure about this?' Ortag said. 'They may have asked you over to broker this secret accord, but for all we know they might just want to turn a few more heads into Slaves.'

'They might,' Drem conceded. 'But I don't think they will. These are scary people but they're not stupid, and this meeting is in both our interests, far more so than the four of us with implants in our heads.'

This was a bluff, and he hoped it would hold until he got what he needed. There was no way the team would have let him go alone – he might be the leader, but they were his commanders – and it had taken a lot of convincing and a great deal of lying even to get them to approve this trip. Drem couldn't reveal the existence of the algorithm or his deal with Terden, so he'd concocted a number of what he believed were fairly solid stories that used the basics of those facts. Eventually his teammates had been assured that they would be safe, and agreed to the journey.

'I hope you're right, son. I truly do,' Ortag said, and went off to prepare, leaving Drem alone in the chamber with Verena.

They did not speak.

Increasingly, he saw her as the last vestige of a life old and false, rapidly fading in memory. Despite all the setbacks and all the people who had let him down – he glanced at Verena, then back at his hazard suit – he had never lost faith in the good work he had done among the Sisters. It was not even the work itself he believed in, but the ideal that lay behind it: that people should be saved from harm, and that human lives mattered.

But his brother and family were dead, and an entire colony had been murdered at the whim of one man whose kind heedlessly lived on. No matter how many lives Drem saved, that man was still out there, untouched; and his brother was still locked in a casket, unforgiven by his own people for being who he was.

Finding out about Verena and then about the Raiders, and the luck he'd had with securing their funding, had all rekindled the angry fire for a time. That anger had faded, leaving behind a dogged, weary purpose – and the terrible knowledge that Drem possessed ideals that were and always would remain incompatible.

He regretted it immensely that he could not serve both roles, of saviour and avenger. He was tired, and he wanted no more than to rest and wait for the inevitable end to take him, but that was no longer an option. He had a man to murder, and others like him; and a long, cold regret in his heart.

As they hovered in the hangar's mouth, Drem thought how odd it was that he had never landed on a fertile planet. He had been to innumerable colonies in his time, from tiny things that barely had enough rock to stand upon, to massive moons where even the areas not locked in by artificial gravity nonetheless held you firmly in place, locked down, forever. The single planet he'd visited in recent times was barely that, more a rock turned rich man's toy. Just once, he thought, he'd like to stand with his bare feet on something meant to hold life.

Wherever that would be, it wouldn't happen here. There had not even been an autogenerated voice welcoming them to what was otherwise a gigantic colony. They had sent a docking request, and their welcome had been the opening of hangar doors.

This place would not receive unexpected visitors. They had passed through an acceleration gate, shunted forth by technology they did not understand towards a place they could not prepare for.

They had weapons on their ship, but decided not to bring them. Whatever they faced in this parasite of silver and metal – nearly encapsulating the entire moon, Drem realized in horrified amazement – might be amenable to reason, but hardly gunfire.

As they disembarked, the first thing everyone noticed was the decrepitude. There was dust everywhere, debris on floors and disconnected or torn wires dangling from the walls. From what little the ship's onboard scanners had been able to tell them, this was a research facility, but it was clear that not many visitors had come here of their own volition.

Another hangar area not too far from them – a much wider one, meant for industrial-size ships carrying large amounts of cargo – was spotlessly clean and also, Drem noticed with a grimace, filled with equipment that looked very much of a containment persuasion.

They passed down a long hall. Nobody spoke. They had their hazard suits on, mostly from habit and a feeling of isolated safety, but the helmets were open and they breathed in the unfiltered local air. Everyone agreed they didn't want to risk being unidentifiable in the face of the mindless, and Drem was privately relieved that Verena wouldn't be able talk to him on private channels.

The dust faded away as they went further in, and the wires clung to the walls. There were more of them, sealed and fastened, row upon row that connected everything like veins in a body. Some of those wires terminated in immobile sensors that seemed completely inert and inactive, as dangerous things tend to be. Drem had no doubt they knew the Sisters were here.

The hall, wide enough to let the group walk side-by-side many times over, retained its size as they crossed the threshold into the main square; but what would have been a thronged core of activity in any other faction was a deathly quiet expanse among the Sansha. Hangar windows gave way to multistacked floors on either side, each the height of two men, that were dotted with what looked like innumerable entryways: open doors that led into shadows. It was like a beehive in winter.

They walked on, their feet thumping on the metal floors. Drem could not keep from glancing up at the openings. There couldn't possibly be this many pathways in the station, he reasoned, so these had to be closed-off chambers.

He kept looking. He saw no movement. A quiet thought at the back of his head, remembering the carnage of his past rescue missions, reminded him that this did not indicate lack of life.

'Drem,' someone behind him whispered, and he saw it. In one chamber, then the other; so inert he detected them almost as much by the movement of air and dust around their forms. Sansha's army. The True Slaves.

There was one in every chamber. Most were almost completely hidden in shadows, but if you knew they were there, knew what you were looking for, the subtle curves and outlines of mechanized humans could be made out. Drem knew that if he were to put his overhead into action, it'd be lit up with hundreds ... He looked to the heights, swiftly counted at least two dozen floors ... maybe thousands of the quietly burning points of life.

As they passed on, the halogen glare from the misty roofs reached them at last. They saw faces now: half-human, glinting in the light, covered like the moon was covered. Every one of them looked down on the team with dead sockets that only sometimes held human eyes.

To their relief, the blueprint directed them down a side corridor; still with the same high ceiling and walls that remained fairly wide, but far from the agoraphobia of the hives. They came upon a body, sprawled face down close to the wall. It was larger than a man should be; the modifications that covered its body made it hard to tell where metal gave way to flesh.

Yaman nudged it with his foot. It barely shifted; the dead are heavy, after all.

Drem wondered if it had been directed here; on some mission that had not ended when this unit lost contact with the hive mind, but merely transferred on to the next available body, this one left here and forgotten. Or perhaps the person – it had to be a person on some level, he thought – had stumbled in here to die, like some great beast operating on orders older than any technology, wandering off the beaten path for the final, endless journey.

He was so lost in thought he didn't hear the rumbling. It came up from another corridor, one they'd passed without noticing.

He turned, and when he saw it, he ran. There was no time to yell.

The thing chasing them was a massive metal heap, like a ball of screeching anger. It smashed into a side wall, careened off and hurtled in their direction, the lights on its carapace glowing like vast angry eyes.

The team conserved its breath, keeping panic at bay and focusing on the running. Behind them they heard the twangy crashes as the metal monster tore cords off walls and sheared through hardened metals as it hurtled toward them.

They came to a fork, two side paths veering off the main one. 'Split, I'm centre!' Drem yelled. Ortag and Yaman went down the right side, Verena the left, while he kept running. A tearing noise that sounded like a scream went off behind them.

Drem risked a look over his shoulder and saw the thing shoot out something like a metal wing, leaving fist-thick grooves in the wall as it tried to slow for a turn. He stopped and caught himself thinking *no no no* as it flew off down the left corridor, after Verena.

Drem jittered on the spot, thinking fast, then ran back and headed down the corridor, after his lover, with the monster between them.

At a distance he saw the metal thing propel itself forward, and in front of it, glimpsed in its wildly careening turns, was the running Verena. Beyond both of them, Drem saw with an acid panic, was a wall. Whatever this corridor led to, it had been sealed off.

He saw Verena slow a little, looking desperately at the sides, but there was nothing she could climb. He cursed himself to the end of the world and back for not having brought the weapons, and frantically went through his gear as he ran, trying to think of something to use. His hands closed on an object his mind told him was important, and for a precious second he tried to think what it was before he realized he was clutching a bomb. The spoke bomb. The bomb that would dig through walls.

'Toss it!' he screamed as loud as his lungs would let him. *'Toss your spoke!'*

He was closing in on the monster, and beyond its metal bulk he saw Verena pull out a spoke bomb, turn it to narrow and throw it at the wall they were rapidly approaching. The explosion rattled the teeth in his exposed head. Metal shards flew all over, leaving a dent in the wall; a tiny hole with nothing on the other side but metal. A waiting place for execution.

The thing smashed against the wall just as Verena dived into the opening, barely missing her. Drem grabbed one of the metal pieces and hurtled it edge first at the metal monster, but the piece merely bounced off its bulk. It backed up, then crashed into the wall again, leaving a deep dent. Verena crouched inside the hole, kneeling with her head in her hands.

Drem screamed in anger, tossing another spoke bomb at the thing as it prepared for another onslaught. It hit, attached, and blew the monster's back wide open.

Drem ran up to it with bloody murder on his mind, but when he saw what was inside, his legs nearly gave out, his body feeling like someone had punched him in the gut.

Inside the shell, now exposed like the undeveloped embryo in a cracked egg, was a small body. It mewled at them, its voice gurgling as if liquid had seeped into its small lungs.

The machine was much taller than Drem, but this thing was the size of a six-year-old child. Its body, which seemed boneless – and *was* nearly boneless, Drem realized with a shudder – had been fitted and shaped to conform to the machine, whose innermost crevices it filled like liquid will a mould.

He walked up to it, crouched down. Its eyes saw him and it moved, pistons shuddering as parts of its body designed to be immovable tried to reach for him. It revolved inside its housing on something resembling a small gyroscope, and in the infinite moment that followed, Drem understood at last what the Sansha were.

It tried to hug him. Its pistoning hands reached out and it tried to touch his face.

A patter in the distance resolved to True Slaves, running in unison. Behind them they tugged a machine that hovered over the ground. They attached it to the metal shell that held the creature, which slowly dragged across the ground until it was locked in a magnetic embrace with the hovering creation. There was a loud hum, and the machine gyrated, turning the shell upwards. It was a transport for rogue units.

They wheeled it away, still mewling. When Verena crawled out of the hole at last she took Drem into her arms and held him there as they sobbed.

These were Sansha's children. Whatever this one had wanted with

Verena – to get closer, to assimilate her into the Nation, or to achieve some kind of natal union – and however deadly it might have been, the basic drive behind it had been that of a child's.

Drem desperately tried to think of it as a clumsy attack, because to acknowledge what it might truly have been, with all the desperation that entailed, also meant he would have to reframe the entire Sansha's Nation as the most terrible victims in the history of New Eden. A nation of metal children whose endless scourge for recruits was driven not merely by an implanted need for recruitment, but a constant craving for human warmth – and whose mad drive to remake the rest of the cluster in their image was nothing more than the attempt to eliminate the idea that it could be anything else than it truly was: a world where they were always outside, looking in.

He wondered, not for the first time, what kind of a man would work with people like this. He felt like he wanted to puke out his own heart.

They reunited with the others and moved on, feeling numb – which was better than disgusted and panicked, though not by much – and followed Drem's given directions to the colony core. There was no hesitation. Sisters would let nothing keep them from reaching their objective: not carnage, not personal risk, and not the myriad mental terrors they might have to suffer.

They talked in quiet tones along the way, if only to hear their own voices. It was hypernormal speak that ignored entirely what had just passed: status checks, team coordination, visuals they all saw but described to one another just the same. They walked over bridges at great heights and saw metal soldiers training in the distance, and over great transparent nanoalloy floors that covered repairs and replacements below, bodies having implants removed from them and others forced back in. Underneath his feet Drem spotted faint outlines of several metal heaps that looked not unlike the one who had followed them. He thought about the broken ones; lying there, unable to speak. The mewling. Like dead cells in the body, awaiting disintegration.

They ended up in a meeting hall guarded by Sanshas with more implants than human skin. The guards were large beasts, bulked up with metal, their hands multifaceted instruments. They did not have weapons; they *were* weapons.

Drem stepped forward and said, 'I am here to see your leader.'

One of the creatures regarded him with unblinking eyes and said, in a voice that was either rarely used or simply synthesized, 'You will be scanned.'

'Do it,' Drem said.

Its torso, half encased in metal, opened up to reveal a pile of miniature drones. They lay in a basket-like container full of a viscous, oily substance, in a position that was, to Drem's lurching disgust, exactly the same as a human stomach.

'Stand still. If you engage, they will erase you,' the guard said.

He did. The drones rolled their way out of the basket and clanged on to the floor. They began to vibrate, and smoke, and Drem could feel the heat coming off them. It smelled, he imagined, like something being cooked – burnt – in stomach acids.

When the drones had dried themselves off, their vibrations ceased and were replaced with a quiet thrum. One by one they arose, rising up to face height and hovering there as a cluster of insects. They each had a lens turned to Drem's face, and floated so close that he could see his oily reflection in their convex surfaces.

They stared at him for a good length of time before retreating to their oleaginous compartment.

The guard said, 'You can enter. They cannot.'

Yaman, unable to contain himself, said, 'What the fuck kind of scan was that?' Drem heard the barely contained tremor in his voice, and imagined his own would sound much the same.

The guard remained silent for a moment, then said, 'The final one.'

'Meaning?'

'You have all been scanned already.'

Drem turned to Yaman and said, 'They probably have bioscanning equipment embedded in the walls of this place.'

'Then what the hell were those things doing just now?'

Drem looked back at the guard. His terror had momentarily

pushed him into a calm place of inquisitiveness and clarity. 'Setting the tone,' he said. 'All right. Let's do this.'

The guard gave him a slow glance, its metal head turning until its eyes – or whatever glowed in those dead sockets – were looking directly at him. It repeated its directive that Drem could enter, and that the rest of the team would remain outside.

And it demanded he strip naked.

Drem heard a snort, and looked to see Yaman struggling to remain inexpressive.

He turned back, but there was nothing approaching sympathy in the eyes of the Sansha.

'You're serious,' he said.

'You can enter. Alone. Unprotected.'

'Can I at least keep my underwear?'

The silence was punctuated only by the quiet ticking of thoughts and metal gears.

'No,' the beast said.

'Is there anything ... anything ... moving on the other side of this wall, other than the one person I am supposed to meet?' Drem asked.

The beast said there was not, other than the guards.

'We'll turn our backs,' Ortag said. 'Let's just do it. I want out of this madhouse more than I've wanted anything in the world.'

Drem raised an eyebrow at him.

Ortag shrugged. 'We've got spoke bombs, admirable as that thinking was. They've got these.' He nodded his head towards the guard. 'We're dead either way, they decide on it.'

In that quiet land beyond terror and adrenaline, Drem sighed and began to dislodge his gear.

It took a while; Sisters hazard outfits were not designed to come off easily. Once he was down to civilian clothes he tried not to hesitate or think of embarrassment, a stupid concept in this of all places. Ortag looked up at the air and Verena down at the floor, though as he removed the last patch of clothing he caught her stealing a glance.

Yaman, of course, exclaimed, 'Motherfucker, you *shave*?' at which the other two crouched to their knees, looked down at the ground and roared in laughter.

He left his clothes in a pile and walked up to the gate. It opened, and the guards turned to offer him passage.

'Think there's a draft,' he murmured, wringing a few last snorts from the others. Anything for humour here in this wretched place.

He walked through, and the doors closed behind him.

Machines purred everywhere. Little things of metal and electricity skittered about on the floor. On the walls were great transparent tubes that held bodies suspended in ectoplasm: clones on life support. There were large blocks in the distance, bright and connected like dew drops in the web, which he expected were performing the colony's calculations, and others beyond, which were likely the visible sections of the atmosphere generators. This was the centre.

In the shadows stood guards, immobile and only breathing.

He walked on, trying not to think of the way the dust was settling on the sweat of his skin. He itched. Ahead was some manner of core, an open space with a dais buffeted by a lot of cords and connecting cables.

As he got closer, he saw that there was a human sitting in a throne on the dais. The person – a man, and naked, too, in so far as what remained of his flesh – conformed to his seat, which curved around him. The cords ended in him, though Drem knew they did not stop at the surface.

Drem stopped in front of him and waited.

The man's lips parted, and a voice issued forth, saying, 'I am Sansha Kuvakei.'

Drem said nothing.

The lips twitched into a smile and said, 'You do not believe me.' It was raspy and worn, as if spoken by punctured lung and tattered cord; each word precisely enunciated as if it might be the last.

'Whatever I'm talking to, I'm sure is the great leader himself,' Drem said. 'But that's not what I'm looking at.'

The man's bald head was full of wires, gossamer filaments wavering from his head, connected to the chair with enough slack to let him move.

'I see the world through other people's eyes,' Sansha said.

Drem couldn't help but glance at the bodies floating in vats.

'Yes,' Sansha said.

As if on cue, every single body in the room opened its eyes, their glares fixed on Drem. He clenched his teeth so hard in shock that his jaw ached.

'I can see I upset you,' Sansha said.

'Whatever gave you that idea?'

'You shrivelled up.'

Drem's mouth dropped open. He was still trying to think of something to say when he realized that the hoarse noise he was hearing came from the expressionless face. Sansha was laughing.

'You are a dangerous man,' Sansha said, in that same dying wheeze. 'I have come to know of you.'

'How did you hear—' Drem started, when his brain caught up with his ears. Not heard; come to know. 'From the people you took. Your zombies.'

The face trembled in a little nod. 'You have almost convinced that witch of the Angels to give you confidential information. You have spoken to the Rabbit himself and woven his money in with your madness. And now you have made it here. I apologize for the rambunctiousness of my child, incidentally. I fear I have neglected it.'

Drem quelled a shudder. 'If you know all this, then you know what I intend to do. I hope it hasn't reached the capsuleers.'

'It has not. I also know who might talk, for my new slaves have no secrets from me. I have been in contact with the others, let them know. Any person who might have been a security risk no longer is.'

Drem, appalled, couldn't help but ask, 'Do they sometimes feed their own people to you, just so you can feed them back what was in their minds?'

The old man did not respond, which was answer enough.

'You know what I want from you,' Drem said. 'And you likely know the basics of what it's for. I won't promise I'll pull it off, but if I can, it'll be a great boon for you. No more capsuleers getting in your way. No more battleships coming in to destroy your forces as you descend on outer space colonies. And no more Sisters, mucking it all up by foreseeing your plans.'

'Yes. You are the one who has been stopping my advances,' the old man said. Those wet eyes stared at him. 'You are a driven man.'

'People have been hurt, subjugated, and now apparently even murdered for my plans. I'd better be.'

'Let me tell you about purpose,' Sansha said. 'It will eat you up.' He swallowed slowly, but it made no change to his voice. 'I was a pioneer of my time. I laid the foundation of a beautiful world, kept free of worry and strife. I built a galactic empire. But in my pride I did not see that the world disapproved of my plans, and eventually they came and they brought me down. I should have made concessions. I should have had more sense. There was no way I could have succeeded, with the odds thrown at me. But when it came to that, there was no way I could stop, either. I was no better than all those poor children of mine, stunted with a purpose that never would let up.'

The old body took a deep breath, its lungs rattling with the effort. He continued, 'You are a remarkable man, with a vision of a new world some would welcome and others call a travesty. I have never seen anyone do what you have done, and I know more about you than you will ever understand. If there is anything I can do for you, I will do it; not for the profit or for the reason, but for the simple act of helping someone take the right step on an old path that I recognize so terribly well.

'But I advise that you be utterly sure of what you plan to do before you engage. Once you start – you will be changed, irrevocably, into something that you may not be able to live with.'

Drem did not say anything. There was nothing to add, and nothing to amend. The man in front of him, or whatever mind behind it, spoke the truth.

'Are you sure in your purpose?' Sansha Kuvakei asked him.

He breathed in deeply. The air was stale and caught in his throat.

'I don't know,' he said at last, standing there naked.

The old man nodded again, the thin cords in his head trembling. With obvious effort he raised one hand and reached out to Drem, in a manner uncomfortably reminiscent of the child inside the shell. 'Come closer,' he said.

Drem stepped forward, up to the dais, and kneeled in front of the old man. Sansha gently stroked his cheek and lay a hand on his hair, as if he were a wayward son.

'If you are. When you are. I will give you what you need,' he said, his voice quavering. 'You beautiful monster.'

15

Ralea walked down the ship's metal corridor, trailing her fingers along its ridges and grooves.

She was en route for a rebuilding of some kind; her and hundreds of thousands, all in tandem on a great trail of caravans that snaked its way through space. If she looked out one of the many viewports on this vessel she would see cruisers and battleships floating along beside them, the guns on their great hulks silhouetted against the vermilion nebulas.

In the Minmatar Republic, a person could work for their own people, in support of ideals that not only honoured the individual but *demanded* individuality and the ability to care for others. The republic was famed – or notorious – for its tendency to cobble together a working machine from ingredients of imperfection, and to place function far over image. They had done this in all sectors of their society. Their politics were those of arguments and pride, their technology had evolved from crude machinery on a resource-scarce world to starships seemingly held together by solder and defiance, and their social ideology was based on living in a republic torn to shreds by the Amarr, who had in ages past invaded and stolen entire societies for enslavement in their own empire.

The caravans were headed into the complete unknown. Nobody knew what this massive construction project was all about. There was guesswork about a space station, or a planetside superstructure that would be unassailable even by the kind of galactic weapons used against the Minmatar in the great rebellion. These days there was a unified state of mind among them, detectable even to outsiders like Ralea, of a great renewal; of creating something important in an environment where everyone was valued. They were not casting off their past, but neither were they getting mired in it like the radioactive muck it could sometimes be.

Her ship alone held thousands of people. It was an industrial hauler once used to house livestock, and it had taken depressingly little reconfiguration to fit humans instead. The Minmatar were experts at customization.

She walked on, taking an upward route. There was a constant muted roar behind the ship's walls, mixing the hum of its engines with the susurrus of the people who lived down below. As she ascended, floor after floor, the roar lessened, quieting to little more than the faintest of whispers. Metal gave way to synthetics and leather, too; and to glass. Ralea could see into other rooms, rooms of leisure: chairs and sofas, holovids running, drinks freely available. The closer she got to the top – the part housing those who would be overseeing the grand project – the more luxurious life became. Just like it had been back on the station, all those ages ago.

She stopped when she saw something glinting on the faux-wooden floor. The floor material was made of a dyed synthetic, etched and varnished so that it looked like parquet tiling. Touching it with her bare fingers gave her a tingle of dread, as if stroking someone's cheek and finding it wasn't truly human. She bent and swiftly picked up the item.

It was a metal shard – flat and sharp enough that she could feel its edges scrape her fingers. How it had gotten here she had no idea. She slid it into her pocket, feeling nicely conspiratorial, as if the marks of some gatecrashing down-below prole had been hidden from the watchful eyes upstairs.

Possibly she could forge a necklace of it. File it down, punch a few holes, make something useful. That was the Minmatar way. Make something out of next to nothing.

She envied them, and hoped she'd be able to make some small contribution. All she wanted, after this long journey, was to be of value; someone who had something good come out of all her work.

She moved on, walking down the corridors of glass with the metal shard in her pocket.

Heci's quarters were up here, on high. Ralea knocked and entered without waiting for a response.

Her friend was sitting in a soft lounge chair, snacks in hand, watching a holovid being broadcast. 'Hey, you're just at the good bit,' she said. 'The dude's pulled his gun out, and his shirt's half torn off. Take a seat. Want something to eat?'

'Thanks, I'm good,' Ralea said, sitting in a chair beside her. It conformed automatically to her natural weight and posture, making her feel she wasn't so much sitting as put in a gentle, caring stasis.

'How's the grungy parts?' Heci asked her.

'Down below? About what you'd expect, I guess,' Ralea said. 'People keep to themselves, but there's no trouble, no violence. There's a quiet hope down there.'

'There is up here, too,' Heci said.

'How're things going?'

'First let me ask you how you're doing down there. If I was dealing with the same Ralea I pulled out of the gutter all that time ago, I'd never have let you live in the poorhouse level all by yourself.'

'It's not a poorhouse, it's just . . .' She thought about it, stroked a strand of hair behind her ear. 'I don't know. I like being useful. There's something about that level of society that's like a slow breath, in and out. I can feel it. I can't feel it up here.'

'So you like handing out baby wipes and bread,' Heci said, cocking an eye at her.

'Rather than attending cocktail parties and smooching dignitaries? God, yeah,' Ralea said and grinned. 'Actually, hand me that Caldari takeout.'

She accepted the box from Heci and continued, 'It feels like I'm making a difference down there. Small difference, I'll admit, but the results are clear and immediate. I'm looking forward to continuing that line of work when we get to the construction site. Whatever they'll have me do.' She licked some grease off her fingers and handed the box back. 'How's your life up here with the cream? You're here as an agent proper, yeah?'

'Yeah. I've been in contact with some people back at homeworld, and apparently I'm still considered just a hapless accessory to your life of crime.'

Ralea rolled her eyes. 'So you get carte blanche to come back when you like.'

'Oh, they'll question the shit out of me. But I've got a good record, no drugs and no major crimes, and they've no solid reason to believe that I'm here of my own free will. Besides,' she said, 'I know a few guys up in Justice. They wouldn't want to inconvenience me.'

'No more than they've done in the past, right?' Ralea said.

'Baby, nothing those guys did with me was inconvenient in the slightest,' Heci said, winking at her. 'Anyway, I figured that if I'm going to be returning anyway, I might as well pick up the title again. I can't say if the higher-ups on this ship are impressed with the line of work itself, but it's a title, and they've responded to that. I even met Wkumi Pol, the Brutor tribe leader.'

'Serious?'

'Nice guy. Speaks like he believes it.'

'Don't they usually?'

'Yeah, but . . .' Heci hesitated. 'You know, you're around the Matari for long enough, you get to hear it all. Enslaved as an empire, violated by the Amarr, countless of their people being torn out and put to work, restoration, revolution, blah blah blah.'

'I know,' Ralea said darkly, remembering the monastery.

'But this time, there's none of that. It feels . . . not like they're trying to leave it behind, which I doubt they'll ever do, but like they're looking towards the future. Enjoying, *relishing* being able to think about something other than rebellion and the Amarr. Even the ones like Wkumi, who has to be gung-ho about liberation within his tribe, you can practically see them breathing a sigh of relief at having something new to do.'

'Whatever they're doing out there, do you think it's good enough to warrant a mindset like that?' Ralea asked her.

'I hope so. They're certainly playing it close to the chest. Nobody'll say a word about what they're going to build or why. People get paid for their efforts and that's enough.'

'Maybe that's best,' Ralea said. 'For hope, and a little peace.'

'Speaking of peace,' Heci said, 'you cannot get in trouble. You realize that? If you give them reason, they will find you. If your name crops up on any records here, it's over for you on this trip. They'll spot you at any empire checkpoint from now on, even in the republic proper, and you'll have only a day or two before they swoop in and take you. There's no other place you can go except for the pirates in lowsec.'

'I know,' Ralea said. 'I'll stay in the shadows.'

She went back to her quarters, snacks consumed and movie finished. Her friendship with Heci was as strong as it had ever been, but there was a new kind of comfort in her presence that had its roots in loss. It was getting to be time to leave, go down separate paths, and the two women intended to do so with all the grace and kindness they could muster. So they spent the hours together now with no real aim other than to wait for the inevitable final parting. Like an old couple.

Ralea grinned. If either one of them had been a man, they'd . . . Well, she allowed herself to imagine that they would have been meant for each other, in their own quiet way, though she suspected there would have been plenty of drama. She doubted she would feel this close to any person ever again, and although that saddened her, it also drew into light the new purpose in life she had started to discover. She simply did not want that kind of closeness on a personal level with anyone else, nor did she want any other manner of satisfaction that revolved solely around her own pleasure.

At the same time, she knew she had to maintain a proper distance from those whom she served, lest she be sucked into a system that took her autonomy and imposed its own morals on her. The Minmatar Republic and its mysterious initiative was the only option she had left among the four great empires. It would not have been her first choice, but she hoped it could be her last; to hide, and to start anew.

The floors where she lived were mostly long corridors,

interspersed every now and then with an open space for gatherings, talking and general breathing. Although she wasn't Minmatar the people who lived here didn't seem to particularly notice her presence, which she treated as a kind of badge of honour. She was convinced that she looked just like someone who could be on this journey with the rest of them, not there simply as a high-class traitor in their midst.

Most people earned their keep here, and so did she. Some of them worked for the ship itself, either in maintenance or general operation. She could have done that – she was a fast learner and had some theoretical knowledge of starship operation – just as she could have moved upstairs and done more diplomatic work, but she barely considered either as a viable option. There was caretaking to be done, in helping the small society onboard the ship to function without crises, and in it she found exactly the kind of fulfilment of purpose she needed. She was apart from those who needed the help, which gave her the necessary emotional distance to do the job, and she saw the results almost instantaneously, both in those to whom she handed supplies and in the general calm of the people she served.

She entered her quarters, tired after a long day, and started getting ready for bed. As she stood in front of her bathroom mirror she drew out the metal shard and laid it against the grooves in her face. It could almost be lodged inside them.

Those wrinkles and crow's feet came not from old and hard times, but from newer and better ones, and each spoke of an exertion she cherished. She remembered seeing people who looked this worn: sometimes old folks who had clearly enjoyed a long life; sometimes drug users, the ones who'd risen from the ashes of their own selves, for whom she always thought this kind of weariness was from the drug use. It wasn't, she realized now. It was from the survival itself.

It took a lot out of you. It had to, if anything new was going to make its way in.

From outside came the high-pitched crying of an infant, echoing and meaningless.

*

The next day was full of the same activity and pleasure as the day before, and of the same tiredness at its end. By the time she got home it was late in the evening.

Everything on this level was made of corridors, each of them lined with doors leading into people's temporary little lives. Ralea was walking slowly, enjoying the ache in her muscles. A young boy went past her at the speed children possess when they're saddled with a purpose, until he reached a door much further down the corridor. He looked around, then unlocked and opened it, and stepped in swiftly. This was the same door, Ralea thought, from where the infant's crying had come last night, as it had for several nights in a row now.

She had seen that boy many times before. She remembered his face from the throng, as one does when children are a little too polite and quiet.

When she got in, she used the spotty shipline access to open her work terminal, and looked up the residential information in the quarters the boy had entered. She was only checking up on things, she told herself. Just being a little curious.

He lived there with his mother and younger sibling. Father was unaccounted for. The mother's name was registered, but the children's were not. This was a flight from home for many people, and if you passed basic criminal checks you weren't expected to give up too many details. Heci might be able to get more information, Ralea thought, but it wouldn't feel right to ask.

If that woman was taking care of her two kids, she likely wouldn't have a lot of time to work, and thus wouldn't be getting much of anything, money or supplies.

Ralea remembered her now, peering out from a door only slightly ajar, her hair not quite held back in a ruffled ponytail. The woman could probably go out for medicine and food if necessary, save for that haunted look in her eyes. Ralea had seen dead expressions like that, though most often they'd been buffeted by layers of mascara and the false rosy shine of injections that were rebuilding burst blood vessels around the cheekbones and temples, after the women had walked into doors, or fallen down passageways all the way to station core. Right.

She slept uneasily that night, under sounds of crying, dreaming of blackened walls and people with too many teeth in their faces.

The next day, at work, she set aside antibiotics and other basic meds, along with some freeze-dried food. She funded it from her own pocket – she would be a philanthropist, not show favouritism – thinking how good it felt to help others.

She took the supplies home and waited. After some time she got tired of listening for sounds and looking out the keyhole, so she left the apartment and sat herself down on the stairs that led to her corridor, placing the bags of stuff beside her. Not many people passed by, and those who did paid her no mind.

The boy came at last. Ralea called him over and he obeyed, standing next to her with his head bowed. When she told him in a gentle tone to sit, he sat.

'I have something for you,' she said.

He looked up at that and gave her a dull gaze that tripped past her eyes and settled on her shoulder, and the wall behind her. She couldn't decide whether that look had a lack of thoughts behind it, or simply too much experience.

She indicated the bags. He did not move, though he nodded a little towards her hand, as if he wanted to look.

'It's medicine and food. I figured you guys might need them,' she said. When he didn't move, she asked, 'Does your brother cry a lot?'

He looked directly into her eyes then, clearly unsure if she was serious. 'Sister,' he said. 'It's my sister.'

'Well, some of this stuff will keep your little sister from crying. And that will give everyone in the apartment some rest, which I imagine you guys could do with.'

When he didn't respond, she broke out her secret weapon. 'I do want something in return.' She could almost see a little light dim in his eyes, and it broke her heart. This boy had not been abused, she was almost certain, but he'd grown to understand, far too soon, that nothing came for free.

She leaned in close and said confidentially, 'I want you to scout

out the ship for me and count the supplies in the nearby sectors. There are huge stacks of food, medicines and other necessities, and I don't trust all the local operators to tally them right. You may have to do a little maths, but it's nothing you can't handle. I doubt they'll let you pull anything off the shelves but you can certainly get close enough to count.'

The light came back. He looked directly into her eyes and nodded eagerly. This was a job. The boy understood jobs.

'The meds and food will be in my apartment, waiting for successful completion.' She would not offer him advances. They were dangerous omens for any job, they and the people who offered them. 'Once you're done, knock on my door. You can give your report in the hall and I will give you what you earned.'

He nodded swiftly.

'Go!'

He rushed off. She could have sworn she saw a little smile on his face.

It took him the whole of that evening and the next full day that followed, but in the late afternoon, as she was headed back to her quarters, he tracked her down.

'You're done already?' she said, only in half-mock surprise. There was a lot of stacked goods in every sector, and counting it would have been beyond the focus of many adults she knew.

He nodded. 'I didn't have anything to write on, but I hope that's OK. I just memorized the numbers.'

He said it with such innocence and fervour that she felt a pang of guilt. Of course she should have given him a datapad of some sort.

He seemed to read her mind, and said, 'It wasn't that hard. I had to count the first sector a few times, but I made up a system and then it got easy. You want the numbers?'

'Absolutely. You want me to bring the supplies, so we can sit on the steps?'

'No, um . . . can we go to your quarters for it? I promise I won't be there long.'

The request surprised her, but she quickly assented. They went to her quarters, and the boy took a seat in the hall, next to the bag that held the medicines and food she had promised him.

'I do have a living room in here. It's got seats,' she said to him in a gently mocking tone that brought out a big grin.

'It's fine, Miss. Thanks. I'd rather just sit here.'

'OK, then.' She took a seat beside him. The wall felt chilly against her back. 'But before we start, I need to know your name.'

He looked a little spooked at that, so she swiftly added, 'I can't be taking data from anonymous sources, now can I?'

That seemed to mollify him. 'Felarn. Or just Fel.'

'Which do you prefer?'

'Fel, please.'

'All right, Fel.' She clapped her hands together. 'Let's hear the numbers.'

Fel leaned his head back and looked up at the empty wall. He started to recite counts for medicines, for frozen and dried food and liquid supplies, all of it partitioned by sectors. He'd even acquired numbers for electronic parts of various kinds, which made Ralea suspect that security could be tightened in certain parts. He recounted all of this in a breezy tone of easy remembrance. It was not a memorized sequence of numbers, drilled in by incessant repetition, but clearly based on a system. On the few occasions where he paused, his lips kept moving slightly, and she saw he was working out the numbers from some manner of base principles. She was impressed.

After the recitation was through, she clapped again, softly. He blushed.

'There are a lot of grownups who couldn't have done what you did,' she said.

He shrugged, not meeting her gaze, and got up. 'I have something for you, Miss,' he said.

'Ralea, Fel,' she said.

He nodded, put a hand in his pocket and carefully pulled out something wrapped in cloth, handing it to her.

When she unwrapped it, she found a small metal plate, half the size of her palm, flattened out into a mostly circular shape. One part of it was slightly fractured, and had a sharp nib stand out, as if it were a tail trying to unfurl.

'Be careful. It's sharp,' Fel said. 'I wanted to give it to you. It looks like Minmatar.'

She stared at the plate for a long time. She had seen that logo embossed all over the ship, and she remembered seeing it on mission reports so long ago. It was the Minmatar faction logo. She did not cry, but she took a deep breath and spoke very calmly. 'Thank you,' she said, placing it in a pocket. 'I will keep this with me always.'

That same evening, the child's crying did not last as long as it usually did. In the evenings that followed, it eventually stopped completely.

She met Fel one afternoon, spotting him on the steps as she was heading back home after a late evening's walk. She took a seat beside him, and they watched the world go by for a little while.

'How's your mum and sister?' she asked.

'They're fine,' he said. 'Thank you for the food and medicines.'

'Thanks for the counting. Maths-head.'

He grinned.

'I imagine it can be tough, just the three of you, on this long trip,' she said to him.

'It's all right. We don't mind. Mum says she prefers it when people don't ask too many questions.'

He'd said it in such a straightforward tone that Ralea decided it probably hadn't been a warning to her. 'She keeps to herself?'

'Yeah. We're laying low, she says.'

Odd choice of words, Ralea thought, but entirely understandable if they were running away from someone rather than something. 'Do you miss being back home?' she asked carefully, not wanting to awaken any memories of an unpleasant father.

'Yeah, sometimes. It was nice.'

'Lots of space, friends to play with?'

'Yeah, and the pool was nice too.'

That made a little less sense. They did not look like people who'd come from riches. Nor did she imagine that a mother with one child and one infant would rush off so suddenly if there were any chance that she might be leaving behind wealth that could help her raise her children.

Ralea did a little mental shrug. It really wasn't any of her business anyway, she reasoned. 'You told me your name, but what's the name of your little sis?'

He smiled at that. 'Jaana.'

'That's a really nice name, like your mum's. Krenalia, wasn't it?'

'No, it's Aziza,' he said. His eyes went wide, and he immediately added, 'No, Krenalia, I mean!' He blushed heavily, breathed in and out a couple of times. 'Sorry. Aziza's my nanny. She took care of me a lot.'

'Your nanny?' Ralea asked in disbelief.

He looked at her for a while. 'Yeah. Well, she's my aunt, too,' he added casually.

She heard it and tried to quell her suspicion, telling herself she shouldn't do anything to risk her stay on this ship.

That same evening, after dithering about it for entirely too long, she called Heci on the shipline and asked her about refugees.

'Oh yeah, they're all over this caravan. I can't imagine there's a single ship without a few of those.'

'What about the criminal checks?'

'This isn't high court, hon. They check hard for explosives and weapons, but if you're just someone looking to start a new life, well, they seem to sympathize. People flee from all kinds of things,' she said, in a tone whose meaning wasn't lost on Ralea. 'If there's anyone here who really shouldn't be, and I've heard we might have our share of those, they'll be well hidden from sight.'

'I'm sure they are,' Ralea thought. She couldn't imagine this single mother of two would be running from anything other than evil men and a hard life.

Something itched at her mind. 'What have you heard about stowaways? Did Wkumi Pol talk about them? That's not the kind of stuff that gets let out, or spoken of in casual conversation.'

'Oh, they aren't casual. Our conversations, I mean. Other things are.'

Ralea rolled her eyes and snorted.

'Whaaat?' Heci said.

'You total whore,' she said.

There was loud laughter on the other end of the line. 'So who're you worried about? The woman you mentioned earlier, the one with the kid?' Heci asked after catching her breath.

'I don't know. No. Not really. I'm probably just wondering.'

'So what's her name?'

Ralea ignored the question. 'How're the men up top? Anyone a prospect for more than just a temporary thing?'

'What is the name of this woman, Ralea?'

'Let's just drop it.'

'Hey, what the hell?'

'Look, no. No. It's not going to be like that. It can't fucking be.'

Heci quietly and gently said, 'We didn't get to where we are by being stupid, hon. And you brought this up for a reason, like it or not. I'll bet my clit that there's more to this than a name.'

Ralea looked around her, at these metal cells. She wondered how far she would have to divorce herself from the humanity that surrounded her in order to find her own.

'She's here under an assumed name,' she said. 'Her registered name is Krenalia, but that's likely the name of a nursemaid they had back in the old world. Her son lied to me, said it was his aunt. They had money, too.'

On the other end of the line, Heci sighed. 'You're doing it. You're getting into trouble.'

'I'm just listening to people!'

'Then stop listening! Do you have any idea what'll happen if you get caught here? There'll be nowhere else for you to go! Argh!'

'Look, I'm sorry. I know I shouldn't be doing this. My brain can't help but latch on to this kind of stuff, where something is wrong and someone needs to step in and fix it.'

'Just like you did in the State, and back at the Amarrian retreat,' Heci said. 'Sometimes I think you're doing this stuff just so you can get into trouble and move on to somewhere else.'

'I'm not. I'm really not,' Ralea said. 'I think.'

There was silence on the line.

Eventually Heci said, 'What's her real name?'

'Aziza.'

Ralea knocked on the door of a woman she had never spoken to but nonetheless knew was a liar.

No one else was in the corridor. It was late and people were likely tired.

There was absolute silence on the other side of the door, too, and Ralea promised herself that if all she was about to accomplish was wake up the baby, she would *build* the family a house in a new home at the end of the journey. A house with a pool. And a nursemaid.

There was a shuffling, followed by more silence. Ralea could feel invisible eyes on her.

The door opened a crack. A frizzy-haired head with dark eyes hovered into view.

'I live in this hall.' Ralea said. 'I know your son, Fel,' she added, as if that were a secret key to admittance.

The woman regarded her, then stepped aside and opened the door. Ralea walked in. The woman closed the door behind them.

The quarters were similar in design to Ralea's, though these had – understandably, she thought – a lot more belongings in them. There was an extra room that she thought might belong to Fel, though the door was closed, as were the doors to what, if the architecture matched, would be the main bedroom and the bathroom.

She walked into the living room. It had baby clothing and some toys, and a datapad sitting on a table, but it was remarkably clean. Ralea couldn't imagine the effort that must go into keeping these quarters clean with a child and infant resident. Her own apartment seemed to radiate dust and cruddy dirt wherever she looked.

The woman walked past her into the living room, bearing two glasses. She took a seat on the couch and poured water from a jar into them. Ralea couldn't quite figure her mood, nor get it to match with any persona she had imagined this woman to have: neither the abused housewife she'd thought of at first, nor the shadowy mystery she'd considered more recently. The woman was not afraid of her, but wary. Not wary, alert. Awake. Waiting.

Ralea said, 'I wanted to see you, just briefly, and thank you for your son's work for me the other day. I hope the medicines I gave him were of some help.'

The woman nodded. Ralea leaned forward, picked up a glass of water and took a sip. She had wanted to reassure herself there was nothing out of the ordinary, and even as she was being given that reassurance, it failed utterly to calm her mind. Heci's words rang in her head. Maybe she was just hunting for problems; injustices to correct.

Ralea sat there for a few moments before the silence pushed her to her feet. 'Anyway, I'm sorry for bothering you. Thank you for the water.' She started to walk away, far more disturbed than she felt she ought to be. Whatever the purpose for her visit, it hadn't been fulfilled, and Ralea wasn't sure that she could leave this apartment before dredging up at least a nominal peace of mind.

'Actually, could I use your bathroom?' she said brightly. The woman nodded, so Ralea went in and locked the door after her.

She sat on the floor, her face in her hands, breathing in slowly for a minute. When she looked up again, she was struck by how clean this room was, too. Bathrooms shouldn't be this spotless, not on dirty Minmatar caravans headed to nowhere, with tired parents and children in tow.

She closed her eyes tight and gently rubbed them. She wondered if she was turning entirely too paranoid for her own good. It would do her good to settle down into whatever work the Minmatar offered. She kept rubbing her eyes as she considered whether she could apply for work in some sort of emergency assistance. She seemed to be good at helping people.

When she opened her eyes again there were little stars hovering about in her vision. She blinked them away and tried to focus on the stark bathroom in front of her, with its varnished walls and unimposing decor. The floor seemed to have a few dark scratches, down where the floor met the wall. She leaned forward and touched them to ground herself. She needed imperfection right now, and the ability to accept it in other people – that they could exist in reality even if they failed to embody the sane, sensible ideals in her head.

When she pulled her fingers back the scratches came with them.

She looked quizzically at her fingertips. As she inspected them there was a noise outside: a series of dull, rhythmic thumps.

The scratches fell from her fingertips and on to the floor. Ralea realized they were tiny little black hairs. Beard stubble.

She got up and unlocked the door and stepped out, and she'd taken a first step into the corridor when there was a dull explosion in her head and the stars returned with a vengeance.

She was on the floor now, crawling, but it was hard because she couldn't see well and her hands wouldn't move. When she pulled at them, they were pulled back. Her wrists were being pushed onto the small of her back. Someone was holding her wrists. Someone was on top of her, holding her wrists. There was a thunderous knocking. Voices said something she didn't understand.

She managed to turn her head enough to see the frizzy hair hanging over her. Her wrists seemed to be entangled, but she pulled at them and the restraints gave way. A voice cursed.

There was a sharp pain in her shoulders as she was yanked up to her knees, then set on her unsteady feet. She was facing the exit door, and the thunderous knocking was coming from its other side.

It fell silent for a moment, then was followed by a bang loud enough to leave a ringing in her ears. The door flew open and a group of black-clad people stormed in.

Ralea tried to turn and look at who was holding her, but a sharp pain at her throat made her freeze up. She looked as far as she could down to one side, and saw that a hand by her neck held a knife.

A woman's voice hissed in her ear, 'I knew you'd come for us! I've been waiting, you little traitor.'

The black-clad troops yelled at someone to stand down, back off and face the wall. Behind them, Ralea glimpsed Heci's anxious face staring in.

There was a knife against her throat. People were yelling and screaming, and there was a knife against her throat.

She went for it before she could think. Tears sprung forth, and in her most helpless, tremulous voice she started wailing, 'Don't-killmedon'tkillmedon'tkillme.' She let her body tremble, which it readily did, and prayed it would cover the movement of her hand sliding into a pocket. She pulled something out, felt for the edge with her thumb and hoped the woman's eyes were focused on the black agents, then sighed loudly and let herself sag down as if fainting. The woman caught her weight, as she'd hoped, and loosened the blade's pressure on her throat a little. It was enough for Ralea. She turned her head quickly, feeling the flesh on her skin slice open from the sharp knife, saw where the woman's leg was, and pulled out of her pocket the gift, the Minmatar metal plate. She brought the sharp point of the metal plate on to the woman's inner thigh as hard as she could, pushing it with her hand. It tore into her captor, and Ralea yanked it upwards, carving even deeper, into flesh and meat, as the woman screamed and grabbed for her hand. Ralea swiftly let go of the plate, turned and grasped at the knife-holding hand, caught a hold of its wrist and held on for dear life as she twisted away from its grasp. She kept turning, and with all her strength wrenched the arm down until the knife dropped from the womans' arm, clattering on the floor. When she saw the woman's other arm rise, she set one leg, exhaled sharply and drove her other knee as hard into her stomach as she could.

The woman gave out an explosive wheeze and collapsed on to her knees. Before the troops could reach them, Ralea grabbed her frizzy hair and pulled her head up so that their eyes met. 'I could have killed you,' she hissed at the woman. 'Remember that.'

Troops moved past, silent now, and Heci's guiding hand found her arm and led her out. They sat down together in the corridor, not saying anything, the salt of Heci's tears mixing with the blood coursing from the flesh wound on Ralea's throat. There came noise from the apartment, of things being torn apart and of a man's voice raised in anger and then in pleading. When the men came out, she saw the infant in one of the black-clad soldier's arms, then a strange man being dragged out in cuffs, then the boy being held by another soldier. The boy's eyes stared at her as he was carried away. None of the doors in the corridors ever opened.

*

'He was a war criminal.'

Ralea lay on a soft couch in Heci's apartment. It had conformed itself to her back and was gently kneading her muscles, which were tense like metal cords. Her eyes were closed. She was thinking of distant lands, far away from the empires.

'Are you asleep, hon?' Heci asked her.

Ralea shook her head very slowly. 'Keep talking.'

'He was a war criminal. Aziza was his wife. They had some contacts in a station we're going to dock at, so likely they planned to jump ship there.'

'What did he do?'

'I . . . haven't been told,' Heci said. 'Not by the people who truly know. There are stories but they conflict in details. He wasn't a nice man, that's all they agree on.'

'Give me examples.'

'I don't have any. Apparently it's not so much any particular action, as the man's complete lack of restraint. No Amarrian was safe from him, and he treated them like paper dolls.'

Ralea sighed. 'You've got to be pretty damn nasty for the Minmatar to reject your efforts in the struggle for freedom.'

'What turned them against him is probably half due to the PR value. They still need outsiders to sympathize with their cause. They're not going to get that while some rogue agent of theirs is brutalizing the opposition.'

'And they really won't admit what this man had been getting up to?'

'Knives,' Heci said with an audible shiver. 'He likes to use knives. That's all I've heard from the top.'

The couch kept kneading Ralea's back as she tried her best not to consider this.

'What's going to happen to him?' she said eventually. 'How are they going to try him?'

'They're not,' Heci said shortly.

She sat up. 'What?'

'You've got to understand the situation. There's a lot of hope surrounding this entire trip. For once in its life, the Minmatar Republic has something else to look forward to than more bloodshed and fighting with the Amarr. They won't let anything detract from that. Also,' she sniffed, 'this guy still has supporters. I don't know who they are, but they're high up, and they're not going to let him be tried. They won't risk that he might speak, say who cleared his way. Some of them probably even believe in the cause.'

'Gods,' Ralea said, stunned.

'This new thing, this project, some people in the republic are going along for the ride just to wait for it to fail. They don't believe in anything but the old cause, to get back everything the Amarr Empire took and reduce it to glowing dust. To them, this guy's a hero. They'll let him disappear somewhere he can't do harm. They celebrate their own people, even those who've done terrible things.' Heci sat next to her, put a hand on her shoulder. 'I'm sorry.'

'They're no better than all the others. They really aren't,' Ralea said.

Heci sighed, looked at the floor. 'I wish I could disagree with that.'

'I have to get out of this, Heci.' She looked at her friend, slowly shaking her head. 'I have to get out.'

'You don't want to join in the rebuilding?' Heci said. It was hardly even a question. Her name had come up in reports. There would be no career for her at the end of the journey.

'I've had enough of people and places that're rotten to the core.'

'Oh, I'm sure there's some job you could find somewhere, if you lay low and get a new name—'

'But it has to be for the right *cause*. That's the thing,' Ralea said. 'No matter what nation I'd end up hiding in, I couldn't just follow along with the others, work at ground level, if I knew my efforts would eventually support nothing I believe in. The Gallente and their worship of the physical, the Amarr and their empty spirituality, the Caldari and their lock-step ways, and now this. The Minmatar say they're anti-slavery and pro-liberty, but they've played the martyrs for years, and when something like this comes up they refuse to take on any responsibility for their own acts. Whatever they are, I want no part of it. I cannot *stand* corruption among those who claim to be helpers and benefactors.'

'You've been thinking this over for a while, I see.'

Ralea nodded. She was thinking, as she had been doing increasingly often, of a meeting she'd had with someone in her past life; a meeting where she'd taken to heart entirely the wrong lessons.

'All the same,' Heci said. 'I'm not sure you can ever find a place that doesn't have its dark side. This was one man you encountered, Ralea. One bad apple.'

'And the ones who hold him up,' she said bitterly. 'All the branches on the tree.'

Heci said, 'So, what are you going to do? It's obvious you're going to have to run, but you better understand that if you talk about dying one more time, I'm trussing you up and taking you back to the Federation.'

Ralea grinned and said, 'Don't worry. I think ... I need to do what I should've done from the start, though I doubt I would have appreciated the choice. I needed this. And I love you so much for going through it with me, Heci. I hope you know that.' She smiled at her friend, who smiled back.

'It's been fun,' Heci said. 'And whatever you're going to tell me is probably going to be stupid and crazy, but I'll back you all the way.'

'You're sure about going back to agenting, then?'

Heci nodded. 'I've gotten assurances that things will be cleared up when I go back.' She shrugged. 'I think I knew it all along, just like you. Just needed the time to see it.'

Ralea nodded in turn. 'Not me. I need to help others. It's atonement, partly. No politics, and no secret scheming.'

'Whatever it is,' Heci said, 'I swear, if you ever need anything, I will be there for you. In the tower, with the capsuleers.'

Ralea took her hand and gave a brittle smile. 'I know.'

'So where are you going to go? Who are you going to devote yourselves to?'

'The only ones I can,' Ralea said. 'The Sisters of EVE.'

16

Drem walked slowly through the forest. The sun shone through the atmospheric shielding far above him, warming the air and casting great leafy shadows on the ground like a darkened net. His shoes kicked up a little dirt with every step. He had been walking since morning.

They had requested temporary leave after the Sansha visit. Given their status, the request was accepted without question. The Sansha were a dark kingdom, possibly second in potent horror only to the Blood Raiders, and there was no penalty for Sisters who needed a reprieve from the risk of capture and implantation. They were now in a Sisters sanctuary in an unspecified system, where the only purpose was R&R, and the calls that came in were on anything but emergencies.

There were options for socializing and plenty of options for solitude, too. The area Drem was traversing had started as a vast, tended public park, years ago. All who visited had gravitated toward its overgrown sections, until eventually its custodians decided simply to let it take care of itself. Trees had grown and taken over; lakes had formed with a little help and pushed against the grass; and whatever paths lay through the dense forest were there on the whim of the flora.

The custodians ran scans on the place every now and then, to ensure a total absence of dangerous visitors. Occasionally they would bring in a few easily domesticated birds and rodents. Otherwise they left the forest, and everyone in it, to themselves.

Drem found his way to a fallen log that lay by the side of a lake. The lake was not too large; he could throw a stone across it with ease. Something was swimming on the far side, a dark brown bird of some sort that paid him no notice.

He'd needed data and capital and secret technology, and he'd extracted promises for two out of three.

Two out of three wasn't bad, he thought. A small chuckle escaped his mouth. Two out of three, well, that was *all right for now.*

He was finding it a little harder to think straight, these days. He hadn't slept much, and the reason was, the reason was, the reason was . . .

He rubbed his eyes and slowly breathed in the forest air.

He had two of the three things he needed to avenge his family. And the third, the data, could be acquired somehow. Bit by bit. Nevermind that the chances of getting caught would rise exponentially – and he'd probably get taken out by the Blood Raiders long before he could even get to that point.

But if he ignored that minor problem and assumed he had all three components, and if he circled back to the original plan, then everything was ready for execution. There was only one small problem.

The whole thing was still impossible.

Completing the plan on a grand scale could be done with lots of planning, years' worth of it. He could carefully insert hired agents into the capsuleer hardware upkeep crew, to the point where they could start pulling in more of their own people. That would eventually create an inside team to implant every single detachment chamber with the Sansha hardware, have it worked into the pilots' heads without their knowledge, and, at some armageddon moment in the distant future, drive them to their deaths.

But the test case was different. The test case could not wait for years. The pilot – *the* pilot – lived in those quarters, and they would need to be infiltrated before he could move. In order to get to him, and to prove this whole damn scheme could work at all, Drem would need more than generalized access codes provided by a pirate.

He had thought this over for innumerable sleepless nights. He had tried to figure out how to use all this data in order to breach the capsuleer sanctum. The more he studied the token datapackage that Hona had sent him, with its tiny fraction of extant data, the more he realized what an insurmountable problem it presented.

For every kind of intrusion plan he could think of, the one irreducible component they all had in common was someone on the inside, someone working with him to get them into the holiest of holies, the capsuleer quarters, where no damn access code would work without a real proper human being behind it. He simply could not do it alone, no matter how much money and information he had.

And that someone would have to forfeit their life, much as he had. There would be no going back. Eventually – perhaps not right away, but eventually – the plan would be discovered, either through failure or successful execution, and when that time came the authorities would scour every log in existence, and they would find out about the test case, and they would find whoever had helped him out.

The fallen log's surface was dry and cracked. When Drem picked at it, it came off in flakes.

He would need someone on the inside, and he didn't have that and never would, and he was perfectly, utterly, absolutely content with letting the whole damn thing die right there.

He threw one of the flakes at the bird. It dropped into the lake an arm's length away. The bird didn't care.

The plan was sunk. He wasn't going to pull it off.

He closed his eyes, leaned back and took a deep breath. He felt the forest in his lungs. It was possible he was smiling. It was also possible he had known this all along. He was not a murderer.

He leaned back a little more, taking in the air and the sun, lost his grip and nearly fell off the log. He scrambled for balance and managed to right himself, leaving nail marks in the bark during the process. As he cleaned the crud from under his fingernails, the bird squawked, as if mocking him.

The sound made him chuckle, and before he knew it he was roaring loudly with laughter that erupted out of him like a volcano.

He covered his face with his hands and kept them there until he quietened down.

A flutter told him the bird had flown away. The sound reminded him of that faint, brief barrage a Sisters agent learned to recognize as the first indications of an electrical fire, right before it burst out of a generator and incinerated whoever you were trying to pull out of a wreckage. Or perhaps it was more similar to the rattling of ocular orbs, rising from the stomach of a mind-controlled animal in the halls of the dead. One or the other.

It occurred to him that he might be edging close to a breakdown. He wondered what could have brought it on. He'd lived a crisis-free life up until now, really.

He was going to have to run. From the Raiders, and from this whole mess. Go underground. It didn't seem fair, but it was the only way out that made any sense. He had needed absolution, for having allowed – it *felt* like allowed – himself to lose his family, and for screwing up the aftermath of his brother's death. The rescue work had allowed him to forget all this, to express in action his love for humanity and for one specific other person, until it all turned dark and rotten.

And then he had needed all this time and effort merely to admit that he didn't want to be a murderer, never had wanted it. He needed to be an avenger, but it was his lot to save lives, not take them. He had found who he was, useless as that knowledge might be to him now.

If he did not have the Blood Raiders on his heels – hell, if he had reached the Sisters by any other route – he honestly would have been content, if not completely happy, spending his life in their faction. Even knowing he was sleeping with a woman who slept with others, working with a man who cared nothing for the future, and destined to end up a pockmarked angel himself, some time down the road – the rescues made up for it. The saving of life still trumped everything. It was his purpose, or at least the only one, apart from revenge for Leip's death, he could imagine fulfilling.

And Drem thought, with logic as clear as water, that one of the benefits of being a dead man was that one need tell no lies.

*

'Hi guys. I need to tell you something.'

Ortag and Yaman and Verena walked into the grove. They were in the forest, near another, smaller lake – a pond, really – and there were several seats about, small benches hewn out of stone or carved out of wood. Drem couldn't imagine doing this inside a room of glass and metal.

Each of his teammates sat down and looked around. 'This is nice,' Yaman said. 'This is really damn nice.'

'You haven't been here?' Drem asked.

'No, been hanging out in the rec centres for the most part. Either working out or watching vids. Having a proper vacation.'

'Our man doesn't want his body polluted by oxygen or sunlight,' Ortag added, picking up a small branch and running his fingers over it.

'Dude, I worked hard for this pale tan.' Yaman rolled back his sleeves, extended an arm. 'You don't get blue veins like this on just anyone.'

'What's up?' Verena gently asked Drem. He hoped, with all the force of the knot in his stomach and the grip on his heart, that he wouldn't disappoint them too badly.

'I haven't been truthful to you guys. Not at all,' he said.

He paused. The outlines of what he wanted to say, the main points, were clear in his head, but he didn't know how to explain them. He had never confessed something like this before.

'I'm . . . a traitor,' he said.

That caught their attention.

'All this time we've been working together, I've been doing it under false pretences.'

'Those people you saved, they were pretty real, son,' Ortag said.

'They were, but that wasn't the point. It wasn't done for them.' Drem hesitated. 'Well . . . not at first.'

'What have you been doing?' Verena asked. It sounded odd to hear it from her.

Drem took a deep breath, of earth and trees and water, and began to tell them.

They sat entirely still for most of his story, which he recounted standing, his body unable to hold still. His admission of the secret purpose he had created behind his work – from the innocent start of wanting the capsuleer's name and it's connection to their strange mission to Hona's asteroid, to the evil plan he'd concocted among the Guristas and how he'd followed up on it on that terrible colony of loneliness with Sansha's Nation – it all rang strangely in his ears, as if he were telling them of someone he'd once known.

He followed it up with the details of his plans: to acquire confidential information from the Angels, funding from the Guristas and experimental hardware from the Sansha, and to breach a capsuleer's quarters to see if they could slowly gain control of his mind, later to recruit workers in key places and expand the project to every capsuleer in space. He explained who the subject of this test case was going to be.

All of this he recounted to the team in the full expectation that they would simply get up and leave, disgusted with how he had perverted the Sisters credo in his private quest for revenge. To his gratified amazement they remained there, still listening, their expressions unreadable.

He finished up by telling them the plan was incomplete – in small part because of the minimal support he expected from Hona, but mostly due to the lack of someone with high-level access and a definite willingness for self-sacrifice – and why it was not ever going to come to fruition.

The three teammates looked at one another for the longest time.

'I've been running a scheme behind your backs the whole time. I am so sorry,' Drem reiterated.

'Drem ... We know,' Ortag said, looking at the branch in his hands.

'What?'

'We always knew,' Verena said as well.

'You ... the ... wait, *what*?' Drem said, before he utterly lost his grip on the words.

Verena said to him, her tone clad in velvet, 'There is within the Sisters of EVE a smaller, clandestine group that has recognized the threat of capsuleers and the immense, terrible destruction they've brought to people's lives all over New Eden. This group does everything in its power to counteract that threat. When you arrived at our station, with your history, we immediately put a watch on you. And when you started asking around, not to mention requesting all sorts of strange information through our databanks, we started to pay very close attention to you.'

'You spied on me,' Drem said. He sat, if only so his legs wouldn't collapse from underneath him.

'We eased your way. You think a rookie acolyte would ever have been able to look up all the information you did? Or get all those paths cleared for him? You've done amazingly well—'

'Let me say something,' Ortag interjected. He looked directly at Drem, though his expression was hidden behind his greying beard. 'The kind of career you've had with us, that would've happened whatever you were planning. Whatever else has been going on, you're easily the most impressive newcomer I've seen come to this organization in a very long time. You've impressed the Angels and the Guristas, and hell, probably the Sansha, if anyone knows their mind. And us. You've impressed us.'

'Well, that's fucking nice,' Drem sighed and rubbed his fingers over his eyes. He was swaying in his seat. Everything felt a little up in the air right now, a little fuzzy around the edges.

'It's real fucking nice,' he heard Yaman say. 'We've saved thousands of people. Whatever the hell else you were doing, that counts.'

'I'm sorry, I just ... you knew? You really, all this time, you were simply using me?' Drem asked them.

'We were saving people, son,' Ortag said. 'And he's right. We didn't know what you were up to, but heuristics on the data digging you were doing back at the start indicated that it'd be sensible to let you do it. Even if it posed a risk to us.'

'I never intentionally—' Drem said, but Ortag raised his hand.

'I know,' he said. 'Doesn't matter, either way. I'd willingly die if it meant ridding the world of those rats in the sky. And the further along you got, the more of a reason we had to help pave your way.'

Drem looked at the three of them. They were the same people

he'd known all along, and the same ones he'd trusted with his life, but now they all seemed like actors. Just as he had, all this time, he thought. He'd been so caught up in his own agenda that he hadn't realized other people had minds and plans of their own. No wonder they had gone along so easily with all his ideas, no matter how crazy or self-serving. No wonder almost everything had worked out. His mission had been their own, even before he'd even seen it fully formed.

Verena said, 'We know about the data you need from the Angels. We know about the money from the Guristas. We know about the Sansha and the technology they offered you. It's a wonderful thing, Drem. It all came from your mind, even if we pushed it along. We've tried so hard to find an angle, but even when we thought we'd found one, like with the Book—'

Ortag shot her a look. 'That's not important now.'

'The what?' Drem said. He had no desire to change the subject, but the idea of these people knowing more than he did about anything felt completely anathema. When they didn't respond, he half-yelled, 'Answer me!'

Ortag sighed. 'You remember Hona?' he said.

'Yeah.'

'Last time we tried something of this magnitude, with the Black Mountain project, it went very wrong. Hona got pulled in. She's pretty much the only survivor, if you can call it that. She's not exactly enamoured of us, and I'm amazed she even wanted to see you, knowing as she probably did exactly what you would eventually try to pull off.' He picked up another branch, used it to scratch the back of his hand. 'That's by the by. We have a real chance now. We've funnelled resources your way because we believe you can do this. We believe it's a necessary thing. Don't lose heart now. You're so close.'

Drem said, 'Do you . . . are you listening to yourselves?'

'We represent greater forces, Drem,' Ortag told him. 'They want what you want. *We* want what you want.'

He thought of greater forces. Of having his plan pushed along. And in a tiny nova of hurt and anger, he thought of all the little things. The letter from the Angel captain, delivered through Verena, and the willingness with which they'd gone to meet Hona. The offer from the Gurista overseer, and the strange talk of trust with the Rabbit. The cold, terrifying audience before Sansha himself, when he spoke of his contact with *others*. It hadn't just been other pirates. It had been the Sisters themselves.

And the night of betrayal after he'd told Verena she was his one and vital anchor. He looked at her in sheer agony.

Her expression was unreadable. 'I'd made sure you were on the right path, but you were getting ready to leave it. I pushed you back,' she said.

In the near-silence, the birdsong felt like nails scraping on metal.

Burying his head in his hands, he said, 'Do you have *any idea* how crazy this is?'

'You seemed to believe in it pretty good,' Yaman said.

He looked up in rage and astonishment. 'I was fucked up! I lost my family and damn near killed myself in some delusional attempt to make up for it! And even when I came up with this mad plan to take revenge on everyone, some tiny tattered shred of sanity that was left in my head made it so that the plan couldn't possibly work!'

'The only thing you need is high-level access,' Ortag said.

Drem quieted, forcing himself to take deep breaths. 'In theory, yeah. For the first raw run. And nobody here has that. Data can be had but pre-existing access can't. The plan is dead.'

'We'll see,' Ortag said.

Drem fixed him with a look. 'You are not going to find someone with the kind of access I would need, but say that you could, I am not going to take part. The last few months of my life have changed the way I think. This is wrong. This is murder.'

'And what was done to your family?'

'Has nothing to do with this. The Sisters of EVE are dedicated to saving lives and no matter what crazy ideas I or anyone else may have, there is absolutely no justification for twisting that purpose into anything like I was going to do. It's wrong. That's the end of it.'

'You do realize, son, that we'll proceed without you.'

'Not without my go-ahead, you won't,' Drem said. 'I don't care what information you spied from the factions; you won't be getting anything from Hona's people or the Guristas, and I very much doubt even the Sansha will assist you. You may have set these things up, but I was the one who made the deals, based on my own reputation and nobody else's. Anyone thinks they can do different, let's see them take a walk with the Rabbit, or walk into the middle of a zombie factory and talk to the face that speaks for Sansha Kuvakei.'

He stood up. They did not speak as he walked away. He kept going, perfectly calm, one step after another, and when after an hour's walk he came to another lake in the woods he strode right into it, took a deep breath, dunked his head underwater and screamed so hard he thought his lungs would bleed.

Days passed. Drem took himself off comms and stayed out of the way.

He spent half his time being furious and the other half feeling like a total moron. He had saved lives with these people. He had grown to believe in the cause they were supposed to represent. All the anger, bargaining and sadness – everything he had gone through – had made him what he was now.

Late one night he walked within visual distance of the team's quarters, and stood stock still, looking at them from a distance.

All that was over now. He'd have preferred to simply jettison Verena and all the rest of them into space, but in the absence of that satisfying option, he simply did not know what to do.

But that pilot was still out there. The datapackage from Hona had named him and given his whereabouts.

And his brother lay dead in his microsealed coffin, cold and unburied.

His head felt heavy. He was very, very angry, and his mind was moving entirely too fast; making connections, looking above and behind every piece of fact, trying to find a way to tie it all together before the angels of death and blood came to claim him. It was exhausting and it felt futile, even as he couldn't stop, for there was really nothing else for him to do.

He had half decided to run after all when Verena walked up to him. She'd been so quiet, or he so lost in thought, that he had no idea how long she had been there.

'We found someone,' she said.

'Good for you,' he said, not knowing what she meant. 'Am I being replaced?'

She stared at him, and for a gut-wrenching moment he thought she might cry. Then she visibly pulled herself together and said, 'No, Drem. We found what you needed. A recent convert to the Sisters, still on active long-term leave from her old job. A capsuleer associate with high-level access. An agent.'

He stared at her. The core of hidden connections came to life.

'We can do this, Drem. We really can. We can do this if you don't leave, if you don't leave and you do this with us, we can make this work,' she said, the words spilling out of her mouth.

The anger that arose in his mind threatened to burst out of his mouth, but he kept it in check, if barely. A crystal cold was settling on his mind, forcing him to see options he hadn't realized until this moment.

'I need to think a little,' he said and started walking away. He hesitated, then softly added, 'Don't give up hope.'

Her smile was so full of warmth and relief, he couldn't bear to look at it.

It was a long walk. The core of ideas unfurled itself, spreading its black arms like the Red God, open to take in everything it touched. It was a long walk, and it was a long time to think, and Drem felt the connections take hold in terrifying ways.

By the time he found that pockmarked face, waiting for him on a bench by the lake, he knew exactly what he would do. The anger had turned to a vicious kind of glee, and it was all he could do to hold it back.

'Verena spoke to me,' he said, in a tone he forced to be affectionate.

Ortag regarded him. Eventually he said, 'And?'

'Who is this agent?'

Ortag looked out at the lake. There were no birds there; no movement of any kind, other than gentle waves lapping at the shore. 'I'm sorry,' he said. 'You came into our lives like a gift from heaven.

For the longest time I believed that you were simply going through the same awakening we did. We have all been there. We've all lost someone, one way or another. Because of *them*.'

He looked at Drem. 'So if you feel we have betrayed you, son, I truly am sorry. Sometimes our causes get the better of us.'

Drem swallowed quietly. He knew what needed to happen, but he did not know what to say.

Ortag saved him. 'This woman, her name is Ralea. She lives not far from here. H sector. I haven't heard her whole story, and she's not inclined to share it all right now, but I'm given to understand she's been through a long, hard tour of the empires, on the run for the most part. She told us we were the right ones for her, given all that she's seen. However you may want to look at it, I can't say I disagree.'

Ortag gave him another look, and this one sealed Drem's intention. It wasn't a look of sympathy, though Drem had no doubt the man felt for him. It was not a look of rejection, nor of betrayal – Ortag accepted him and, apparently, still expected him to accept them in return.

From this old man's bearded face and his calm, nonchalant voice that constantly belied his devious plans; whose knowledge that Drem might be the sole linchpin in those plans; from this supposed saviour of lives who carried murder in his heart, came a look of desperate hope.

Drem nodded to him, and made himself smile. 'I am going to pay her a visit,' he said. 'To explain.'

Ortag hesitated, so Drem laid a hand on his shoulder and said, as gently as he could, 'Don't worry. Don't. We're on the same team. And after tonight, she will be, too.'

He rang the bell outside her quarters and heard it sound inside. A few moments later the door opened, and a woman about his age, maybe a little older, looked at him with a familiar mixture of curiosity and weariness. He had seen that expression before, though rather less pretty, whenever he looked in the mirror. Its lines traced a map of times past and old agonies.

'I'm from the Sisters. My name is Drem,' he said.

'Hello Drem. I'm Ralea,' she replied. She did not open the door any wider, but neither did she seem to be nervous at his appearance. She merely stood there, waiting to hear whatever he had to say.

'You've just recently joined the Sisters,' he said.

'Yes,' she replied.

'Why, may I ask?'

'Because I wanted to do good,' she said, a little annoyance creeping in.

He regarded that face, and its lines; and its eyes, which were distant but sharp, taking everything in from a great distance. She met his gaze without wavering.

'Why did you really join?' he asked, there in the darkness.

She kept looking into his eyes. Eventually her gaze softened a fraction, not in acceptance, and certainly not yet in trust, but in approval. Acknowledgement, perhaps.

She said, 'The rest of the world and I, we don't get along. We tried, but it didn't work out. We don't see eye to eye.'

It took him a moment to realize he was nodding. 'So what brought you here?'

She looked around, taking in the darkness behind him. 'The Sisters, they seem to treat people right. Maybe they're the only ones that do. I had a lot of things go wrong, and a lot of people let me down, until there was very little left except a drive to do good and a faith I could find others who wanted to do the same.'

'You believe in the Sisters.' It was hardly a question.

'I do,' she said.

'Then you and I, we need to have a talk,' he said. 'Is it OK if I come in?'

She looked him over. 'I think I want to hear what you've got to say,' she said, 'but you're going to stay out here for the time being while I call a couple of friends and tell them I'm having a visitor over.'

He gave a small smile that he hoped didn't make him look like a predator. 'That'll be fine.'

'Good. And besides,' she said, with a small smile of her own that spoke volumes of sense and confidence, 'if the background checks turn up anything I don't like, they can still come over to help remove your body.'

His laughter felt better than anything had in a long time.

It took a while, but she eventually returned to the door, a carefully blank expression on her face.

'So, those background checks go all right?' Drem joked.

She seemed at a loss at how to answer. Eventually she said, 'You've been to places that I didn't imagine many Sisters had. There are ... connections that you may not have been aware of.'

Drem raised an eyebrow. 'How so?'

'I think you had better take a seat,' Ralea said, stepping aside to let him in.

When he left her quarters at dawn they had the exact same taut, steely expression on their faces. He headed to his own apartment, where he composed a long message to Hona, encrypted it with a key that had been located in her datapackage, and sent it to Captain Kiel Rhan. He attached a note to Rhan explaining that this packet contained the details of a plan that should convince their mutual friend of its righteousness, and asking that he forward it as soon as possible.

A few minutes later he received acknowledgement from Rhan, and only a couple of hours after, he began receiving transmissions from an unknown source. Hona had approved of his plan. He was more relieved than he could say.

He went to the forest one last time to meet with the team.

'I want to apologize for acting the way I did,' he said, quite calmly. 'It was inexcusable.'

They began to speak, but he raised a hand. 'I ask forgiveness from you and from the people who backed you in your work. I've come to my senses. I've thought it over and I've gotten my head right. And I've convinced Ralea to join our cause.'

'Drem ...' Ortag began, then faded.

'There's something you should know,' Verena said. 'About this agent. And about something she did.'

'She contacted some people last night, and then she ran some checks,' Yaman said. 'Our people are monitoring her, same way we monitored you back in the day. They were curious about the data she was requesting, but they didn't put it all together until it was too late.'

'I know. She told me.'

Verena said, 'I seriously tell you, we didn't know—'

'That she was the one who issued the capsuleer his mission? The mission that ended up with him destroying the colony I lived on?' Drem said in an icy tone.

Verena fell quiet, and nodded her head.

Drem said to them, 'Think of it as a . . . test. Of good faith. She told me about it, and I convinced her to join our side. That should be all the proof you need that I intend to see this thing through to the end. Besides, the fact that she's effectively giving up the only chance she has of having a life in the empire means a lot to me.'

And he realized he would never know if it was coincidence or not. Or even if these people had known. The cabal might have planned it without telling them.

He looked at them. The expressions of relief on their faces were palpable, and he smiled. 'With your permission, the two of us can leave immediately and start the trial run. I would have liked for you to join me, but we all know that this plan can only ever accommodate people who won't be returning. And with this . . . particular case, I should hope it's obvious why one of those people will be me.'

They stood up and walked over to him. Ortag clapped a hand on his shoulder, Yaman shook his hand, and Verena gave him a deep, tight hug that lasted forever. He buried his head in the crook of her neck and breathed in deeply.

They promised to trust him with this mission, Ralea at his side; and in that forest, they let him go.

PART III

Rebirth

17

It took their caravan a long time to arrive at the station. Neither Drem nor Ralea minded. He needed the time to steady his nerves. She needed the time to adjust to yet another drastic turn in her life.

They got along well. Drem found, much to his surprise, that he liked telling her stories of rescue missions past. His comfort with the revisitation of those memories depended entirely on the listener, and in her he encountered a rapt attention combined with care and deep insight. She wasn't disturbed by the amount of blood and suffering that inevitably followed the recounting. Agents, she explained to him with a savage amusement, had a high tolerance for carnage, seeing as how they were the architects of destruction for a reasonable portion of all celestial deaths. She took care not to mention one fateful mission she had ordered, and he avoided that same topic.

The darkness that haunted some of Drem's stories seemed a little less gloomy when he spoke them aloud to her. He felt a measure of guilt about ruining her chances to do rescue missions of her own, but she reassured him that it was all right. She was used to adapting by now. After their talk she had seen a lot of things differently.

In turn she shared her stories of past lives, cycling through the last few months in the different empires and eventually going back – with a little trepidation that was easily overcome by the distance of time and the comfort of Drem's interest – to the agenting period, and her encounters with capsuleers. She told him how those people lived, and it was testament to her delivery and charm that the stories of the high life and those who lived it did not constantly remind Drem of the one who'd become the focus of his own life.

In between conversations they spent most of their time either studying mission data, or looking out of the viewports and letting the reality of their plan settle in their heads. Sometimes they looked at each other, most often when one thought the other wouldn't see it.

Doubt, that self-destructive catalyst for failure, was not an option. Both people had learned this in their previous careers. There was only one nervous moment when Ralea looked up and realized Drem had been staring out of the port for a long while, his mind getting lost in the darkness. When he turned to her, he said, 'Are you sure your credentials are up to this?'

She made sure to keep her voice calm and free of worry. 'Agents are safe. No matter what else I've done, they can't start processing my case until I'm back in Federation space, and even then there's a guaranteed two-day sanction period for me to prepare my arguments. In that period I have to retain uninterrupted access rights. I'd only risk losing them if I did something I shouldn't on Federation soil.'

'And you're absolutely sure that *killing* someone doesn't fall under that?'

She shrugged genially. 'What can I say? We're the elite.'

'Well, let's hope,' Drem said.

She walked over to him and put a hand on his shoulder. 'It's going to be fine. We're going to go in there, follow your plan, use your money and my access rights, make our way up the levels in that station until we get to the quarters of that capsuleer. And then we'll do what we need to do. It's really going to be all right.'

He turned away from the port, looking at her and giving a small smile. She squeezed his shoulder.

He said, without rancour, 'I'm not sure which one of us you're trying to convince. Are you sure you're comfortable taking this all the way to the end?'

She thought it over. 'Honestly, I've caused so many deaths in my career that what we're about to do – to someone like *him* – won't change anything, one way or another.'

He looked at her for a while, not saying anything.

She met his gaze, then said, 'Shit, I just realized how that sounded. Look, I . . . I really didn't kill them. Your family.'

'Ralea—'

'But I was responsible, and there are *no words* to express how sorry I am. Same goes for a lot of other things I did when I was an agent. But this one journey we're now on, the way we're going to break everything open, it's going to make up a bit for that. It has to. Not completely, not by a long shot, but at least it'll close the door for good on something I need to let go of. A system I despise, and people who've ruined it.'

'That's not what was on my mind,' he said. 'I simply thought this affected you more than you were willing to let on.'

She looked at the floor. 'Guess I just confirmed that, didn't I?'

'You were a piece in a larger machine. Remember that. It's what I've been telling myself. It wasn't just you. And we're going to make it right.'

As the station hovered into view they made their final preparations, and just before they were due to dock they approached one another and hugged tight.

Landing was remarkably easy, with none of the shuddering tremors Drem had long since started to associate with arrival on stations. He reminded himself that this mission could not be run on instinct. This was not a war-torn lowsec colony where he could march in and take charge under authority of the Sisters banner. Ralea likewise reminded herself that this was not an Amarrian religious retreat, nor an assembly line for a Minmatar renaissance. She was no longer an outsider, observing a new world; but neither was she an agent again. She would have to act as if she belonged, and remember that she did not.

They came in at one of the lower levels in the station, not that far from its churning, dirty core of operations. The sheer number of people she saw on the other side of the hangar entrance area astounded her. This was a truer life than the one she'd known, certainly, though it was true in good part because anything that sounded, looked and smelled this way could be nothing less than real.

It was easy to pass as one of the crowd here. Checkpoints were present, certainly, but control checks were far less stringent than the ones they would encounter higher up in the station, and Drem hoped, based on the personnel and security schematics information he'd received from Hona, that making his way up the line in this manner would be easier than trying to barge in at the top level would have been. One did not simply walk into a capsuleer's quarters.

As they made their way through the throng and walked unnoticed past the first checkpoints, Drem was amazed by his own assurance. Of course it was important not to look suspicious or nervous, but it went beyond that. He felt calm, very calm, but it was a calmness that was more of a willed control, born of all those moments when he was about to unearth something living from the wreckage. It was the emotional encapsulation, like a shield, of the deep-set knowledge that whatever happened next might turn out fine or wholly not alright at all, but either way he'd need to keep a cool head to deal with it.

As they walked through the main walkway, buffeted by the noise of thousands going about their business, Drem felt that calm sink even deeper, until he was entirely cold and hyperaware. Those same instincts that kept him under control also helped him take in signs of danger – the creak of a support beam or the crackle and hiss of loose elements – and they were warning him.

He turned his head a fraction to either side, taking in everything he could: every face, every body, every motion that seemed a hair out of tune with the river of people in which they were all immersed.

Ralea kept looking straight ahead but asked him, in a low tone, 'Everything all right?'

'We're in danger and I don't know why,' he murmured.

'Nobody would touch us here. Too many people for an explosion, too much interruption for a sniping.'

'Then we're probably being followed. Let's change up our pace, but stay on populated routes.'

It took a long march through the crowds, but at last Drem said, 'I've got them. There're two, but they split up every now and then. They're on your side, just past the entrance to Engines 36-8B.'

'Got them. You're good at this,' Ralea said, in a tone almost free of tremor.

'You get used to spotting a rock out of place, you can see people clear as day,' Drem said.

'We cannot kill these men,' Ralea told him.

'I know.' He thought it over as he walked, and kept his eyes on the environment. The houses and stores here were as grungy as the people, and sold almost anything on the grey side of legality. 'In absence of my own equipment, I'm used to relying on local resources, and that starts with the people. You got that datapad?'

Ralea took a small, silver pad from an inside pocket. 'Personnel check?'

'Yeah.'

'What am I looking for?'

'You know stations better than me. Take Hona's datapackage, see if you can match the locales we're seeing with its personnel files. We need allies here.'

She consulted her pad, looking around every now and then as if she were a tourist verifying a map. Drem caught on; she wanted to make it look like they were headed for whatever location she'd choose, instead of making a sudden and unannounced beeline for it. He looked around as well, making sure to keep his eyes on the buildings rather than the people. He didn't want to tip his hand by accidentally locking eyes with their pursuers.

'I've got something,' Ralea said. 'There is a tech and hardware store coming up. Owner is an ex-pirate by the looks of it. Definite Angel connections.'

'They allow those people to operate here?'

'If you were only a small-timer, yeah, they'll overlook it. The real crimes happen on the higher levels,' she said in an acid tone. 'But this one's different. He's got weapons experience and some reputation among the Angels. This kind of track record should've barred him from the station.'

'How come he's here, then?'

'Someone wiped it for him. I guess he wanted a clean start. I don't think this data even shows up in official Angel records. It looks like keylocked notes, internal ones. I have no idea how this friend of yours even got access to them.'

'Best not to ask, I think. You think this man will help us?'

'I did a quick cross-check and he's got some distant family saved by the Sisters. I can't connect it directly to you, but it was at the time you were working for the Angels. And he's got tons of hardware; there's apparently a small warehouse behind his store, judging by these station drawings. If we want to supply ourselves with something, or recruit any backup, this is the best place to do it.'

'Sounds perfect. Let's go,' Drem said. They made their way through the crowd, taking care not to elbow anyone aside or look like they were too eager for the safety of a commercial building. Drem hoped their pursuers would have the sense to wait outside, unseen. He didn't want to kill anyone, and he certainly did not want to have his mission interrupted.

They made it to the building, fronted with large windows of transparent nanoalloy. Drem risked a glance at their reflection and did not see anyone bearing down on him from behind. With a sigh of relief, he passed through the door.

It was quiet and chilly inside. Long racks held necessities and tech of various sorts, lit up by halogen from high above. At the other end of the store Drem glimpsed a burly man sitting behind a counter. 'That him?' he asked Ralea, and she nodded.

They walked up to the counter. There were a few people browsing the racks, but nobody within earshot. The man, who looked to be in his late forties and had hairy skin that covered muscles like wires, gave them a brief look and said, 'What do you need?'

'Help,' Drem said.

This drew the man's attention proper, and Drem handed him a code key. 'This is us.'

The burly man ran it through his scanner. Drem did not see the results, but knew they would prove his Sisters credentials. They would also, on subsequent entrance to the station's general datalogs, disintegrate into a heap of indecipherable bits. No trace; no trail.

The man handed back the code key. 'What can I do for you?' he said in a much lower tone.

'We're in trouble. Being followed.'

'You want me to call out some guys?'

'No, can't afford to get noticed. You have a quick list of materials on sale?'

The man thought this over. 'I do. I have lists.'

Noticing the plural, Drem murmured, 'We don't need weapons. We can't afford to get scanned or caught.'

The man shrugged. 'There's weapons and weapons,' he said.

'I hate to say this,' Ralea said to them, 'but unless we can figure out a way to trap these guys, we're just going to have to go for them.'

Drem thought it over. 'Ralea, can you look up any part of this station in our vicinity that doesn't have human monitoring, and that can take a bit of a beating?'

'Sure.' Many station compartments had been built, or left unfinished, solely so they could take the brunt of any damage occurring either from outside assaults or internal incidents. The slang term for these was 'leg space'.

Drem turned to the former pirate. 'Can I get a quick browse through those lists?'

The man handed him a datapad. Drem scanned through it, making a few notes. Finally he showed the notes to the owner. 'I need these if you have them, and quick as possible. Some of them are verging on illegal, I hope that won't get you in trouble.'

The man looked at him, and tapped the list in his hand. 'For someone like you, I have these.'

'We also need some preparation space.'

The man thumbed toward a side door. 'Out in the back. Welding, electronics, anything you need. I'll key you in, then get the things from storage. Five minutes, if you have them.'

'That's fine. Thanks very much for this. We won't be long.'

The owner shrugged. 'Anything else?' When they didn't respond, he added, 'Your faces, you look like you're going somewhere dangerous. Unarmed. I don't like doing that to a Sister.'

Drem looked at Ralea, who shrugged. He looked back to the Angel. 'Well . . . we'll need a distraction once we leave this place. Something to shake off these hunters, temporarily.'

The man's face split into a grin. He took the notes and silently added one item.

Drem read it. It said, 'Multispectral grenade'.

Not too long after, they exited the store. Drem now had a backpack. Ralea's outfit protruded ever so slightly at odd angles.

The crowds had started to thin a little with the waning day. Drem and Ralea made sure not to look in any particular direction. They started to walk out back to the main street, then made an abrupt turn and headed back towards the store, passing quickly down a small alley to its side. Drem risked a peek and saw from the corner of his eye two indistinct figures moving swiftly through the crowds, not at a very high speed but with definite tones of confrontation in the assuredness of their motion. He said to Ralea, 'Toss it in eight,' and silently counted down as they went deeper into the alley. The moment before he hit zero, he took good stock of his surroundings, then closed his eyes and ran. Ralea took off as well, and right behind them he heard the patter of chasing feet. There was the whirr of a multispectral being set to visual range, the plink of its landing on the street and then the quiet thunk of its activation, followed immediately by two voices howling in pain and shock. The patter ceased immediately, and was replaced by the thumps and clunks of two bodies collapsing and rolling around on the ground. Drem thought he heard one of them retch.

Ralea whispered, 'Safe?' and he nodded, still running, before he realized his eyes were still closed. He was so used to running blind, working off a mental map rather than whatever debris was in his way, that he didn't need to see. He said, 'Yeah, let's gun it,' and they ran at full speed, eyes open, toward the bowels of the station.

It took them a while to get there, partly because they relied only on pedestrian, nonsealable paths, and partly because they didn't want to lose the chase entirely. The direction they'd taken could only lead to a limited number of locations, all of them deeper in the uninhabited core of the station, and of those, only a couple led back into the station proper and the higher levels. Drem was headed for one of those interim locations and expected his pursuers to do exactly the same.

Multispectral grenades were multifunctional and often nasty devices whose legality depended on their use. The same grenade could be used for a kinetic blast, a thermal dousing or a visual effect, and could also be adjusted for strength. Hence, a kinetic blast could topple over trashcans or, at the other extreme, quite thoroughly disentangle a human victim; while a thermal hit could incinerate the same, or merely burn scorchlessly on all available surfaces with just sufficient heat to hold back whoever was in pursuit. Its kaleidoscopic functions diffracted all available light, and at low levels – the ones that didn't quite fry the synapses – made the victim feel he was trying to run through a world of broken mirrors. A vicious migraine, a high level of nausea and an all-over cranky disposition were unavoidable results.

Drem's backpack clanked. He pushed it up a little higher on his shoulders.

They eventually arrived at a narrow junction that opened up into a large hall, unmonitored and empty apart from a mass of metal debris that littered its floor. Leg space was often used for storage, particularly of station parts that did not serve any purpose other than eventual hull upkeep.

Once they were in the hall proper, Drem unshouldered his backpack and pulled out various metal parts, each more intricate than the last. While he fitted some of them together, Ralea stood watch. She looked around and said, 'You think this place will do?'

Without looking up, Drem said softly, 'It's perfect.'

She smiled and looked towards the entrance, waiting for their pursuers to pass through.

It didn't take long. Drem had only walked a couple of times around the hall, setting up his gear, when they heard noises right outside. Drem shared a look with Ralea and hurried over to her, adopting a casual stance with his hands in his pockets. Clearly these people were not worried about being caught, which meant they were assured of their own capabilities, and had taken care that no witnesses would be near. This was good.

They passed into the hall, two men in loose, grey clothing that shone faintly with threads of golden red. Now that Drem could look at them properly he thought something in their faces looked quite familiar, even unnervingly so, but he couldn't quite place it. Too many pirate factions over too long a time period. He realized with a wince that he had ignored the possibility that they might be empire agents, but forgave himself the lapse in judgement. It was extremely unlikely that the empires would have found out about his plans, much less commissioned secret agents to stop him. If they were affiliated with the empires then everything was already lost, and that was simply not an eventuality Drem intended to contemplate.

The hunters took their positions, standing a few arm's lengths apart, their hands hanging by their sides. Drem did not see weapons yet, which concerned him a little. These men would be angry and annoyed at the multispectral grenade. They would want a little payback before finishing the deal. But unless they had impeccable intelligence on him and Ralea, they should at the very least have guns trained on them. They seemed to expect their presence alone to be intimidating.

Something about that idea caught on in his mind. He decided to explore it a little, and said, 'You really shouldn't have come here. We're on a private mission.'

'There's nothing private with people like you, little acolyte,' one of them said.

The realization hit Drem like a bomb. '... Oh, you fuckers,' he hissed, at his opponents and everyone they represented.

'What is it?' Ralea whispered at him. 'Who are they? Do you know them?'

Drem glanced at her for half a second, then turned immediately back to the two men, afraid that his face might have given away its mind's secrets. 'Blood Raiders. They're Blood Raider agents.' No wonder they'd seemed so cocksure. Their kind would be accustomed to terrifying people into obeisance by their presence alone.

'Your flight ends here,' one of them said.

'I suspect you don't know why you're doing what you're doing,' Drem said.

'You're planning to ruin our hunting. That's all we need to know, you fucking traitor.'

'I don't suppose you'd believe me if I said I was on your side?' Drem asked them.

One of the men raised a gun.

'Guess not,' Drem said, and to the Blood Raiders' surprise unslung his backpack with a deep sigh. 'So it's all over.'

He was impressed with Ralea, who held herself entirely still after hearing the codephrase. Drem pressed a small catalyst in his pocket and held his breath. There was a hiss from somewhere as equipment started to overload. The Blood Raiders stepped in, as Drem knew they would; they wouldn't want to waste all that close-combat training, and besides, Raiders liked to look into your eyes.

The hiss rose to a crescendo, tumultuous and trembling, and just as the gun-toting Raider turned to see what was happening, Drem threw his backpack at them and dropped to the floor. The beams above their heads, laced with explosives, blew apart with surgical precision and plummeted to the floor, showering the two Raiders with deadly metal just as the ad-hoc spoke bomb in the backpack blew open around them and shot out the laces of its lifesaving grid. The last Drem saw of the agents was two astonished expressions, too stunned to even fire a shot as the roof caved in around them. He thanked the gods for leg space and all the motley garbage that could be found there.

Once the dust had settled, Drem and Ralea moved toward the pile of rubble that now lay on top of their would-be killers.

'That was ... amazingly accurate,' Ralea said. 'I didn't think you could make it fall this precisely. All I have on me is a little dust.'

'I learned from the masters,' Drem said. She gave him a wondering look, and he said, 'You don't go roaring into half-exploded asteroid colonies unless you know a little about how they got to be that way.'

He walked closer to the rubble. From the way it curved at the centre, he surmised the spoke bomb was still holding. He put his face up to the metal and yelled, 'If you can hear me, try to conserve your air! This section of the station isn't part of regular operations, which you probably know since you were planning to kill us here, so the first autodetectors that arrive won't immediately be scanning for life! Also, I suggest you not activate any weapons, lest the spoke grid give way and you get pulped! I've seen it happen and it's really not that pretty!'

There was no sound from within the rubble.

Drem brushed some dust off his hands. 'Let's go,' he said to Ralea.

She cocked her head at him, but said nothing, and started to walk out of the hall with him.

As they made their way out, Ralea's silence hanging over them like a weight, Drem angrily muttered, 'We should've taken them out right away.'

'You were the one who wanted to find out more about them,' Ralea said to him. 'Care to tell me anything? Why were they after us? And why did you recognize them?'

'I don't know,' Drem lied.

They passed back into the station proper. Ralea was clearly annoyed at him, but worked through it by taking control. They started making their way up the station levels, and as she had far more experience of proper, fully operational stations than Drem did, he gladly relinquished authority to her.

The Angel database from Hona proved invaluable. There were detailed records on almost every fixture in the station, covering everything from resident individuals to intangible processes. The records provided information on who could be bribed and who had connections – a vital thing for any proper pirate needing to do business on the station – but also contained algorithms that could generate short-lived access codes, written off as anomalies in the immensely complicated station control systems. Identities were worn for a few minutes, then discarded, and backstories were memorized equally.

They used a portion of the Gurista money, routed through proxy accounts that reached to lowsec and back, to float them up through the lower levels, most of which were dirty enough that they only needed a little grease for passage. As they ascended it was increasingly not the guards who received their money, but carefully chosen shopkeepers, vendors and tradesmen, most of whom, encouraged by Drem's unhesitant spending and Ralea's genial chatter, willingly vouched for them with their friends in the guarding, overseeing and checkpoint control professions. In one of those encounters, the seller even complimented Drem on his choice of equipment.

'I can see you know what you're talking about when it comes to repair equipment for small-scale electronics. It's like fresh air, I tell you. Most people in this place, they couldn't fix their damn holovid without frying their eyeballs out in the process. Here, you can have a third off that one,' he said and winked.

Drem, whose past missions had included thousands of operations on local equipment that was charred, leaking or actively on fire, muttered a slightly embarrassed thanks and started offering to buy something else to offset any loss, but Ralea took over and spent a good twenty minutes in conversation. When they left the man, they had – to Drem's amazement – a good number of confirmed contacts who would gladly help them get to the higher levels, plus a couple of new ones that Drem hadn't even considered approaching before. As Ralea explained to him, once a person had staked out a sufficiently respectable niche in the business of corruption, favours became the currency of choice, while direct bribes turned into warning signs.

On the few occasions where their paths could be expected to cross those of an incorruptible lower-level official, they dug into the Gurista funds again and purchased on-site identicleaners. These created temporary aliases for them; not enough if anyone decided to do deep background checks, but sufficient to pass through a few gates if they didn't arouse suspicion otherwise. The cleaners were expensive, but Ralea decided to err on the side of discretion, lest any word of their antics with the Blood Raiders should come back to haunt them.

Once they'd ascended to even higher levels within the station, even this was not enough. The money flowed from them at a progressively faster pace, and the identity concealment turned from identicleaning and access codes to bodymods – retinal, subdermal – and immensely complicated subroutines that allowed them to defeat the complex bioencryption they encountered; but as they passed into the higher and better-monitored sections of the station the duo eventually had to resort, however uncomfortably, to variations of the truth.

On one of the interim sections Drem was stopped by a guard who inspected his fake identity, then looked at Drem and said, 'This isn't you.'

'I'm sorry?'

The guard said, 'I've seen people from that part of the world, and they're easygoing, civilian, usually kind of pudgy. You've got a Navy air about you. Is there anything you want to share, or you want me to start running deep checks?'

Drem's mind went into panic. His mouth took over, and a story of half-truths involving rescue from a ship attacked by Blood Raiders and convalescence at a Sisters outpost didn't help matters much, either.

Ralea took over instead. Using her extensive mission agent background and myriad extant station access codes, she concocted a story that didn't get them through but at least convinced the guard not to call in assistance. When her own backlog of VIP codes failed to do the trick, she excused herself and contacted an old associate, one who had returned to agent work and whose codes thankfully proved sufficient. With these codes in hand, Ralea's presence provided enough authority to finally float them through with smiles and excuses on the guard's behalf. In this haven of wealth, money inexorably gave way to bluff as the coin of choice.

Ralea's codes and connections, combined with her knowledge of the social mores that came with the upper class of station citizenry, turned out to be invaluable, and reinforced Drem's belief that the whole plan would have been doomed without her presence. This was her world now. She walked with the air of complete assurance, projecting the unassailable fact that she belonged exactly where she was. In some of the checks they weren't even questioned, and it wasn't until the guards noticed Drem tagging along behind her that eyebrows were raised and ID cards needed to be produced. His knowledge of shift schedules, encryption methods and security systems, and of how structural supports worked in times of stress, was entirely useless here.

They had gotten so very close to the top level when they were stopped by a guard, a man dressed in social black clothing, not a hint of security gear about him. Brute force was not welcome here. The man stood in the way of Ralea, inspecting her ID card, and said, 'I'm afraid this is not acceptable, madam.'

Drem saw Ralea draw herself up to her full height, like a titan in launch. 'Explain,' she said.

The guard drew back just a fraction, but set his face and said, 'It's neither broken nor false, madam—'

'I should think it's not.'

'—and it verifies perfectly in our local system, on all checks. But for some reason the out-of-station checks on its secondary codes aren't being processed.'

'That is not my problem,' Ralea said. And it wasn't, Drem knew. It was a problem caused by internal rerouting, where the tracers sent off-station to check the veracity of these ID cards were funnelled through lesser-priority datapaths and lowsec colony databases, all of which were in tacit support of this project and none of which were much inclined to serve these requests with any kind of speed.

'Madam, this level is granted safe for capsuleers, and while your ID looks pitch-perfect, I'm afraid that without this last background check I cannot—'

'I have seen people who turned themselves inside-out,' Ralea said in a voice so soft that it choked the guard into silence. 'I have spent an age with Amarrian priests, deciphering the details of Scripture. I have run a Caldari team of warriors, and stood face-to-face with Tibus Heth himself. When I was threatened with my life, a knife against my throat, I left the assailant in *ruins*.'

She walked up close to the man and looked straight into his eyes. 'The force of all these things and more, you will find coming your way if I am made to wait here. I have spent more time among the capsuleers than you and everyone you know. If you have any inclination to let your day go by as any other, you will let me pass.'

The guard stood there, rooted to the spot. Drem held his breath.

After an age of doubt, the guard nodded his head and stepped aside, murmuring an apology. Ralea ignored him entirely as she stormed past, Drem following on her heels, into the station's inner sanctum, into the holiest of holies: the top level, the home of immortals, the capsuleers.

18

The capsuleer rotated his camera drones to get a better look at the Gallentean station, with its gentle green curves and myriad of viewports. The Gallenteans liked their sunlight and their view of space.

He called up the mission details and studied them yet again. They'd come from an agent he had never worked with before, someone named Heci, and were far too lucrative to refuse. But it did require he dock at this particular station and that he disengage from his capsule.

The idea of leaving his capsule unnerved him. It was something he had never grown used to, and not merely because of the discomfort inherent in the extraction process. There was a deeper kind of disgust to being shoved back into the body – that limp, fragile form.

Nonetheless, he wanted to check it out. At the very least it would net him some really good money, though he hoped there would be something more to the deal: an encounter with angry new enemies, some new series of protected structures that needed reducing to rubble, even something precious left behind in the wreckage of his wake. The endless repetition he endured every day for hours on end held some comfort in routine, but he'd become so good at it that it barely got his heart rate up. These days he'd taken to blowing practically anything to pieces simply to set it ablaze.

There was some pride in the cause to be had, certainly. Most of those missions required him to venture into lowsec areas and cleanse a pirate scourge that had taken root, with only the occasional request for him to ferry sensitive data across lines of danger, along with the rare and rather bizarre request that he procure some amount of ore or other for a starving component assembly line. All of these were important, and so time-sensitive that routing them through that faction's usual Navy systems, with all the inherent red tape and interdepartmental strife, was unthinkable. When a mission was given to a capsuleer, a free agent, its needs trumped bureaucracy by default.

Likewise, most of the profits he reaped from the missions, he gave to his alliance, a coalition of capsuleers fighting for much greater things than merely the efforts of an empire faction. He had risen high in this alliance and been granted great trust, but even as his compatriots engaged in vicious warfare with others of their kind, he found a kind of peace in undertaking his missions. Occasionally he'd fly support in fleet battles, with hundreds of ships clashing like lightning in the sky, but he was of more use here, tearing up the pirates and their colonies, and bringing the spoils back to his legion.

His ship hovered up to the docking bays. Only once he was nearly at the mouth of the great station did its scale hit him. From this angle it dwarfed the planet that it orbited, and the sun beyond it as well. Thousands of viewports looked up to him, and the maw of the bays seemed ready to swallow him whole. The docking bays alone easily contained the bulk of his ship and many others, and it seemed to him that a structure like this could only have been made by something greater than mere men.

And as his ship glided toward the mouth of the station, its columns of lights glinting off his metal carapace, it felt like more than a place made by gods: it felt like it had been made for him.

A voice informed him that his docking request had been accepted, and the fuzziness at the edge of his consciousness meant that he would soon be detached from his ship's processes. He hated this part of the jaunt; he truly loathed it.

He relaxed as best he could, let the ship float on through the invisible waves, and accepted the inevitable.

The mind, shorn of input, made up a reality of its own, composed of morphing silhouettes lit in neon against a black background of nothingness. These things did not exist; they were not even the fading remnants of eyesight blocked off from light. The very physicality of the capsuleer's body decreased to the point where everything – every limb, every cell, every ghostly sensation – seemed to him disembodied, no less of a fantasy than the amorphous shapes he saw before his eyes.

He did not know who he was at this moment. He had been one kind of animal, with the input and thoughts that came with floating in space, and soon he would be another, bound by gravity and flesh. This limbo was as close to a real death as he would ever come, and that idea – not of the event itself, which he had experienced many times, but of the void, the nothingness that was sure to follow for an eternity – frightened him more than anything else.

The synaptic twitches of his other life began flickering into his consciousness. He was increasingly aware of weightlessness: not the true absence of weight that followed on being disembodied and thus having no real corporeal presence, but the feeling of his existent corpus being suspended.

His back ached. The umbilical cord, a solid mass of metal connected to the plugs that dotted his spine, was entirely unforgiving when it came to movement.

His vision was not back yet, but the halogen shapes seemed to have stopped hovering about so much. An increasing fuzziness to their form lent them the verisimilitude of real things, waiting out there for him.

His body twitched. He grasped at nothing, and felt not so much the movement as the supple give of whatever surrounded it. He tried not to think of how capsuleer bodies floated suspended in ectoplasm. It would be in his lungs. It would be in his nose and mouth and in his lungs.

His feet were cold. His body was pulled down increasingly, and he realized something was in fact touching his feet; he had floated down and was standing on the capsule's bottom. It wouldn't be long now. A shuddering lurch indicated that his pod had clamped in place. He must have already passed through decontamination, scanning and nourishment injection. Time truly flew.

He gritted his teeth and waited for the flood.

There was a muted hiss followed by a series of clangs as the pedestal locked itself into place beneath his pod.

In a rush the liquid fell past him, a thick waterfall that pounded his back and left him collapsed and shivering. His body cramped up in tune, expelling the same viscous ectoplasm from his insides. He was held up by the cord, which locked into his back and suspended him like a single-string puppet. He still had his eyes closed, for there was nothing here he wanted to see. Droplets of ectoplasm cascaded over his back. He felt the pull on his skin as the cord slowly lowered him to the pedestal, giving out a muted whine. The cold air of the capsule detachment room flowed over his body as the pedestal descended, taking him out of the capsule and into the room proper. Were he to fall from this height, to be disconnected from the cord and tumble from the pedestal, he would break like an egg.

The pedestal slowly lowered, and several seconds later clicked into place. The cord lowered him as far as he could go, until he was crouching with his head between his knees, then loosened from his back with a click. The sudden loss of support made him drop on his hands and knees.

He vomited up the last of the ectoplasm, feeling it gush out of his mouth and his nose, and trying not to instinctively inhale lest he swallow it back down or choke on it. The sludgy fluid dripped down into a grate.

He was a rich man by any standard. Of the trillions of people in this world he belonged to a percentage so elite it was barely measurable except by its distance from everyone else. He could buy anything. He was immortal, feared, hated and worshipped.

He dry-heaved a couple of times, his hoarse retching echoing off the metallic walls.

And as he looked up, his blocked ears detecting the dull thuds of footsteps, he saw a repairman walk up to him with a strange smile, and he had a moment to wonder what the hell this person was doing in his private chamber before the back of his head exploded into pain and light and oblivion.

Hazy sounds found their way into his head, gently pushing at a throbbing headache. When he opened one eye, then another, all he saw was a gloomy darkness without movement or sense.

He closed his eyes and tried to think. The haze slowly ebbed away, though the headache remained.

After a few breaths he hazarded another look, and this time he managed to figure it out. He was sitting in his favourite chair in the middle of his quarters, the lights were shaded, there was quiet music playing, and something was very wrong.

'Welcome back,' said a woman's voice from somewhere behind him.

His head ached.

'I want you to understand something,' the voice said. He heard soft steps, and the speaker moved into view. It was a woman, probably late thirties, quite attractive in a worn, outdoors sort of way. She was dressed in the outfit of a repair worker, one of those people the capsuleer never really noticed. Her movements were definite, in the manner of someone who brings them to completion whatever the opposition. He felt an immediate attraction – less, he suspected, out of any romance than out of a need to imagine this situation as more leisurely than it undoubtedly was. He also felt like he should know who she was.

'I'm listening,' he said. It came out as a whisper; his headache made the words echo inside his skull.

'You are about to make a simple choice. It won't be a pleasant one. I doubt you'll ever understand the reason, but the consequences should be eminently clear. One option will greatly inconvenience you. The other will cost you your life.'

The woman stood directly in front of him. She leaned forward, putting her arms on each side of his. She smelled of work and activity. Her eyes, alive with incredible power, held his locked in a gaze. 'There is no getting around this. Money, power, influence, they all mean nothing in this room. You're dealing with a force stronger than anything you can wield.'

'What force?' he whispered.

'Revenge,' said another voice.

There was someone else there, just at the corner of his eye, sitting in the dark.

The woman apparently noticed his glance. She rose and said, 'Don't look in that corner. It is not a good corner for you to look into. The man sitting there would very much like to see you dead.'

'I don't want to die,' he told her, and he meant it. He tried very hard to remember if he'd seen this woman before. She looked familiar, but she didn't match anyone he knew. He wondered if she was someone's family – a close relative, maybe a sibling.

She took a seat on the couch that faced him. 'I don't have quite the emotional involvement in all of this to bother with watching you suffer. Nor do I really have any ethical qualms about murdering you.' She leaned in, and he instinctively tried to do the same, but the burst of pain in his head kept him stationary. 'I *have* killed before, you see. It gets easier. But my friend here, he hasn't. And even as he wants you to go through the same agonies as he has, I know he also wouldn't mind if you made it easy on us, freaked out and made enough trouble that we would simply have to take your life.'

Whatever this choice they were going to give him, he did not expect it would be pleasant. He decided to stall for time. 'Who sent you?'

There was a snort from the dark corner. A man's voice said, 'Nobody. Not anymore.'

'You did not get in here on your own,' he said. 'You're obviously not repairmen, either.'

'Of course we're not,' the woman said.

'Plan was to sneak in here while you were away and install a piece of hardware in the capsule detachment chamber,' the man said from the darkness. 'Deep enough you wouldn't notice it. It'd do some things to your head, and if they worked we intended to run the same plan on as many capsuleers in New Eden as we could. You people would never have seen us, and by the time we progressed to the final stages, it'd be far too late for anyone.'

Despite his present worries, he couldn't help but ask. 'What would have happened?'

The man appeared to think this over. He said, 'Incremental adjustments of behaviour, through alterations on a cellular scale, until thoughts that might once have been completely mad now seem entirely reasonable, even the ones that could easily lead to your own death. It's a little like how hatred works, come to think of it.'

The chair creaked gently as the man stood up. He walked into the capsuleer's line of sight. Dressed in the same repairman outfit, he was a little younger than the woman but equally worn, and there was something in his eyes that seemed to look beyond the capsuleer and the very room they were in. Whatever went on in that man's mind, it was not something the capsuleer particularly wanted to experience.

'Who *are* you?' He still couldn't remember who this woman was, and he was certain he'd never seen the man in his life.

'We . . .' The man looked toward his companion. 'We represent a power that isn't much enamoured with the capsuleers. They keep that attitude secret, and not even I knew about it until the time came to put the plan into action. But I decided I didn't want to kill all those people.'

A tiny hope bloomed. 'So you really don't want to kill any capsuleers at all.'

'Not really,' said the man. 'Just you.'

'I don't want to die,' he told his captors. His croaky voice sounded embarrassingly pleading.

'Neither did they,' the man said, absent-mindedly.

'Who?'

He saw the woman give her companion a warning look. Maybe if he could keep them talking, they'd reveal something he could use, or there'd be someone who would check up on him. He had no doubt these people could subdue him.

He blinked hard, tried to clear his mind. Some other path; some other path than death. 'Could I get a glass of water, please?'

They loomed over him.

'Forget I asked,' he sighed. The effort of speaking made his head hurt – it was as if something was poking into his eyeballs from behind their sockets – but he didn't dare stop. 'Did another capsuleer send you here?'

They gave each other strange looks, and he plunged ahead. 'That's it, isn't it? Who was it? Someone from another alliance?' When they didn't respond, he gasped and said, 'Not in my own! Who was it? Tell me his name and I'll pay you twice as much, several times as much, if you go into his quarters instead.'

'Nobody . . . no one in your alliance is out to get you,' the man said. He seemed to be keeping his voice intently under control. 'Though I'm amazed at how quickly you people start to eat your own.'

The capsuleer stared at him, then at the woman, who had turned her face away from his sight and was hugging her shoulders. She trembled a little, and snorted a couple of times.

He tried to smile without making it look too fake, but all his muscles seemed to want was to tense up and never let go. He wondered why nobody had come looking for him.

'We've deactivated your security system, cloning and all, while we do our vital repairs,' his male captor said, inspecting the badge on his jacket that bore the repairman insignia. 'Those repairs, they're tough work.'

'People will know I'm here. I came in on a mission,' the capsuleer said.

'Maybe they'll match your docking logs later, yes. But nobody is expecting you here, or waiting for you.'

'No, there's an agent—' He stopped. Comprehension slowly dawned. He sighed, and said, 'No. There is not an agent.'

They shook their heads.

He said, quietly, 'Shit . . .'

They nodded.

'What did I do to you? Who did I kill?'

'Everyone I knew,' the man said.

'Is there anything I can do?'

'Nothing. All there is left is retribution,' the man told him.

He sighed deeply, closed his eyes and leaned his head back in his chair. His body was feeling moderately better, but even so he didn't think he could take them on. Not until he knew what they wanted from him, and had, possibly, the adrenaline of last resort flowing through his veins.

'All right,' he said, eyes still resolutely closed. 'What do you want from me?'

'You belong to an alliance,' he heard the man say. 'Your people trust you.'

'Yes.'

'You give most of your spoils to them, and they, in turn, leave their possessions unprotected from you.'

He swallowed dryly. 'Yes.'

The man's voice hovered somewhere in the distance, detached from place and time. 'You are going to rob your alliance of everything they have. You will take their funds and transfer them to a proxy. You will take their belongings, both commodities and modules and entire fleets of ships, and what you cannot sell you will liquidate for the minerals. All the proceeds will go to the proxy. Then you will send your alliance mates a message explaining how you robbed them, shut down all their rentals of every factory, lab and office in New Eden, resign from the alliance, and go on the run. Forever.'

The capsuleer's eyes popped open. He started to rise, a scream roaring up his throat, as the man's fist smashed into his face so hard that he was lifted up in the air, spun around, and dropped right back on the floor. The blow and the landing's impact hurt so much that he lost his sight for a moment, and the afterpain went all the way down to his testicles, as if all the nerves in his body were being clamped in a vice. It hurt so much that he retched on the floor, dazedly marvelling at how viscous the outcome looked, until he realized it was the last remnants of half-digested ectoplasm that had been floating around in his system.

'Capsuleers have some funny ideas about ethics,' the woman said. 'And the one thing they seem to hate more than anything else is a thief. You do this, and you'll be judged. We'll leave you with enough to get by, and you'll need it, because every member of your alliance will hunt you down until the end of time. Every time you wake in a clone pod, you'll live only long enough for them to find you again.

You are going to destroy their life's work and they will never forgive you.'

'I can't do this,' he said. 'I can't do this. Please don't make me do this.'

'All right,' the woman said. She walked over to a nearby shelf and picked up a glass bottle, hefted it, then swung down hard on a wooden settee. The bottle broke in two. The woman walked back over to the capsuleer, who had raised himself up to his knees in supplication. 'Then we'll cut your throat,' she said to him.

'Do you understand what you're asking me to do?' he pleaded. His face was wet, though whether from tears or the spattering of bile, he didn't know.

'You will die a thousand deaths, hunted wherever you go, for the remainder of your natural life,' the man said, quite emotionlessly. 'Everything you knew and worked for will be gone.'

'You're dead,' the capsuleer replied, fear giving its easy way to anger. 'You're both dead.'

'We are,' the woman said to him.

'You will be erased,' he said, the anger now overriding any sense. 'There won't be a shred left of you.'

The woman walked up to him and grasped a hold of his left hand. She shifted her grip to his pinkie finger and twisted sharply with a crack.

The capsuleer yelped with the instant influx of stinging, burning pain. Tears welled up in his eyes. He tried to pull his hand back, but the woman held fast on to the broken finger.

She said, 'After we leave this room, our identities will be gone. Our trail will already have started to fade at the station's lowest level, with temporary passes expiring and proxies going dark. This process will continue until it reaches us here, at which point there'll be nothing left of us. We will leave as ghosts. Nobody will admit they ever employed us, especially if they look to be embroiled in a capsuleer fight. The group who planned to kill all your people will break themselves in half rather than allow any trace linking us to them. And you—' she twisted the finger, and the capsuleer yelped, '—nobody will ever believe your claims that two civilians simply waltzed in here, backed by oceans of money and top-secret data, and forced you to do what your people have been doing of their own accord to everyone else in this world since your kind first found its way into all our lives.'

She let go of his finger.

He sat there, idly cradling it, knowing he was lost. 'So that's it, is it,' he said, not as a question.

'Yes,' she said. 'You'll do as we say, and run.'

He raised his head to her and asked, for confirmation rather than out of defiance, 'Or?'

'Or I'll slit your throat.'

He sat there, considering this. He felt calm now, as one would when having gone beyond bearable horror. This was the end of him. It was nearly equal to an absolute death.

His two captors stood there, staring at him. The man seemed ill at ease. Eventually he barked at the capsuleer, 'That's all this is to you, isn't it? Characters on a screen, and a locked-on target. How can it mean so much and so little all at the same time? What kind of human being are you?'

The doomed man couldn't help but smile. The woman raised the bottle in warning, but his smile was without ego or rancour, and she lowered it again.

'I'm a capsuleer,' he said.

Epilogue

The lounge was cold but neither man seemed to mind. Through the viewports could be seen trains of caravans pouring in and out of the station, and amidst the river of their flow there hovered still the solid rocks of capsuleer vessels. The rose-red nebula lit everything up with the glow of setting suns.

The Blood Raider regarded him stoically. 'I should be wary of spending any time near a man with your track record. Everything you've accomplished is enough to mark you permanently in our books.'

'As a threat?' Drem asked him. They sat side by side, facing the outside world.

The man leaned forward, regarded the ships. 'As an anomaly. Someone to be reckoned with. We have a hard time with people who don't fear us, much less ones that can dance around our people like you did.'

'Speaking of which. Those two agents of yours, they get out all right?'

'They did. They're the laughing stock of our entire undercover agency, but they'll live.'

'Good.'

'Which is more than can be said for that Sisters cabal you exposed. Amazing, how a faction dedicated to the preservation of life will viciously react when it finds out about traitors in its midst. They've done things to your people even I wouldn't have thought of.'

Drem nodded. Wherever his old teammates were now, he didn't know, and he was certain he didn't want to know. The price had been paid.

The man regarded him. 'You've really been on a strange quest, haven't you? If even half the reports I've read are true—'

'Let's just say it needed to happen,' Drem said. He reminded himself that this man was not his friend, nor were the people he represented in any way safe associates.

The man sat up again. 'All right. Business, then?'

Drem nodded. 'Tell me what they decided.'

'Wasn't much chance of anything other than what you expected. They agreed, fully and completely.' He hesitated, then added, 'You know, if we had *known* about your double bluff, we wouldn't have sent those agents.'

'Nobody could know. I didn't even tell my associate that I'd been in contact with you.'

'How'd she take it?'

Drem gave him a look.

The Blood Raider laughed. 'Is she here?'

Drem shook his head. 'She's not anywhere. Neither am I, any longer.'

'You do realize that considering what you've done for the faction, your past sins will be forgotten. You're always welcome among the Blood Raiders.'

He nodded as if he believed the man. 'Thanks. I'll keep that in mind. Doubt I'll be returning to the fold, though.'

'Well, that's your call.' The man shrugged. 'The money will be put to good use. We're certainly grateful that you foiled the Sisters plot, but I can honestly say that the money alone would have granted you favour with Omir Sarakusa himself.'

'That's good. But it's not what I asked for,' Drem said.

The Blood Raider agent said, 'That's right. It's not.' He pulled out a datapad, called up an image, and handed the pad to Drem.

The datapad showed Leip, Drem's brother, in an airsealed coffin. He looked exactly the same as he had in his bed, on that morning so long ago. The coffin sat on top of a pedestal decorated with Blood

Raider insignia. It was the farewell ceremony. It was the burial, at last.

'His name has been entered in the Book of the Dead. It can never be stricken.'

Drem ran his finger over the picture.

'What are you going to do now?'

'I don't know. Live a long life, if I can. Do some good,' Drem replied.

He looked at that picture for a long time. Eventually he handed the man back his datapad, thanked him, stood up and slowly walked away, toward the undocking bays. The red nebula lit his way.